After the Break

Also by Penny Smith
Coming Up Next

After the Break

PENNY SMITH

FOURTH ESTATE · London

First published in Great Britain in 2009 by
Fourth Estate
An imprint of HarperCollins*Publishers*
77–85 Fulham Palace Road
London W6 8JB
www.4thestate.co.uk

Visit our authors' blog: www.fifthestate.co.uk

1

A catalogue record for this book is available from the British Library

ISBN 978-0-00-731528-4

Typeset in Minion by
G&M Designs Limited, Raunds, Northamptonshire
Printed in Great Britain by Clays Ltd, St Ives plc

Mixed Sources
Product group from well-managed
forests and other controlled sources
www.fsc.org Cert no. SW-COC-1806
© 1996 Forest Stewardship Council

FSC is a non-profit international organisation established to promote the
responsible management of the world's forests. Products carrying the FSC
label are independently certified to assure consumers that they come
from forests that are managed to meet the social, economic and
ecological needs of present and future generations.

Find out more about HarperCollins and the environment at
www.harpercollins.co.uk/green

To my brothers and sister

CHAPTER ONE

It is a well-known fact that celebrity game shows are only for those who crave fame, more fame or fortune. The producers of *Celebrity X-Treme* had trawled the usual suspects for their new show, set in Norway. They were trying to get the last two people to sign up, but had already decided on a number of possible storylines. They wouldn't be so much manipulating (an accusation they vehemently denied) as helping things along.

A meeting of executive producers, producers and directors had been convened at the headquarters of the production company before many of them flew out. Siobhan Stamp, the striking woman who would oversee the entire thing, stood at the front of the room. She was slim, with translucent skin and deep-set blue eyes, which were always lined with kohl pencil. Today her strawberry blonde hair was tied back loosely, and a few tendrils had been teased in front of her ears. 'I know we've been through the list over and over again, whittling it down and discussing it *ad infinitum*, but I thought I'd just make sure we're all singing from the same hymn sheet. So, let's go ... Denise Trench.'

A picture of her appeared on the screen behind.

'Lead singer in Label. Two hits. Won the Eurovision Song Contest. Twice in rehab – alcohol and drugs. Single. Ageing woman-about-town.'

The picture changed to that of a page-three model who had been allegedly 'comforting' a Premier League footballer after his marriage split. 'Crystal Blake,' said Siobhan. 'Tony Belt, of Arsenal, says he's categorically not dating her, and never has. Which seems likely, considering she's willing to do *Celebrity X-Treme*. Young, but not as dim as you might think.'

She turned to look at the next photo, of a woman who bore a striking similarity to Naomi Campbell. 'Tanya Wilton. Has had a two-year relationship with Howard Elph, the shadow environment minister, who has since ended his marriage. But they are no longer an item. Seems to have no visible means of support.'

One of the male producers sniggered. Tanya Wilton was a natural G cup.

Siobhan smiled at him. Little did he know it, but she had plans for him. She paused. Looked back at the screen. 'Flynn O'Mara. Astrologer to the stars. Married to her manager. Two children. Columns in the *Mail* and various glossy magazines.'

The handsome face of a soap star filled the screen. 'Peter Philbin. His contract hasn't been renewed. He says it's his choice. He wants to go travelling, possibly trace his real parents in Jamaica and Ireland.' She had imbued that sentence with a degree of cynicism.

'Dave Beal,' she went on. 'Comedian of the old school. Fifty.'

There was a sharp intake of breath – he looked at least fifteen years older.

'Hasn't worked on television for years. Mostly lives abroad. Did very well out of the property boom. Unlike Steve Flyte ...' The face of the man who had been in all the papers talking about his divorce from a renowned cocaine-snorting actress appeared behind her. 'DJ. Confirmed heterosexual.' She left it there. Everyone knew that he batted for both sides. 'Helping out when they're busy', as one member of staff had put it.

'Paul Martin. Columnist/rent-a-quote, getting a higher profile by the week. Says he's doing this to have an insight into the world of the celebrity. Often to be seen at premières, parties, nightclubs, et cetera. And ...'

She turned to check.

'Alex Neil. Clothes designer. Gay. Single. No long relationships. Finally, Katie Fisher,' she said, trying not to sound venomous. 'Katie used to be one of the main anchors on *Hello Britain!*. She got sacked. Did a late-night series called *Start the Weekend*. Currently dating Adam Williams, one of the owners of Wolf Days Productions.'

She looked down at her notes. 'Now, as you know, Katie Fisher and Flynn O'Mara are not confirmed as yet, and a couple of others are waiting in the wings. In terms of stories coming out of the show, we do anticipate at least one relationship. And when I say relationship, I don't necessarily mean one resulting in marriage. But if we can all keep our eyes peeled – you know the sort of thing we want. I don't need to tell you that the success of this will rest on what keeps viewers on the edge of their seats. Will he, won't he? Will she, won't she? They've all got massive egos. That's why they're in this show. We want flirting, we want fights. We want confrontations, conflagrations. We want a soap opera. Let's give the audience the best reality TV show they've seen in the last decade.'

Katie Fisher had not set out to be a television presenter. She had wanted to be a journalist ever since she could remember, and had been ecstatic when she had got a job as a cub reporter on a local newspaper. She had worked her way up from there to the job she had loved as co-host on the number-one breakfast show.

When she looked in the mirror, she saw a woman in her forties with clear skin, wavy auburn hair and green eyes. On a good day, she felt passable. On a bad day, she felt almost too dreadful to approach the front door, let alone walk through it.

What the men who fell in love with her saw was a woman in her prime with sparkling eyes and a body made for the bedroom.

Katie had made enough money during her years on the prestigious sofa at *Hello Britain!* to have a flat in Chelsea overlooking the river, and a pretty cottage in Dorset, which she had bought after she'd done a chat show in a nearby village. It had seen a lot of use during her relationship, now ended, with land-scape gardener Bob Hewlett. He lived in a beautiful house near her parents and was one of her brother's best friends. He looked like a blue-eyed Richard Gere, had the most attractive forearms and a cat called Caligula.

Months of bliss had been brought to an abrupt halt by a stray remark from a friend, who revealed that Bob's protestations of faithfulness during a temporary split had been overstated. He had apparently indulged in a fling with a marine biologist called Clare McMurray, who continued to keep in touch.

Katie discovered her jealous gene, which she had previously thought missing.

One of her great friends, Dee – the weather presenter at *Hello Britain!* – wasn't convinced that this was the end of Katie and Bob. She had never seen Katie as happy, funny, silly and full of the joys of life as she had been with Mr Hewlett.

Katie and she met up at the gym they had joined in a drunken pact at New Year. They were now familiar with the café's offerings, rather less so with the inside of the adjoining gym. They sat drinking herbal tea in their tracksuits, having done no more than change into them. Dee had (as usual) claimed fatigue from the early mornings. Katie had (as usual) pleaded idleness. The window was open, allowing an occasional waft of vaguely fresh air to blow through.

'Yes, I know I did the dirty on Bob first,' said Katie, taking an accidentally noisy slurp of her tea. 'He lied to me, though, for months. And that is unforgivable.'

'To be fair,' said Dee, '*you* probably wouldn't have told *him* about that bloke, Krishnan Casey, if it hadn't been in the papers.'

'How on earth can you remember his name?' asked Katie, impressed.

'He was very good-looking and I always remember very good-looking men.'

'Well. Anyway,' said Katie, 'the point is, I only kissed him. And kissing someone is not the same as going to bed with them. Not in my book.'

'But you'd split up. Bob was a single man to all intents and purposes. He thought he could go at it with impunity.'

'Her name was Clare.'

'Sorry?'

'You said he was at it with Impunity.'

'If you don't want to discuss it, then tell me to shut up. I don't feel like dealing with your crap punning today.'

'Oooh,' sang Katie, lips pursed.

'No. Really. I'm knackered. Simon's being a total tit and keeps hunting me down in corridors to tell me I'm shit and that he doesn't know why I bother. Why can't they get a different editor? I don't believe the entire success of *Hello Britain!* rests on his skinny arse.'

Simon had been one of those responsible for Katie leaving the show. He was a vindictive man with sparse hair and a penchant for weak tea with sugar.

'Try not to worry too much,' said Katie, immediately solicitous. 'He can't get rid of you, you're too popular.'

'You know that's only as true as my last press cutting,' Dee responded. 'The only reason he wouldn't sack me is because he sacked you. If he got rid of another presenter, it would look bad.'

'To lose one presenter is unfortunate. To lose two is careless.'

'Exactly.' Dee smiled, reaching back to untie her dark hair from the elastic band she had shoved it into for the alleged workout. 'It's exhausting. I say something on air, then wait for him to come and tell me how rubbish it was. It's doing my head in. It's got to the stage where I start a sentence and then, because I'm worried, I don't finish it. So it actually *is* shit. As he says it is.'

They sipped their infusions, contemplating the man they both disliked.

'Which flavour is this?' asked Katie.

'Passionfruit and vanilla, I think. Why?'

'They all taste the same. Like tangy hot water. They always smell nicer than they are. What's yours?'

'Mandarin and grapefruit.' Dee offered it, and Katie took a sip.

'Yup. Tastes like mine.' She put down her own cup, pondering the infidelity question. 'It's about honesty. At any stage, Bob could have told me he'd shagged that woman. But he didn't.'

'He only lied by omission.'

'No. He lied. I asked him what he'd got up to while we were in limbo—'

'Separated,' corrected Dee.

'Whatever. And he said he'd missed me – and that's mostly what he did. Pined. Or some such tosh.'

'You can miss someone and sleep with someone else, can't you? To get over it, perhaps?' asked Dee, raising her eyebrows questioningly.

'In that case, he should have told me,' said Katie, emphatically.

'Maybe he thought you wouldn't understand. You can be a bit, erm …'

Katie smiled at her friend as she searched for the right word. 'Yes, I know I can be stroppy. But he should have tried. It was much worse the way he did it. Anyway. It's all over. For ever,' she said, standing up and draining her cup.

Dee reached for her bag and sighed. 'Well, I think it's a crying shame. You two were brilliant together.'

Katie looked arch. 'I've got a date tonight.'

'Oh, yes?' asked Dee, her eyes alight with enquiry.

'With Matt Damon.'

'*No*. Really?' Dee demanded disbelievingly.

'No. Not really,' Katie agreed. 'The next best thing, though. Adam Williams.'

'Oh, God, he's *gorgeous*,' said Dee, elongating the word, and trying to zip up her overflowing gym bag.

Adam Williams and Nick Midhurst were co-owners of Wolf Days Productions, the company that had produced *Start the Weekend* in Dorset.

They were both extraordinarily handsome. If Adam looked like Matt Damon, then Nick bore more than a passing resemblance to Ben Affleck.

'He's not only gorgeous, he's also very nice,' said Katie, running both hands through her long hair, bringing it forwards over her face and peeping seductively through the strands. 'And he isn't a lying toe-rag,' she added provocatively.

'Bob isn't a toe-rag,' Dee asserted, rising to the bait. 'And this is all a bit quick, isn't it? You finish with one, and another pops up before you've put the lid on the pen, or whatever the expression is.'

'Bonnet on the pig?'

'Whatever. So how did *that* happen?'

'He phoned me.'

'And?'

'And asked if I was free tonight.'

'And this was?'

'This morning.'

'And you've waited until now to tell me?'

'I was building up to it.'

'You were toying with me, is what you were.'

'I admit to a certain amount of toyness,' said Katie, with a laugh. 'And now I'm going to spend the rest of the day getting ready. Should I have my legs waxed and my bikini line done?'

'Absolutely not,' said Dee, horrified. 'Go out with your legs like a plucked chicken and walking in a funny way?'

'I don't walk in a funny way after my bikini wax.'

'Well, they aren't doing it right, then.'

'How can they do it in the wrong way?'

'Not taking enough off.'

'This is *not*,' said Katie, 'a top-trumps to see how much of a trim one gets. I refuse to have it bald, like some pre-pubescent schoolgirl. I'm an adult, with body hair. One doesn't have to have an entire bush under which to shelter when it's raining but one does need a little tidy-round from time to time.'

'All right,' said Dee. 'Don't get your knickers in a twist. Talking of which, do you have to wear awfully big pants to cover up the, er, hedgerow?'

Katie smiled. 'Enough already. If I can't wax, I'll have to go out as a scary hairy Mary. Which means trousers or a skirt and boots.'

'Well, while you spend many happy hours pondering your outfit, I'm going home to kip. Oliver and I are off to the cinema tonight.'

Oliver was a proctologist, and a great friend of Katie's doctor brother Ben, who was now a consultant anaesthetist at a large London hospital.

'Well, wish me luck, then,' said Katie, putting on her coat and pushing the chair in towards the table.

'Good luck – as if you need it.'

Katie was glowing. Her hair was shining, her green eyes glittering with anticipation.

'How the bloody hell do you look so good, considering your vast age?' asked Dee.

'Oi. I'll have you know that early forties is the new early thirties. And, in all seriousness, not getting up at sparrow's fart every morning is one of the greatest aids to youth. I'm finally getting my beauty sleep. In fact, the only fly in my ointment is the lack of a job, and therefore a certain restriction on my spending.'

'Oh, OK,' said Dee, with exaggeratedly weary acceptance. 'I'll stump up for the tea.' She made a slow move towards the till, shoulders slumped.

'Cheers,' said Katie, picking up her sports bag. She caught up with Dee, gave her a kiss on the cheek and left her. As she got to the door, she turned. 'Give my love to Oliver,' she called. 'I'll ring you tomorrow and give you a blow-by-blow account.' She made a suggestive face.

'You are disgusting,' said Dee, without looking up from her purse.

Katie's evening was everything she had hoped it would be – and more.

Adam was charming, witty, and very, very flirty. He and Nick had both fallen for the presenter of their show the first time they had seen her. But Nick was away supervising filming in France, and Adam had stolen a march on his rival. He had absolutely no intention of letting his business partner know that he was seeing Katie for dinner – or that she was single.

As soon as he had heard on the grapevine that Katie and Bob had split up, he had begun his campaign. He was enough of a hunter to let her think he knew nothing of the separation and was merely after a discussion of future projects in a 'more comfortable environment than the glass box that is my office'.

It had been an unnecessary subterfuge.

Katie considered dinner with any man to be a prelude to intimacy. 'They may *say* it's about work,' she bragged to her friend Kirsty, whom she'd phoned from the back of a cab on the way home from the gym, 'but if it was, they'd do it where I couldn't pounce on them.'

'Aren't you going to let him do the pouncing?' asked Kirsty, who was pregnant with her second child and couldn't imagine anyone wanting to pounce anywhere.

'We may do a double pounce,' Katie pronounced.

'With a triple salchow?'

'Absolutely. Followed by a … erm …'

'Ha. Stumped, my little fat friend,' said Kirsty, triumphantly.

'I think you'll find that *you* are going to be *my* little fat friend before too long,' said Katie, sliding to the other side of the cab as the driver swung round a bend too fast. 'How's it going?'

'Vomiting a lot, which isn't great. Actually, I wouldn't mind so much if I thought I could eat more without putting on too much weight. But I'm eating dry biscuits to keep it down, and I'm going through two packets a day. And then I've got this awful craving for pickled beetroot. I get up, throw up, eat biscuits, throw up, eat pickled beetroot, get heartburn, go to bed and start the cycle all over again. *And* I have the midwife saying I've got to hold off on the biscuits and not eat so much beetroot. At the moment I've got spots round my mouth from being sick, got red pee, red poo and Fred has left a deposit of something on one shoulder.'

'You poor thing,' said Katie, solicitously. 'Nothing I can do, I assume?'

'Take Fred off my hands occasionally?'

'If you're desperate enough to ask *me* to take him, you *must* be in a bad way. Of course I will. But you know I'm not that good when they're little. In a couple of years' time I'll be taking him out and about all over the shop. Tea at the Ritz. A tour of the National Gallery. Whatever.'

'He'll be three in a couple of years' time.'

'Well, the Science Museum, then.'

'He'll be three.'

'You see? I'm hopeless when they're like overgrown foetuses. I mean, honestly, what *do* you do with a one-year-old?'

'Play with him?'

'He'd get bored.'

'You mean you'd get bored. Enjoy your dinner. The idea of flirting with anyone in my current state makes me feel sick. You know, I always wondered why they called it morning sickness when it can strike at any time of the day or night. I've taken to chewing a nub of toothpaste to take away the taste.'

'Do you spit or swallow?' asked Katie with interest. 'As you know, one swallow doesn't make a girlfriend.'

'You are rude, crude and disgusting. I am now putting the phone down.'

'Enjoy your beetroot,' said Katie, pressing end call and putting the phone into her bag.

Back home, she had a shower and washed her hair, making sure that the conditioner was the nicest-smelling one she had. She let it dry naturally as she padded round the flat, slowly getting ready. With the towel wrapped round her waist, she opened her wardrobe doors and surveyed the contents. First things first, she thought, and took out her brand new, vertiginous, purple Gina shoes. They were not exactly practical. She could barely walk the length of the sitting room before she needed a rest – but they were beautiful. It wasn't often you got such a jewel-like colour. As soon as she had slipped them on in the shop, her head had buzzed with the busy refrain, 'Neeew shoooes.'

She put them on now and stood in front of the mirror, admiring the way they made her feet look so small and elegant. She dropped the towel. Hmm. Probably better with clothes.

She took out a little black dress with discreet fringing, which she had been thinking would be perfect. Had it always been so snug a fit, she wondered, as she tugged at the zip? She flicked back her hair from her now slightly sweaty face and stood up straight. Omigod, she thought. I look like a singed woodlouse.

Over the next hour, she became more frantic as she realized that virtually everything was too damned tight. Hot and bothered, she eventually chose a stretchy silk shirt, stretchy black skirt and large stretchy belt, all bought when she was going through a fat phase. Or, at least, she'd thought it was a fat phase.

It was bloody annoying how, as you got older, the phases became more frequent and longer-lasting. And how you could put on three pounds in a day, but a month later, you were still struggling to take it off.

Life, she thought. A constant battle to keep everything in place. If only steamed vegetables and pineapple were enough to keep the soul alive. She applied the bare minimum of makeup and, having checked that she looked as good as she could under the circumstances, she left the flat.

She usually tried to be a smidge late for dinner, but a taxi pulled up immediately, so she was – as usual – bang on time.

Adam, who was used to his ex-girlfriend sometimes forgetting to turn up at all, was pleasantly surprised to find Katie sitting at the table when he arrived. She was drinking a glass of tap water. 'I know. Not exactly racy, is it?' she said, after kissing his cheek, rather self-consciously.

To kiss or not to kiss? Too late now, she thought, gulping water to cover her confusion. First dates – if this was a first date – were always a mixture of excitement and trepidation. Not unlike opening a packet of fig rolls …

The restaurant was expensive, with heavy white damask tablecloths and elegant wine glasses. She assumed it had been chosen because it shrieked neither seduction nor business deal, but rather the quiet confidence of a platinum card.

Adam had also chosen his outfit carefully. He had started with his tan Longines watch and worked outwards. He was wearing a navy Paul Smith suit with a lilac shirt. Katie could barely look at him, he was so handsome.

After an initially shaky start, when he had talked vaguely about some of the projects he was working on, there had been an unspoken agreement that they were not there to discuss what he could offer in the way of programmes, but more about what he could offer in the realm of a merger.

As the dinner progressed, and the wine bottle emptied, they covered the gamut. Katie heard herself telling Adam how to cook aubergines: 'Slice in half, face down on a non-stick tray, bake for half an hour. Lovely with honey.'

And Adam was surprised to find himself telling Katie how he had always coveted a pair of X-ray spectacles he had seen in the *Beano*: 'I wanted them originally to see through this ant-house I had, and then, latterly, women's clothes.'

'Of course.' Katie had nodded understandingly.

At one point, she deliberately brought in Bob's name, making it clear that she was no longer with him.

'Oh, I wasn't aware that was all over,' he lied. 'Sad,' he lied again. 'Not for me, I hasten to add,' finally being truthful, 'but I remember he came down to Dorset on that first evening of the chat show. On his motorbike, wasn't he?' he asked, knowing full well he had been. He and Nick had gone to look (and drool) over it. Not only did he know that Bob rode a motorbike, he knew what model and even the state of the tyres. The bastard obviously raced it.

'Yes. But it's definitely over,' said Katie, making sure she hadn't been misunderstood.

He got it. 'Well it's always horrible when it doesn't work out,' he said, his fist balled into a valedictory salute under the table.

The restaurant was warm and cosy, the candles were guttering, the glasses empty. It was time to get the bill. Katie was feeling as smooth and melting as the chocolates that had come with her coffee.

Outside, she shivered, despite her coat.

'Cold?' Adam asked, wrapped in his cashmere jacket.

'A bit.'

'Let's see what I can do about that,' he said, and enveloped her in a warm hug that turned into a tentative kiss. Her response was everything he had hoped it would be. She almost fizzed with electricity.

Katie was in heaven. In stumbling words, between kisses, she invited him back to her flat, where cloud nine was superseded by clouds ten and eleven and eventually every silver lining in the sky seemed to be lying in front of her.

A few months' later when she had introduced him to her parents, they had been cautiously complimentary. They had driven up to Yorkshire in Adam's Jaguar, a sleek car with a throaty purr that was incredibly sexy. Just the feel of her thighs on the leather seat made Katie feel in the mood. It had been a balmy evening, with the scent of grass cuttings wafting through the open window.

It had all gone well until Adam had left half of his *pot au feu* of braised pork belly, as though it had been a restaurant.

All attendant members of the Fisher family were horrified. Katie's father, Jack, was an enthusiastic chef who spent hours poring over recipe books and watching television cookery shows. He didn't approve of leaving food. You took what you wanted and ate it all. Unless you didn't like it – in which case, you shouldn't have taken so much in the first place.

Katie's mother, Lynda, who was more than happy to let her husband do all the work in the kitchen, had been brought up by parents who had struggled to make ends meet, and she didn't approve of waste. And Katie was a pig, who couldn't understand why anyone wouldn't eat every single mouthful of her father's delicious food, then go back for more.

By the end of the weekend, Adam had partially overcome their distrust of a man who could leave food on a plate, and had charmed them. His major Brownie points had been accrued when he had praised a painting in the dining room, which he had correctly identified as a posy of peonies. It had been executed by Lynda during her artist phase, and derided by her family as reminiscent of the rear view of a family of baboons with their heads down a well.

'Mum is what we call, a keen … erm … trier,' Katie explained, as Adam admired a pottery vase in the kitchen while they were making coffee. 'That was originally a milk jug but, as you can see, its handle melted in the kiln. If you look closely, you'll also notice a small hole in the bottom where she failed to supply enough clay. Hence the dried flowers. It's like living with an overgrown primary-school child.'

'Oi,' said her mother, coming up behind them as they considered her creation. 'I'll have you know that was modelled on one by a famous arts-and-crafts exponent.'

'Called Slipshod,' said Katie.

Her mother smiled. 'I've left it to you in my will,' she said.

'Gee, thanks, Mum. Just what I've always wanted. Do hope you've left *Baboon Anuses on a Summer's Day* to me as well. Or does *anus* become *anii* in the plural?'

'You are a rude and ungrateful girl. If I were you, Adam, I'd have nothing more to do with her.'

He nodded. 'You're absolutely right. No one could ask for more than a beautiful painting of peonies and an homage vase,' he said, rhyming homage with *fromage*.

'Homage vase!' puffed Katie. 'What are you like? It's a piece of clutter.'

'My daughter, as I'm sure you're aware by now, considers everything to be clutter,' said Lynda. 'She would probably live in a sterile lab, given the choice. Every home she's had, you feel like you're sitting in a show house. Can't put your tea down without her tidying it away. And never anything in the fridge. Prisoners make their cells more homely.'

'Hey, Mum,' said Katie, a bit hurt by her mother's comments. 'I'm not that bad. Honestly. Just because I can't be doing with all the dust. Do you know, we shed an entire outer layer of skin every two days? That's a whole human. This vase has probably got one of Mum's legs and Dad's ears on it.'

Adam smiled. 'Actually, I'm afraid I have to blot my copybook and confess that I, too, live a slightly minimalist life.' He made a face of apology.

Lynda harrumphed and put the vase back on the windowsill. 'Shall we have coffee in the garden since it's such a nice day?'

They took the tray out to where Jack was pinning back some of the trailing roses, which were threatening to swamp, rather than cascade over, a small wall near the greenhouse.

'It looks lovely out here, Dad,' said Katie, gazing about her and sniffing appreciatively. She loved coming home to the grey-stone house, even if her mother did sometimes make her feel unwelcome by using her old bedroom as a repository for the detritus from her discarded hobbies. 'Incidentally, Mum,' she said, pouring milk into her coffee, 'I think Hercules may have rolled in some fox poo. He was smelling very ripe when I passed him.'

Hercules was their ageing Labrador.

'Wretched dog,' said her mother, without heat. She took her coffee, raised her voice and, without looking round, said, 'Jack. Your dog has been rolling in fox poo.'

He was lost in contemplation of a hollyhock and didn't respond.

'Jack. Hercules smells,' she said, louder this time.

'Oh,' he said. 'I'll get on to it. Excellent. Coffee. Have you poured me one?'

Katie passed him his cup and he took a big gulp. 'Your mother's turning into a right old cantankerous trout,' he said quietly, but with feeling.

'Was she ever different?' asked Katie, who had always had a difficult relationship with her.

He didn't answer but put his cup back on the table and went off to get some secateurs.

'Are you going to wash the dog, Jack?' asked Lynda, annoyed.

'I'll do it in a minute,' he responded curtly.

Later, when Katie phoned to let them know they had got back to London safely, her father told her that he had taken up fishing to get out of the house more. And, in passing, he mentioned that Bob was a frequent companion.

She hadn't said anything at the time, but that night, lying between crisp sheets and reading *Private Eye*, Katie acknowledged a twinge as she thought of her father and the handsome landscape gardener casting their lines into the cool waters of the river.

All her friends loved Adam, but Dee had expressed reservations. 'He seems just a teensy-weensy bit self-obsessed,' she told Katie, during a drunken night out with the girls.

Now, eight months on, Katie had to confess that she was beginning to feel she came a poor second to his business. He was expanding Wolf Days Productions, and they were taking on new staff. He did invite her to some of the business dinners, but they were dull, involving talk of editing suites and cabling. She had tried to lighten one up by brightly announcing that coconuts killed 150 people a year. Adam had had the temerity to tell her to be quiet. In front of everyone. It had taken her so much by surprise that she had immediately phoned her friends to discuss the state of her relationship.

She met her perennially single friend Kathy at their favourite budget café, its gay plastic tablecloths covered with garish pictures of vegetables. They ordered enormous frothy cappuccinos. Katie took all the foam and chocolate sprinkle off the top of hers and ate it before she addressed the matter in hand. 'He seems really keen one minute, then cools off the next,' she said. 'I know he's busy businessing at the moment, but it's making me feel needy. And I *hate* feeling needy.'

'Maybe it's because you don't have a job,' said Kathy, who was juggling two, and still not earning enough to make ends meet.

'Thanks for reminding me.'

'Well, you are what you do, and you've done bugger-all of any consequence for rather a long time.'

Katie had been limping along by writing for newspapers and magazines, hosting awards ceremonies and standing in for people on local radio. 'There's not much about,' she said ruefully. 'I was offered *Celebrity Masterchef*, but I hate cooking anything that's not vegetable soup. And I couldn't do the meat thing. A mate of mine, who was training to be a chef, gave it all up after he had to debone a whole pig. Apparently shot the shoulder ball, or whatever it was, into an enormous trifle made by the head pastry chef. Nobody saw it happen, but he was convinced that if he confessed the pastry chef would kill him. And that if he didn't, he'd be up before the beak for killing a trifle-eater with E. coli or whatever you get from uncooked pork.'

'Tapeworms.'

'Nope. Don't think it was a tapeworm. Anyway, he said he felt sick, drove home and never went near the place again. He presents some show on BBC4 now.'

'Food?'

'No, thanks. Unless they have one of their special lemon meringue pies. Why? You hungry?'

'I meant, does he present a programme about food?'

'Oh. No. I think it's vaguely intellectual. He was telling me something about Einstein's brain being bigger in one area than another and scientists trying to work out whether it developed like that or had always been that way. It seemed to me that it was a bit difficult to prove. I mean, it's not as though you can cut the top off people's heads to look at their brain – like peering into a boiled egg – to find out whether nature or nurture is responsible for what's going on in it.'

'What was his answer?'

'I don't recall.'

The inside of the café was steamy. Katie rested her hands on her cup to warm them. 'Hey, talking telly for a minute, did you see that beast Keera Keethley on *Hello Britain!* this morning?' she asked.

'Why do you watch that programme? It only annoys you,' said Kathy, who had witnessed the hurt Katie had suffered when Keera had replaced her on the *Hello Britain!* sofa.

The new presenter was exotically beautiful, with long black hair and blue eyes. She was also hugely ambitious, and employed publicists to make sure she was constantly in the public eye. She rarely drank alcohol, appeared at all the right events and in all the right places, and never left the house without checking in a mirror … unlike Katie, who had appeared in numerous periodicals and publications coming out of the wrong sort of places in the wrong sort of state.

'So what did she do this morning?'

'She was interviewing this chap from some massive quango about what they were going to do for consumers. And then – because, as we know, she's as thick as a Scotch pancake – she asked in that sugary little-girl voice she does, "But do you have any teeth?" And he looked bemused, smiled and said, "Of course I do." And then *she* looked confused. And Rod Fallon rescued her with, "Yes, she obviously doesn't mean it literally. What Keera means is what teeth does your organization have?" And then there was a two shot with Keera looking thunderous. It was hysterical.'

'You know, *Hello Britain!* suddenly sounds like it's worth watching,' said Kathy, rolling her eyes.

'Yes. All right. Maybe you had to be there.'

'Anyway. As for the Adam stuff, I'm sure he's in love with you, just as they always bloody are.'

'Being, as I am, the most gorgeous creature alive,' said Katie, deadpan.

'Frankly, I don't know what it is. You're an ugly muppet with no personality. It must be the smell of your feet,' said Kathy, glancing at her watch and doing a double-take. 'Damn. I really have to go. Enjoy your relationship for what it is. That's what you tell me when I occasionally get lucky. See you.' She grabbed her things.

CHAPTER TWO

All was not well at *Hello Britain!*. The ratings were down, and the editor was blaming everyone but himself. To be fair, it wasn't entirely his fault. He had had a new male presenter foisted on him by The Boss. Rod Fallon had all the presence of a sock. He had been brought in as a safe pair of hands to replace the previous male presenter, who had been unveiled as a kerb-crawling sex pervert. Mike had been the consummate break-fast-television host. He had looked good, sounded good, and could do a good interview. He had been able to turn a difficult situation into must-watch television with a sense of aplomb. Rod could do a passable interview – period, as they would have said in the States. He was grey in every sense of the word. And that, coupled with the easy on the eye, but essentially dim Keera Keethley, was not pulling in the viewers.

Simon gazed out of the window, his hands shoved deep into his trouser pockets, pulling the thin material tight over his bony haunches. As he waited for the news editor and the producers to come in for their morning meeting, he mulled over what was needed to give the show a boost – something that everyone would be talking about.

He turned as they walked in. 'Morning,' he said nastily. 'Not a good one, frankly, was it?'

The news editor, Colin, was taken aback. 'Oh. I thought it was. Bounced along. Lots of content,' he said.

'Flat as a tea-tray and about as inspiring,' said Simon, sitting down and tapping some of the keys on his computer. 'There was nothing that would have got me tuning in. We could start with some intelligent bloody conversation. What the hell was Keera doing asking what a potato clock was when Rod quite clearly said he'd got up at eight o'clock?'

'I think she thought it was funny.'

'We both know she doesn't think,' said Simon, bitchily.

Colin was surprised. What he couldn't have known was that Keera could no longer be bothered to flirt with the programme's editor. Knowing that she wouldn't be sacked now that Katie and Mike had gone, she had no further use for the little tête-à-têtes she'd had when she'd first got her feet tucked firmly under the famous *Hello Britain!* sofa.

Consequently, Simon's view of her had altered. The stirring in his loins was still there when he caught the glimpse of thigh and panties she flashed so regularly on the show it had almost become her trademark, but her lack of intelligence grated. That morning, she had called some starving Africans 'emancipated'. You could get away with that sort of mistake if you were seen as innately clever. People assumed you knew the right word. The problem was that Keera probably didn't.

'Right,' said Simon, clenching his small buttocks in the pale blue trousers. 'I have decided that we need one of our presenters out and about. Next week we'll go on the road. We'll do OBs every day.'

There was a subdued groan. Outside broadcasts were a recipe for disaster. There was disruption, chaos … and that was just the presenters' and crew's home lives. There was so much to organize, so many things to go wrong, and therefore more reasons for bollockings from Simon, who relished them.

'I want a different town every day. You can forget about Northern Ireland, but I want one morning in Wales and one in Scotland. One in the north, one in the south-west, the other wherever. But not London. And I want a proper reason for us to be there, not some made-up crap. Now. What have we got for tomorrow?'

The rest of the meeting was conducted in the usual bear-pit manner, with one person being picked on for a special mauling.

Afterwards they spilled out in silence.

'I don't see why it's so awful to do OBs,' Kent, the producer, said to Heather, wrinkling his nose in confusion. 'I've never been on one, but they sound like good fun.'

Heather was a senior producer, and had been there long enough to have seen knee-jerk reactions to low ratings before. They never worked. Only one thing did, in her opinion. Good content. Good interviewees. And good interviewers. She couldn't be bothered to explain that to Kent. He was besotted with Keera and would have been happy to watch a three-and-a-half-hour programme of her applying her lipgloss. Mind you, she thought wearily, it would be a damn sight cheaper than going on the road.

She wished she'd taken the job at the BBC when it had been offered five years ago. It had been a lot less cash, but she wouldn't now be dreading going on the road with Keera. She was difficult enough to nursemaid when she was at the end of a button hard-wired into her ear …

In his office, Simon sat at his keyboard and rattled off an email to Rod, Keera and Dee. He smiled. Sending emails that he knew would disrupt his presenters' lives was one of the delights of the job. He wondered how long it would be before he got the phone calls, and in which order they would come. He looked at his watch.

Keera was having a meeting with her new agent. At least, she was hoping he'd be her new agent. She had accidentally sacked the first one. She really didn't like it when things were unplanned. She had phoned to tell him to pull his finger out. 'I really should be doing better than I am,' she had said. 'I'm a high-profile presenter but what have I been offered? Nothing that I want to do. You need to get out there and be hustling on my behalf. It's up to you to make it happen. I said I wanted my own show, and I see no sign of it happening.'

She always liked to hear herself sounding firm. In control. Serious. She even drummed her burgundy-lacquered nails on the table as she was talking, admiring the way they looked.

But he had told her that if she felt like that, perhaps it was time for them to part company. Taken by surprise, she had agreed.

The agent had not been unhappy. He was relieved to see her go, despite the money she brought in for his company. She was high maintenance, constantly demanding more meetings, more action, more show reels sent to more people who couldn't possibly have anything to offer. He could do without her running his staff ragged in pointless exercises.

So Keera had phoned Matthew Praed, who was considered one of the best. He also charged a punitive commission, and demanded his clients follow his advice even if they felt it was against their morals, principles or best future interests. For her first meeting with him, she had chosen a slim-fitting black suit and high red stilettos.

'Obviously, most people know me as a war correspondent and journalist,' she said, to his amusement, since most people knew her for the naked photo shoot she had done shortly after joining *Hello Britain!*. 'But I don't really see myself as a newshound.' She crossed her immaculately stockinged legs, giving him a flash of black-lace panties. 'I want to be more famous than the people I interview. Actually, I probably am more famous than most of them. But I want to be someone whose name is so well known that I'm just Keera, no surname required. I know that sounds a little, perhaps, ridiculous ...' She tried out the latest smile she had been practising, which involved a shy look up through her fringe, then polished it off with the laugh she felt she had almost perfected. As it rang out, she wondered whether there should be a touch more bass. 'But if you can't be honest with your agent,' she finished, 'then who can you be honest with? I suppose my dream job would be my own show. Michael Parkinson, only younger and more female.'

Matthew was not surprised that she wanted her own show. Every presenter did. And he liked her sheer determination and naked ambition. It was what had driven him from his first job in a relative's nascent porn-film business to the *über*-agency he now ran out of a smart address in London's West End. He had many famous names on his books, and was well aware of the money that could be made at the high end of television. Normally he would have turned over a breakfast presenter to one of the five agents who worked for him, but he decided that until he had added her to his burgeoning number of bed notches, Keera would be under his aegis.

Matthew Praed was a renowned philanderer, and few women had not succumbed. He was a committed collector, and a commitment phobe. Today his well-honed body was clothed in an Ozwald Boateng brown suit, with a thin orange stripe, and a white T-shirt. 'Absolutely,' he concurred. 'One should always be honest with one's agent. Best to set out your stall straight away. What else are you doing at the moment apart from *Hello Britain!*? And I assume you'd leave the programme if the right job came up?'

'Too right I would,' she responded with alacrity. 'And as for other things that I'm doing, well … all I keep getting offered are programmes where I have to strip off.'

'Hmm. Perhaps that's understandable, considering that you've done a number of photo shoots where you've appeared naked.'

'Yes, but I don't have to tell you how different it is doing a photograph naked and being naked doing a television programme.'

'Of course not,' he said soothingly. Before their meeting he had enjoyed looking through the magazines and newspaper articles featuring Miss Keethley. She was a very knowing model, he thought. 'So where would you draw the line?'

Keera pursed her lips. Then, worried that she might not look very attractive in that pose, she relaxed them. She made sure her voice was well modulated and began to explain. 'As I said, I don't want to be seen only as a journalist. But I'm aware that the news side of it does carry a certain, erm … What's the word?'

'Cachet?' he supplied.

'Yes. Probably,' she said. She had thought a cachet was something you kept your jewellery in. But obviously not. 'And I don't want to lose that entirely by prancing about in my swimwear.'

'I see,' he said, smiling encouragingly and glancing towards her short skirt as it edged up slightly.

She was delighted to notice that. 'Apart from hosting my own show, I think what I would like to do,' she said, wriggling slightly in her seat, 'is to keep that journalistic allure, as it were, while actually going more entertainment-based. You know that I got the job on the sofa because of my war reporting.'

It had been something of a standing joke in the newsroom. Her first report had been so unutterably bad that the producers had had to write the rest and fax them to her so that she could rehearse them. What she had done well was deliver the words. And obviously no one could dispute that she had actually been in a war zone – albeit a very well-protected part of it.

'So I'm talking more … Oh I don't know … more *University Challenge* than *Love Island*.'

Matthew was enjoying this meeting. He liked Keera's *chutzpah*, no matter how misguided she was. He tried not to let his face show his incredulity. *University Challenge*! 'I think Jeremy Paxman's got that pretty well wrapped up,' he said, 'but I get where you're coming from.' He leaned back in his chair and crossed his ankles, admiring the soft leather of his Italian brogues. 'I'm sure we can get something brewing. If you're OK with our terms and conditions, I'll get my secretary to send over a contract. And in the meantime I can start setting up some meetings. I have quite a good relationship with Wolf Days Productions, who are big players in the television world, as you know,' he said.

She nodded. 'They were one of the ones who wanted me to do a programme wearing nothing,' she said, with a complicated sigh that was supposed to indicate it was understandable that everyone wanted a piece of her.

'Yes, well, they've always got something on the go, and it doesn't hurt to put your name out there,' he said, then dragged a large desk diary towards him. 'How are you fixed at the moment date wise?'

She reached into her Chanel bag for her BlackBerry. She noticed that an email was waiting from Simon, and quickly read it. Damn, she thought, as she scrolled through to her diary. 'Well,' she said, 'if we're talking about a one-hour meeting, max, I can do a week on Monday straight after the show. It'll get me out of the morning meeting at *Hello Britain!*, which is always tedious.'

'Better give me a few more days, just in case. And maybe tell me your free afternoons and evenings. Sometimes they can be more productive.' He jotted down the dates she gave. 'Good. I'll come back to you when I've firmed things up. And, as I said, I'll get that contract written up with our terms et cetera. It's all pretty standard. On the assumption that you sign, welcome aboard,' he said, standing up and holding out his hand.

She stood up, too, aware that her skirt had ridden up and was nudging the top of her thighs. She pulled it down a little. 'Thanks very much,' she said, taking his hand. Look at me being all businesslike, she thought. I'm like Reese Witherspoon in *Legally Blonde.* Only better, because I'm taller and, though I say it myself, better-looking. Better-sounding in the name department, too. Witherspoon. That is just so … so … withering. She made sure her handshake was firm, but not too firm.

Matthew, meanwhile, was contemplating how attractive she would look spreadeagled on his leather bed.

* * *

Outside, on the pavement, Keera phoned Simon. She was skilled enough in the politics of office life never to let her annoyance show. 'Hello, Simon,' she said, 'Keera here. Are you busy?'

'Not for you,' he said, adjusting his trousers and checking his watch. He was out by an hour. Must be losing his touch. Although he'd been right that she would be the first to ring.

'Just to let you know that obviously I'm delighted we're going on a little roadshow,' she said. 'Brilliant idea. I was just wondering whether it was worth one of us staying in the studio because, as we know, with the best will in the world, things can go wrong and you could do with a safe pair of hands to anchor it.' She really didn't want to be traipsing round the country meeting the *hoi polloi* and being pawed by local dignitaries. It was so depressing.

'Hmm,' said Simon, pretending to think about it. 'So we'd have Rod back in the studio, you mean?'

Keera laughed her new laugh. Only lower. Finally, she thought. Absolutely pitch perfect. 'Whatever,' she said, pertly. 'Although, as the main presenter, I was actually thinking that perhaps it should be me …' She tailed off.

'Oh,' said Simon, examining the chewed cuticles on his left hand and smiling to himself. 'I saw the main presenter as the one who was going to be at the hub. And the hub will be wherever we're going to be. The other person will be the co-anchor, and there'll be less for them to do. Which was why it was going to be you. But if you're happy with Rod being main presenter for the week …'

Keera had been caught out. She had insisted on being described in all correspondence as the main presenter. How very annoying.

'Keera?'

'Yes, still here. Sorry. I couldn't hear you. I'm standing on the street and a lorry just went past.'

'I said that the main presenter ...'

'Yes, I heard you,' she snapped.

'Oh. I thought you said you hadn't,' he said, pretending he'd believed her.

'I meant I hadn't quite heard you. Or wasn't sure I'd heard you correctly. The thing is ... well, to be honest, I have a number of evening corporate events, which I'm hosting.'

'Well, I'm sorry about that,' he said, not sounding even remotely sorry, 'but you're going to have to sort that out yourself. I'm sure you'll be able to get to one or two. You won't be on another continent, after all.'

She realized she had been comprehensively snookered. That idiot Rod would get the cushy job of sitting on the sofa, while she trailed round Britain staying at hideous hotels with the camera crew, interviewing the general public. Hateful. *And* she would be losing money. There was no way she'd be able to get to and from the corporate gigs if she was in the wilds of bloody Wales, for bloody example. At least it wouldn't be annoying for her new agent because they'd been set up by the previous one.

She phoned Matthew to see if *Hello Britain!* could force her to go if she decided to put her foot down.

36

'Moot point,' he said, moving his chair back from the desk and imagining her in lingerie. 'You could push it if you wanted. But it's a high-risk strategy. It might result in them not only sticking to their guns but demanding a change in your contract – and you really don't want that. On balance, I think you'll have to grin and bear it. As soon as we know where you're going to be, we can book cars or flights or whatever. And those corporates you absolutely can't do – well, I'll have a word with your previous agent. Since he arranged them, it's up to him to farm them out to someone else. I can always help him with names from our books, too.'

How annoying, Keera thought, as she hailed a cab home. She'd earmarked that money for a new car. A Mercedes SLK convertible in silver. Or possibly black. She'd have to check which one looked nicer with her hair – silver might be a better contrast.

Her co-presenter was also annoyed about the arrangements for the week of outside broadcasts. Rod had assumed that he would be the one going on the road, and had told his wife and daughter. He had been looking forward to getting away from home.

And, to complete the hat-trick, Heather was annoyed, too. Simon had decided that there was to be a plastic-surgery strand the week after the OBs and that, to save on health and safety issues with the public, producers would volunteer to undergo the procedures. He already had candidates for Botox, fillers and ears pinning. He had persuaded Heather to have her eyebags done. It had been a double whammy for her. Number one: she didn't fancy going under the knife, even though it was a local anaesthetic and she'd be straight out. Number two: she didn't think she needed it. But when she'd told a friend how she'd been press-ganged into having her eyelids sliced off, her friend had told her she was lucky. Lucky!

Katie Fisher caught up with all the gossip late that afternoon when she saw her senior producer friend, Richard, who had finished his stint of overnights and was about to have four days off. She caught the tube and an overground train to Twickenham, then went into a delicatessen where she bought a bottle of white, a bottle of red, some cheese, olives and a box of chocolate-covered ginger, to which she knew he was partial.

'Provisions,' she declared, as he opened the door.

'Thank goodness for that,' he responded, with a smile. 'We were down to our last weevil.'

'You look like shit,' she said, giving him a hug and moving a small dumper truck off one of the chairs.

'Why, thank you, kind lady. I wish I could say the same for you, but sadly you look great. Have you done something new to your hair?'

'Washed it. It's probably shrunk. You know how it is.'

Richard ran his hand through his receding hairline. 'That's not kind. Mine's not so much shrinking as disappearing. I've got to the stage where I talk about past events as "when I had hair".'

'I'd feel sorry for you, except you're such a damned fine figure of a man that you look more handsome without it,' she declared.

'I knew I liked you. Let's open the first bottle of wine and have all our week's units in one fell swoop. When do you have to go?' he asked, opening the tub of olives and putting them on the table.

She looked at her watch. 'I've got a few hours. Enough to do at least six or nine units, I'd have thought. Where are the children?'

'Oooh! Are these chocolate gingers, you naughty young lady?' he asked, picking a piece of sticky tape from the side of the container. 'They're out with Louise. We have a very small window of opportunity before we have to escape to the shed to continue drinking in peace and quiet.'

'How are they?'

'Oh, you know, a chippy thirteen-year-old, a clingy ten-year-old, and a noisy three-year-old, whose new lorry you almost sat on. Sometimes I wish I'd had the snip.'

'You love 'em.' She laughed and poured the wine. 'Cheers.' They chinked glasses and there was a companionable silence as the liquid eased its way to the right places.

Richard and Louise had met as producers on *Look West* – and, in the throes of new love, he had swiftly given in to her demand for impregnation. Then she had quite reasonably said she didn't want to leave it too long for another. He really couldn't remember the third occasion, which had resulted in Brett. He claimed she had got him drunk on his birthday and the next thing he knew she was handing him the white plastic stick with a line through the middle of the window.

'I do love them,' Richard confirmed ruefully, getting up to go and get a board and a knife for the cheese, 'but they're knackering. It would help if we didn't both work. What with me doing mostly nights, and Louise doing mostly days, we should have it all covered. Instead we're always trying to sort out the gaps. God knows how single parents do it. I'd have to build some sort of cage to stop the children getting out. I thought it was bad enough when they were little and keeping us up all the time or getting into trouble. Now, we're just a glorified taxi service. Daisy and Andrew have a bigger sporting and social life than we ever did. Even Brett gets out more than I do. Does life have to be this hard?'

'You could try being sacked as the anchor of Britain's foremost breakfast-television station and finding another job that paid as well.'

He smiled. 'Can't Adam give you a job?'

'He's got me in to do voiceovers here and there. But all the things he's been working on since we've been together have needed a different presenter from me. Or he puts my name down and the commissioning editor says they want someone else. I could do with losing about fifteen years and eight stone.'

'Don't be silly.'

'Television companies demand young flesh. Or less flesh, more youth.'

'Blessed are the young, for they shall inherit the National Debt,' he said.

She grinned. 'Very funny.'

'I think a comedian said it.'

'It's so annoying when they say it first. I like the one that George Burns said about how when he was young the Dead Sea was only sick.' She picked out one of the larger olives.

'Anything at all in the pipeline?'

She sighed and puffed out her cheeks. 'The usual. I get by on articles for newspapers and magazines and hosting corporate events.'

'At least you haven't got a thirteen-year-old stomping round the house, telling you she hates you and shutting herself up in her bedroom and picking her spots, or whatever she does.'

'Aaah. Bless her little cotton socks. I remember Daisy when she was a sweet girl who adored her daddy. I still use her expression when I'm blow-drying my hair and it goes static.'

He raised his eyebrows questioningly.

'This hairbrush is making my hair ecstatic,' she reminded him.

'Oh, I'm sure she'll come out the other side,' he said. 'After all, it's puberty, not a life choice. It's predictably tedious, though.'

'Andrew hasn't started it yet, has he?'

'No. Something to look forward to. And Brett, when he's not banging his head on the walls and developing his lunge technique, is adorable.'

'Takes after you. Oh dear. I think my glass has got a hole in it.'

'It's a trick one. It always does that. I think mine's got a slow leak, too.' He leaned over and topped up the glasses. 'There's also the smell. Did you have a bedroom that needed a public-health warning slapped on it when you were a teenager?'

She looked horrified. 'Do you know to whom you're talking? Little Miss Tidy! My mother used to ask me to give a room a lick and a polish and she'd come in to find me behind the sofa trying to get the pile up on the carpet where the feet had been.'

'Daisy goes berserk if you so much as suggest she wouldn't get so many spots if she washed more often, put her clothes in the laundry basket and didn't live in a pit.'

'I hate to break confidences, but Dee's still like that. I once found a cheese sandwich welded to the underneath of a fake Tiffany lamp.'

He laughed.

'Talking of which, how are things at the funny farm?' she asked.

'Rod Fallon's the dullest man on earth. He's so dull, that I almost long for Mike to be brought back.'

Katie made a face.

'I know,' he said. 'I kept telling you he wasn't what he seemed.'

'I still can't quite believe it, though. I didn't think he had much of a sex drive.'

'Hey, that's a good one. A new version of kerb crawling. Get it?'

'Yes, I get it. Doesn't take a genius to get it,' she said, in a quelling tone.

'Yes, but I got it first.'

'I wasn't aware it was a competition,' she said stiffly, and took a big slurp of wine. Then she smiled. 'But 'oo would've thought, eh?'

'Do you remember where you were when you heard he'd been arrested for kerb crawling?'

'I was doing my first programme in Dorset for Wolf Days Productions, if you recall.'

'Of course. Do you keep in touch with him?'

'You are joking? He was the one who wanted Keera in and me out, if you remember!'

'Oops. Sorry. I plead breakfast-television lag.'

'Talking of jet lag … did you know that it's worse if you travel west to east because it's easier to stay up late than get up earlier? And that in hamsters Viagra improved recovery by fifty per cent?'

'Where do you get all this bollocks from?'

'Wikipedia. Amazing what you find to do with your time when there's lots of it. Strange thing, time. When you're young birthdays take for ever and ever to come round. And now I'm … erm … thirty-six,' she said carefully, both of them nodding at the lie, 'I feel like I'm on a time-travelling escalator. It's like being at Yo Sushi! with them rushing towards you on the conveyor belt before you're even done with the first one. My mum used to tell me I'd get to the point where I wouldn't celebrate birthdays. I thought she was absolutely bonkers. Mad as a box of frogs. Off her chuff.'

'Oh, those simple days, when all you had to worry about was whether you were going to get picked for the football team. And whether you were going to have sex with Jackie Fenter.'

'Attractive, was she?'

'No. Available.' He cut another slice of cheese.

'Whoops. My glass appears to be empty again. It requires more units,' she observed.

'Help yourself. My arm's getting repetitive strain injury.'

She reached for the bottle. 'You were telling me about Rod Fallon. The man with the charisma of plankton.'

'Dull. Dull. Duller than any dishcloth. As dull as a smudge. I know they wanted to make sure we didn't get another Mike, but he's like a wet blanket, extinguishing any spark. Manages to render an exciting story dreary within a minute. And, as I predicted, Keera walks all over him. She's become a monster.'

Katie loved hearing Keera bad-mouthed. 'What's she been doing?' she said, eyes sparkling. She put her elbows on the table and leaned forward for the full gory details.

Richard smiled at her obvious relish. 'You are so bad,' he admonished her. 'However. You know I told you she'd insisted it was written into her contract that she was the main presenter?'

Katie nodded.

'So she nabs whichever interview she wants. Talks all over him. And she's taken to wilfully mishearing him because she thinks it's funny. Today she talked about a potato clock when he said he'd got up at eight o'clock. And she wouldn't shut up. One interview had to be slashed to a minute and a half because she overran so much. Oh, and – you're not going to believe this – Rod was taken out a fortnight ago by Derek in Wardrobe, to brighten him up.'

'Fantastic. I wondered why he was beginning to look like a fruit salad.'

'And then they waste all this money by dragging him to Savile Row. I ask you.'

'Must have cost them a fortune.'

'And he's not happy.'

'Bless.'

'And neither is Keera. She says it makes her look like she's a backing singer.'

'Bless.'

'Exactly. We've stopped it now, because it's boring, but we started having a verbal sweepstake on what fruit he'd resemble next.'

She looked at the big clock on the wall. 'How long have we got before we get swamped by children?'

'I'll give Louise a ring,' he said, and stood up to get his mobile phone out of his pocket. He had a short conversation. 'Half an hour,' he announced.

'So drink up. And tell me more.'

He shook his head. 'You're an addict. OK. Another Keera story, then. She was telling us she'd gone to see *Swan Lake*. She's been trying to up her cultural quotient. So she said to Heather, "And then the owl died at the end."'

Katie laughed. 'She did not!'

'She did. And Heather said, "Are you sure you don't mean the black swan?" Keera looked at her in that way that you know the penny's suddenly dropped, and said, "Whatever." I tell you, it was one of the funniest things. It's a shame she didn't say it on air.'

'Talking of daft things to say,' said Katie, 'did I tell you about my appearance on *Saturday Morning Kitchen*, or whatever it's called? Afterwards, they asked me if I could do a few random statements, like what's my favourite ring tone or whatever. So I said yes. And they asked me about my favourite snack to have in front of the telly. I said, "Are you rolling?" They said yes. So I said, "My favourite snack to eat in front of the television is cock porn. Sorry. Did I just say cock porn? Can I do that again?" So they said yes and I started again. "My favourite snack to eat in front of the television is cock porn. Did I say cock porn again? I did? I mean popcorn. Obviously." And I had to do it three times. *Three times.* I hadn't even got the excuse that I was knackered from the early mornings.'

As Katie and Richard broached their second bottle – and the children arrived back to find them giggling uncontrollably at the kitchen table – Dee, the weather presenter, was getting ready to have a bath … and was about to make a splash both literally and figuratively. Later, she blamed it on the tiredness that afflicts all breakfast-television presenters.

She had taken the tube to Highbury and Islington, then hoofed it to Oliver's house. Feeling hot and sweaty, she had given him a big kiss and belted upstairs to go and wash her feet. With hindsight, she should have had a shower. But at the time it had seemed eminently sensible to stick them in the bath. After all, it was only her feet that needed a freshen-up after running about in thick nylon tights. She couldn't explain how it had happened. She had washed one foot in the high, clawed-foot bath, then lifted the other and fallen backwards. Scrabbling to keep her balance, one foot had gone into the loo, beside the bath, and then there was a funny sound as it went round the U-bend. Boy, did it hurt! She yelped, tears came into her eyes and she collapsed onto the floor.

Oliver, while trying to be comforting, couldn't help laughing. 'What an idiot,' he said, gently cradling the ankle in his hands. 'You know what? I think you've broken it.'

And she had.

He had driven her to A and E, where she had been put in plaster and sent home with painkillers. She phoned the television station from the car to warn them that she was going to be on crutches for a bit.

The next morning in the makeup department, Dee was explaining what had happened. 'I can't believe how stupid it all was. You couldn't make it up. One minute I'm washing my feet, the next I'm upside-down with one of them stuck in the toilet. I would have laughed if it hadn't been so painful. What a thoroughly thick thing to do. Thicker than an Aran sweater.'

'Ah. They're lovely and warm, though,' said Vanda, the makeup artist. 'Just like you,' she said, cloyingly.

'Creep,' laughed Heather, who had come in to tell Dee that there was a problem with her weather graphics.

'Whereas you,' said Vanda, with a sidelong look at Heather, whom she liked, 'are like a sweater from a pound shop. Not very warm at all.'

'And an odd shape,' added Heather. 'Or maybe a jumper made out of different yarns. Mixed up, confused and liable to fall apart on a cold wash!'

They all laughed as Keera floated in. It was her new way of walking. She had been watching an Audrey Hepburn film and decided that languid was the new black.

'Something funny?'

'No,' said Dee, her grin still lingering.

'Well, you're all laughing.'

'Just deciding what kind of jumpers we are. I'm a thick Aran sweater,' she began.

'Well, I'll be a superfine cashmere with a hint of silk, then,' said Keera.

There was a small silence.

'Yes. Good. Excellent choice,' said Dee.

Keera sashayed out of the room to check her outfit.

'"Excellent choice," mimicked Vanda. 'What are you like?' She shook her head.

'Well, I hadn't explained why I was thick, had I?'

'She didn't give you a chance. And she'd never have got it, anyway.'

'No. If anything, she's a double-ply thick jumper with moths.'

'Or maybe a big hairy sweater!' said Vanda.

They giggled.

Keera swayed back in. 'Oh, my God! What's happened to your leg?' she shrieked, as she suddenly noticed the plaster on Dee's ankle. Her voice was much higher than she'd meant it to be, so she added another sentence in a lower range. 'Are you going to be out of action for long?'

'Broke my ankle washing my feet.'

'I assume you're kidding?'

'Nope. One foot in the bath, one foot out of the bath. Staggered about, foot went in the lavvy, broke my ankle in the U-bend.'

'You're making that up,' said Keera, aghast.

'God's honest,' said Dee.

'Well. How, erm …'

'Idiotic?' smiled Dee.

'Um. Yes,' said Keera. If she had put what she thought into words, she would have said, 'How weird. And how incredibly annoying, because that is *so* going to make it into the papers.'

It wasn't that Keera was short of column inches, but she absolutely hated it when anyone else got them. She'd have to phone her publicist and see if there wasn't something he could do.

CHAPTER THREE

In a minimalist flat in Chelsea, the radio alarm clicked. Ten o'clock. It was the most beautiful crisp, wintry morning. The sun was shining in a pale blue sky, there was a light wind, and a bird was chirping somewhere nearby.

There was no reason for Katie to put an alarm on, but she felt that grown-ups ought to have some sort of structure or things would start to go wrong. Not that she had *always* believed that. In the weeks and months following her sacking from *Hello Britain!*, she had relished the shapelessness of her days. Afternoons running into evenings, late evenings running into two days later ... the strangeness of looking at her watch and not having a clue whether it was five in the morning or five in the afternoon. But that had become boring in itself. Boring and, much worse than that, it had made her fatter and spottier. Eating outside normal hours resulted in endless snacking from nearby fast-food outlets – and organic chocolate was still chocolate.

She stretched and eventually pulled herself away from *Woman's Hour* on Radio 4 to make herself a pot of tea. She clicked her computer on, and as it hummed into life, she pulled a couple of eyelashes out as she contemplated the day. For some reason, gently pulling on eyelashes until one gave itself up made her feel happy. She examined them closely. Good thick bulbous roots.

'I feel heppy,' she said out loud, in an upper-crust accent. 'Oi feel 'appy,' she said again, using a really bad East End accent. 'Eye feel haffy,' she said, stretching her lips really thinly, and keeping her teeth together.

She spooned loose leaves into the teapot and put a mug, a strainer and a nice milk jug onto a tray. Even at her most slovenly (and slovenly, for Katie, meant socks worn two days in a row), she liked a proper tea tray. She went back to bed, pulled the duvet up and grabbed her laptop as her tea mashed. '*Je suis heureuse*,' she said huskily, with her head on one side as she clicked on her emails. '*Ich bin* happy,' she reiterated, with her chin jutting forward.

A number of little boxes popped up, and Katie (happily) went through them. 'Hmm,' she said, as one opened with a job offer, passed on from her agent's office. She read it thoroughly, then went back to the beginning to read it again.

On *Woman's Hour*, they were discussing wages. 'Because of the difference in wages for men and women, basically for one month of the year, women don't get paid,' someone was saying.

'Oh, yes, they jolly well might,' Katie said to the radio, getting out of bed to find her phone.

She called her agent.

'Jim Break.'

'Katie Fisher,' she announced.

'Well, hello, Ms Fisher. I can only assume you're calling about the offer from *Celebrity X-Treme* that I sent you on email last night.'

'That I am,' she said.

'And what are your thoughts?'

'Well, my first thought is what a lot of money. My second is … what is everyone else being offered? My third is … who *is* everyone else? My fourth is … has it bloody well come to this? Because we both know that unless I get an offer of a job pretty damn smartish, I'm going to run out of savings. There's a limit to how many articles I can write about being a woman in her forties on television. Or a woman in her forties *off* television, to be more accurate. And guesting on shows where they've run out of guests.'

'Well, going through those questions in no particular order … I agree that you haven't exactly been inundated with offers. But you need to think very hard before taking on something like this. It could be the worst career decision you've ever made. You know as well as I do what the producers will be hoping to get from you. And they'll be doing all they can to make sure you either do the things they're expecting … or look like you're doing them.'

'If you're talking about the drinking and the men, I think we can safely say that I'm over that. I haven't been hammered for months, and I am, of course, going out with the scrummy Adam, thank you very much.'

'Well, my advice – for what it's worth – is not to do it. Yes,' he pressed on, sensing her interruption, 'I know you need the cash and it *is* a large sum, but is it large enough to live on for the rest of your life? Even if you do get a few things off the back of it, you'll soon find them drying up if you've ruined your credibility.'

'That's all well and good but I need to eat in the meantime. Do you know anyone else they've asked? And what they might have been offered in the filthy-lucre department?'

'I think they're doing a trawl at the moment. I know some of the names. Not people you'd probably want to spend a fortnight with. As for the cash, no idea. It'll depend on profile, obviously.'

'When do they need to know by?'

'As soon as. But I honestly do think you'd be wise not to. You know, the other thing is that if you go into this, people will think your career's on the skids.'

'It kind of is.'

'No, it's more in the doldrums.'

'Doldrums, skids, whatever. The one thing it's not is on the up.'

'One programme offer, and you'd be on the way up. That's all it takes,' he said.

'Which is sounding suspiciously like what actors say. And that is *not* why I became a journalist.'

'It's hardly a journalistic job, this one.'

'But I could use it as one. Maybe write a book off the back of it. Or something,' she said lamely.

'Hm. I'd bet you a pound to a bunch of grapes that at least one other contestant will claim the same reason. Anyway, you asked for my opinion, and that's it. Don't do it. Enjoy the fact that they're willing to pay such a lot of money for the dubious pleasure of watching you make a complete tit of yourself and say no.'

'OK.'

'OK yes or OK no?'

'OK, I'll think about it.'

'All right. What are you up to?'

'Drinking tea.'

'As one does. Well, have a good morning, and I'll speak to you later.'

Katie put the phone down and took a long draught of tea to warm up her nose. The air was positively frosty. Then she picked up the phone again, and dialled Adam.

He answered on the first ring.

'That was a very speedy response,' she said, putting her mug down on the bedside table and snuggling under the duvet.

'That's because I saw who was calling.'

'Oh, good,' she said coyly. 'What are you wearing?'

'Is this a dirty phone call?'

'Only if you make it one. I like to know what you're wearing, so I can imagine it.'

'A navy suit, a cream shirt and a tan watch.'

'A tan watch?'

'Yes. Why? You don't like tan watches?'

'I'd have thought a silver one would go better.'

'You know nothing. Are you still in bed?' he asked suspiciously.

'No,' she said briskly, sitting up.

'Yes, you are,' he said, laughing. 'I can hear the sheets rustling.'

'I *was* up,' she said guiltily, 'but then I got back into bed because I was cold.'

'Yes. Of course. I believe you.'

'Anyway. Listen. I know we weren't supposed to be seeing each other tonight, although I've forgotten why. Was it one of your meetings? But could we, at some stage?'

'Hold on a second,' he said, and she heard him leafing through what she imagined was his diary.

She slurped some tea.

'Nice,' he drawled.

'Sorry. Got my lips in the wrong order,' she said.

'Is ten o'clock too late?' he asked.

'No. That would be brilliant. How about going to that new bar that's opened in Soho in that street that's erm, sort of perpendicular to the one that runs parallel to Regent Street? Or do I mean adjacent?'

'Journalism is so good for the communication skills. I assume you mean The Rag Room?' he asked.

'That's the one. Oh, good. Something to look forward to.'

'Nothing in the diary until then?' he asked sympathetically.

'Tons. I really ought to get on. There's a bit of dusting needs doing behind one of my books,' she said, with dignity.

'Well, don't be late for The Rag Room,' he admonished, 'I know how dusting can drag on. You start with one book and before you know it you're dusting behind another.'

'Am I ever late? Of course I won't be. And, in all seriousness, I do have a meeting at twelve. See you later.' She pressed the little red phone icon. Won't, she thought. Won't. Funny word. Even funnier when you consider that it's the short form of 'will not'. Why don't we say 'willn't'? I will marry you or maybe I willn't.

She grimaced. Maybe I willn't because I haven't been asked. Would I say, 'I will,' if I was? That's a difficult one.

She wriggled further under the duvet, and pressed her non-phone ear into the pillow to warm it up. Maybe I should put the heating on. Or maybe I willn't. She smiled. She might ask Adam later if he knew why it was 'won't'.

She didn't have a meeting, but she didn't like to think of him picturing her lying in bed all day like some latter-day Hollywood starlet. 'Ooh, 'ark at me, Hollywood starlet,' she muttered to herself, as she sat up again and drank the rest of her tea, making exaggerated lip-smacking noises for the sheer hell of it. 'Hollywood tartlet, more like. Or Stollywood tartlet. Hey, maybe I will have a vodka martini tonight. A nod to the old days.'

Since she'd been stepping out with Adam, as she liked to describe it, she had cut down drastically on the alcohol consumption, but there was nothing in the world like a vodka martini. The oil from the two olives lying on the meniscus. The smell of the vermouth. The way it almost crept into your mouth and past your throat, coating it with a glow. She started to salivate at the memory.

She tried to conduct an internal debate about the pros and cons of doing *Celebrity X-Treme*, but large wads of money kept hanging over the proceedings so she gave up.

She could not have known just how much Siobhan Stamp wanted to get her on the show – that she had been given a big budget for the fee by Lamplight, the production company. And that she was already laying the groundwork for a spot of skulduggery by seducing one of the confirmed contestants, Paul Martin – not that she needed much of an excuse to seduce a handsome man but the prospect of killing two birds with one stone was delicious.

Siobhan was facing a late night working on *Celebrity X-Treme*. She would have been pleased to know that not only was Katie more than halfway to accepting the company's kind offer of £150,000 for three weeks' work, but that she was going to appear in the newspaper the next day in a very unflattering pose. She found it therapeutic seeing a woman who had bested her – even if she was unaware of it – not looking her best.

The *Hello Britain!* roadshow was on its fourth day and Keera had had enough. As she had predicted, Dee had been hogging the headlines with her broken ankle. She'd been an '… and finally' on the late news, and had appeared on two afternoon chat shows. It wasn't exactly Anklegate, but Keera had been relegated to a supporting role in both senses of the word – not only a shoulder to lean on as they were making their way to the outside broadcasts, but once at them people were all over Dee and virtually ignoring the star presenter.

She opened a bottle of water from the minibar and elegantly sipped. She had been sent the duty officer's log from the morning, with all the calls that had been received, and looked through it as she sat on the bed, her suitcase open at her feet, its contents immaculately folded.

A man called Kevin Drayton had rung in: 'I watch your programme regularly. Obviously I'm not well.'

What a rude man, she thought, before reading on.

'I've been housebound for some years now. Could I please have Keera's autograph?'

Oh, she thought, not as rude as all that, then.

Miss Pam Franks had called: 'When are Girls Aloud coming in?'

Girls Aloud. She didn't think they'd been booked to come in any time soon. She'd have to have a word with the head of entertainment. On a need-to-know basis, she did need to know these things.

Dave Gilbert: 'Could I please come and visit because I love everyone on the show. Apart from Dee, who is very annoying. She always says it's going to rain and then it doesn't. Her hands are too big.'

Excellent. She'd make sure Dee saw that one. She wondered if there was any way of making the last two sentences disappear, since it somehow made Dave sound less sensible.

Four doors down the corridor, Dee had found one of the Sunday supplements from the week before in her suitcase. She was searching for a particular shirt that she could have sworn she'd put in. She wanted to wear it for her appearance on a local television station. The bed was piled high with clothes, makeup, hair-drying paraphernalia and a vase. Oliver had threatened to send flowers and it was best to be prepared. She swept the vase and an odd sock to one side and sat down to read her stars: '*Capricorn*. A decision you make in the next few days could have a major effect on the rest of your life. Don't rely on other people to make it, even if you trust them. The planets are promising much – but will only deliver if you take the initiative.'

Ooh. I wonder if I'm going to be offered a new job. Or maybe Oliver will propose. Or perhaps *I* should. She had another look. Yes, that would work. Or was it only a decision when you had to make a choice between two things? As in accepting something offered. Because otherwise, surely, you made decisions every day from the moment you got up to the moment you went to sleep. As in should I put this magazine down now and get on with the packing? As in; should I make sure I haven't missed something interesting in this before I get on with the packing?

She looked through the rest of the magazine, ending up at the problem page. 'I love my husband,' she read, 'but I have been having an affair since we got married. My mother-in-law is very rich. If I stay with my husband, I can get some of the inheritance when she dies. But if I stay with him, my lover says he will leave me. What should I do?'

Dee was horrified. That was exactly what was wrong with marriage, these days, she thought. Her own husband had had a fling with an au pair. Then she had found her new boyfriend in bed with a male hairdresser. People were disgusting, she thought. Claiming they were in love with one person, then going off with another. She put the magazine in the bin. Was *that* the decision that would make the rest of her life different?

She put the vase and the sock in the suitcase – forgetting to check where the other one was – then chucked everything else in haphazardly, along with a seriously full hairbrush. She leaned firmly on the bulging case and clicked the fasteners with difficulty. After a cursory look in the bathroom, she dragged the case out of the door, and let it close behind her.

At eleven o'clock, as the maids entered the hotel bedroom to find Dee's cleanser, mascara, nightie and one pink sock, Katie was indulging in one of her favourite activities. Tidying.

She had got up an hour earlier and eaten four pieces of toast with sliced apple and Marmite, then decided that she was going to do a pre-emptive spring clean. Unlike Dee, she had not read her stars. They shared a sign, but she rarely read it, and paradoxically put that down to being a Capricorn. An earth sign. Sensible. No time for that namby-pamby nonsense. She couldn't see how one twelfth of the planet would be having a good day, no matter where they were. Capricorns around the world were being tortured, becoming single parents, being put in jail, discovering they were ill, losing socks … yet apparently they were all about to travel or meet the perfect person. It didn't help that her birthday was three days before Christmas, so generally people bought her a birthday-cum-Christmas present. It made you feel rather bitter about birthdays and birth signs. Although Adam had given her a beautiful Cartier watch.

She spent a blissful day cleaning and de-cluttering. There were few things more satisfactory, she thought, as she sat cross-legged in front of a cupboard, than looking round and seeing a mountain of items to be disposed of at charity shops or in the bin.

And then there were the surprises. She had found a picture of herself, which she had believed long lost, with an Olympic weightlifter. She had interviewed him when she had been on the newspaper. It made her smile. She had written an article full of innuendo, which the news editor had threatened to spike unless she rewrote it. The trouble was that the name of virtually every lift had a double meaning, and for a girl who liked a pun, it had proved irresistible. The snatch. The jerk. How on earth did sports commentators do it? 'What a magnificent snatch. What a superb jerk.'

She remembered Mike, the pervert co-presenter on *Hello Britain!*, once saying, 'Congratulations on your Brazilian,' to the manager of a football team that had bought one of the world's best defenders. She'd had to explain to him later why she had barked with laughter. If you were a Brazilian, could you have a close shave? she wondered. She put the black-and-white photograph into a packet with a few others.

And that, she thought, is that.

She stood up, and went to get a whole load of bin-liners. She checked her watch. Perfect. Enough time to get to the Oxfam shop before it closed, then to Marks & Spencer for some groceries.

By the time she got home with her food, she was feeling too weary to do much. She put the vegetable curry into a pan and tried to work out a way of not dirtying another for the rice. In the end, she had it with toast.

Later, in the bath, Katie pondered life's conundrums. Why do the English call condoms 'French letters' and the cap the 'Dutch cap'? Why do the French call syphilis the 'English disease'? Who makes up jokes? What is a homonym?

She squeezed an in-growing hair on her leg and was then worried that it would look spotty later. Hopefully, Adam will be so busy elsewhere that he won't notice, she thought rudely.

Hair and hare. I'm sure that's a homonym. Or is it a homophone? There were days when all her English grammar lessons came back to her. And other days, like today, when she would be hard pressed to tell her oxymorons from her synonyms.

If you're bald, put a rabbit on your head because from a distance it looks like a hare.

She wished her bath was bigger. If she sank down until her chin was in the water, her knees were chilled and if she put her knees in, her shoulders got cold. She ran the hot water, moving her knees to one side to avoid scalding them.

By the time she got out of the bath – swaying and holding on to the radiator because of the rush of blood to her head – she was cranberry-coloured. She opened the bathroom door to a welcome blast of cool air. When she could stand unaided, she went into the bedroom, opened the wardrobe doors and perused the contents for fifteen minutes, deciding what to wear. She pulled out a soft brown dress that didn't need much ironing. Anyway, the heat emanating from her body would get rid of the creases. She matched it with a pair of high suede boots. The underwear choosing took four times as long. If underwear was going to be seen by a man, it had to produce no bulges and it had to go with the stockings. And that was another dilemma: stockings or tights? Stockings always went down well, in every way, but tights gave a smoother line. And then there were hold-ups, which some men found more attractive than stockings and suspender belts. It was all bloody exhausting.

Katie loved young relationships, but you wasted an inordinate amount of time on clothing. The *only* good thing about a comfortable old relationship was comfortable old clothes. Otherwise it was boring. It was like having cheese for the rest of your life – there would come a moment when you simply had to have something else.

Katie liked it when men held the door open for you and gave you flowers and gifts and wanted to kiss you all the time. She loved the electricity that flowed as your lips were about to touch. She could have lived on it for ever. She was a romantic who, deep down, was holding on to the hope that if she found the 'right' man, she would stop feeling like that. Was Adam the right man? He was bloody handsome. Funny. Intelligent. Good taste in music. Fit as a robber's dog. Ticks in all the right boxes … but was he Mr Right? Her soul-mate? Her sole mate for the rest of her life? God, that was scary. For the rest of her life.

She went over to the CD player to put on some loud music to stop the voices in her head. Muse. *Black Holes and Revelations*. She sang along to the words she could remember.

Excellent. She went back to the underwear drawer. Brown silk with a turquoise ribbon threaded through, and Wolford hold-up stockings. So much easier to decide when death and destruction were coursing out of the speakers.

Katie did a mental bit of air guitar, and then, with her head bobbing in rhythm to 'Starlight', she picked out a sheer petticoat to iron out the bumps. She checked in the mirror. Dress. Boots. Gold earrings. Perfect. Or as perfect as it was going to get, she thought, peering at herself again. Getting older was a nightmare. Every day another crow's foot. There must be no crows left with feet. Stop it, she remonstrated. Like there's an alternative to getting older. She gave herself an imaginary shake, tied her hair back loosely (to make it easier to loosen later), turned Muse off and set out.

She would have been gratified to know that Adam had been unable to concentrate fully on his meeting because he was thinking about her. Katie was unlike any of his previous girl-friends. He had always gone for women who were high mainte-nance. He hadn't *known* they were high maintenance until it was too late. They had seemed normal. Then they had half moved in with clothes, toothbrush and bags, and he had discovered that they took absolutely hours to get ready, that there was a drama if the manicurist couldn't fit them in, that one wrong word brought on a crisis. It was exhausting.

Katie was refreshing. She was beautiful, made him laugh, and was sexy – in fact, sexier because there were no tantrums. There was none of the rowing that had marred his other relationships. She had *joie de vivre* in spades. And the peachiest of bottoms. Just thinking about her was making him hot.

He dragged his mind back to the meeting – Nick was staring at him. Was he supposed to have said something? He brought his attention fully into the room.

'Would you agree to that?' asked the man from BBC Factual.

Adam thought quickly. 'What do you think, Nick?'

Nick slightly raised his eyebrows. They were talking about an antiques project Adam had masterminded so it was basically up to him to sign it off. 'It sounds fine to me,' he said.

'Good. Then that's what we'll do,' Adam said, and looked at his watch. 'Tell you what, I have to go now. Any odds and ends, we can discuss on the phone, yes?'

As they left, Nick asked mildly, 'What were you thinking about when you were supposed to be making the deal?'

'Suddenly remembered there was some stuff I'd got on the computer, and I'd forgotten to save it. Debating about whether I should go back to the office and sort it.'

'Cool,' said Nick, who clearly didn't believe him. 'See you tomorrow, then.'

Much, much later, between cotton sheets, the decision was made. Adam and Katie lay tangled together. She was snuggled down, with barely the tip of her nose showing, while he had most of his torso and one leg on top of the duvet.

'How can you bear to have so much flesh exposed to the elements?' she muffled.

'I think you'll find it's tolerably warm out here. We have this new-fangled contraption called a boiler, which is linked to something we modern-day humans call central heating.'

'It's freezing.'

'There's something wrong with your thermostat.'

Katie giggled.

'What?' he asked.

'When I was growing up, we had a really dodgy boiler,' she replied.

'Called your grandmother,' he interrupted.

'Cheeky. No she was not. We had this really dodgy boiler—'

'Can't believe you call your mother that.'

'Stop it. If you'll let me finish … We used to have this really dodgy boiler.' She lifted her head and gave him a hard look, as if she was daring him to speak again. 'And periodically it would have to be riddled. When I look back at the winters at home, they were punctuated by shouts of "Has anybody riddled the boiler?", which is just ripe for comedy. But either we weren't as crude, rude and disgusting as we generally are now, or that expression was not in our lexicon.'

'It was a more innocent time.'

'Maybe.'

'Well, you only have to look at children's television programmes then and now,' he said. 'They're more knowing today.'

'*Teletubbies* wasn't knowing.'

'*SpongeBob SquarePants*? It's filth. Pure, unadulterated filth.'

'*SpongeBob SquarePants*?' She laughed. 'Or are you talking in the cleaning sense?'

'I was watching it last night. It's sheer pornography. This bloke Bob sponging down a woman with square pants on.'

She chortled and put her nose below the duvet.

'What are you doing?' he asked, with a throaty growl.

'Warming my nose up,' she muttered, through the feathers. 'I think you're the one with a dodgy thermostat.'

'How the hell would you cope in the cold weather in Norway if you decided to do *Celebrity X-Treme*?'

'Good point. I assume there'll be central heating,' she said, hopefully.

'What? The Norwegians have mastered the art of centrally heating their countryside?'

'It's called global warming. We're all helping,' she responded, wriggling onto her front and propping her head on her hands. 'You are awfully handsome,' she said, gazing at his chin from close range.

Adam smiled down at her and kissed the tip of her nose. 'You're rather scrumptious yourself. But, really, on a purely basic level, are you up for *Celebrity X-Treme* in terms of the chilliness of the environment? If you find this cold, how on earth are you going to cope with minus thirty, or whatever it could be?'

'I'm sure they'd provide me with adequate clothing. They wouldn't have us freezing to death. 'Elf and safety would have something to say about that.'

'And what about playing the game?' Adam looked down at her, as she lay in the crook of his arm.

'You really do have one of the best profiles of anyone, ever,' she said, caressing his emerging stubble.

'Is that a profile when you can only see my chin?'

'Well, what else could you call it? An anti-file?'

'Idiot,' he said, stroking her shoulder. 'And *you* have the silki-est skin of anyone, ever.'

'Why, thank you kindly, sir.'

'But you haven't answered the question.'

'What was it again?'

'Do you think you can manage to do a reality show without coming a cropper?'

'I don't know. It depends who the other people are, I suppose. I'll probably hate them all and look like a narky git.'

'"Git". What a very elegant word,' he commented.

'Onomatopoeic, I would say. Gittish behaviour. Just saying it makes your mouth into a long, disapproving line. Try it,' she prompted.

'Gittish behaviour,' he obliged her. 'I concur. It's probably impossible to say with your mouth any other way.' He tried it. 'Goatish. Ah, interesting.'

'You see? Anyway … it's impossible to know whether I can play the game or come out of it in a muppetish way.'

'You do make up some interesting adjectives. I suppose what I'm trying to say is that you have to be prepared for them to edit the programme in a way that's not in your favour. And it seems to me that those who come out of these things best are the people who are perhaps the most innocent – to come back to what we were talking about earlier and those innocent times. And innocent is possibly the last adjective I would ever use in your general direction.'

'I open my nostrils upon you. I spit in your general direction,' she misquoted, from *Monty Python and the Holy Grail.*

'Your mother smells of elderberries and your father was a hamster,' he continued.

'Hmm. I do see what you mean, though.'

There was silence for a while.

'The thing is …' she said slowly '… that there is also the matter of the money …'

'Yes. It is quite a lot. But not if it's the end of your career.'

'That's what my agent says. But could it really be the end of it?'

'That's a million-dollar question. It could radically alter how people view you, and therefore have a radical effect on the sort of jobs you get offered. But you know all the pros and cons, you don't need me to tell you. What's your gut feeling?'

'I wish people wouldn't ask me that. I don't have gut feelings. Unless I've had a large dish of chillies. But it could be fun. I could maybe get a book out of it.'

She felt him smile. 'What?'

'You could, of course,' he said, 'but if that's an excuse for why you want to do it, it's a pretty poor one. You might as well be honest and say you're doing it for the cash. If the money was less, how much of a difference would it make?'

'I don't know. I've done that in my head already. Obviously it would make some difference, particularly if they were offering bugger-all. I'd just say no. Funnily enough, the thing that would make the biggest difference is if I could find out who else was going.'

She thought for a moment, then sat up abruptly and looked directly at him. 'Hey. Do you think *you* could?'

He put his leg under the duvet and gave a little shiver.

'Ha. Told you it was cold.'

'It was an involuntary shiver such as one gives when a tickly hair gets up one's nose.'

'Was not. You're cold. Let me feel that leg.' She reached out and caressed his firm thigh.

'Mmm. Nice,' he said.

'Couldn't agree more,' she concurred.

'I could try to find out,' he said slowly, thinking about who he knew at the production company. 'But you know how they treat these things – like they're covered by the Official Secrets Act. And sometimes they honestly don't know until the last moment.' He paused. 'I get the impression you're more tempted than not.'

'Yes, I think that would be fair.'

He hugged her to him and dropped a kiss on her hair. 'Mmm, you smell good.' He closed his eyes and inhaled the scent of her hair. Katie melted and curled herself round him. The duvet sighed.

And so it was that Katie found herself in northern Norway at the beginning of March, in a hut, on the first night of filming for *Celebrity X-Treme*. There were bunk beds and bedrolls on the floor. It was the luck of the draw as to who had been assigned what, and Katie had pulled a short straw. She tried to get comfortable in her sleeping-bag as she listened to the snoring coming from the one on her left. She stifled a giggle. A bag in every sense of the word.

Denise Trench was the singer in a pop band that had had a couple of hits and won the Eurovision Song Contest before disappearing from view. The band had been about as trendy as a pair of pale nylon slacks. Their fan base was an army of women of a certain age, who smelled faintly of wee. Nowadays, Denise was more famous for her colourful sex life, and her occasional forays into bottles of Jack Daniel's followed by stints in rehab.

Katie sighed and wriggled around in her sleeping-bag again. Whichever bit of her ended up touching the bedroll became instantly chilled and started to hurt. This is ridiculous, she thought. If I hadn't bought that bloody cottage in Dorset, if I hadn't spent my money on holidays, if I hadn't taken my eye off the ball, if I hadn't trusted Mike and he hadn't stitched me up and got me sacked from *Hello Britain!*, I could have been coasting towards a happy early retirement instead of lying here in a ruddy shed with a draught and a whole load of people I'd rather see shot and mounted. On a wall. Obviously.

She thought back to the conversation with Adam. He had warned her, but she hadn't listened. She had been seduced by the noughts on a cheque. Had thought she'd be able to cope with it. Oh, God, she groaned inwardly. I used to think people were numpties to appear on these wretched programmes. And now I'm one of them. How has it come to this?

She wriggled again, and merely succeeded in twisting her thermal pyjamas so far round she felt like a human Mr Whippy. She raised her bottom, unscrewed her pyjamas and humphed back down. She was freezing. It was no good. She was going to have to get out and put some more clothes on.

She rolled the sleeping-bag down, wriggling like a caterpillar, and crept out, instantly alerting the producer on duty in the gallery, who was watching the bank of television monitors in front of him. He pointed it out to the director, who mixed from a shot of Denise Trench snoring like a warthog and gently breaking wind.

Mark, the producer, was bored already, and hoping he could wangle a move to daytime. Nights were so tedious. So far this evening he'd got barely five minutes' worth of good stuff. The best bit had been some kind of movement going on in Peter Philbin's mid-region. The girls would like that. Particularly since one of the camera angles had got his fully muscled-up chest emerging in all its glory. That would go into the storyline they were hoping to manipulate in which the handsome soap star would end up in some way, shape or form with Crystal, the model. He checked on the camera which was pointing at her to see what she was doing. Sleeping prettily, with her lipgloss surprisingly intact. She was so much better-looking without all her usual makeup, he thought.

He watched Katie as she tiptoed past the others, and boosted the sound.

'Who's that?' whispered Tanya Wilton, who was close to the door.

The woman more infamous than famous after a fling with a politician was having a fitful night.

'Sorry,' murmured Katie, 'I've got to get more clothes. My head feels like an ice cube.'

'Mine too,' said Tanya, quietly.

'Do you want me to pass you something? I've got a spare hat.'

'Could you? That would be great, thank you.'

Katie tiptoed to her suitcase, which she could see in the dim light of the moon, shining through the uncurtained windows, and rummaged through its contents. Her years as a presenter on breakfast television had stood her in good stead for pitch-of-night rummaging. Even at home in the flat, she hardly ever put the lights on if she had to get up in the dark, preferring instead to move around partially blind. So here in Norway, at three o'clock on a frozen spring morning, she was in her element, mentally logging where everything was. She found her hat and then, buried underneath, discovered a balaclava. Lovely, lovely balaclava. Thank goodness her chin was going to be warm. She also found a scarf and her sheepskin mittens and crept back past the sleeping bodies to Tanya. 'There you go,' she whispered, handing over the hat.

She snuggled back into her sleeping-bag, and pulled on her balaclava, wrapped the scarf firmly round her neck and slid on the mittens. Within half an hour she was finally warm enough to sleep.

Up in the viewing gallery, Mark peered closer at the camera. As daylight cast a gloomy glow, it was quite clear that the erstwhile queen of the breakfast sofa had crammed an enormous pair of green pants on her head, the stout gusset protecting her nose from the cold, her closed eyelids nicely framed by one of the leg holes. The producer and director shared a smile. That would *definitely* go in.

At six o'clock, they handed over to the early birds. The story producer was the glorious strawberry blonde Mark rather fancied. 'Morning, Siobhan,' he said, unfurling himself from the seat.

'Hi, Mark. Anything happening?'

'Not a huge amount. Peter having an early-morning fumble. Katie with a pair of knickers on her head.'

'Really? May I ask why?'

'Think she mistook them for a hat.'

'Ah. Yes. Easily done. Same number of holes. Not.'

'No, seriously. She was rooting around in her case in the dark.'

'Why didn't she use a torch?'

'Probably trying not to wake the others.'

'You don't think she did it hoping for air time?'

'Watch the tape. It didn't look like it to me.'

Siobhan went over to talk to the director as Mark gathered up his belongings. 'What do *you* think?' she asked.

'Looked genuine to me,' he answered, yawning and stretching. 'Actually, even if she did it for effect, it's still pretty funny. And not much else has happened. I think we're going to have to stop wearing them out during the day. Four hours on that ice assault course yesterday – I was exhausted just watching them.'

'I'll have a word with the activities people,' she said, 'but they seem keen on distancing us from other reality shows by having them out and about. Otherwise it's just *Big Brother Does the Jungle* in a cold place. It seems to be holding up well so far, ratings wise. As soon as we start the voting next week, the senior executives will probably have another look at it. I'm going to get a coffee – do you want anything?'

'No, thanks. I'm whacked. I'm going to get straight off as soon as we've done the handover.'

Mark picked up his holdall and walked over to the desk to join the other overnighters as they ran through the storylines that were emerging. Page three's Crystal was being flirty with Peter Philbin. Denise Trench was doing lots of ranting at columnist Paul Martin. Alex Neil, the outrageously gay designer, was getting very close to the DJ Steve Flyte, who appeared to be enjoying the proximity. Tanya Wilton was continuing to spill the beans about her fling with the politician to Flynn O'Mara, 'astrologer to the stars'. Katie Fisher was falling over a lot. And Dave Beal, the alleged comedian, was still telling jokes that failed to raise a laugh.

Mark straightened up from where he was leaning on the desk. 'I also think it might be worth keeping an eye on Katie Fisher and Paul Martin. There might be something going on there.' He turned to lob his plastic water cup into the bin and failed to notice Siobhan's slight smirk.

Siobhan was a man's woman. She dressed for men. She studied men. She hunted men. She hated women. She particularly hated successful women. It didn't matter that to Mr and Mrs Average, as she thought of them, with their drudge-end jobs, she was successful in the exciting world of television. She was a bitter woman. She had chips on her shoulder. And they were well-nurtured chips.

Many years ago, when she had cherished dreams of being a presenter, she had been beaten to her ideal job of hosting *Hello Britain!* by Beatrice Shah. She had been covering holiday shifts, and had thought it was a done deal. After finding out that her position had been usurped, she had stormed into The Boss's office to demand an explanation. He had looked surprised and said she had never been considered. That under no circumstances would she *ever* be considered after research had shown her to be out of touch with the viewers.

'Out of touch with the viewers?' she had shrieked. 'What do they mean "out of touch"?'

'Apparently you sound snotty, for want of a better word,' he had said. The Boss was not an unkind man, but he hadn't taken to Siobhan. She was too ballsy for his liking. He preferred a more emollient woman. She did an efficient job, but her predatory nature meant that some of his male staff had confessed they felt hounded.

'Look, I'm sorry if you were under the impression that you were a shoo-in for the job. But I was told Simon had said there was no point in you applying for the post.'

Siobhan had gritted her teeth. Simon hadn't told her. And she *had* been given the impression that she was a shoo-in for the job. And she knew exactly why he hadn't seen fit to let her know. She had literally been sleeping with the enemy. What a fool. What a waste of her unquestionable talents. She wouldn't have minded so much except that he was such a very inadequate lover, with an unattractive pouch of fat under his stomach and rather girly pink nipples. She curled her lip derisively. Lover! No love involved on either side. A business arrangement that had worked out well for him.

He would pay. She would make him pay.

A week later, she had gone into his office and told him she was pregnant. If an etiolated man could have been said to blanch, then he did.

'I don't know whether you and your wife,' she imbued the word with venom, 'would be prepared to bring up the child as your own?' She let the sentence hover for a moment. 'No. I thought not. Well, in that case, I suggest you hand me a cheque for the abortion at a private clinic. If you need the bill for your records, I will obviously supply it.' She raised her eyebrows. She was hoping he wouldn't demand proof, but if the worst came to the worst, she was fairly sure she could cobble something together.

He had been only too keen to write her a cheque – it seemed a small price to pay for the months of illicit sex he had been enjoying. Sex with attractive women had been in short supply. His wife – a woman of limited intelligence – had married him in haste after a threat of deportation. If he had been single, Simon would have been bragging to all and sundry that he had been bedding Siobhan Stamp ... possibly even that she was pregnant with his super-sperm. He handed over the money and watched her departing figure with regret.

She had left the station, and reported from various windy locations up and down the country for smaller and smaller television companies. Her failure to be nice on the way up the presenting ladder had contributed to her descent and, eventually, with hatred in her heart, she had taken a job as a producer for a company called Wolf Days Productions. In the year that she had been there, she had made no friends. Her colleagues – mostly women – were either slightly scared of or loathed her.

They recognized a vulture when they saw one, even one in sheepskin clothing from Joseph.

She had, to her delight, managed to ensnare one man. She had been proud to announce her seduction of Nick Midhurst, one of the bosses. Keeping her claws sheathed, she had managed to charm him into her bed. Not for her the tenet of discretion being the better part of valour. That had been her downfall.

Nick had faced such a barrage of fury from his staff that he'd had a rethink and brought the blossoming romance to a swift end.

'Very wise,' said Adam, when informed. 'Apparently she's poisonous. Good worker, and very easy on the eye but, according to virtually everyone here, not the most pleasant of people.'

The company was a friendly one, and everyone was encouraged to air grievances to stop the backbiting that was endemic in the industry. There had been a steady stream of people going in to complain about their latest recruit.

She had seemed to accept the end of the affair with equanimity, and continued to work hard. But she had blotted her copybook irretrievably by trying surreptitiously to add Adam's scalp to her belt. She had sent him a flurry of explicit texts, which he had shared with Nick. And that had sealed her fate. Her contract had not been renewed.

'She has a circular bed and black satin sheets,' revealed Nick, darkly, after she had cleared her desk.

'Urk,' said Adam, making a face. 'Or was that pleasant?'

'No. Very slippy. And you know ... she's not quite as beautiful without all the makeup. To be honest ... sort of eel-like. And,' he added, 'she makes quite a lot of noise.'

Adam raised an eyebrow.

'It begins with a miaow, then works up to a full-throated roar,' he said.

'Goodness,' remarked Adam.

'I have neighbours,' said Nick. 'Albeit a field away. I was worried they'd come round to see whether I was setting up a safari park.'

They left their office to find everyone breaking out bottles and biscuit barrels of celebration.

'I hadn't realized she was *that* unpopular,' murmured Adam, taking a small plastic cup of champagne.

Siobhan, re-entering an hour later to collect a contacts book, had found a full-scale party going on. There had been a hideous silence as she stalked across the office, opened a drawer and extracted her property. She had nodded at the revellers, strode back across the office and slammed the door behind her.

There was an explosion of noise as it shut.

'Phew,' said Gemma, one of the young producers. 'I thought for one awful moment that she was going to put some kind of evil spell on us.'

'I know,' said another producer, Rose. 'She'll no doubt be casting nasturtiums upon us as we speak.'

'Aspersions, I think,' muttered Adam.

'That too,' said Rose.

'And that isn't the same as casting spells, anyway,' added Gemma.

'Whatever,' said Rose, flicking the 'what' and 'ever' signs using her middle three fingers.

Siobhan, meanwhile, was walking determinedly out of the building. 'I will prevail,' she muttered under her breath. 'I will get back at them. All of them.'

And, earlier than expected, she had found her chance.

At *Celebrity X-Treme*, she was the producer in charge of following up possible storylines and, boy, was she going to manipulate them. After the names of the contestants had been finalized, and before a frame had been shot, she had taken Paul Martin out to dinner. She had Googled him. Thirty-seven years old. Columnist. Handsome with thick, sandy hair and blue eyes. Single. Rich enough. Obsessed with television and football.

One thing she had discovered during her career was that few men would turn down the offer of free sex from an attractive woman. Within a week, she was manoeuvring him just where she wanted him. 'Could I call this being in the pole position?' she asked, as she shimmied into the bedroom where he had been waiting.

She had made one fatal mistake. She had taken off her makeup before emerging from the bathroom. Her deep-set eyes receded, and her translucent skin became blue. Her pale lips looked like a snake's.

Paul Martin was keen to make his mark on this game show. He wanted to get into television, and that meant staying in the contest as long as was feasibly possible. Preferably, he wanted to win. He knew what Siobhan's role was, and how useful she could be. And it helped that she was a cracking-looking bird. Until that moment …

Still, if he had to have sex with a woman who, without makeup, looked like a gonk, then so be it. He could have done without the black satin sheets. He hadn't thought they existed outside the pages of his porn stash. But here they were. It was enough to put you off your stroke. And what was it with the baby-doll nightie and the high-heeled fluffy mules, which were click-clacking on the back of her heels as she sauntered towards him with a sultry smile?

Generally, he went for exotic, dark-haired beauties like Keera Keethley from *Hello Britain!* who, he felt sure, would never have bought a carpet with flowers etched into it such as the one he was looking at. He took a deep breath. Right, he thought. Here we go. Concentrate. He closed his eyes and threw himself into the breach.

The next-door neighbours looked at each other over their glasses as they sat in bed, reading.

'The cat's out again,' said Mrs Smith, wearily, as the miaowing grew to a crescendo from the other side of the shared wall.

CHAPTER FOUR

Katie blew gently on her fingers as she listened to the morning briefing. Dog-sledding. Excellent. This was what she had worked towards all her life. The very pineapple of her career, as Mrs Malaprop said in *The Rivals*. Sheridan. Or Sheraton? No. That was a hotel chain. Concentrate. Concentrate. Which is a strange word when you come to think of it. Because it can mean undiluted orange juice. Why did the man sit looking at the carton of orange juice? Because it said concentrate. Is undiluted concentration a tautology?

Oh, no, she thought, now I've missed more. If I wasn't so tired … It can't be that difficult. Stand on the ruddy sled. Unhook snow anchor. Foot off snow brake. Collect items *en route* in return for treats for your team. Hardly rocket science. If my fingers haven't dropped off from frostbite, that is. That would be vaguely amusing, handing over a trinket and a dead finger. She wondered if it would come away like a scab … a slight sucking noise, and then a bit of a pop?

'Sorry?' she said, as the trainer asked her a question.

'I asked if you were OK. You appear to be sleeping standing up. Did you hear what I said?'

'Yes, yes,' she said hurriedly.

'What was it?'

'It was … It was … Actually. No. I didn't hear. Sorry.'

'Right,' said the trainer. 'This really is important. I'm not here for my own benefit. I'm trying to make sure that you don't injure yourselves. Or the dogs. So, to recap for those who have dozed off, make sure you keep your foot on the snow brake when you go downhill so that you don't catch the dogs' paws. Keep your feet on the brake when you bend down to release the snow anchor. And always have your snow anchor thus …' He hooked it over the side of the wooden shopping-trolley-shaped sled '… so that you don't take anybody's head off if you go careering past them. Not that you should. Because we'll be docking points for silly, stupid or dangerous riding. In the worst case, we'll send you home. All the items to be picked up are heavily wrapped with two stiff handles sticking up to make it easier. The enterprise will be timed. But it's more important that you do this safely. And since it will all be filmed we can even retrospectively ban anyone who has flouted those safety rules. The routes are clearly marked. Team A will follow the blue flags. Team B will follow the red flags. You nominate three members from your team. I'll give you twenty minutes.'

Katie stamped her feet in her enormous Arctic boots. One of her toes had been dead when it went in and it wasn't about to kick into life any time soon.

'One hoof beat for yes, two for no. Good horse,' said Paul, nodding at her feet as he went past.

'Are you in my team today?' she asked. 'Only I get so confused with this Team A and B stuff. Why can't we all be on the same team?'

'They want competition. Frrrriction.' He rolled the *r*, and made a suggestive face.

'I just want to be voted off and get home so I can read a bit of friction at home in my comfortable bed,' she replied.

'I cannot believe you're saying that already. It's two weeks out of your life. Get over yourself. I'm going to nominate you to do the trial. Give you something to think about instead of dreaming of home. Aren't you enjoying any of it?'

'My favourite things so far are: the snoring of my female companions every night, the loud guffing coming from your room and the deadly stench coming into ours, the smell of the drop loos and the stalactites of poo in them, the cold, the hat hair – oh, and the pointlessness of most of it.'

'Well, tell them you're going home and give them back the money,' he said caustically.

'Ay, there's the rub,' she said ruefully, tripping over a rock.

'Mind that rock,' he said, deadpan.

'Thanks. It's because of my dead toe.'

'Do you want me to give it the kiss of life?'

She barked a laugh. 'I think it needs more than a kiss.'

'I give very good foot.'

'And that means?'

'Well, it's like good head, only with feet.'

'Saucy,' she said appreciatively. 'I hope they're not tuned into our mikes.'

'We'll never know,' he said, lying.

Siobhan had told him what they'd be looking for, and he knew that he and Katie would be heavily featured.

'I wonder if they're watching us at home, or if we're the final nail in the "celebrity-" ' – he made quote marks in the air – 'reality-show coffin. Would you watch if you were at home?'

'I suppose I would if I knew someone in it,' she said, after thinking for a moment. 'Or if I saw clips of it somewhere and it looked good. I was hooked on the ice dancing. And the dancing, for that matter. On the other hand, they did go on for ever and ever. I'd grown a beard by the time it was over.'

'An interesting use of your time. Big beard?'

'Full Captain Haddock.'

'Nice.' He nodded appreciatively as he held open the door to the central hut for her.

She stamped her boots on the doormat to get rid of the snow, and put them neatly to one side. She then removed her enormous snowsuit and hung it on a hook. They opened the interior door to a wall of warmth coming from the newly stoked fire.

'Why can't it be this cosy at night?' She groaned.

'Because someone would have to keep it going – and make sure we weren't all burned to a crisp by a stray faggot,' said Denise Trench.

'Are you talking about me?' asked Alex Neil.

Katie shook her head and went to stick her toes on a piece of warm slate. 'Shall we get this sorted, then?' she asked. She looked around. 'I'm only being bossy because … because, as you all know, I *am* bossy. Does anyone actually *want* to do this task?'

Four people nodded.

'Remind me. Whose team are you all on?'

Paul and Crystal were Team A.

Peter and Tanya were Team B.

'In which case, we need one more of each. Who can we bludgeon into this? Denise? You fancy it?'

'No. I'll do the washing-up.'

There was a slight groan. Denise was the kind of washer-upper who merely moved the dirt around. A dog would have licked the plates cleaner.

'Flynn?'

'I'll do dog feeding and dog-poo shovelling afterwards. Those lovely ickle doggies are so bliss,' said the astrologer to the stars.

'Dave? You'd be great,' Katie said sarcastically.

'Don't mind if I don't. I have a cough coming on. A fer-cough, that is.'

'Terribly amusing,' said Katie, who found his idea of comedy deeply unfunny. 'What will you do instead?'

'I thought I might tidy my rheum.'

'Ha bloody ha,' she said, normally the first to appreciate a bad pun. 'And really?'

'I don't know, Miss Bossy Boots. There's always something needs doing that I can do.'

'Alex?'

'I honestly don't think I'd be very good at it.'

'Steve. It's got to be you.'

'Why? Make one of the others.'

'This is ridiculous. I'll have to go myself, even though I don't want to. If nobody else volunteers, it's the short-straw solution.'

They all looked at the fire.

Katie sighed and went to get the straws out of the box.

She didn't see Paul's foot move slightly, and before she knew where she was, she had cannoned into the table.

'Whoops. The straw that broke the camel's back,' said Dave.

'Are you all right?' asked Paul, solicitously, scrambling to his feet.

'Mm. Yup. Think so. Just a flesh wound on the leg. And one of my arms has been wrenched off completely. It's all right, though. No one needs to worry. I've got spares on the other side.' She rubbed her thigh. 'I'll be covered with bruises. At this rate I'll be able to do join the dots.'

'Maybe you'll find it looks like a lovely big walrus,' commented Alex, bitchily.

'How kind,' said Katie, sarcastically, smiling gaily at him. If she hadn't marked him down as a horrid little queen, she would have been upset by his constant references to her weight.

She started picking up the straws, then hobbled over to the rest of them to find out who would be the sixth member of the dog-sledding teams. 'Please let it be Dave,' she prayed.

But it was Steve.

'I can't believe I'm doing this, when I've got a perfectly good bus pass waiting for me at home,' he said.

'You're here for the same reason as the rest of us,' said Katie. 'We need the money. Or the profile. Or both. And the sooner we get on with it, the sooner it's over.'

'I'm really looking forward to it, actually,' said Peter, flexing his biceps and doing a drum roll on his washboard stomach.

Crystal gazed at him admiringly with her big blue eyes. 'So am I,' she simpered.

'I can hardly wait,' said Tanya, standing up and going to put on her snowsuit.

'Do you need me to rub that thigh down later?' asked Paul, as he and Katie made their way to the sleds.

'As in with a block and a piece of sandpaper? You make it sound like it's a dodgy bit of pine cupboard.'

'Nothing wrong with a pine cupboard.'

'And nothing wrong with my leg that a warm bath won't sort out.'

'I'll be able to check that out for real with our hot-tub action tonight,' he whispered close to her ear, bringing her out in goose-bumps.

'Are you flirting with me?' she asked him, looking directly into his eyes, and accidentally at his mouth while she was at it. Stop it, she thought. You've got a man at home. You're just isolated and you need a hug.

'I may be,' he said, giving her a knowing look. Good, he thought. All going according to plan.

The cameras had caught the conversation on a long shot, and although the sound was low, it could be boosted in the edit. Siobhan had been alerted by one of the producers, and she made sure the director had clocked it too. This was like taking candy from a baby, she thought. 'Let's make sure the drinks cabinet is stocked high for this afternoon in the hot tub,' she said. And then, she thought, light the taper and stand back for fireworks. If that wasn't a hopeless metaphor, considering the damp.

She sat at the back of the gallery, debating what she needed in an ideal world. A drunken kiss and a fumble between Katie and Paul would be perfect. It was odd watching a man with whom she had been intimate getting intimate with another woman. But she was the puppet-master so it gave her a rather perverse thrill. She used sex to get what she wanted, and there had been no danger that she would fall for a man she considered vain and stupid enough to think she wanted him to win for love.

Looking at Paul dispassionately on the screen, she thought she saw signs of dissipation and a weak mouth. Tasty, though. She'd give him that.

She switched her gaze to another screen where Crystal and Peter were talking together. They were about as intelligent as krill, she thought, but in the edit, we can play up the romance to get the audience tuned in.

Thinking of newspaper pictures, she fancied a good close-up of one of the older women's cellulite. And Steve either nutting Alex or kissing him. She smiled.

The director smiled back at her. 'Looking good?'

'Oh, it's looking very good,' she responded. 'I'm going to have a quick word with the cameramen. And woman,' she added, remembering the lone camerawoman who would be covering the Jacuzzi shots.

She stood up, stretched and, out of the corner of her eye, noted that Katie had shot out of frame, catapulted from the dog sled in a perfect arc, as she had tried to take up the snow anchor. Her bottom had virtually filled the screen at one point, replaced with a surprised eyeball and a spot erupting near her nose.

An excellent bit of tape, she thought. Nice when a plan came together.

Siobhan could have spoken to the cameras on their earpieces, but it was easier to talk to them face to face and explain exactly what she needed. She shivered in the freezing air as she slid her Hermès sunglasses quickly into place. The bright white snow was brilliant with the sun bouncing off it. She crunched over to one of the snowmobiles and raced off.

Katie could have done without falling off the sled before she had even started the race. Bloody dogs. First rule of television: never work with dogs. Second rule of television: never work with dogs like Denise Trench. What a hateful old battleaxe she was. I hope I never turn out like that, she thought, bitter and twisted. And drunk.

She was standing on the snow brake, trying to stop the dogs hurling her down the slope again. 'Concentrate. Concentrate. Concentrate,' she muttered to herself, like a mantra. Then made the fatal error of looking to her left, where Paul Martin was nonchalantly tapping one foot on the snow brake, the other on the rung of the sled.

Was it possible? He was smiling seductively at her. How could that be? He was wearing an Arctic suit, snowboots, mittens, a balaclava and sunglasses. But he was definitely giving her the come-on. She frowned and looked down at her boots, then took one hand off the sledge to fiddle with her goggles – just as the dogs, barking and straining to be off, were given the green light.

It was one of the scariest things she had ever done. The dogs stopped barking and tore round the course. Crystal fell off on the first bend. Steve was crouching in an unorthodox position, hanging on for dear life. Katie was bouncing about like a dried pea in a blender. At one point, her sled appeared to be a foot off the ground and about to overtake her dogs, the lead animal glancing round to see what had happened. She tried to grasp the handles of the weighted bags as she went round, but whipped past three in a blur and only managed to get the fourth because the sled knocked into it. At the sixth, she finally fell off, and was dragged the last two hundred yards, shovelling so much snow up one of her trouser legs that she looked as if she had lop-sided elephantiasis.

'That's exactly what you should do if you feel you might be getting a bruise,' said Paul, admiringly, as he sauntered over to her. Put lots of ice on it. And such an easy way to do it, you clever thing.'

She lay bruised, battered and winded in front of him, as one of the cameras zoomed in to take a close-up. 'Thanks for your solicitude,' she gasped. 'No. No. Don't help me up. I'm fine. Just a modest amputation here and there.'

He bent down and gave her his hand, bracing his foot against one of hers. 'Up you come, you snow queen,' he said.

She could feel his muscular body under his suit. He really was a very attractive man, with big, slightly shovel-shaped hands that were brushing snow off her legs and bottom. Her heart lurched. She was remembering other hands. A landscape gardener's hands. What was wrong with her?

She was in love with Adam. How had a vision of Bob suddenly come striding into her mind? She could see him as clearly as if he was standing right in front of her. His heart-stopping smile. The way he ruffled his hair until it stood up after he had been working in the garden. His broad shoulders. The golden hair on his forearms.

She gave herself a mental shake. Then a physical shake. And strode away from the group with a grim face.

'What's up with her?' asked Crystal, who was standing next to Peter.

He shook his head. 'Dunno. Who cares?' he asked, admiring the curve of Katie's rump in her tight snowsuit. From the back, he thought, she was surprisingly attractive for an older woman.

I care, thought Siobhan in the gallery, metaphorically rubbing her hands with glee.

At that very moment Bob was sitting in a boat on a reservoir in Yorkshire with Katie's father. Jack had rung that morning. 'Lovely day. Do you fancy it?' he had asked jovially.

Bob, who hadn't been up for long, wandered out into the garden with the phone to check whether he did or didn't fancy fishing. Considering it was only the beginning of March, it was a beautiful day. There was a gentle breeze and a hint of a nip in the air. But otherwise it was a very good day to hang out and see if the trout were nibbling. 'Oh, go on, then,' he said.

'How long will it take you to get ready?'

'Maximum half an hour. I can't move anywhere without a coffee. I'm assuming the reservoir?'

'This time of year, any other suggestions?'

'Yeah. Right. Brain not quite in gear. Shall we stop on the way for breakfast?'

'I've already eaten. A bowl of porridge with an assortment of nuts and raisins, a sprinkling of cane sugar and a dash of maple syrup.'

'Do you ever eat as us mere mortals?' laughed Bob.

'You mean just porridge with honey?' asked Jack, considering the question.

'Exactly.'

'No. Can't see the point,' Jack replied. 'I keep an extensive larder and I like to make use of it. But this isn't getting the baby bathed. I'll pick you up in three-quarters of an hour to give you adequate preparation time. I'd suggest a nice set of thick thermals – it's going to be blasted cold on that there reservoir.'

'I was thinking T-shirt and shorts,' joked Bob, and went to make his coffee.

When he and Katie had split up, he had thought that his relationship with her parents would also founder. But partly due to them being near neighbours, and partly through Jack and Lynda's persistence, he had become very close to them, particularly to Jack. He was very like Katie in his sense of the ridiculous, his love of language and his guilty look when he caught himself in the middle of a story he really shouldn't be telling. His mouth would suddenly go into a Wallace and Gromit line that made Bob hoot.

He was already in his wellies when Jack arrived. He put his fishing gear and a carrier-bag of food and drink into the boot.

The older man nodded with approval at his attire. 'Good hat,' he said, checking out the colourful article on Bob's head. 'Are we going to put on a show for the fish?'

'You mean tempt them up with fishy renditions of plays and films we've loved?' Bob considered the prospect, his head bobbing gently in time to the music on the car radio, as they drove off. 'We could start with *A Fish Called Wanda*. Or is that too obvious?'

'Not terribly inventive. How about … *A Fridge Too Far*?' suggested Jack.

'Nice. Do you think a trout would know about a fridge?'

'Well, go on, then. Think of another.'

'*Lord of the Flies!*' he exclaimed.

'Good one,' said Jack. 'Love this song. It reminds me of Katie.' He smiled as he reached forward and turned up the Scaffold singing 'Lily The Pink'. They joined in raucously with the chorus, Bob harmonizing at various points.

Mention of Katie's name always turned a knife somewhere in his stomach. But it passed. 'Katie's favourite was it?' he asked, only his slightly tense hands giving it away.

'Yes. You could pick any line and she'd know the rest of it. It was one way to get her to take disgusting medicines.'

Bob Marley and his Wailers superseded the Scaffold, and they hummed and jigged in time to the beat.

The wind had picked up as they approached the reservoir, and they shivered as they got out of the warm car.

'This is where we have second thoughts and decide to go and have a fat boy's late breakfast at the greasy spoon,' said Jack.

'I can hear the trout from here,' said Bob. 'They're calling your name.' He cupped his hands and, with his lips pursed in a trout pout, very quietly intoned: 'Jaaaack. Jaaaack.'

Jack smiled.

Bob removed his offending headgear and put it into the boot, retrieved his bags and put on a thick thermal hat.

Jack reached in and struggled to remove an enormous hamper.

'My God. What have you got in there?'

'Lynda,' he responded.

'You've finally done it, then,' said Bob, giving him a hand.

'Actually, she really is pissing me off at the moment. It would be nice to get an occasional thank-you. Or some acknowledgement that I'm even there. I think sometimes she'd only notice me if I was dead and decomposing in the middle of the hall. And even then I'd just be an irritating blob on the carpet.'

'Not that bad, surely?' queried Bob.

'Bad enough,' said Jack, grimly. 'Now, what do we fancy? Start off on the bank and then get a boat if it's not working? Or straight into the boat and bugger the bank?'

'Oh, let's just do the boat. With that massive hamper, we're rather hampered. As it were.'

'You will not consider it a hamperation as soon as you see what we've got for lunch. And I've also brought a number of snacks for your delectation and delight. There's soup. Fresh bread. Oh, and I put some leftover blackberry and apple crumble in too.'

'I might as well leave my paltry offerings in the boot,' said Bob, raising his eyebrows.

'Tempt me,' challenged Jack.

'A Mars bar and a Bounty. An out-of-date cheese and pickle sandwich. Two apples. Overcooked sausages. A meat pie of dubious origin. It was in the fridge and it hadn't gone green. And … something else.'

'A stomach pump?'

'And … four spring onions,' said Bob, triumphantly, as though he had won *The Generation Game*.

Jack rolled his eyes. 'I'll go to the fishing lodge and sort out the boat, then,' he said. 'You take the hamper down.'

'I'm just a muscle Mary to you, aren't I?'

'Exactly,' Jack threw over his shoulder, as he went off to pay for the boat and the fishing licence.

Later, sitting comfortably in the boat, they prepared to cast off.

'What are you going for?' Jack asked.

'I,' pronounced Bob, 'am getting out the big guns. I am going to lob in a dog-nobbler.'

Jack nodded dubiously. 'Well, one can't help but admire your bravado. I, however, will be doing a hare's ear or a March brown.'

'You're after a starter, then, while I'm pulling out dinner.'

'If you pull out anything at all.'

'There's an enormous ten-pounder with my name on, just waiting for me to cast this lure,' said Bob, confidently.

'Yeah. Right. I bet you ten quid that my ear beats your nobbler.'

'Done.'

As early morning gave way to mid-morning, and mid-morning retired hurt before midday, the two men continued to cast their lures and put the world to rights.

Jack had not been kidding about the lunch. 'There's enough to feed the cast of *Ben-Hur* here,' Bob mumbled, through his starter of beef carpaccio and sesame oil.

'It's in case we get marooned.'

'A distinct possibility here in the wilds of Yorkshire, on a reservoir.'

There was a lull in the conversation as they addressed themselves to lunch, washed down by a bottle of fine red wine.

'Wonder how Katie's getting on,' said her father, as he adjusted his position to allow the food a freer passage.

Bob allowed his heart to get back to a regular beat before he asked, 'Were you in favour of her doing it?'

'What do I know about television? I just told her to think about the worst that could happen, and if she could deal with that, then, yes, do it.'

Bob took a slurp of wine. 'But the worst could be massive injury. Limbs off. Frostbite … death?'

'Doubt it. Anyway, I meant in terms of loss of dignity.'

They were quiet for a moment.

Jack was thinking about his own dignity, which was being eroded by his wife. In the past, his advice to both Katie and Ben had been that decisions taken were better than decisions forced. Perhaps now was the time to take his own advice.

Bob was thinking about Katie and how dignity was a word he would be hard pressed to use in the same sentence. Funny. Adorable. Gorgeous. Sexy. Bright. Beautiful. He gazed at the sun glinting off the water. If onlys sparkled in a line. 'Hey,' he said. 'Trout. Hand me my rod.'

In the car on the way home, slowly warming up, Bob couldn't keep the glee from his voice. 'So when will I be getting my ten quid, then?' he asked.

CHAPTER FIVE

Jim Break was sitting in front of the television with the most enormous steak roll and a tomato. He took a huge bite and, after ten minutes of chewing, addressed his girlfriend, Amanda, who was sitting on the other side of the sofa reading *Psychologies*.

'You're sure this is a balanced diet, then?'

She glanced up, putting her finger on the line she was reading so that she wouldn't lose her place. 'You said you wanted some protein so you've got some protein. And the tomato's good for your prostate.'

'It's chewy.'

'What? The tomato?'

He shook his head at her stupidity ...

She continued, 'Good for your teeth if the steak's chewy. What's up with you, anyway? You've gone grumpy on me. You were perfectly happy about it before we sat down. You could have had some of my hummus and vegetables, if you'd wanted.'

He turned back to the television. 'I told her not to do it,' he said, watching his client's bottom virtually pressed up against the screen, followed by a large spot and a bit of nose.

'She needed the money,' said Amanda.

'I know. But it doesn't look good. It looks like she's on another downward slope. She'd only just got sorted out after being sacked from *Hello Britain!.*' Jim had been Katie's agent since her first job in television, and she had made him a tidy sum when she had moved to the hallowed breakfast-television sofa. Then she had got sacked, appeared all over the newspapers being drunk and disorderly, and almost been done for assault after a night out on the town. There had been the chat show, which had lasted for two series – then nothing. Female television presenters in their late forties were not exactly in demand.

He watched Katie trip over again. 'They're trying to make it look like she's either dyspraxic or a dipsomaniac,' he said, shooting a jet of fat down his top as he took another bite of his roll.

Amanda went back to her article, which was about whether it was better to rip off a bandage that was stuck to the skin or to do it slowly. She chomped a carrot as she read. 'Interesting. What do you think?' she asked Jim. 'Pain wise. Short and sharp or long and less sharp?'

'Hmm. Short and sharp, I'd say.'

'And you'd be wrong,' she said. 'Apparently, the brain copes better if it anticipates a longer amount of low-level pain than a short amount of agony. That's interesting, eh?'

'Hmm. This programme's operating on the same principle. It's too painful to watch. Look at her now.'

Katie Fisher was attempting to back into the outside Jacuzzi without revealing too much of her bottom and thighs. A sneaky camera shot showed everything.

'She won't like that,' said Amanda, on a sharp in-breath.

Then there was silence apart from the commentator on the television, who was drawing their attention to a mishap about to happen.

Katie, edging backwards, missing her footing and splashing inelegantly into the hot tub, legs akimbo, face an evocation of surprise.

Amanda laughed.

Jim tutted. 'How she can keep her credibility after this is anyone's guess,' he said disapprovingly.

'She'll be all right,' said Amanda. 'She's proving she's like the rest of us. It's what she's always going on about anyway – that no matter what you do, who you are, we're all basically the same underneath. They'll love it. You never know, it might be the making of her.'

'More like the unmaking of her. And if I was her new bloke, I wouldn't be too happy about the way she's canoodling with Mr Martin.'

They continued to watch as the storyline switched to Crystal, the ex-page-three model, and her open-mouthed adoration of the terminally dull but exceptionally well-hewn Peter Philbin.

'That is a very attractive item,' commented Amanda, then devoted herself to her magazine again.

In her extraordinarily messy flat, Dee was in bed, watching *Celebrity X-Treme* and eating low-fat, low-carb, low-sugar, low-taste biscuits – she was on a diet. She was halfway down the packet and was now at the crucial tipping point: to continue, finish the packet and get rid of the evidence, or to stop and eat something with a little more nutritional value?

She looked again at the ingredients. They appeared to be the components of a dirty bomb. Her fingers hesitated. Then she took another and popped it into her mouth whole as the ad break came to an end. She snuggled down under the duvet as the biscuit softened. All that snow and ice was making her feel cold.

The phone rang. She glanced at caller ID. Oliver. She swallowed quickly. 'Hi, handsome. Is it important? I'm watching Katie on *X-Treme*.'

'Shall I come round? I'm about five hundred yards from your door as we speak.'

'Go on, then.' She threw down the phone, turned the TV volume to ear-splitting and, with one eye on the screen, hurriedly tidied up. Or as much as she could with her ankle in plaster. Dee claimed that only boring people had immaculate flats. She liked to misquote Erma Bombeck: 'My second favourite household chore is tidying. My first being hitting my head on the top bunk bed until I faint.'

She stuffed three more biscuits into her mouth as she went past the bed to the laundry basket, and almost choked on the dry crumbs. She cleaned her teeth, spitting soggy biscuit and toothpaste all over the wash-basin, then lobbed everything in the bathroom into a carrier-bag lying on the floor, which already contained disposable razors she hadn't disposed of. In the absence of air-freshener, she sprayed perfume round the flat. As she cleared five mugs in various stages of fermentation from the coffee-table, the doorbell rang.

Dee did a final check in the bedroom and, after poking a pair of grubby knickers under the bed, let Oliver in. She had met him at a comedy club where he had been hoping to make his mark with tales from the world of doctoring. Specifically, the bottom end of doctoring. His material had been good, but he had been overcome with a rare attack of nerves. He had made such a hash of it and had confessed afterwards that the insertion of a small pine tree up his rectum without lubricant would have been marginally more pleasant.

'Have you ever done that, then?' Dee had asked, with interest.

'Not without lubrication,' he had replied.

They had agreed later – much, much later and with far fewer clothes on – that their relationship had essentially started from that moment.

Oliver gave her a massive, warm, wraparound kiss as he came into the flat, wearing his rumpled doctoring clothes and smelling of hospital. 'Going deaf, are we?' he asked, as they shuffled, glued together at the hips, into the bedroom.

'Just listening out for Katie,' she mumbled into his mouth, before reaching for the volume control and turning it down.

They crunched heavily onto the bed.

'I think you may have large bed-bugs, which we've squashed,' he said.

'I think you may find it's a packet of biscuits,' she replied, pulling back the duvet to reveal a crumbly mess.

'Was a packet of biscuits,' he corrected.

'Sssh – Katie.' She gestured at the screen. 'Oh. She won't like that – *I* wouldn't like it,' she commented, as Katie's hips and thighs were shown in unforgiving close-up.

'I've seen worse,' Oliver said. 'Much worse. And, anyway, it's the insides that count.'

They cuddled together for the last twenty minutes of the show, and as the credits rolled, they began the serious part of the evening, emerging from the duvet half an hour later, comprehensively covered with beige biscuit crumbs and looking like scampi.

'You smell much better now,' she muttered into his neck.

'I can't smell a thing. There's an overriding scent of perfume in here. But you are very edible.' He picked a large piece of biscuit off her hair. 'Just out of interest, why is Katie doing this?'

'Money. And because it sounded fun. Apparently.'

'Doesn't this devalue the product?'

'It would have done years ago, maybe. Nowadays, it's almost *de rigueur*.'

'But this is a woman who would have been doing stories about ... oh, I don't know ... famines in Africa, floods in Bangladesh, bank meltdowns, sleaze in politics, and there she is falling backwards into a Jacuzzi with her swimming costume riding up and a man who's not her boyfriend making eyes at her.'

'I know,' said Dee, slowly, 'but she's not, or rather she wasn't, that kind of serious. We're not talking John Humphrys here. Katie would be the last person to say she was a *serious* journalist. More a journalist who could tackle serious issues. Can I use the word "serious" any more, do we think?'

'Seriously ...'

'It's about integrity. If you have it, you retain it. And I'm almost sure ...' She trailed off. 'I'm almost sure that Katie will therefore ... although ... on the other hand ...'

'On the other hand?'

'Yes. Anyhow, it's pointless talking about it. She's doing it. And she's got another week or so to go. The newspapers have done very little about her so far. You must have seen all the Crystal–Peter Philbin stuff, though. Gives them an excuse to feature a lot of pictures of them both without their vests on, despite the chill in the air. Oh, and about that alleged comedian Dave Beal and his awful jokes. Nasty piece of work. Wouldn't be surprised if he didn't turn out to be a wife-batterer.'

'Do you need me to go so you can get some sleep?' asked Oliver, suddenly noticing the time.

'Probably. Although I'm not doing much tomorrow apart from *Hello Britain!*. I could always have a nap when I get home mid-morning.'

He drew her to him again. 'In that case, the doctor may start practising his bedside manner again.'

'Oooh, Matron,' said Dee, sinking down on the bed.

At *Hello Britain!* they were all watching *Celebrity X-Treme* with varying degrees of delight.

Richard, who was putting the show out the next day, was considering sending a round-robin email reminding people to vote. Or would that put Keera's nose out of joint? He couldn't see the harm in it. No one from *Hello Britain!* was in it, so it wasn't as though there was a conflict of interest. But Keera was a tricksy character, and there was no point in getting on the wrong side of her.

He looked at his watch.

Where was Heather? His producer wasn't normally late. He asked the runner to give her a ring at home.

'There's no answer. And I've rung her mobile and it goes straight to voicemail,' said the runner.

'Shit,' Richard said. 'Can you just do a double-check to make sure she's on shift? I may have got it wrong.'

He hadn't.

He left a message on her home phone in case she had overslept, then phoned again and left a louder one. He took her address from the computer and gave it to the runner. 'She normally drives herself in, but get the cab company to go round and ring on the doorbell. Tell them not to leave until they've knocked her up.'

The runner smirked.

'Don't be smutty,' Richard said. 'And get them to ring us as soon as she's in the car.' He turned back to the screen, and smiled. Katie was making very good television. He did wonder whether Adam would be happy with the flirting going on between her and the columnist. The two were sitting in the hot tub telling jokes.

'What does it mean when a man's in your bed, gasping for breath and calling your name?' asked Katie.

'That I was obviously unavailable that night,' responded Paul, with a smile.

'Nope. It means you didn't hold the pillow down long enough.'

'Mine was a better answer.'

Tanya Wilton raised the subject of affairs. 'I always say that if it has tyres or testicles, it'll cause problems,' she said.

'Hear hear,' said one of the watching researchers, whose car had recently given up the ghost.

Richard started flicking through the first editions of the newspapers to see if there were any stories they should be covering that hadn't been picked up. There was a photo of Dee with a specially made wellington boot that a company had made for her for outside broadcasts. She looked very pretty. He sighed. That would put Keera in a bad mood.

It didn't look like they'd missed anything. An item about old-fashioned sweets might be useful for what they called pres-play, where the presenters could ad-lib about the sort of thing that usually got the emails and texts coming in. Proper gobstoppers with tiny aniseeds in the centre, he thought. They were good. Your jaw ached for the whole day. And as they got smaller, you could lightly knock them against your back teeth.

'Do you remember the joy of a wobbly tooth?' he asked a researcher who had come up to ask him how long he needed for a VT.

'Yes,' she said, surprised. 'Are we doing something about milk teeth?'

'No.' He smiled. 'Reminiscing, that's all. I used to love it when you wiggled your tooth and there was that pleasurable pain. And then you pulled it out and got a taste of blood and a hole in your gum you could stick your tongue into.'

'And when it was one of your molars, your tongue would ache from having to curl up to feel it.'

'Um. Great, though, wasn't it?'

'Too right. How long for the war piece, by the way?'

'One minute twenty. We're stuffed for time in the news bulletins today.'

His attention was drawn back to the screen – Katie and Paul doing more flirting. He knew it was how it had been edited – but, really, she must know what she's doing, he thought, as she came out with yet another of her dreadful puns.

'You see, the difference between a stoat and a weasel is that a stoat is stoatally different and a weasel is weasily distinguishable,' she was saying, as she zipped up her snowsuit.

'And that,' said Paul, his face quite close to hers, 'is why we love you. It's stoatally crap, but the fact that you find it hysterical is funny.'

And they laughed together as they walked out into the snow.

Richard shivered. He shouted to the runner, 'Any luck with Heather?'

'Oh. Sorry. Forgot to say that they rang the bell, but couldn't get any answer, and they've had to get the car to somewhere else now.'

'For God's sake, I needed to know that,' he said, annoyed. He tapped his fingers on the desk. She was an hour late. 'Can you ring the police and see if there've been any accidents between here and Twickenham?'

The runner picked up the phone.

On *Celebrity X-Treme*, Flynn O'Mara was telling a rapt audience about the different star signs. 'It's about the other influences as much as the sun sign. If you're a Virgo, for example, with Cancer rising, then you're more likely to go into the caring professions than, say, a Virgo with Gemini rising when you'd be more suited to the media because of Geminis' natural fear of boredom.'

Richard thought astrology was a lot of bollocks, but he did know he was a Gemini. Weird how you knew that sort of thing even if you had no interest. Like he knew that Jimmy Choo made shoes and that newspapers could be used to clean the windows. Mind you, at least that was useful. Knowing someone was a Taurean was hardly going to influence your decision as to whether they were suitable to build an extension to your house.

The runner came over. 'No accidents.'

Richard closed his eyes and stroked the top of his head. Where else could she be? He looked over at a researcher who was monitoring the bank of television screens to see what they were covering news wise. 'Rav, you drove in today?'

'Yes.'

'Can you go over to Heather's and keep your eyes peeled along the way in case something's happened to her? Maybe her mobile's conked out. She drives a battered orange Volvo.'

'Will do,' said Rav, standing up and stretching.

He was relieved to get out of the building – and get a sneaky fag in. As he walked past The Boss's office, he saw one of the producers stretched out on the sofa, sleeping. He cast a quick glance behind him, then went to the door and shut it. Everyone on breakfast television operated below par – it was the nature of the beast. Let sleeping producers lie, he thought. He took the lift to the basement car park and lit a cigarette. He had a drag and spotted an orange Volvo. Shielding the cigarette, in case Security was watching on CCTV, he approached the vehicle. There was Heather, slumbering over the steering-wheel, oddly bruised beneath both eyes.

* * *

In Norway, Siobhan was working out her strategy. She knew for certain that Katie and Paul were not going to get voted off, but she wanted to make sure the editing backed up her plan. Everyone was watching the programme go out. The bosses seemed happy. She caught Mark's eye. He winked at her. She smiled back – a moment of collusion. He had made it clear that he was attracted to her.

She needed a possible fall-guy if things went wrong. She put her fingers to her lips. He would be perfect.

Mark sidled over. 'Worried?' he asked solicitously, his hand on her shoulder.

'No.' She smiled up at him. 'Working something out.'

'Anything I can help with?'

'Don't think so. Although …' She put her head on one side, considering.

'Shoot,' he said encouragingly. 'Come on. You can trust me. What's up?'

Trust him? Like hell. A friend had recently sent her a card with a female praying mantis saying to a male, 'After we have sex, but before I kill you, I'm going to need your help with some shelves.' That was what men were there for. Sex and odd jobs. 'I was wondering if you knew any computer whiz-kids for a project I'm trying to set up away from here,' she said slowly.

'What sort of project?' he asked.

'A website. I can't tell you more than that. It's in the early stages, and I don't want to jinx it. It may come to nothing.'

'I see. Mum's the word,' he said, tapping the side of his nose in the age-old gesture of secrecy.

She hated things like that. Clichés. Space fillers. People saying, 'I have to say,' when they absolutely didn't. 'At the end of the day'. 'Basically'. He could have simply said, 'I see,' and left it at that. Her face did not reveal her irritation. 'Of course,' she said sweetly. 'As you say, mum's the word. So, do you know anyone who could help?'

'Well, you need a web builder. And I know someone who specializes in that sort of thing.'

'It may involve phone links.'

He thought for a second. 'I'll give him a ring and find out. How soon do you need it?'

'As soon as ...'

'I'll text him, then. Shall I give him your mobile number so you can discuss it?'

'I'll probably need to meet up with him, talk it over face to face,' she said. 'If it all works out I'll treat you to dinner. How does that sound?'

'That sounds very fine, thank you,' he said, and gave her shoulder a squeeze.

I bet he thinks that's a subtle come-on, she thought. Poor fool. Men are so bloody easy.

CHAPTER SIX

It was a sparkling morning in northern Norway. The Sami were making sure their reindeer had survived the night – it had been a blisteringly cold one, down to minus thirty with a strong wind. Outside the hut, those who hadn't been in the dog-sledding the day before were drilling through the thick ice of the lake to get water.

'If I'd known it was going to be like the Girl Guides, I'd've told them to stuff it when they asked me to do this bloody show,' wheezed Denise Trench, her nicotine-laden lungs gasping in the frosty air.

'Why don't you go and tell them you want out, then?' asked Alex, his piglet-like ears tinged with pink, his breath spouting in spumes against the blue sky.

'Maybe I will,' she replied, bending down to pick up her bucket of water and slopping most of it back into the hole.

'Oi,' said Dave. 'Careful what you're about. It'll take us twice as long if you're going to keep throwing half of it away.'

'Oh, shut up, moron,' she responded, deliberately pouring a little dribble of water by his feet as she made off across the frozen lake.

The cameramen, filming the incident for inclusion in that night's viewing, made sure there was a close-up of Dave's expression, and his muttered 'Slapper.'

By the time Denise stomped into the hut, her bucket contained barely a cupful of water.

'Oh dear,' said Crystal, as it was poured into the barrel. 'Is it difficult today?'

'Like pulling teeth.'

'Funny expression that,' commented Katie, coming into the kitchen wearing an odd assortment of clothing. 'Does it mean that it's like a dentist trying to pull teeth out, or like the person having to put up with the pain of the teeth being pulled out? Or am I refining it too much?'

'I used to love pulling my teeth out when I was little,' said Tanya. 'That nice sucking feeling when it gave way and the hole you could stick your tongue in.'

'Yurk. You are, like, so *weird*,' said Crystal.

'But, weirdly, I agree with you,' said Katie, going over to put some bread in the toaster. 'I also think it's weird that the plural of tooth is teeth, but the plural of booth is not beeth. The English language is full of paradoxes. Or should that be para-doxii? Does anyone else want toast, by the way?'

'Yes, please, all carbohydrates gratefully received,' replied Paul, who had moved in to take up the favoured spot by the fire.

'Anything to soak up last night's alcohol.' He gave Katie a knowing look. She smiled innocently back at him.

'A boy at school used to eat his scabs,' he said conversationally.

'This is so *gross*,' exclaimed Crystal.

'Oh, come on. Bet you were a scrubby little nose-picker,' he said, leaning into the heat.

'No, I was not,' she said petulantly. 'I bet *you* were.'

'I doubt there's anyone who doesn't – or didn't – pick their nose. I wonder if there's anyone who will ever admit to *eating* it?'

'Interesting,' said Katie, thoughtfully. 'Is it, perhaps, one of the last taboos? You can admit to adultery. There are those who are only too keen to confess to murder, even. But eating your own bogeys? Even if I did, or had, would I own up? I doubt it. Which means that no one will ever know the extent of the problem. If problem it is.'

'It's perhaps more of a problem if you stick them somewhere,' added Paul. 'A pilot friend of mine had a mate who stuck them on the underneath of the seat. He'd get into the plane, try to adjust it and there'd be a mass of crunchy bogeys in great stalactites under it.'

'I'm getting *out* of here,' said Crystal. 'This conversation's making me feel sick.'

'Why don't you go down to the lake, then, and bring up some water?' asked Denise.

'Because that's your job, since you didn't do yesterday's team event.'

'Doesn't stop you helping.'

'Why should I?'

'Your "boyfriend" is down there.'

There was a short silence as the toast popped up. 'Butter?' Katie asked.

'Yes, please. Have we got any Marmite left?' asked Paul.

'Think so. But you'll have to put your own on. It's something even one's mother doesn't get right.'

Crystal went towards the door. 'All right. I *will* go down to the lake but only because you didn't bring up enough water. Not because Peter's down there.'

'Of course not,' said Denise, sardonically. She reached for her cigarettes, and flicked her lighter.

'Not in the hut,' said Katie.

'OK, Herr Kommandant,' said Denise, nastily, making a snappy salute and stalking outside.

'She's what we call a right mardy cow.'

'"Mardy". There's a word. What does it mean?' Paul asked.

'Moody.'

'Are you a mardy cow, Miss Fisher?'

'I don't think so. But, then, it's like being mean. Do we ever know that we are?'

'Do bullies know they're bullies?'

'Some of them must. Others probably think they're being funny. A friend of mine once accused me of being a bully because I used to flirt with this young guy at work every morning.'

'No,' said Paul, mock-horrified. 'You? Flirt?'

'Um. I know. Hard to believe. So, this friend accused me of abusing my position. Said the guy was probably too scared to complain about me because I was a presenter. I stopped it immediately. Many years later he told me he was really sad when that happened because it had perked up his mornings ...' She stumbled to a finish. 'Which makes it sound like I'm marvellous when actually I was trying to make the point about bullying. That it's like the difference between sexual harassment and flirting. Maybe it depends on whether you like the person doing it. If you don't—'

'Then it's an industrial tribunal.'

'Exactly. And if you *do* like them ...'

'You have sex with them,' he finished promptly.

She laughed. 'Obviously.'

'Talking of which?'

'Talking of which? What? And let us not forget that there are cameras here. And that anything we say may be taken down and used in evidence against us. And that we have no recourse to an industrial tribunal.'

'I enjoyed last night. That was all I was going to say.'

Katie's mouth formed an O. 'But that implies we had sex!' she said instantly.

'No, it doesn't.'

'It does. I think we ought to stop this conversation immediately. Do your toast.'

He turned to his plate and meekly applied the Marmite.

* * *

In the control room, Siobhan was beside herself with excitement. 'Excellent,' she said. 'That gives us a final out on that little storyline, I think. Can you get us all a celebratory coffee, please?' she asked one of the runners.

Paul seemed to be following instructions. She wondered how Adam was responding to the nightly broadcasts – and how he would react to tonight's after she had finished the edit.

That afternoon there was a meeting between the senior executives, the senior producers and the producers to discuss how things were going and whether there needed to be any tweaking. 'Do we need to have more stuff in the hut?' she asked, as everybody scraped their chairs and got comfortable. 'I'm only asking because that's where all the good stuff's happening.'

'But it's only happening there because of what's going on outside, surely,' said one of the senior executives, leaning back in his seat. 'You wouldn't have got them in the hot tub again the other night if it hadn't been for the ice-climbing, and the massaging stuff without that rather mad tug-of-war type thing.'

'I just think we could do with less jauntering about, Mal, and more down time. With drink,' she said, with a look.

'I reiterate. We're only getting the storylines because of the outside activities. The bonding that they're generating is influencing what's happening inside the hut. Obvious, really,' he said pointedly.

Mal, a fat, sweaty man with a penchant for pies, had taken issue with the way that Siobhan seemed to be leading these discussions. She found him as appetizing as a spleen, and had done nothing to get him on-side.

'What do you think, Pamela?' Siobhan asked, turning to the other senior executive.

Pamela had been doodling on her pad since the meeting started. She had immaculately manicured nails and the sort of sharp trouser suit worn by the military leaders of a junta. 'Difficult to say, really. There's an element of truth in both statements. Perhaps a compromise. We chop an hour off the outdoor stuff and give more alcohol as a reward. Even if they haven't earned it. How does that sound?'

Mal and Siobhan nodded agreement.

'How do we feel that the outside is going, in general?'

'We could do with more close-up shots,' said Siobhan. 'In editing, we've always got loads of long shots but not enough of their faces.'

'Camera crew have got their work cut out already,' commented Mal. 'They can't rush around in those bloody great Arctic suits, stuffing their cameras up people's noses. Quite apart from anything else, we'll get the celebs putting on an act.'

'Like they're not already,' sneered Siobhan.

'It'll be worse if the cameras are closer.'

'I disagree.'

'Pamela?'

'How about we appoint one of the cameras to try to get closer, no matter where they are? We might get random shots of the wrong celebs for the storyline, but we can always cover it in voiceover.'

'Fine,' they said together.

'Anything else?' asked Pamela.

'Have we decided who we'd like to go?' Siobhan asked her.

'Not yet. For my money, we could do without Alex and Steve. And Flynn and Denise aren't coming through on the female side. You're the one who's seeing all the shots. Are we getting the full picture?'

'I think so,' she said.

Mal piped up, 'Denise is just a drunken old bag who smokes and doesn't want to do anything. And if Flynn makes one more pronouncement about the moon being in ruddy Venus ...'

'She *is* an astrologer,' Siobhan reminded him.

'Oh, *is* she?' he asked sarcastically, 'I had no idea. The point *is*,' he emphasized, 'that she never says anything interesting about it. She just makes all this shit up and says that that's why X is doing whatever they're doing.'

'Well, I think Flynn should stay,' said Siobhan. 'She makes me laugh. I think Tanya should get the chop. Tanya, Denise, Alex and Steve.'

'Right,' said Pamela. 'Let's assume that Denise, Alex, Tanya and Steve are incidentals, and concentrate on the others. Anything else?'

There was a swift discussion about other storylines, and then it was back to the gallery.

* * *

The hut was fugging up. Tanya and Denise were slugging it out over the washing-up. 'Could you just rinse the things before putting them in the rack so I can tell whether there's muck still on them?' asked Tanya, handing back a plate with appliquéd egg.

'Who gives a toss? They're only going to get dirty again. Wash the frigging dishes yourself, if you're so ruddy particular.'

'I would. But then that would mean you'd done precisely sweet FA in the last twenty-four hours. Apart from sitting on your lardy arse.'

'How *dare* you?' Denise turned from the sink with a plate she'd been tickling with the sponge, and thumped it down on the draining-board so hard that it cracked.

Peter and Crystal, sitting very close together on a chair by the fire, stopped speaking and looked over. Crystal whispered something and Peter stood up.

'Hey,' he said, going over to the sink, 'shall I take over on the washing-up?'

'No,' said Denise, firmly, through gritted teeth.

'Yes, please,' said Tanya, smiling sweetly.

'I'll do the drying, then.'

He took the tea-towel from Tanya, giving her a swift nudge in the ribs.

She stomped off to get her snowsuit. 'I'm going out for a walk.'

'Don't forget the briefing's in half an hour,' shouted Katie, as the kitchen door shut behind her.

Paul, who had been filling his water bottle, made his way over to her.

'They're getting on like a house on fire,' he whispered. 'Should I take extra water out with us in case we need to throw it on the flames?'

'I think you're supposed to throw a damp towel on a kitchen fire, aren't you, not water?' she whispered back.

'That's a chip-pan fire.'

'Have they had their chips, do you think?'

'Let's hope one of them has.'

The camera lights above them glowed red. In the control room, the producer logged the time code.

At *Hello Britain!* Keera was having her first ever setback. She had been called into the editor's office. She sat down, expecting to be told how marvellously she had done with the Round Britain tour. Instead, Simon had told her to brush up on her general knowledge, and her general knowledge of the news in particular. He fiddled with his mug of weak tea as he spoke, and his knee jigged.

'I assume this is because I didn't know that that pop group had split up,' she asked, biting her lip.

'No, it isn't. Although if you're going to say you didn't know one of them had gone solo, best not to compound your mistake by saying they must have split up recently. It gives that bloke whose name I've now forgotten the right to say – which he did – that it happened some time ago and that you did the interview when they announced it.'

Keera's brows came together mutinously.

'Before we get on to the particulars, I also wanted to say that it would be better if you avoided words you don't understand. You said the other day that the difference in the atmosphere was palatable.'

'What's wrong with that?'

'The word is "palpable".'

'Oh.'

'And I seem to remember telling you before that a rhetorical question is one that does not require an answer, not a difficult question that *you* don't know the answer to.'

She looked at his bony hands as they continued to caress the mug. 'Do you think the viewers actually care?' she challenged.

He turned towards the computer and clicked a couple of times. 'So, last, erm, Tuesday. This is one example of shoddy interviewing. You were talking to a man who was in the middle of hundreds of lorries and cars blocking the M1. And you said, and I quote, "I'm talking to you while looking at the pictures from a helicopter above you, and all I can see is a mass of lorries and cars. What can you see?"'

'So?'

'The only answer he could have given you was the answer he did give you – "I can see loads of lorries and cars." What else were you expecting him to be able to see? Chimpanzees swinging through the trees carrying bananas? Polo matches on the hard shoulder?'

Keera kept quiet. It didn't sound so bad to her. And other people made mistakes, didn't they?

Simon turned back to the computer. 'Last Monday you asked an Alaskan who had moved to Texas how he liked living in America. You asked subsequent questions that reinforced the impression that you thought Alaska was another country, as opposed to the largest state of the United States of America.'

'I think that's an easy mistake to make,' she said petulantly.

'It is not. Read newspapers. Expand your knowledge. If you don't know something, ask before you go on air. That's it. You can go.' He swung his feet under his desk, dismissing her by clicking on an icon and checking his emails.

She stood up and strode through the door. Ugly little man, she thought. What was all that about? She couldn't believe it was because of a few questions that weren't her fault. She phoned Matthew Praed.

'Hello, Keera. How are things?' he asked, leaning back in his chair and running his spare hand through his hair. He imagined her lithe body lying beneath him. He had taken her out to dinner a couple of times. Instinct told him she was about to fall into his hands like a ripe plum.

'I don't know. I've just had a meeting with the editor, which was less than satisfactory. I need to know how much longer my contract has to run. And, also, when I am going to get a new show so that I don't have to worry about this one?'

'Do you want to meet up tonight, and see if there are any stones we've left unturned?' he asked soothingly.

'I've got to work tomorrow.'

'We could make it an early one.'

She hesitated. 'All right, then.' She sounded excited about the prospect of dinner with him.

They would look so good together. Keera Praed, she thought. It had an exotic sound to it. She imagined the wedding. A big, socialite one, full of celebrities.

In the car on the way home, her driver kept up a running commentary on what was happening on the road and hummed along to the songs on the radio. Keera asked him tersely to be quiet. She was trying to visualise her wedding dress and he was getting in the way. The driver pulled a face, but shut up. Apart from an occasional hum, he managed to say no more until she'd got out.

Her bad mood evaporated as she opened the door to her flat. Sitting on her beige sofa, she thought how perfect she would look if she was being followed by cameras right now. She was wearing chocolate and cream, her black hair glinting in the mid-morning sun shining through the big window. Gazing at herself in the huge Venetian mirror propped up against the opposite wall, she crossed her legs to see if that made them look more elegant. Then she uncrossed them, and simply rested them together at a slant. Difficult. On balance, uncrossed. She leaned forward, and cupped her head in one hand. No wonder she got so much fanmail from obsessed men. She really was extraordinarily beautiful.

'And welcome to *The Keera Show*,' she said, with a little wriggle in the seat.

That did sound good. What did stupid, simple Simon know about television? He'd never presented anything. Apart from the audience figures and things. Which wasn't at all the same thing. Now that she'd had time to mull over what he'd said to her, she dismissed it. Nobody she knew would have given a damn about the Alaska-America business. And as for that motorway question, that was the fault of the thick lorry driver. No. Something else was going on here.

Had she phoned her editor, she would have discovered that it was nothing more than the usual wounded animal inflicting pain on another. The shareholders were after their pound of flesh. The Boss had told Simon to sort out the programme to try to get revenue up. In the absence of anyone else, Simon had gone for the easy option. Keera cocked up on a daily basis and hadn't massaged his ego for a long time. In his eyes, presenters were overpaid monkeys who turned up for a few hours a day and read aloud for a living – they needed to be slapped down regularly. It was people like him who put in the hard graft and ought to be remunerated. He should have taken that Channel 4 job when it was offered. He conveniently forgot that it would have involved longer hours for less money and working under a woman. And he despised women more than he despised presenters.

* * *

Keera, meanwhile, had put him out of her mind and was concentrating on the evening ahead. It took her all afternoon to get ready. A final pose in front of the gigantic bedroom mirror showed that it had been worth the effort. Her blue eyes gazed back in satisfaction. She smiled the smile she had been working on ever since she was tall enough to see herself in the bathroom mirror at home, picked up her Dior handbag and walked to the door, Christian Louboutin heels clicking on the floorboards.

CHAPTER SEVEN

That night, millions tuned in to watch the latest episode of *Celebrity X-Treme*.

'Tonight,' the commentator said, 'it's like a bad production of *Henry VIII*. We've got debauched, breaded, fried, debilitated, bedded, survived.' As he said each word, the screen showed a close-up of those involved.

Dave Beal, legless.

Paul Martin, with toast.

Tanya Wilton, smearing cream on a very sunburned face.

Alex Neil, being taken off the slope on a stretcher.

Katie Fisher, pursing her lips as Paul whispered in her ear.

Crystal Blake, lying in the snow laughing and whipping off her goggles.

'The day's task was cross-country skiing,' said the commentator. 'With a difference. They had to work as a team to decipher clues and gather hidden treasure, which could be exchanged for food and drink. They experienced varying degrees of success. And cracks are already starting to appear.'

The celebrities were shown standing together, with Katie upsetting Alex.

'Language is strange, isn't it? Like, you could say someone was down to earth, but if they were *small* and down to earth, it could be misconstrued. And the same if you were standing next to someone really small, and you said you were dwarfing everyone.'

'I assume that's a dig at my size,' he said, with a tight smile, 'and it's not remotely funny.' He turned round, fell over, landed awkwardly and, in a freak incident, sprained his wrist.

The programme turned to Tanya's sunburn. Shots were bundled together of everyone stopping to put on sunblock. 'Black don't crack,' she said, when offered cream. The picture cut to her putting aloe vera on her burned nose.

Crystal and Peter, looking like an advert for toothpaste, were shown being cute, particularly when she fell over, and her long blonde hair was covered in snow.

And then it was Katie and Paul's turn. They were pictured getting very close, with Paul saying, 'You have sex with them. Talking of which, I enjoyed last night ...'

Katie smiled shyly.

'Oh, yes, they're getting on like a house on fire, those two,' said the commentator, as Paul said quietly, 'Should I take extra water out with us in case the flames start melting the country-side?'

* * *

At Wolf Days Productions, everyone was being very careful not to mention *Celebrity X-Treme* within earshot of the bosses. Gemma and Rose stood by the water-cooler, gossiping.

'Do you think he was watching?' asked Gemma, taking a sip from her plastic cup.

'He can't have been, or he'd be in a shit mood because of Katie copping off with Paul Martin,' said Rose, in a scandalized voice. 'Or allegedly copping off. Could just be editing, of course. We'd have seen it, otherwise, wouldn't we? The actual moment.'

'Yup. 'S not difficult, is it? Would you do it with Paul Martin?'

'Yeah. Course. He looks like Daniel Craig. And he's got, like, a six-pack or an eight-pack or something. Did you see his biceps straining under that T-shirt when he was getting into his Arctic suit?' asked Rose, taking more water and gulping it down.

'Whoah. Well cool. And he's got such amazing blue eyes. He is cute with a capital Q.'

'Or a capital C, even.'

'Whatever. I bet Katie fancies him,' pronounced Gemma.

'Course she does. You can see it in her eyes. You can do all sorts of things in the editing suite, but you can't change what your eyes are saying, can you?'

Gemma thought for a minute. 'Look into my eyes.'

Rose stared into them, her head slightly forwards.

'Well?' asked Gemma, finally having to blink.

'Hmm,' Rose said. 'They're saying you were out too late last night and you wish you hadn't drunk that tenth vodka shot.'

'Oh, God. Are they all bloodshot?' Gemma closed them and pressed on her eyelids.

'Like that's going to help. And, no, they're not. Or no more than normal.'

'Gee, thanks, Peanut Head. Anyway, what they were really saying was that you're a fat slag with the breath of a hyena.'

'Ta, Pig Face. *Does* my breath smell, though?' asked Rose. She licked her hand and sniffed. And giggled at Gemma's face. 'It works. You lick your hand, let it dry and smell it. And that's what your breath smells like. Honest.'

'I believe you. Thousands wouldn't,' said Gemma. 'And, no, your breath doesn't smell.'

'I know. I've just smelled it.' Rose grabbed a final cup of water and walked away. 'However,' she threw over her shoulder, 'you do smell like an armpit.'

Gemma laughed. 'Cheers,' she said, going to her desk to plough through the list of people she had to phone now that she was in charge of *Dare to Bare*, a new show for Channel 4.

Nick came into the office, carrying a take-out coffee and smelling divinely of almond croissant.

'Mm. Edible,' said Rose, looking up from her computer as he went past.

'I know,' said Gemma. 'Shame he'd never look at either of us.'

'I was obviously talking about his croissant,' said Rose, with dignity. Then she smiled. 'Do you think we're doomed to a life of singleness, interrupted by occasional unsuitable shags?'

'Speak for yourself. I have a perfectly respectable man, thank you,' said Gemma, who was dating a singer in an 'up-and-coming' indy band, which had been up-and-coming for some years.

'Don't make me laugh. Is Dracula respectable?'

'Dracula?'

'How many love bites can you get on one neck? It is *so* uncool once you've left school.'

'*One* love bite. And that was on the first date before he knew how sensitive my skin was,' declared Gemma.

'He sleeps in a coffin. He's as pale as death. He's got a killer bite. He's Dracula.'

'Ha!' exclaimed Gemma. 'Got you. Dracula doesn't kill you with his bite. He makes you undead. So.'

'So what? He still kills you in real life. You're not technically alive if you're undead.'

'You're not dead, though, are you?'

'Technically, yes.'

'Technically, no. Anyway, I've got to get on. I need six new guinea pigs before Nick or Adam have my guts for garters.'

Guinea pigs were not what Adam was considering at that precise moment.

He was admiring himself in front of the mirror and pondering the day's attire.

His reflection showed a tall, attractive man with a washboard stomach and a smooth, muscled chest. Membership to a select gym had been his ex-girlfriend's last gift to him before she had left him, and he had developed an almost lover-like relationship with it. He could spend hours there, losing himself in contemplation of a single muscle. A small part of him was appalled by his obsession but he wasn't about to stop going any time soon – particularly when the results were so bloody marvellous. He reached forward and picked out a navy Gucci shirt and a pair of faded jeans. He opened another cupboard and chose a pair of brown, fashionably distressed boots. He slipped a pair of Ray-Bans into his pocket, and left the flat.

A photographer, who was hoping to get work for one of the tabloids, started taking snaps of him, running backwards to get the shots as Adam walked along the road to his Porsche. He smiled at him in a friendly way even though his space had been invaded. Katie's experiences had taught him that if you ever spotted a photographer you should try to look as pleasant as possible for as long as possible. That way, it was harder to illustrate a hideous article with a hideous picture.

He was driving along listening idly to the radio when an item about pensions caught his ear. He wondered if it was possible to make an interesting television programme about pensions. Take five people who had made financial choices, say, ten, fifteen, twenty years ago. What had happened to their pensions, and who was best off? He viewed his own retirement with fear and loathing. He couldn't imagine how anyone was supposed to have fun without a company to play with. On his way to the gym, he had seen a woman bent double pushing a shopping trolley. Would he be the sort of older person who was unable to unscrew the lid of a jar? Unable to get through childproof packaging? Unable to get up once he'd fallen over?

He smiled – Katie could probably tell him what that felt like.

So. These five people's finances would have to be similar, but their choices different. And then you'd see the results of investments in stocks and shares, or houses or commercial properties or Premium Bonds or whatever.

He turned into the underground car park next to the office, and sat there for a minute, trying to think of other ways of investing. Offshore? Leaving everything in a bank on the highest interest rate? Buying a sheep farm in Wales and living off the fat of the land?

He was still pondering this as he swung in through the double glass doors. He didn't, therefore, notice the hush that immediately descended as everyone tried to look busy. He went straight into Nick's room. 'Nick. How many people do you know who have prepared adequately for their old age?'

'As in got enough jumpers and made sure their boiler's working?'

'Twat,' said Adam, in a friendly way. 'I mean, as in pensions.'

'I don't know. Not something we talk about down the Old Slug and Limpet.'

'So. What do you think of this idea?' And he outlined the programme.

Discussion over, Nick could contain himself no longer. 'Assume you were watching last night?' he asked, wandering over to the window.

'Of course.'

'And?'

'And it's obviously all in the editing suite, just as we imagined it would be. As I said to Katie before she went, they'll do whatever they can for ratings. And I discovered that the hideous Siobhan Stamp is in charge so she'll be doing her best to make Katie look shit.'

Nick pulled a face. 'I didn't know that.'

'Found out before Katie agreed to do it. So no surprise that she's already trying to find a way to make us pay. Told you she was poisonous, didn't I?'

Nick had actually been hoping that *Celebrity X-Treme* would provoke a hiccup in Katie and Adam's relationship. Not in a nasty way. But as a little payback. He wondered, again, how Adam had done it. He had come back from a trip away and discovered them virtually living in each other's pockets. It didn't help that Adam had been in such a good mood since. He had to admit, they were a very handsome pair. He had seen a photo in one of the gossip magazines in which Katie, her long auburn hair tied back at the neck, was smiling up at Adam.

'I'm actually hoping,' his friend broke into his thoughts, 'or should I say, slightly hoping, that she'll be among the first to be voted off so she can take the money and not lose too much of her dignity. But I doubt it. She's making good copy.'

'Hmm. I hate to throw a tiny spanner in the works here, but the papers aren't going to let you off that easy. Have you seen them today?' He lobbed one over, folded to the page.

Adam looked at the headline: 'Is Paul Martin Getting His Column Inches?'

'Stuff and nonsense, as my granny used to say. All bluster and whatever that other word is. Baloney. No. Bluff. Bluster and bluff. Or, in Anglo-Saxon, bollocks.'

Nick grimaced. 'Still, bet you want to ram his teeth down his throat.'

'Depends. I'll get Katie's view before I do that. If he's done anything to warrant it, they will, of course, be pushed so far down his throat he'll have to clean them by sitting on his tooth-brush. Does that make you feel better?'

'Much. Thank you. And now I come to think of it, why would she go with that tosser when she's got another ugly tosser already in the bag?' asked Nick.

'Still not got a girlfriend?' asked Adam, mock-sympathetic.

'Cock off,' Nick responded.

Adam picked up the rest of the newspapers and disappeared to his office.

In the part of Nick's brain marked 'Sex/Beer' he had filed a picture of Katie and him. It was never going to happen now – too weird – but she was his kind of girl, and really not Adam's. When she had first walked into the office, he had felt a stirring in his loins. It continued to this day whenever he thought of

139

her. He had taken to having extended breaks if he knew she was coming in to avoid a difficult situation. Maybe he should take a leaf out of Adam's book and begin heavy gym work. Getting drunk was quite useful but the effects were too fleeting, and it always made him feel rather maudlin.

In Norway they were doing a fancy-dress slalom. On the practice runs Katie had fallen over every time. 'I have lumps the size of a small mountain range arriving on my leg,' she said to Paul, as he leaned on his poles waiting for his second ski down the mountain, 'or maybe they should be described as foothills.'

'Ah. The famous punning.'

'Just funning punning. You haven't fallen over at all, have you?'

'Nope. I'm imagining an enormous net ready to catch me. It appears to be giving me unwarranted confidence,' he said, with a grin.

'And I'm imagining an enormous hard thing just waiting to hurt me,' she told him.

'You must be thinking something similar to what I am right now,' he said, with a wink, as he set off down the slope.

Tanya moved closer. 'That boy is incorrigible,' she said, nudging her.

'I know. But he's a laugh,' replied Katie. 'How much longer have we got before we have to do this wretched nonsense?'

Tanya untangled her ski gloves and poles, and peered at her watch.

'About half an hour. Why?'

'Wondering if I can manage to break something only moderately important and retire hurt before I get voted off.'

Tanya smiled. 'Do you want to leave?'

'Not exactly. It would be fantastic to win, obviously, but a large part of me thinks that's as likely as a tortoise winning the annual reef-knot-tying contest. It would be better to leave of my own accord.'

'I think we all feel a bit like that.'

'Do *you*?'

'Well … no. But, then, I've got nothing better to do so I might as well stay here and enjoy myself.'

They stood leaning companionably on their ski poles as Denise headed tentatively down the slope in a snow-plough position.

'I'd enjoy it more if that tragic apology for a woman wasn't constantly winding me up,' commented Tanya.

'She really is a curmudgeonly old beast, isn't she? It goes against the grain to be civil to her. The temptation just to tell her to – I don't know – take a flying leap …'

'Let the force be with you, I say,' replied Tanya. 'Maybe we could both shovel her off the side of the mountain. Are you going now or shall I?'

'You first. I'm debating whether I have enough arnica tablets to deal with another bruise.'

Tanya adjusted her feathery ear-muffs. 'No,' she responded to Katie's unspoken question. 'They don't keep my ears warm at all. But they do look pretty, don't they?' And the question was left in the air as she launched herself forward.

Sighing, Katie gave it a few minutes and shuffled into position. Here we go, she thought grimly, pushing firmly on the ski poles.

She was doing very well, by her standards, until a spectacular fall about twenty yards from the finish. She completed the course on her bottom, legs akimbo.

Paul rushed to help her up. 'Hey,' he said, dusting snow off her back, 'that was a fast time.'

'Of course it was. I didn't use my feet for the last part,' she said, massaging her bruised rear.

'Here, let me do that,' he said solicitously, reaching round.

'I think not.' She laughed unsteadily because the tumble felt as if it had dented more than her pride. 'Oh, God, that feels nice – not.' She groaned, her fingers checking the damage. 'That's going to be one hell of a lump.'

'Maybe you should go down the next one on your front,' he suggested.

'Ha-ha. Ouch. Oop. That really does hurt. You know, it sounds a bit wimpy, but I'm going to have a word with the doc and ask him if I should call it a day.'

'Chicken,' he said.

'And what do you mean by that?'

'I mean I saw what you did before the "accidental" accident. And don't think you're going to be out of this before they vote you out. That's all.' And, with a meaningful look, he wandered off.

She bent over to take off her skis while she had a little think. By the time she raised her head again, she had decided that she would – unfortunately – have to pull herself together and do the wretched fancy-dress slalom.

She limped over to the doctor, a suave man in his fifties. 'Doctor, doctor,' she said.

'Yes?' he asked wearily, waiting for the inevitable joke.

'I feel like I'm a pair of curtains.'

'Pull yourself together. You can do better than that.'

'Feel like I'm a dog?'

'Get on the sofa. Not allowed on the sofa. And again?'

'How about … I've only got a week to live?'

'Good news, though. The patient in the next bed wants to buy your slippers?'

'You're good,' she said appreciatively. 'Final chance. Oh, you've got a fly on your nose?'

He thought for a minute. 'It's got no wings. It must be a walk?'

'Excellent. But, actually, you really do have a little fly on your nose. Or a speck of something.'

He rubbed it off. 'And what can I do for you? Or did you just come over here to discover whether I knew every doctor-doctor joke going?'

'I fell over and now I hurt everywhere. Should I be worried?'

'Anything you can't move?'

'My ears.'

'Could you move them before you fell over?'

'No.'

'How many fingers am I holding up?'

'Two spring onions and a tree. No. Seriously, though, I'm not concussed.'

'In that case, take some paracetamol-based tablets to bring down the swelling. And be more careful.'

'You have got such a wonderful bedside manner, Doctor,' she said flirtily, smiling through her lashes.

He was a regular fixture on a number of television programmes, was attractive, smelled nice and had an impressively firm torso. She did like a man who could distinguish his metatarsal from his dorsal fin.

'Hold that smile for much longer and it'll turn into a rictus grin,' he warned jauntily.

'Do you see many of those at the surgery?' she asked interestedly.

'Not this time of year, no.'

'Migratory, are they?'

'You must be thinking of the borborygmi.'

'Oh. Yes, now I come to think of it, I was.'

'Stomach rumbles, in case you were wondering.'

'Obviously, I already knew.'

They watched Peter sliding sideways and almost taking out one of the safety struts before leaping to his feet and punching the air.

'I must say, this is a young man's game,' said the doctor. 'I went out skiing this morning and overdid it. I'm fifty-four this year—'

'You look brilliant,' cut in Katie.

'How kind. Anyway, I ache all over. Not as much as you will, though ...'

Crystal came over. 'Paul's worried about you,' she said. 'Are you all right?'

'He is, is he?' Katie said dismissively. 'You can tell him I'm fine. So fine, in fact, that I'm going to ski over the rocks next time to make it more exciting.'

She watched Crystal go back to Paul, her blonde hair cascading down her back. 'Utterly stunning,' she commented.

'Yup,' agreed the doctor.

'I suppose I'd better get back,' she said wistfully, glaring with dislike at the start of the fancy-dress race where the organizers were stretching across a tape. They had strung a host of red balloons at the finishing line.

Half an hour later the contestants were in their outfits – wigs, feather boas, humps, fake noses and moustaches.

Katie took her time, didn't fall over, but was last. 'I was so worried before I set off that there was a small pile of bricks where I was standing,' she told the group.

Crystal looked confused. 'I didn't see any bricks and I came down after you,' she said.

'You know,' said Paul, 'I used to go out with Tessa Sanderson. But she chucked me.'

'Did she?' asked Crystal, concerned.

'Stop taking the piss, you two,' said Peter. He put an arm round Crystal. 'Paul's making a joke about the fact that Tessa Sanderson was a javelin thrower.'

'Was she?'

'You see,' said Peter, throwing a glance at Paul, 'some people don't remember the Old Days.

'Fatima Whitbread?' asked Paul.

Katie bit her lip, trying to remember the punchline. Her frown cleared. 'No. Guffed in your Grolsch!' she declared.

He smiled approvingly.

CHAPTER EIGHT

Siobhan was with the VT editor, her truncheon-like big toes, with bright red nail polish, right on the edge of the table. He found it a gross infringement of his human rights to have them so close to his workspace, but she was renowned for her vicious streak so he kept his mouth tightly shut as he obeyed her orders. 'Go back again to where Paul is talking to Katie at the top of the mountain,' she said.

Obediently he spooled to the sequence.

She leaned forward. 'Time code ten thirty-eight,' she said, as he played it. 'We'll take it from where Katie says she's thinking of a hard thing and his response.'

He pressed the button.

They watched as the columnist made his comment, and winked.

'That's a bit out of order, isn't it? It makes it sound like it's entirely a conversation about his, erm, manhood?'

'If I want your input, I'll ask for it. Otherwise shut the fuck up or I'll have you taken off the production,' she said, not looking away from the screen. 'Now put in the section where she's skiing and falls over.'

He did as he was told, harbouring evil thoughts, as he spooled forwards.

Siobhan called the time codes and he cut the pieces together. It really was above and beyond manipulation. He wondered if he should complain to his bosses – but he might end up sacked for his trouble. Actually, what did he care? The celebrities were all a bunch of losers getting paid a fortune for making tits of themselves. He'd get tanked up and forget about it as soon as his shift was over.

He continued to cut the tape, and paste over the cracks with shots decided by Siobhan. Katie's fall and rub down from Paul, her flirting with the doctor …

Siobhan was extremely happy. She stood up and stretched in a way that she imagined was sexy and lithe.

'Bitch,' said the VT editor to the door as she left – but not loud enough for her to hear. He had a mortgage to pay.

As the VT editor was lining up his fourth bourbon on the rocks, Bob Hewlett, landscape gardener from Yorkshire and erstwhile lover of Katie Fisher, was absent-mindedly opening a bottle of Rioja in the kitchen at his house in Hawes. He was in a quandary. He stood picking at one of his sideburns and debating his options. His girlfriend, marine biologist Clare McMurray, was gorgeous, but he could no longer deny that the ghost of Katie hung over their relationship.

Normally Bob felt that he was very good at getting on with things. The past was the past. Move on. But a newspaper article about Katie being in *Celebrity X-Treme*, illustrated with a photograph of her smiling, had given him such a punch in the stomach that he felt queasy.

It had been his decision to end their romance after her drunken kiss with a man in a nightclub. Actually, he could have got over that – but she hadn't seen fit to warn him that it might be in the newspapers, and that had been cowardly. And how could he trust someone who'd fall into someone else's arms after a few drinks?

Their rekindled affair had been snookered by his own dalliance with Clare, which he hadn't told Katie about. Well, he'd been single by that time, hadn't he? Deep down, he knew he should have brought it up. Sauce for the goose et cetera. The time had never seemed right, though. And, anyway, why should he? Yes, he should have done. All right, all right, all right, already.

He poured a tumbler of wine. Why did life have to be so blasted complicated? Why did brains have to keep on raking up stuff instead of leaving it in a pile to mulch down and melt away? He had a fantastic woman. Sex on tap – or as on tap as it was possible to be when the two of them lived so far apart. But could he imagine her as the mother of his future children? Could he have children? Did he want children?

Oddly, when he'd been with Katie, he had imagined the two of them with a brace of progeny running round the house,

Caligula the cat being joined by a dog, a hamster, stick insects, a collection of handmade pottery dinosaurs, potato-cut paintings ... sticky fingerprints on the walls and sticky kisses all over his face.

He was quite lost in contemplation of this idyll when Harry phoned to ask him if he fancied a quick snifter down the pub. 'I'll ask Clare,' he said. 'She's just packing her bag to go to Wales or Ireland or wherever the hell she's off to now.'

He called up to her. 'Do you want a drink at the pub before you go? With Harry?'

He spoke to Harry again: 'Fine. See you in ten.'

Harry lived in the next village, with his wife and daughter Elizabeth, to whom Bob was godfather. He was one of the few people who knew everything there was to know about Bob's love life. He was already at the bar when Bob and Clare arrived.

'How's work?' Harry asked her, as he tried to catch the landlord's eye.

'Great,' she said. 'Up to my ears as usual. Studying sea vegetables at the moment.'

'Fun?'

'Interesting. And cold.'

'Are you doing all right, Bob?'

'Fair to middling, as Dad always used to say. You know. I miss him as much now as I did when he died. Too late now to ask him whether it was fair to middling or whether he couldn't be bothered to say anything else.'

'Which means that work *is* fair to middling. Or is it crap?' asked Harry, as they stuck their pints to an unwashed table, and Clare sipped her glass of lime and soda water.

'No. Work is definitely fair to middling. I'm ever hopeful of *the* big project that'll make me a fortune.'

'Remain optimistic at all times,' said Clare, jauntily.

'As you know, Harry, it's difficult in the current economic—'

'Climate,' Clare helped out. 'Although I'm finding the climate quite challenging – one day I need a thermal suit, the next it's T-shirt weather. Spring. Not easy when you're out.'

Bob didn't continue.

'How's the watch business?' she asked.

'It's fine. Could be better,' Harry said.

Clare's mobile beeped. She flicked it open. 'That's the answer to the question you were asking earlier,' she said to Bob. 'Apparently that song was written in 1967 by Mike d'Abo from Manfred Mann and then it was performed by Rod Stewart in 'seventy and the Stereophonics in 2001.'

'Oh.'

'As I said.'

'Yep.'

'We were having a dispute about "Handbags and Gladrags", Harry.'

'Great song.'

'Agreed. I can't remember if that was the name of the album as well. I may AQA that one, too. I should get a BlackBerry. It would save me a fortune on texting. Do you ever use the service? It's brilliant. Text any question and they send you back the answer.'

Harry shook his head. 'I work from home. I Google.'

'O to work from home. You boys are so lucky. No bosses.' She looked at her watch. 'I'd better go. Only time for a quick one. Arf, arf. Very Finbarr Saunders and his double-entendres.' She drained her glass and stood up.

'Thanks for a wonderful day, my little sausage,' she said, kissing Bob on the top of his head. 'Well worth the detour. See you soon. 'Bye, Harry.' She waved as she bounced off to the door.

There was a small silence as both men gazed at their pints.

'All going well, there, is it?' asked Harry, sensing that Bob was not happy.

'It's fine,' said Bob, taking a long swig of beer. 'I think I'm going to get a packet of crisps. Do you want anything?'

'A proper answer when you get back?'

'I'll work on one,' said Bob, heading back to the bar.

He bought four packets of crisps – one packet each, one for sharing and one for his dinner. He hadn't been shopping and there was nothing in the house but tins of things he didn't fancy. He threw them onto the table. 'A smorgasbord for your delectation and delight.'

'And the answer to the question? I'm only asking because you've got a face like a smacked arse and you look like shit.'

'You're no oil painting yourself. Twat,' said Bob, picking up the packet of cracked-pepper and sea-salt crisps. He opened them slowly. 'Do you ever think you should just stop thinking and get on with it?'

'In every area of life, or one in particular?'

'Clare is gorgeous. She's virtually my dream date. Tall, leggy, red hair, et cetera, et cetera … and a marine biologist. If I'd written out a list of requirements when I was sixteen and in a permanent state of erection she would have ticked every box.'

'I can hear an enormous "but" coming in.'

'Yes. It is.' He paused for two sips of beer and another handful of crisps.

'Katie?' prompted Harry, who had been through the whole sorry saga.

'Exactly,' sighed Bob. 'I don't know whether it's because she's in the papers all the sodding time with this show she's in or …'

'Or what?'

'Exactly.'

'That doesn't make sense.'

'Neither does what I think.'

They sat there companionably drinking their beer, while the hubbub around them rose and fell. Eventually Harry broke the seal on another bag of crisps. 'So what is it, then?'

Bob looked up from his consideration of the foam at the side of the glass.

'I think it's because Clare doesn't need me. She's too independent. I think I want someone to look after – even if they don't think they need looking after. Clare is always keen to come up here and hang out any weekend that she's free …

sometimes, like today, come up for just one day. She's fun. Et cetera. Et cetera. Yes, I know I keep saying "et cetera". But she also pisses me off big-time. You saw that this evening, with her finishing my sentences. And, yes, again, I know …' he said, seeing Harry raise his eyebrows '… I know everyone pisses us off at some time or another. And there's also another major irritation. We'll be lying in bed, and we'll be nattering away. And something will come up, as in that question about Rod Stewart's song, and she's immediately on to it.'

Harry smiled.

'Yes, I know I'm a bloody big Googler too, but this is beyond the pale. I reckon she'd Google or AQA in the middle of a – in the middle of a … whatever … if she could get her fingers to the mobile or the keyboard.'

'When you'd prefer her fingers to be on your keyboard.' Harry nodded sagely.

'Exactly. And that isn't the only thing. She's so capable. She's got her own set of drills and screwdrivers and she was telling me the other day how she's knocking down a wall.'

'That *is* impressive,' Harry said, mouth pursed.

'Well, it's only a small wall, and it isn't a supporting one, but …'

'Yes.'

'Sophie wouldn't do that, would she?'

'Oh, she might if there was a handbag behind the wall in an "impossible to get your hands on" colour. But she'd probably just charge at it with a battering ram under one arm.'

'You see. That's what I mean. She needs *you* to do a proper job. Clare makes me feel less of a … less of a …'

'Less of a man.'

'Well, yes. Not to put too fine a point on it. She makes me feel a bit useless. Like, what am I offering? I'm a prostitute.'

'Prostitute?'

'No. OK. No. But all I'm there for is sex.'

'There are those who'd think that was the best of all possible worlds.'

'Yes. Not me, though. And that's why Katie keeps getting back into my head. She's capable and incapable in equal measures. I want to look after her.' He corrected himself. 'Wanted to look after her … and possibly still want to look after her.'

'Is that because she's with someone else? Is that what this is all about?'

'Oh, I don't know.' Bob opened his third packet of crisps.

'Early dinner?'

'What?'

'I thought you said that that packet was for dinner.'

'I'll get some peanuts. I don't know whether it's a dog-in-the-manger problem or whether I've never really given up on her. Anyway. This is dull, dull, dull. It's been going round in my head so much I don't know what I'm thinking any more, or if I'm using it as an excuse.'

'An excuse for what?'

'An excuse to end it with Clare. What else can I say to her? "I want you to leave me alone because you're too good with a drill bit, you keep interrupting and you've got a Google habit that turns me off'? Not a thumping great reason to end a perfectly good relationship, is it?'

'Unless it's true,' said Harry. 'And you don't have to put it in those words. More to the point, though, is why finish with Clare when Katie's with someone else?'

'I know.' Bob groaned, then laughed bitterly. 'Which is why I'm finding it almost impossible to make a decision. Can I have your life, please?'

'Hmm. You can if you want. I've got a very demanding client at the moment. He wants an original 1950s Rolex wind-up watch to give to his wife for her birthday. He phones me virtually on an hourly basis. Plus I've taken apart a very old pocket watch for another very demanding client, spent about seven thousand man-hours trying to track down parts for it. Sorted it out. And now he's gone and snuffed it. And I haven't the heart to ask his widow for payment since she was a friend of my father's. Oh, and Sophie's pre-menstrual and keeps shouting at me because I haven't done the washing/tidying/dusting the underneath of the skirting board/got her pregnant again. And Elizabeth is being a bully at school and they've told us that if she does it again, they'll have to ask us to take her out.'

'Oh dear,' said Bob, draining the last of his pint. 'Quite puts my little worries into perspective, doesn't it?'

'Exactly,' said Harry. 'Actually, I wasn't trying to put you down. It's just that the grass isn't necessarily greener on the other side. Is all. You moron.'

Bob smiled. 'Another?'

'Yes. Might as well. It's not what you'd call a long walk home from here.'

'And I could have one and walk it off on the way back. I could definitely do with a bit of exercise,' said Bob, tapping his stomach and pushing it out under his fingers. 'Do you think we need more crisps to go with my dinner peanuts?'

'Of course. No calories in a measly old bag of crisps, eh?'

It was nine o'clock. By throwing-out time, they were talking complete gibberish and Harry knew he was going to be in trouble. 'This,' he said portentously, as they stood outside the pub, 'is where it's better to be going home to nothing and nobody.'

'Caligula is not nothing,' said Bob, emphatically.

'Caligula is a cat. A cat is almost nothing.'

'Say that again, and I'll take you down.'

'A cat is nothing.'

'Name your weapon.'

'Spoons.'

'Right. Spoons at dawn.'

'Fine. Now bugger off. I've got a beating to take from my wife.'

They meandered into the dark, as the moon tripped in and out of some clouds that had wandered away with a warm wind moving in from the west.

* * *

Not that many miles away as the crow flew, Katie's parents settled in to watch their daughter make an idiot of herself on television, as her mother put it. Jack said he thought Katie was taking a calculated risk.

'You always stick up for her,' said Lynda, as they sat down on the sofa before the programme began, 'but my view is that she's been lucky. Up until now, her youth has carried her through.' She hoicked the dog's back end from the carpet in front of her favourite television-watching chair. 'I have a foreboding that this will be the final straw. Have you broken wind or is it Hercules?' she asked, her nostrils twitching.

'As if,' harrumphed Jack who, they both knew, had taken to blaming the dog in such circumstances. 'Hercules,' he growled threateningly.

The dog looked up guiltily, sniffed his bottom, staggered to his feet and left the sitting room for his basket.

'Did you put that pan in to soak?' asked Lynda.

'Of course. Don't you worry your pretty little head about anything to do with the kitchen,' he said patronizingly.

'Don't patronize me.'

'As if.'

'And what's this "as if" business? Since when did you start saying "as if"?'

'Since when did you start asking me about putting pans to soak? You haven't been near the kitchen in decades.'

'Let's not have a row.'

'Well, really. As soon as I defend my daughter, you get all quarrelsome.'

'I am *not* quarrelsome. And she's my daughter too.'

'Well, you'd never know it to hear you talk about her. You've always got a down on her.'

'I have not. I've got a more realistic view of her. Now, ssh. It's about to start.'

Nothing more was said while they watched the programme go out.

The dog, who had come back in under cover of *Celebrity X-Treme* and passed out on the carpet, stretched, yawned and broke wind.

'Was that you?' asked Lynda.

'No,' Jack responded, truthfully this time.

She pressed the off button. 'Well, I think she's done enough,' she said.

'Hmm.'

'And when I say done enough, I mean done enough to get rid of Adam. And to get rid of any chance of doing anything else with the rest of her life apart from appearing on more shows like that.'

'You see? There you go again. Cut her some slack, why don't you?'

'You must admit she's coming across as a common little flirt. And although I'm sure she didn't cheat, it was made clear that *they* think she did.'

'I'm going to go and scrub out that pan. Can you take Hercules for a walk?' he asked, as he disappeared into the kitchen. 'Do something constructive, for a change,' he muttered, under his breath. He didn't want to have another argument about Katie – especially since he felt Lynda might have been right this time. Their daughter was coming across as what his mates would have called 'a fast piece', and he didn't like it one bit.

CHAPTER NINE

It was a pitch-black moonless night when the early-morning workers and presenters made their way into the *Hello Britain!* building. The weather, as so often seemed to happen, had held itself in abeyance for the hour or so before dawn. Thunderous rain had pounded down all night, making potholes into puddles. But there was a lull now.

In the makeup room, the conversation would normally have been about the lightning that had disturbed their sleep and the difficulty of the trip into work for those who had driven in from outside central London. But as Vanda flung the makeup bib around Dee, the first thing she demanded was an update on *Celebrity X-Treme*. 'I had to go to bed last night at seven. And remind me to tell you about trying to find my car last night after I finished doing the makeup for a photo shoot. But tell me, tell me!'

'Well, it was a fancy-dress downhill-skiing thing. It was hysterical. She slid most of the way on her bottom on one of the warm-up runs. And then Paul Martin suggested she did it deliberately – although why it matters … It was still funny.'

Heather put her head round the door. 'Graphics are a nightmare. You may not have them up for your first weather.'

'Hm. Is anyone out on an OB today? We could use a shot from their camera to put on the chroma key so at least there's something to look at behind me that's vaguely weather-related.' The chroma key was the blank canvas behind the weather presenter, used to put up images.

'Good idea,' said Heather. 'I'll have a word.' She disappeared.

'What happened to her?' asked Vanda.

'About what?'

'The black eyes or whatever. Has she been beaten up?'

'Oh. That. No. She had her eyebags done for a plastic-surgery strand. They've dropped it.'

'No!' said Vanda, scandalized.

'Now, to go back to *X-Treme* …' started Dee, and they continued to gossip about it until Keera piped up from another makeup chair.

'When does the first evacuation take place?'

Dee stifled a laugh. 'The first eviction is tonight.'

'Who do you think will go?' asked Vanda.

'Well, Denise Trench is hideous. And Flynn O'Mara's irritating me, even though I love reading my stars – her voice is very, very annoying. But Dave Beal's absolutely hateful. I want him and Denise to go first. How about you?' asked Dee.

'Don't know. But it would be nice if Crystal Blake won. She seems lovely.'

Dee wasn't having any of it. 'I cannot believe you want Crystal to win. You obviously want Katie to win. She's brilliant. And giving us some great telly.'

Vanda looked guilty. '*Of course*,' she stressed, 'but if she doesn't, then Crystal.'

Dee smiled. 'Well played.'

'Yes. I agree with you,' Keera said. She gave a tinkly laugh, its first public appearance. 'It's a good job Katie's a cuddly shape, with all that falling over she's doing.'

Dee gritted her teeth, deciding not to rise to the bait. 'Hey, Vanda, what was that story about your car?'

'Oh, yes. So I get back to my car after this photo shoot, so tired I can barely stand, and there's a traffic warden about to slap a ticket on it. So I rush up and virtually go down on mended knee …'

'Mended knee?'

'What?'

'You said "mended knee".'

'You're lucky I can do joined-up speaking I'm so tired. You know I meant bended knee. As I was saying … I go down on bended knee and plead with her not to give me a ticket, because I thought it was a residents' parking area, and I say that I have a resident's permit. And then she says it *is* a residents' parking area, and I suddenly realize it's not my car! And then this man, who's been watching this stuff going on, says there's an identical silver Peugeot up the road that's probably mine. And that's when I notice we're standing by a Peugeot. And my car's a Volkswagen!'

Dee barked with laughter. 'Do I need more blusher do you think?' she asked quizzically, turning her head from side to side as she looked in the mirror.

'I'll adjust it later. Let me get on with my job, and you do yours,' said Vanda, tartly.

'Well, you said you were tired. I was just wondering about the blusher, that's all. Don't suppose you were watching that programme about HIV and Africa last night, were you?'

'How many times do I have to tell you that I was working all day doing a photo shoot, and then so knackered that—'

'Oh, yes. Well, it must have been on before *X-Treme*. And there's this bloke who's a researcher or something. And he's talking about the new initiatives and tests and things. And he says that there's a fifty to sixty per cent less chance of getting HIV as a man if you're circumcised. And then he says ...' she started giggling '... and then he says, that unlike this other thing they're trying out, circumcision's a difficult tool to roll out!' She hooted, as Vanda joined in.

Keera wondered if she had misheard.

For a few minutes, the only sound in the makeup room was the television in the corner, blurting out the early-morning news.

'I really hate this bloke reading the news today,' said Dee. 'Such a pompous man. It's as though he thinks we're all children who don't understand anything.' She mimicked his delivery. 'Do you remember when the *QE2* ran aground and they said on the news that it was being tugged off?'

The two of them were getting slightly hysterical. Early mornings affected people in different ways. Some went quiet. Others went silly.

'I made up a joke yesterday,' said Vanda. 'Do you want to hear it?'

'Go on,' said Dee, using a cotton bud to tidy up some mascara.

'Why didn't Gandalf go to the Middle Earth meetings any more?'

'I don't know.'

'Because he'd managed to kick the hobbit.'

Dee giggled, then looked serious. 'It needs work, though. I mean, there's no reason for him to kick a hobbit.'

'It's Middle Earth.'

'Yes, but that's not enough. He needs a reason for the kicking. Like why did he stop shaving? Because he'd kicked the hobbit. No. That doesn't work either.'

Keera tuned out. This was the sort of conversation she hated. And she wanted to concentrate on thinking about Matthew Praed. For the first time in her life, she feared she had made a mistake. She had slept with him after their dinner date. She had a horrible feeling that she had been used.

It was no wonder that Dee Krammer was still doing the weather on *Hello Britain!*, she thought. Too much time spent watching television and not enough time devoted to her career. She closed her eyes as the makeup artist stroked black eyeliner across the lids to emphasize her feline features.

Dee and Vanda were on the verge of meltdown. 'And then the beavers say to these hunters, "We no longer want to be known as beavers. We want to be called vagina squirrels."' Dee was holding the side of the chair as she guffawed.

'Stop it,' said Vanda. 'Oh, look what you've done to your makeup.'

Dee's eyes had puckered up so much she had two caterpillars of mascara underneath. 'Oops.' The two women quietened as Vanda tidied up.

'I'm going to have to be careful today. I'm on the edge,' said Dee, as she finally stood up and went to the wardrobe department to collect her clothes.

At five minutes to on air, she went past the makeup room again and poked her head round the door. 'And I've just remembered another thing,' she said, tittering. 'Were you working that day we had a winner of something, and we had his name as Mike Hunt?'

Keera was fed up of their nonsense, and escaped to the sound department to put on her microphone before she went through to the studio.

Rod, wearing a lime green shirt and dark green tie, was bemused. Every minor quip he made when they were off air was greeted with gales of laughter by Dee. 'What's she on?' he asked Keera.

'I don't know,' she responded sourly. 'Probably been at the sherry.'

That started Dee off again. 'Stop it,' she gasped. 'I'm not safe.'

In their earpieces, they could hear a row of some sort developing in the gallery, with Richard shouting at the producer of an OB at a shopping centre: 'Well, go to the nearest place and grab some, then … There must be somewhere with people in it … I don't know. Use your bloody imagination.'

The director's assistant started counting down to the end of the ad break.

'Five … four … three … two … one … on air.'

'Cue grams,' said the director.

And the *Hello Britain!* logo was followed by a two-shot of the presenters. 'Welcome back,' said Rod. 'It's eight twenty. Glad to have you with us this morning. We've got a gospel choir from America coming up.'

'So stick around for that,' said Keera, 'but first …' she did her serious face '… we're talking about the elderly, and how many of them don't see anyone from one end of the week to another.' She continued to read, her face not betraying her view that they should all move into homes anyway.

During the ad break, she stood up and stretched. 'Can you turn off my mike?' she asked the sound girl. 'I need to nip out to the loo.'

The girl nodded, while seriously considering leaving the sound up. Then she reconsidered. She needed her job and everyone knew how vindictive *Hello Britain!*'s star presenter could be.

Richard went through to Rod's talkback. 'We've had problems with the next item, the shopping centre. Brent can hear us, but we can't see him on the monitors. They're working on it. He should be with a whole load of early-morning shoppers. You may have to stretch the link to him.'

'Fine.' He reached for a newspaper and turned to an item that had caught his eye earlier. If all else failed, he could use that as a filler.

Keera came back in and sat down. Rod didn't bother to tell her what had happened, and she was wrongfooted by him suddenly ad-libbing about something she hadn't seen in the paper. She opened her mouth to speak, then closed it as he showed no signs of stopping.

In her earpiece she heard Richard say, 'Keera. Throw to Brent at the shopping centre.'

She waited for Rod to stop and then said: 'Now we can go over to Brent to see just how many people are taking advantage of the bargains to be had at the moment.'

Brent was having a miserable time. He and his producer had arrived at the venue to find one homeless man trying to find a warm spot, and a cleaner. Richard had told them to go and grab people from the nearest big building, so they had. The 'shoppers' stood around the reporter, silently gazing at the camera, wearing big labels round their necks identifying who they were and where they lived. Brent did his piece and handed back to the studio.

And immediately, Rod and Keera's earpieces were filled with a rant from Richard, shouting on the squawk box. 'For God's sake! I didn't mean you to go and get people from the ruddy Shady Pines Home for the Terminally Bewildered. I can't believe there was nowhere else … Well, you should at least have taken their bloody labels off. If we do another hit, and I mean if, at least put their labels on their backs if they have to have them on.'

Keera and Rod were still talking to the nation.

'Well, at least they won't be the sort of elderly people who don't see anyone from one end of the week to the other. They've got each other to talk to,' said Keera, in a two-shot.

Rod looked aghast. How on earth was he supposed to respond to that?

Dee, who was standing at the chroma key waiting to do the weather, found it almost impossible not to giggle. Thank goodness she had five minutes to compose herself, she thought, pretending to fiddle with the plunger she used to change the graphics.

It turned out to be one of the worst programmes Richard had worked on. The gospel choir from America had turned up expecting to be paid in cash. Apparently it had been agreed with the finance department, but someone somewhere had forgotten to check whether the envelope was there. He'd had to send every member of the production team to the cashpoint to draw out as much money as they could.

As the closing music played, he leaned back in his chair and gave a sigh of relief, followed by another of resignation, as he went upstairs for a spot of ritual humiliation at the editor's hands. There were days, he thought, when he wished he'd gone into drainage.

In Norway it was a tense day. Everyone was keyed up about the eviction. They had no idea how much air time they'd had or who was being painted as what.

Siobhan had had her way, and they were all to stay inside and play a game of speed Monopoly, with forfeits for those who had the least cash at the end of half an hour.

Paul Martin wandered over towards Katie. 'How are the bruises?'

She laughed ruefully. 'I look like I've been manhandled by an octopus.'

'Interesting. An octopus has three hearts, you know.'

'Does that mean they're very romantic?'

'And very good at massage. They're like me, really.'

'Impossible to buy jumpers for, though.'

'How kind. When can I expect it?'

'Stop it,' she said. 'I'm going to have to get away from the fire – it's making me hot.'

Paul's eyes followed her as she went into the kitchen. Every day he was becoming happier with the position into which Siobhan had thrust him. To be flirting with the only woman he found attractive while knowing it was helping him to win the show was a very fine place to be.

* * *

In the control room, the quiet logging of the cameras went on.
'Mark?'

'Siobhan.'

'I'm assuming you've done a triple check on the phone lines for tonight's eviction?'

'The company in charge assures me that everything's in working order, yes. And we did a run-through in which we put through a specified number of calls and checked that they corresponded. It's all looking good.'

'Fine. We can't afford to have any negative stories on that front. Oh, and I phoned that company you suggested, Compot, about the website. Thanks.'

'No worries.'

She could have hugged herself when she thought of how it was all coming together.

Katie's parents, on the other hand, were coming apart. While she was falling down and wondering whether it was possible to be in love with two people (and feel rather tingly about a third), Jack and Lynda were wondering about their own relationship – or, strictly speaking, Jack was.

While his wife was at a Ladies Who Lunch book-club meeting, he was at home, making apple and parsnip soup. He liked cooking. He liked gardening. He liked home. His wife, it seemed to him, liked to do anything that didn't involve him. Although she appeared to enjoy the fruits of his labour.

He had copied out a quote from a book he was reading, a memoir of a journey on foot from England through Europe just before the Second World War. Some ancient knight had written: 'Live, don't know how long. And die, don't know when. Must go, don't know where.' It ended: 'I am astonished I am so cheerful.' For that, Jack substituted: 'I am not even remotely astonished to find that I am not cheerful.'

He had reached a point at which he could no longer pretend to be at the delta of middle age. He was officially in the sea of old people. He felt like a car that needed love and careful handling because the engine was starting to coke up and the points and plugs were furry.

Having said that, he was feeling surprisingly well, apart from a minor knee twinge. Lynda would have ordered him to the doctor if she'd found out about it. He would go if he thought it was worth it, but their family doctor would no doubt refer him to hospital, with his pursed lips looking like the end of an undercooked sausage roll. And then there would be X-rays, and the verdict: creeping decrepitude. Before he knew it, he'd be on twenty tablets a day and contemplating adult nappies. He peeled another parsnip.

If the Grim Reaper were to emerge from the fridge right now, he'd be – well, annoyed because he hadn't finished the soup but also sad. What a lonely little word that was. Sad.

They'd done a good job with the kids, though. Kind, lovely, intelligent and with a wonderful zest for life. Ben was the best son anyone could ever have had. And Katie, well, occasionally she went mad and drank too much, but everyone had to have a release valve. They could have done without her buggering up their and Ben's relationship with Bob Hewlett, but they had pulled through that one.

He smiled as he remembered the enormous trout Bob had caught on their fishing trip, and how they had eaten it simply grilled with lemon. And the leftovers had been great as pâté. Although, in hindsight, perhaps a touch more parsley.

However, she now seemed to be happily ensconced with Adam Williams. Or was she? He did wish she wasn't such a flirt. And that she hadn't done this television programme. He and Lynda were having so many rows about it. But maybe it was all for the best: it had forced him to consider the deeper malaise. He put the pan on the hob and turned up the heat. It was time to take his own advice. He was forever intoning the mantra: 'Make a decision. Don't let things slide. Nip it in the bud.' Like all advice, it was easier to give than to take.

He had already had a number of conversations with Lynda, and she didn't take him seriously. She got all stroppy and claimed it was his fault, not hers. What she needed was a taste of life without him. It was a high-risk strategy, but he felt sufficiently confident it would work.

He reduced the heat under his soup and went upstairs to collect a few things together. He wasn't sure how much he needed, since he wasn't entirely sure how long he'd be away. He clicked the locks on his battered old suitcase. Was he really going to do this? And was he really going to do it now? For the first time in ages, he was nervous and excited.

A few miles away at the Old Coach House, Bob Hewlett was also making a decision.

It was strange watching Katie on *Celebrity X-Treme*, and even more peculiar watching her apparently getting off with someone else. It was horrible. Fascinating. And yet strangely, deep down, it made him hope. If she was so in love with this Adam bloke, how could she contemplate anyone else?

He phoned Ben, and was surprised when he answered. 'Hey, I was all prepared to leave a message.'

'A rare morning off. I told the hospital to hold all further patients. We've got a lovely big fridge where we stack them until I can get in.'

'What a brilliant idea. How great would that be?'

'I don't know why I've never thought of it before. What do you reckon? Stacked upright or lying on shelves?'

'Upright, like bottles of beer, surely.'

'Hmm. I can see trouble ahead. You'd open the door, and they'd be falling down like skittles.'

'Talking of which …' said Bob, then hesitated.

'Talking of which …' Ben prompted.

'Have you been watching your sister on *Celebrity X-Treme*?'

'Of course. I've Sky-plussed it so I don't miss a single frame. Load of old tosh, eh? What's it got to do with skittles?'

'Eh?'

'You said "talking of which" after we'd talked about stacking people in a fridge like skittles. Do you remember? I'm sure you were there.'

'Yeah, OK. Maybe it was the shape of the skittles that made me think of her. Sorry. Sorry. Don't know what I'm talking about. Too much coffee. Too little coffee.'

'Are you all right?' asked Ben, as Bob randomly wittered on.

'Yes. Really I am, Doctor. Anyway … how do you think Katie's doing?'

'Lots of air time. I assume that's good. That Martin chap's a sleaze-bag. You can see his game sticking out a mile.'

'That's a revolting thought. The Tanya woman's a good-looking bird, though.'

'She most assuredly is. I may get Katie to introduce her to me when they all get out.'

'Do they fly straight home?'

'I think they have to wait for the whole show to end. Or do they? You know, I can't remember what she told me. Why? You want to go to the end-of-show party with Clare?'

'Probably not,' Bob said hastily. 'I was wondering when you were next up in Yorkshire.'

'Are you having a party?'

'No. I'm missing you, passionately, desperately, fervently,' he said theatrically. And then in a normal voice: 'Do I have to have a party to get you up here to see me and your parents? What are you like?'

Ben laughed. 'Well, depending on what Katie's got planned after she gets out of the igloo, we could maybe both come up for a weekend. Although Adam will probably be in tow. If he doesn't ditch her, that is. Mum and Dad will no doubt be wanting to hear all about it. Having said that, maybe they won't. We'll see. Now, I notice from the way the big hand and the little hand are positioned on my rectangular timepiece that I have to go to work.'

'Just before you do, I heard a good line for you the other day. "Support bacteria if you want to be cultured."'

'Ha. I was considering setting up a DIY surgery and calling it Suture Self.'

'Nice,' said Bob, approvingly, as Caligula leaped onto his lap and paddled his claws into his thigh. He winced. He loved his cat, but there were times when he pined for the unconditional adoration of a dog with blunt toenails.

CHAPTER TEN

It had been no surprise to the producers of *Celebrity X-Treme* that the first person to be voted off was Steve Flyte. They had made sure that his appearances on the show had been fleeting and anodyne. Although the public could always go collectively bonkers and do something odd, there had been enough reality shows now for people to realize that if they voted off all the baddies it would be a boring programme.

The two main irritants were Dave Beal and Denise Trench – and Dave had turned out to be a dab hand at Monopoly, putting himself out of reach of voters for the day. Siobhan didn't care which of them stayed long-term. But she had stressed to colleagues and VT editors that she wanted Peter Philbin, Crystal Blake, Paul Martin and Katie Fisher kept in as long as possible. 'Two love affairs from one reality show,' she had said enthusiastically. 'It's never been done before.'

'I can see the Peter–Crystal thing,' said Mark, taking a long swig of his coffee, 'but do we reckon there really is something between Paul and Katie?'

'Have you been watching the bloody programme going out?' she snapped. People needed to believe there was something going on so that the votes she had arranged to come flooding in didn't look suspicious. 'I reckon that after we get Flynn O'Mara off or Alex Neil or whoever we should maybe add a large dash of alcohol to the mix to get things humming.'

'Denise Trench is an alcoholic,' one of the producers reminded her.

'Is that my problem? No, it isn't. She must have to deal with these situations all the time. She can have a scrumptious glass of water or alcohol-free beer. Whatever she wants. A tonic-water cocktail. We could make sure she's out of the way – or work on getting her out next.'

As the puppet-masters pulled the strings, the puppets were having breakfast.

Paul Martin was making coffee and toast for everyone, looking handsome and tousled.

'How come men can be guaranteed to make the most remarkable mess of the smallest task?' tutted Katie, as she came through to collect the latest batch.

'We get taught at our mother's knee,' said Paul.

He buttered the last piece of toast on the work surface next to him, then handed it to her, leaving the knife balanced on top of the marmalade jar. 'We only do it as a cry for help. We need the love of a good woman to change our ways,' he added, as he followed her through to the dining room.

Crystal was eating buttered toast, standing against the window, her blonde hair in a plait down her back. She was wearing just a long nightshirt and a pair of knee-high sheepskin boots. She looked amazing.

'Wow,' he said. 'That's what I came all the way to Norway for. To watch a blonde girl in high boots masticating.'

Crystal looked over her shoulder. 'Sorry? Are you talking to me? I was looking at this beautiful view. Isn't it pretty? So clean. Apart from the footprints on the lake. Do you think there are wolves?'

'Oh, yes,' said Katie drily, looking at Paul. 'There are definitely wolves.'

'Too right there are,' Dave said, with a wink and a nod.

You disgusting little man, thought Katie. I bet you wear a rotting leather posing pouch and have a velour dressing-gown in red. With a hood. 'If you were a wolf would you prefer to wear sheep's clothing or something cooler?' Katie asked.

Crystal looked adorably confused. 'I don't understand the question.'

'You know. A wolf in sheep's clothing. It's already wearing its own coat. Then it has a woolly jumper on the top. It would be very warm. They might prefer, on balance, to be wolves in thin mackintoshes.'

Crystal smiled, amused. 'I'm very warm in my sheepskin boots, so I could be said to be wearing sheep's clothing already,' she said, moving away from the window.

'The thing is,' said Paul, 'that you have to consider the size of the animal, and the number of limbs. A wolf couldn't wear a mac because two of its legs would be uncovered, but a sheep's outfit would fit perfectly because of the similarity in shape. A wolf could possibly wear pig's clothing, but its face would poke out the front.'

'And the other thing is, you can take a sheep's clothing and still leave the sheep intact – albeit chilly,' debated Katie, considering the issue.

'You have a point,' said Paul, taking a swig from his mug.

'So we'll leave it as a wolf in sheep's clothing, then, in the absence of anything more suitable?'

'Are there any other expressions that we should be considering while we're at it? There must be hundreds that could be improved upon.'

'Indubitably. As my father likes to say.'

'And no wonder he likes saying it. It's an excellent word. I go through months of having a favourite word, which I repeat *ad infinitum* in my column.'

'And your favourite word at the moment is?'

'Katie,' he said promptly.

She looked at him for a moment, then burst out laughing. 'You are a hound! Do many women fall for this rot? I assume you favour the scattergun approach in the hope that at least one in a thousand will succumb.'

'I only say it to you.' He lowered his eyelids slightly and looked up through his lashes.

'Bollocks.' She smiled. 'Talking of which, when do you think we'll be getting word on today's task?'

'Wouldn't it be nice if we could just stay here and be all cosy and comfy, and tell each other our life stories? Get to know each other even better.' He slipped his arm around her waist and nuzzled her neck.

'For God's sake, get off me, you idiot,' she said, unplucking his hands from behind her. 'Have you been at the oats again?'

'I'd like to be.'

'Enough. And, actually, I'm not sure that makes sense. Sowing them again – that would work.'

'With you?'

'No. Not with me,' she said sternly. 'I am happily paired up with a handsome, gorgeous man, thank you.' God knew how they were going to edit this programme, and she didn't want Adam or any of his friends getting the wrong impression. Mind you, Paul Martin was a totally appealing package, the sort of man she found it almost impossible not to respond to. It was very annoying. There were days when this man-nonsense almost made her head explode. In the olden days, I would have been the perfect courtesan, she thought. Except you had to make an effort all the time. And not spend a whole day in bed eating buns and watching daytime television. Or an evening out with your girlfriends getting drunk on margaritas and dancing like a squid on a hotplate. She smiled.

'What are you smiling at, girl?' asked Tanya, sauntering up beside her.

'About how I could have been a courtesan in a different era,' she said wistfully, then recalled why Tanya was there. 'Whoops,' she said, guiltily.

'Oh, don't you worry, babes,' said Tanya. 'I wouldn't be here if I couldn't take it. "Courtesan" is a good word, isn't it? Better than some of the others I've been called.'

The bell rang out for them to gather and hear what the day's activity would be.

The instructor told them they were to be pulled by the dogs in giant tractor tyres on a straight course up and down two hills. They could control themselves with small wooden spikes attached to the tyres through loops.

A small man with bandy legs, known as 'Elfin Safety', pointed out exactly what they were expected to do and not to do – and stressed that they would be disqualified if they infringed the rules. 'I would remind you that disqualification means you will not get your fee,' he said, looking from face to face. His final words, said with a sour look, were 'Enjoy yourselves.'

They filed out to the hut where the equipment had been laid ready. Denise Trench began trying on the helmets, careful with her hair.

'You're going to have to get a bigger helmet, love,' said Dave, as he crunched past her. 'And that's never been said to me, ha-ha.'

'They must be rocking in the aisles,' put in Katie, as she joined the queue.

'I bet you have Capricorn as your moon sign,' said Flynn.

'As well as my Capricorn sun sign?'

'Oh. Yes. Quite.' She nodded. 'Cool and calm. But you want to come out on top.'

'I must also be a Capricorn moon, then,' said Paul, resting his head on Katie's shoulder. 'I definitely want to be on top.'

Katie shook him off, irritated. 'I don't know what's got into you today. I think you need some bromide in your tea.'

Siobhan, watching closely in the control room, jotted something down on her pad.

Katie's mother was in a quandary. Her husband appeared to have left her. And left her with a saucepan of parsnip and apple soup. Her first emotion on reading the note had been disbelief, then irritation and a dash of worry. She had the mobile phone they shared, so he was not contactable.

She rang Ben, pretending she was checking when he was next up for the weekend – but either he was unaware of Jack's whereabouts or he was putting on an excellent act. Then she phoned Jack's oldest friend, who sounded surprised to hear from her and rambled on about his latest operation. She cut him off when he started eulogizing about the quality of the stitches. It wasn't that she was uncaring, she reasoned, but she really did have to get on. There was Hercules to walk now that Jack wasn't there, and food to get in, now that Jack wasn't there. And cooking to do, now that Jack wasn't there.

183

She made herself a cup of Earl Grey, sat at the kitchen table and burst into tears.

As Lynda was cuddling Hercules and weeping into his fur, Jack was on a bus to Blackpool. He would have preferred a train – it would have been more romantic to run away from home with the sound of the metal wheels clanking on the tracks – but the connections hadn't worked out, and he didn't fancy drinking endless cups of pale tea out of paper cups on draughty railway stations.

He checked into the Big Blue Hotel and unpacked his suitcase. It felt odd not having Lynda exploding belongings into every corner, and keeping up a running commentary on the state of the place. He arranged his toiletries on the shelf in the bathroom, and cleaned his teeth, then went down to the bar where he enjoyed a cup of strong tea and admired the way that the grey sky met the grey sea so seamlessly that it looked as if a grey seal could swim its way up to the top of the window frame.

Then he went to Blackpool Pleasure Beach and bought himself a pass for the next day. He had a feeling it wasn't going to be busy, with the weather presenter on *Hello Britain!* having forecast a blustery weekend.

The beach was deserted apart from a few hardy souls with their dogs. He hoped Hercules wouldn't miss his customary long walks too much in the days he was planning on staying away. When Lynda took him, she was usually back within half an hour. Labradors were like children, he thought. They needed to be forced to exercise or they turned into blimps.

The sky had now squeezed the sea so heartily that it had started to leak, and he was driven back towards the parade by a clammy dampness round the back of his neck that he suddenly found insupportable. He ducked into Gipsy Rose Bee's fortune-telling abode and, judging by her surprise, deduced that she didn't get that many men of a certain age requesting her predictive skills.

She swiped an envelope addressed to Sharon McKenzie off the table and leaned forward, her plump bosom resting on the obligatory red cloth. She looked at his palms and started her reading.

A quarter of an hour later, Jack emerged into the brightening gloom, looking as surprised as Sharon 'Rose Bee' McKenzie had. She had hit all the nails on the head.

He was going to travel: he had the return ticket right there in his pocket.

He was going to find love: perhaps, strictly speaking, it would be a rekindling of love.

He was lost: well, he *was* carrying a map just in case.

He was in need of fun in his life: yes, he had a pass to the Pleasure Beach.

Things were looking up.

He bought a small polystyrene tub of cockles from a van on the opposite side of the road, and walked slowly back to the hotel, now that the rain had turned to a bracing drizzle.

As he divested himself of his coat and freshened up before going to the bar for a glass of red wine, he wondered how much Lynda was missing him. Or if she was missing him at all.

No doubt there were people who liked being on trains, thought Keera, but she was not one of them. She preferred a chauffeur-driven limousine. There was no point in being a national celebrity if you didn't get the accessories – and it was obviously better if you got them for free. What you wanted was comfort, speed, convenience and no *hoi polloi*. But she couldn't get a car at the last minute, and first class was completely booked. So here she was, with the great unwashed. Despite the lowering clouds, she put on a huge pair of sunglasses.

It was Matthew Praed's fault. She had no idea whether they were having an affair or not. She didn't want to muck up their work relationship by pressing him on it, but she couldn't believe he didn't want to see her again. I bet he's gay, she thought. If only her future career wasn't at stake, with Matthew as her agent, she could have told the newspaper journalist with whom she had a cosy arrangement. Maybe she'd ask him if he'd heard of any whispers about Matthew's sexuality. Or would that get back to him? She decided to phone the reporter anyway. It was probably time for another offensive after Dee's recent splurge because of the broken ankle.

She looked out of the window as the train filled up.

Two women sat down next to her, facing each other over the table. One then stood up again, took off her coat and tried to put it in the rack overhead, enveloping Keera in bits of musty fabric.

'Whoops. I'm so sorry, I can't quite reach,' she said to her friend.

The other, taller, woman came round to help her. Keera caught the waft of damp wool as two coats were flung up.

They were continuing a conversation: 'And so she tells me she's not going out with him. He's not rich enough to be that fat and ugly, apparently.'

They sat down.

'Oh, you know they evacuated the whole building, by the way, because of a man with a pound of sausages strapped to his waist? Obviously they thought it was dynamite. Do you want some of these pistachios?' She got them out of her handbag and they sat companionably cracking open the nuts.

'You've got so many bits of shell down your front, you look like you've been mulched,' one laughed, reaching over to flick them off her friend.

Keera gritted her teeth. Sodding lesbians, she thought spitefully. They were all right when you weren't sitting near them. If just one small nibble of a nut lands on me ... Just when she thought it couldn't get worse, a young woman stood at the end of the table and told her she had booked the seat in which Keera was sitting.

'Booked this seat?' she queried in disbelief. 'How did you book this particular seat?'

'Online two weeks ago, if you must know. But you definitely have my seat. And normally I wouldn't quibble, but there aren't any others.'

'So you expect me to give this one up to you, knowing that I would have nowhere to sit?' asked Keera, her voice getting higher and more strident.

'Well, I'm sorry, but it's you or me. And since I've booked it …' She raised her eyebrows.

Keera – tired from getting up early, annoyed because of the pistachio-eating lesbians, stressed because of Matthew Praed – suddenly snapped. She whipped off her sunglasses and uttered the dreaded words: 'Do you know who I am?'

The woman did. But she was not about to give in. 'No, I don't. But maybe we could phone the last number you dialled on your mobile, and they might be able to tell you who you are,' she said, with a smile.

'Ha. Ha. Ha. How very amusing. Well, I'm not moving.'

The woman pursed her lips, opened them to say something, then closed them again and walked off.

Keera jammed her sunglasses back on and sat back, her heart pounding. How embarrassing. But she had won. And that was all that mattered. What were those rug-munchers looking at? She felt like baring her teeth at them. Nosy parkers. She tried to get comfortable. She closed her eyes. And was woken up by the ticket inspector.

'Excuse me, madam. Could I please see your reservation for this seat?' he asked politely.

Keera opened her purse and took the ticket out.

'And your reservation for the seat?'

The young woman appeared behind the ticket inspector, and smiled sweetly.

Keera could barely speak. That bitch. That total bitch. She hated women. And she particularly hated this woman. She realized she was beaten.

She stood up, banging into the pistachio-eater next to her and scattering nut shells everywhere. She swung her handbag onto her shoulder, almost knocking the passenger's head off. Then, shouting incoherently about having had enough, she barged past the ticket inspector and the holder of the seat reservation. 'I hope you're happy,' she snarled in a parting shot, 'you stuck-up little shit.'

'Thank you, I will be now,' the woman replied. 'And thank you for warming up my seat. Have a good trip.'

'I hope the carriage blows up and you die a slow, horrible death,' shouted Keera, picking up her overnight bag from the rack and rushing to the connecting door.

In the space between the carriages, she stood breathing heavily. What a nightmare. Her heart was racing now. She waited until it slowed down, then strode along the train until she found a space to stand.

Adam Williams was also on the move. He was approaching his second glass of champagne on the Eurostar. He loved trains – and especially the Eurostar. He loved the beautifully restored and improved St Pancras station, and he loved alighting three hours later in Paris and going to the restaurant opposite the Gare du Nord where he would have an enormous bowl of *moules marinières* and chips for lunch. Delicious. He was annoyed that he had had to come on a Friday, but he was still available on the end of a BlackBerry.

Wolf Days Productions was on a roll. Commissioners from every broadcasting organization were beating a path to their door. Nick was thinking of buying another flat in London on the proceeds, but Adam had set his heart on a flat slightly further afield – hence the trip on a work day to Paris. He was picking up the key for a bijou apartment overlooking the Seine, with high ceilings, long windows and painted white floorboards. And then he was going to meet Cécile d'Ombard, who had been recommended to him as an interior decorator.

He leaned back in his seat and closed his eyes for a moment, trying to visualize Katie Fisher on the huge bed he imagined in the space. He couldn't picture her looking tidy on it. She needed to be a bit more Audrey Hepburn and less Jane Russell. He wondered if he could persuade her to develop a gym passion. A stone less would do her the world of good.

Nick finished work early and drove down to his house in Dorset. The traffic was dreadful. He was going so slowly he could have started a relationship with the woman in the BMW in the adjacent lane. Cracking rack, he thought. He couldn't see her face … seventy per cent chance she's a prawn. Delicious body, ugly face. One of those BONPAs – Bed Only No Public Appearances.

He hated driving on a Friday. There was no point unless you set off from London before lunch. If you didn't, a two-hour journey took four. But if you left it later, it had to be after seven which meant he wouldn't get to Dorset until nine. It was odd how he could organize a successful production company but not his life. He should have gone shopping yesterday when he'd had the time.

He leaned forward to press the roam button on the radio. He was a big fan of local radio. Butch, confident DJs, music always a little less than cutting edge. And good names: Radio Eagle, Radio Griffin, Radio Beagle – no, there would never be a Radio Beagle. He put on a deep voice. 'Radio Beagle, broadcasting on a frequency only available to dogs.' He looked to his right. The alleged prawn was now a shaven-headed man in a Mondeo. His mobile rang.

'Nick Midhurst.'

'Matthew Praed.'

Nick's eyes slid to the clock on the dashboard. 'To what do I owe the pleasure?' he asked.

'I've been meaning to call you about a client of mine. Can you talk?'

'I most certainly can. I am currently stuck in traffic. Which client?'

'Keera Keethley.'

'Ah. The beautiful Keera Keethley. We did offer her a job, actually, a programme called *Dare to Bare*. She turned us down flat.'

'Yes, she mentioned it. She's trying to move into other areas.'

'While still working at *Hello Britain!*?'

'Not necessarily.'

'She would leave? For what?'

'Tell you what. Do you fancy meeting up next week and having an informal chat about it? You're going in and out of range. Call me. Or I'll call you.'

Nick put the windscreen wipers on. What filthy weather. Keera Keethley. Well, well. He wondered if *Hello Britain!* knew that their star presenter was actively seeking other work.

CHAPTER ELEVEN

The television viewers had voted. Siobhan and the producers had done a fine job, and Alex Neil was evicted from *Celebrity X-Treme*. 'What's the betting he'll put it down to his injury?' Siobhan asked.

One of the runners came up to her. 'I've been told to ask you about whether Jane can go now because she's not feeling very well. I don't know whether anyone else can cover her shift, though, so we were wondering if—'

'Can I stop you there?' asked Siobhan, and left the room.

The runner waited for ten minutes, then went over to Mark, who was stretching and giving his head a thorough scratch. 'Is she coming back, do you think?'

He looked round. 'Siobhan? I don't know,' he said. 'What's the problem?'

'I need to know if Jane can go early, but there's no one to cover the rest of her shift.'

'How long has she got?'

'She's supposed to be on for three more hours.'

'I'm sure everyone can fend for themselves for three hours. What did Siobhan say when you asked her?'

'She said, "Can I stop you there?"'

He huffed a laugh. 'And then walked off?'

She nodded.

'Brilliant,' he said, shaking his head. He gave her a quick showbiz hug and told her to let Jane off the rest of her shift. He was still smiling when he saw Siobhan on the phone in one of the edit suites. She looked a bit shifty, and quickly ended the call.

'Problem?' she asked, eyebrows raised.

'Nope. I told one of the sick runners to go back early, after you apparently walked off.'

For a moment she seemed nonplussed. 'Oh, that wimpy little girl who was talking to me? Yes. She was boring. Couldn't be bothered to listen any more. Now, I was thinking …'

'Let's hope there's no irreparable damage,' he said, with a twinkle – then wondered if he'd overstepped the mark. 'Joke?' he said, putting up his hands as if to ward off the evil eye.

She grimaced, then gave a fake smile. 'Good. Yes. So. Seriously, I was thinking that we could use Flynn to get the two relationships we've decided on moving along.'

'But I thought you wanted her out?'

'Woman's prerogative to change her mind. Anyway, we can use her until she goes.'

'Everything game wise has already been decided.'

'Yes. I know. I was there when it was decided,' she said cuttingly, 'but that isn't to say that we can't add to the games, maybe with a little astrological twist.'

'No. Course not. Erm. I was looking for the VT editor by the way. Do you know where he is?'

'Haven't a clue. If he doesn't get back in here smartish, though, I'll make sure he never works in television again.'

Mark wondered whether she really thought she had the power. Delusions. The television world was full of people who probably needed psychiatric help. 'Good luck with it,' he said, turning to go.

'What? No ideas yourself?' she snapped.

'Oh, sorry, didn't realize you wanted input.'

'Of course I do,' she said, softening. The electronic lights behind her on the machines glimmered and flickered. One was casting a devilish hue on her face.

Mark pulled a swivel chair closer to her and sat down. 'Right. So you get one of the games and add on something along the lines of, say … one's a Scorpio, and they're supposed to go with a Libra or whatever?'

'Exactly. Although you wouldn't get a Scorpio and a Libra together.' She shook her head.

'Oh. You're an expert, then?'

'No. I just know I'm a Scorpio.'

'Do we know what star signs the four of them are?'

'Shouldn't be difficult to find out. Google them. But then what?'

Half an hour later, they had come up with an idea.

Saturday morning dawned fair with a light breeze. Katie and Paul were up early, drinking coffee and hot milk while they waited for the others to surface.

'What time did you get up when you were at *Hello Britain!*?' he asked.

'A minute past four.'

'A minute past? Why not four o'clock?'

'Over the years it adds up,' she pronounced.

He put his mug down and went to look out of the window at the lake. He thought he could see a reindeer. 'They say deer are taking over the countryside in Britain,' he remarked conversationally, having pointed it out to her.

'What's wrong with that? At least they're not hoodies with knives.'

'They carry ticks, apparently, which aren't good for humans.'

'But not as bad as hoodies.'

'They want them culled.'

'What? Hoodies?'

'Of course. Cull the hoodies. No, they need to cull the deer to save the countryside, they say.'

'Animals. They're a nightmare. You go for a walk anywhere, you can't move for them. Let's start a sticker campaign: "Save the countryside, bomb a badger."'

He laughed.

'What do you reckon we're doing today?' she asked.

'Who can tell? I thoroughly enjoyed yesterday in the tyres. Great laugh. It should be an Olympic sport.'

'Who needs the Olympics when we have the Olympics of life right here?'

'That was very *Hello Britain!*,' he commented.

'Yes, it was.' She nodded. 'I would then have turned to my co-presenter and he would have said …?'

'And he would have said … Let me see … He'd have said something like "You are so right. You are seriously gorgeous and if it wasn't for the Arctic suit, I'd have tumbled you in the snow on day one."'

Katie spluttered out a mouthful of coffee. 'How many times do I have to tell you not to do that?' she asked. 'Now look what you've made me do.' She dabbed at the stain on her tracksuit trousers. 'These are the only clean pair I have. And coffee's a bugger to get out.' She went into the kitchen, and messed about with washing-up liquid and the hot water that was left in the kettle. The devil of it was that she was finding him more and more attractive. It wasn't just his body – although he was a magnificent specimen – it was his quick mind. He was witty, interesting, funny … and, of course, very flirtatious. She could only assume he was single because he wanted to be.

With the stain now a map of the Caribbean islands, she returned to the sitting room.

'Lovely,' he said appreciatively, staring at her crotch.

'Incorrigible.' She smiled. 'I have leave to tell you that you are a rake, sir. A libertine. A squire of dames. A gay deceiver. A philanderer.'

'Nice,' he said approvingly. 'Good list.'

'Why are you doing this? Because it's safe?'

'You look the dangerous type to me. That's why.'

She disregarded his comment. 'Is that why you don't have a girlfriend? You only want what you can't have?'

'I don't have a girlfriend because I've been waiting for you,' he said dolefully.

'Yeah, right.' She tutted.

'No one who had the good fortune to call you his girlfriend could ever want anyone else.'

God, he really was totally scrummy, thought Katie. He was making her all hot and fizzy. Flirting was the best. Better than shoes. Better than silk satin. Almost better than the first kiss – and that first kiss … Talk about fizzing. The moment when your lips met. It made your head spin. And Paul Martin did have the most kissable lips. Particularly when they were parted slightly and smiling as they were now.

'What?' he asked innocently, having read her face very accurately.

'Toast. Do you want some?' She bustled back into the kitchen.

In the control room, the exchange was logged for that night's programme. Judicious editing resulted in a simmering three minutes of air time.

In Nottingham that night, Keera and her mother sat down to a tuna Niçoise supper in front of the television.

'This looks delicious,' said her mother, miserably. She had wanted a meal from the local chippy with a side order of mushy peas and pickled eggs.

'Thanks, Sheila,' said Keera, who had been taught from an early age to call her mother by her name. 'It's a shame the tuna wasn't blue fin and that we couldn't get any of the extra virgin olive oil, which is cold pressed. It does make such a difference to the dressing.'

Her mother, pining for a pickled egg, did not reply.

Keera insisted on watching the evening news. She found it as boring as her mother, but after her 'bollocking' by the editor over her lack of knowledge, she supposed she ought to do a bit of homework. The news was just so wretchedly gloomy and dull – like its presenters. If she was doing the news, she'd wear something to cheer people up.

They sat chewing their leaves and watching the pictures roll in front of them.

Sheila was thinking that Keera had changed quite a lot since she had become the star presenter on *Hello Britain!*. In the past, she would have been happy to come home and have a cosy chat – dish the dirt, tell her the gossip and share a nice Victoria sponge over a pot of tea. Now it was all balsamic vinegar this and truffle oil that. And why is there no hand-squashed, white-cherry, seedless tomato purée in the cupboard? She loved her daughter, but when she had mentioned the change, Keera had accused her of being a stick in the mud.

'Shall we watch some of that American dancing show after this?' she asked.

'Oh, yes,' said Keera, visibly brightening.

'And then I've *got* to watch *Celebrity X-Treme*.'

'Fine,' said Keera.

'Would you do one of those celebrity programmes?'

'I don't need to. They're really only for people who are Z-listers and want to resurrect their careers.'

'Except this is really good fun,' said Sheila. 'Did you see the one with the huge tyres being pulled by dogs? That looked like such a laugh.'

'Yes, but it's not exactly elegant, is it? It's not like *Strictly Come Dancing*, is it, where you actually learn something useful? I can't see that Katie Fisher winning a dog race is going to help her get another job.'

The Prime Minister appeared on a news item.

'How *is* the Prime Minister by the way?' asked Sheila, excitedly. This was the stuff she liked, hearing about famous people, especially if there was a titbit she could pass on to her friends who worked with her at the supermarket.

'He's fine. He's taller than he looks, and he's always really friendly. I think it's only a matter of time before I get invited down to Chequers.'

'Really?' asked her mother, biting her lip with excitement. 'How wonderful.'

'Mm,' said Keera, putting her knife and fork together.

'You haven't finished all your food.'

'It's good manners to leave some on your plate,' explained Keera.

'But there's just the two of us. And it's a waste.'

'Oh, all right,' said Keera testily, and finished the last two French beans and the piece of egg. 'There. Better?'

'Thank you,' said her mother, standing up and taking their plates through to the kitchen. She noticed that they had successfully talked through most of the news.

'Do you want a ginger beer?' she shouted through.

'Is it one of those mixer things?' called Keera.

'I don't know. It comes in a big bottle.'

'No, thanks. Just some water.'

Her mother brought through a glass of sparkling water and a ginger beer, and put them carefully on the crocheted place mats on the side tables. She dragged over one of the pouffes and kicked off her slippers as she relaxed for an evening of television-watching with her famous daughter.

In Paris, Adam was having dinner at the Hôtel Costes with Cécile. They had spent the previous day in a number of shops where he had agreed on the items to be purchased for the flat. He was opposite her now, unconsciously echoing his girlfriend's deliberations that morning on the nature of love and lust.

Cécile was elegant, with a touch of the Catherine Deneuves round the jaw line, and the graceful carriage of a fifties model. Candles threw an alluring light into her brown eyes, flecking them with amber.

'Cheers,' he said, raising the glass of Sancerre.

'*Santé*,' she responded, taking a minute sip of the pale honey-coloured wine.

'So …' he lingered.

'So … what, Monsieur Williams?' she asked, her French accent rendering the brief sentence sexy.

'To return to the question I posed before our second bottle arrived.'

'Ah, yes. Extra-marital afairs. But you know that we in France have a different view of that from you English.'

'And that hasn't changed over the years, with the advent of the Internet, the influence of American culture?'

'We guard our culture more closely than others, as you know. Perhaps it has changed a little, though.' She gave a small nod. 'Do you ask because you would prefer it to be *de rigueur* to have *une maîtresse*?'

'Not that, so much as the acceptance that while you can pledge your love to one woman, you're never going to stop looking at others.'

'Ah. But is it just the window-shopping? Is that not the problem? Very few people like to window-shop without the possibility of buying.'

'And for some people, even looking in the shop window can create jealous outbursts.'

'Yes. It is not easy for partners of window-shoppers.'

'I don't see why it shouldn't be. As long as it doesn't involve the purchase.'

'This metaphor has perhaps run its course?' she queried.

'Yes, let's drop it,' he said.

'Or do I take it there was some ulterior motive for it, which you cannot speak candidly about?' she asked, lifting her chin a little.

'No.' He laughed. 'Obviously, you're a very attractive woman. And there would be those who would misconstrue this intimate dinner. I'm enjoying myself, and enjoying window-shopping – sorry to go back to the metaphor – but I have a girlfriend back in England.'

'And you love her?'

He hesitated. 'Love is a very big word.'

'Oh dear. You sound like Prince Charles and his Lady Di. "Whatever love is." We all remember those words.'

'Maybe it's the English condition.' He laughed ruefully. 'We have a very happy relationship. And, yes, I think I love her. But if that's the case, how come I do so much window-shopping?'

Cécile took his hand in hers. 'Do you want to do more than window-shop?' she asked breathily. He was a very attractive man, and she could see the muscles through the fine white shirt he was wearing.

He gazed into her eyes, and thought about Katie. Beautiful, adorable Katie. If a tad plump Katie. Nothing diet and exercise couldn't sort out. 'No,' he said. 'But I won't deny it's tempting. Pudding?'

'What a singularly 'orrible word. Poo-ding.' She exaggerated the word. 'Thanks. But no thanks. Maybe some *petits fours* and a small coffee.'

She leaned back, and he was aware of the warmth being withdrawn as she took away her hand.

Richard and Louise had spent the evening slobbing out in front of the television after packing their offspring off to bed. He had been regaling her with the story of his fellow producer's eyebag surgery. 'She didn't want to do it, but she was strong-armed into it. They needed to make up the numbers for a plastic-surgery strand. And now they've dropped it. They really are awful. Although, between you and me, she looks a lot better now. She did look like she'd been in a domestic incident for a few days, but the stitches have come out and you'd never know.'

'Should I have mine done?' asked Louise, turning her face towards him.

'You haven't got eyebags.'

'Perhaps not big ones yet. But it's only a matter of time before the clutch bags become fully fledged totes.'

'We'll get you some eyebag splints.'

'How kind. We can get them colour-coordinated.' She got up off the sofa and went to open another bottle of wine.

'Do you think Katie will get off with Paul Martin? Or has already got off with him?' She raised her voice from the kitchen. A friend of a friend of hers worked at Wolf Days Productions and couldn't believe she would cheat on the gorgeous Adam Williams.

'"Get off with" is such a revolting expression,' said Richard, mildly. 'If she had, they would have shown it. They're doing as much as they can to suggest it, but if they had the evidence, it'd be out there.'

'Like extra-terrestrials,' Louise said, topping up his glass.

'If the aliens stopped abducting people in small farming communities in America's Midwest, they'd be in trouble. We'd find out where they came from, and exactly why they insist on using anal probes on humans. What can they find out with a probe that they can't find out by any other means?'

'So do you think Katie and Paul Martin are getting it together?'

'Katie is the most massive flirt. It's second nature to her. But she and Adam seem very happy. On the other hand, she's a generally happy person. I dunno.'

'You do need a nice warm man to hunker down with if it's well below freezing,' she said, giving him a kiss under his ear and snuggling under his arm. 'I wonder what those snowsuits are stuffed with to make them so impervious to the cold.'

'Penguins.'

She laughed. 'Of course. And polar bears. What have you heard about him?'

'Only what I've read in the newspapers. His columns are pretty much like all the others. A rant here and there, bitchy comments about celebrities. Issue of the day. He has a good turn of phrase and they're often quite funny. Sometimes very funny, actually.'

'I think he's a bit of a snake,' said Louise, 'because he knows she's going out with Adam.'

'He can't know how the producers are cutting the show, though. The flirting might be a tiny percentage of what's going on.'

'I'm glad they got rid of Denise Trench. She was revolting.'

'Or she was made revolting in the edit suite.'

'You really do ruin the magic of television,' laughed Louise.

Rod Fallon and his wife had gone out to a charity dinner, dropping their sixteen-year-old daughter Eleanor at a friend's house for a sleepover. 'Although sleepover is a misnomer – precious little sleeping involved, I bet,' he said to his wife.

He was right. Eleanor and Issy were going to a party. They promised, faithfully, that they would be back by midnight. It was being held in a smart townhouse, and had been organized by the older brother of a friend of Issy's, who was the son of a famous musician.

Eleanor was going through a belated parent-hating phase, and needed no encouragement to get drunk. She ploughed straight into bottles of highly coloured drinks, dragging Issy with her.

By the time Issy's mother arrived to pick them up, they were in a terrible state. Her daughter was glassy-eyed, lipstick-smeared, and Eleanor was on a pile of coats, kissing a spotty boy with a stiff quiff and a bent end. As she dragged them both out of the door, the party was disintegrating. There appeared to be some sort of fight going on. As she bundled the girls into the car, two police cars roared up, just in time to witness Eleanor Fallon vomiting down the side of a black BMW.

CHAPTER TWELVE

In the olden days Sunday newspapers took a couple of hours to read, and at the end of the process, you had been informed, tickled and tested. Nowadays, thought Jack, in his hotel room in Blackpool, you felt guilty about the mountain of paper that was discarded before you got to the smidgen you wanted to read. He put the sports section, the travel section, the fashion section, the motoring section and the culture section in the bin, then got back onto the bed to read the news section and the gardening section.

It was another grizzly, drizzly day, so it was with some reluctance that he eventually put the paper into his bag, and went down to Reception to comply with the checking-out time. He had a cup of tea in the dining room, finished reading the paper and, wishing he had bought a mobile phone, made a call from the hotel reception. Then, leaving himself plenty of time, he made his way to the bus station.

It wasn't a packed bus, and he had two seats to himself as he retraced his steps back to Yorkshire, where he took a taxi. A casual observer would have assumed he was going home, since the car followed his normal route, but after a short while, it veered off, eventually coming to a halt outside the Old Coach House.

Bob Hewlett had been surprised, to say the least, when Jack had phoned to ask himself to stay but, within minutes, he had succumbed to the plea for help. He was pleased to see that Jack was carrying a small suitcase, since he had not enquired as to the length of his visit. 'Good trip?' he asked, showing Jack to a bright room at the back of the house, with a beautiful view across the garden to the hills beyond.

'Fine. Uneventful. A careful bus driver, and that's all you can hope for. Perhaps a little too careful. He went round the bends so slowly I could have balanced a cup of tea on my thighs and played a hand of whist. Not unlike how you ride your motorbike,' he said ironically.

Bob was quietly chuffed that Jack had noticed his speediness on his beloved Triumph. 'This is your bathroom, by the way,' he said, pointing to it, two doors down from the bedroom. 'I know the bath isn't very big, but you do have an enormous shower head.'

'Why, thank you kindly. Maybe if I brought my ears forward, you wouldn't notice so much.'

'Ha. I can see where your daughter gets it from,' said Bob, who then blushed slightly and turned on the taps in the basin to cover it. 'Yes,' he said randomly. 'They're working.'

'Were they not?' asked Jack, who hadn't noticed the blush. 'If there's anything I can do around the house while I'm here, it would make me feel better about imposing on you like this.'

'No worries,' said Bob. 'I think everything's all right. If I do notice anything, I will immediately supply you with the proper tools and demand you get it sorted.'

Jack smiled. 'I mean it. It's very kind of you to let me stay. And it really won't be for very long. It may look odd, but I couldn't think of anything else to do that I hadn't done already.'

'I'll be in the kitchen, when you've unpacked and everything,' said Bob. 'I've got the ingredients you asked for. You really don't have to cook for me if you're feeling tired, though. I'm sure I can rummage up something passable.'

'There will be no rummaging up passable food while I'm here,' said Jack, forcefully. 'I'll be right down to deal with that deer.'

He quickly got out his toiletries, washed his face and made his way downstairs. In the warm kitchen, he got to grips with the venison.

'Can I help?' asked Bob.

'No. You can talk to me while I'm wrestling this into the pot.'

The sound of a distant radio could be heard.

'Whoops. Left the portable in the garden. I was digging over the ground ready for some new inhabitants. I'll go and get it. Be right back,' said Bob, as Jack rubbed seasoning into the meat.

'How are things?' he asked, when Bob returned.

'Fine. Fine. Could do with more work but it's ticking over.'

'Love life all right?'

Bob barked a laugh. 'Cut straight to the chase. I assume you've heard the rumour that Clare McMurray and I have gone our separate ways?'

Jack nodded. 'Sorry about that,' he said, washing his hands in the sink. 'I assume your oranges are in the fridge?'

'Oranges?' said Bob. 'Um. I don't know whether I got oranges. If I didn't buy them, is there anything else you can use?'

'I'll think of something. Did you get cranberries?'

'Definitely. Yes. They're in the fridge. And the vegetables. I'll peel those. I've got to do something or I'm going to stand here like a … like a …'

'Lemon.'

'I don't think I have any citrus fruit at all.'

Jack smiled.

'Do you want a coffee while you work?'

'I'm a tea-holic. So maybe a pot of tea? Or a mug of builder's. Whatever you've got. "Coffee" is a strange word, when you think about it. Cough-ee. Like a person over whom one coughs. And, funnily enough, coffee does make me cough.'

'I saw one of those recently in one of the papers,' said Bob, 'or maybe it was an email. "Rectum", meaning to make a mess of them.'

'Testicle. A humorous exam question,' added Jack.

'Nice,' said Bob.

As they smiled together, they were both thinking it was like having Katie there in the room, talking silliness.

Bob was glad that Jack had invited himself to stay. It was the next best thing.

And Jack was glad that Bob had agreed to have him. He wished that Katie hadn't messed up, and that they were still together. He liked Adam, but the man was self-obsessed and spent an awful lot of time talking about work. He couldn't imagine inviting himself to stay with young Mr Williams.

Bob busied himself with the tea, then helped with the vegetables. When dinner was in the oven, they slumped onto the sofa with a couple of beers and put the television on.

'It'll be ready in about two hours,' said Jack. 'Hope that's OK.'

'That's absolutely fine. Not doing anything pressing. Sunday nights are a curate's egg, aren't they? You can't start anything because it's Monday tomorrow and it's too much of a lazy kind of day to go round finishing things.'

'I must say this is very comfortable,' said Jack.

Bob was thinking how pleasant – yet strange – it was having Jack relaxing on his sofa. 'What did you get up to yesterday?' he asked.

'I spent all day at Blackpool Pleasure Beach. I went on the Big One about six times, and have a lot less hair as a result. And then I went on most of the other rides, barging those youngsters out of the way. One of the few advantages of being old. Having said that, you know the worst thing?' Bob shook his head. 'How sad it is these days that a seventy-year-old man can't go round a funfair on his own without attracting the occasional comment about paedophiles.'

'That is bloody sad.'

'But, really, people are obsessed. And the last research I saw said that attacks had stayed static for the last hundred years. I pretended I was with my granddaughter at one point.'

'You don't have a granddaughter, do you?' asked Bob, sitting up suddenly, surprised.

'No. Ben and Katie have so far refused to provide me with one. I had an imaginary granddaughter who was ill and being looked after by my wife, so I was making sure the pass wasn't wasted. That's what I was telling people in the queues. I have no idea whether they believed me or not, but it made me feel better.'

'Crying shame that you had to, though.'

'I know. It's funny … there was a girl on one of the rides who reminded me so much of Katie. About eight, she was. And she was really excited about her new red shoes, but trying to be grown-up and not show it. She kept pretending she needed to stretch so she could admire them. I remember taking Katie out for some new shoes, and Lynda telling me they had to be black for school. But Katie wheedled, and did that thing little girls do when they wind you round their grubby thumbs. We came back with a pair of red ones and I got it in the neck from Lynda. There was hell to pay. At least I'd bought them a couple of sizes bigger, as Lynda had ordered me, so she could grow into them. Of course by the time she did grow into them, they were wrecked. So scuffed there was barely any leather left. And Lynda had refused to splash out on red shoe polish just for Katie's shoes, so they got browner and browner. Katie hated having to clean them. You could see her gingerly putting on the tiniest dob of brown shoe polish because she liked them cherry red.' He sat quietly for a minute, remembering. 'You know, we didn't have a lot of money, but it seemed to me that Lynda and I had a lot more fun then. Or maybe I mean that we had a lot more fun together,' he ended wistfully.

'Another beer?' asked Bob.

'Don't mind if I do. It's a shame we can't go down the pub, but I can't risk someone telling Lynda they saw me.'

'What are you going to say to her when you do see her?'

'Oh, something will occur to me. I'll wing it. Knowing my luck, she'll have decided to go on a round-the-world cruise for a month. Or I'll walk through the door and she won't have noticed I'd gone.'

'Best-case scenario?'

'I walk back in, she throws herself on me like I'm some prodigal husband, we walk off into the sunset.'

'Better make sure you're wearing stout shoes, then.'

Bob went into the kitchen to get more beers, and Caligula came prancing in through the open door to find a comfy armchair. He considered his options and, based on the merest whiff of venison, chose Jack. He padded round and round the lap, raising his paws and expanding his claws as he did so, until he found the optimum position, whereupon he sank into a cat ball and drifted off to sleep with his tail tucked firmly round his feet.

* * *

Keera Keethley was on a train back from Nottingham as *Celebrity X-Treme* went out that night. The carriage was repugnant. She liked the word 'repugnant'. It was a word with three syllables and it made her feel good. Plus, she knew exactly what it meant.

She had enjoyed her weekend away. Her mother had made her feel like a star. Sheila lapped up her tales and came back for more. 'I saw the picture of you in one of the magazines the other day,' she had said. 'You and two men in LA when you went there. You looked great. Such a pretty bikini. I've put it in the scrapbook with all the others. I've started a fifth already. And that's not including the magazines where you're on the front cover. I've kept those whole.'

So here was the cover girl on the train again. Luckily, it was only half full, and she had taken the precaution of bringing a book from her mother's shelves. She was a bit embarrassed about it, but she was holding it under the lip of the table, so no one could see that she was thoroughly enjoying one of Mills & Boon's racier titles. The picture on the front showed a couple in a passionate clinch. The man resembled Peter Philbin. It was a shame he was a soap star, she thought. He wouldn't be good for her image. Otherwise she was fairly sure she could get a date with him when he got out of *Celebrity X-Treme*. He obviously looked after himself. She found she was reading her book with him in the title role and herself as the heroine.

She really ought to begin an earnest hunt for the right kind of man to squire her about town, now that Mr Praed was off the menu. She wanted a man who looked good and had a high-powered job. Or maybe a title.

She got back to her book. The train's arrival in London interrupted a very steamy passage, and she could hardly wait to get home.

After metaphorically notching his bedpost, Matthew Praed had wiped Keera from that part of his mind and was hunting the next conquest – an actress with an icy demeanour and a reputation as a difficult nut to crack. He had a fancy to storm the citadel and fly a flag from the ramparts. He was having an unaccustomed early night, and was idly watching *Celebrity X-Treme* in the absence of anything else while flicking through one of the Sunday supplements.

As Tanya Wilton was predictably booted off (could the producers be any more cynical about whom they wanted out? he wondered), he debated whether she would look good on his books. Or even on his bed. Possibly. He leaned over to the side table, the leather bed creaking as he adjusted his position, to write on a large pad. Crystal Blake's stupendous cleavage had lingered in his mind, but he dismissed it. Too short-term. He couldn't see her going the distance, and she'd bore most of his staff. Paul Martin? Now there was a piece of work. He wondered if he had any representation … and jotted his name down with Tanya's. He recognized the hungry look in Paul Martin's eyes. Truly hungry for Katie – or for fame? Or both?

* * *

Siobhan had had a successful Sunday and was relaxing with a glass of Chardonnay.

Mark's idea for the astrology game had been inspired. The seven men and women had had to put on enormous comedy boots, then run from one roped-off area to another, picking up balloons, which had pictures on them representing the defining characteristics of each star sign.

The one with the most correct balloons would win a specially prepared dinner.

There had been the anticipated grumbling from some of the participants that Flynn O'Mara was obviously going to win. Flynn had said loudly that she hoped they were using a reputable astrology book (i.e. hers) for the characteristics. Dave Beal had sworn comprehensively when hearing the rules of the game, and said he had no idea what his star sign was. Nobody believed him.

It had turned out to be very funny, with lots of crashes and silliness. And Flynn O'Mara had not won because her boots were too big and she couldn't walk in them (she said).

As they had waited for the starting hooter, Katie had examined her footwear.

'I could do with a blacksmith to put metal grips on these,' she said. 'They're going to slip everywhere.'

'Don't blacksmiths do horses? You'd end up getting rehoofed,' said Paul, standing next to her.

'I could become a hoofer. I could become Hoofers Sewell.'

'Ah. Those puns.' He sighed.

To everyone's astonishment, it was Dave Beal who took the crown. Mark had given Siobhan a sideways look as Dave stood under his Scorpio balloons showing sexiness and strength. She had smiled knowingly back at him. Her plan had worked. The celebrities were sharing intimate details of their lives with each other in a way they hadn't done before. And now that the alcoholic Denise Trench was out, they had been able to go to town on the booze. Dave Beal had been revoltingly lecherous with poor Crystal, so they would put quite a lot of that in the final edit to get people fired up.

Another producer came over to speak to Mark.

'Hysterical,' he said, as the producer went back to his station, monitoring the input.

'What?' she asked.

'Apparently Katie told Crystal she thought Flynn might be from the isle of Lesbos. Then Crystal went over and said it was strange having a name like Flynn O'Mara when she was from Greece. And Flynn said, "Who told you I was from Greece when I'm from Billericay?"'

'Excellent on so many levels. That should definitely get in.' She looked at her watch. 'I'm going to turn in for the night. You fancy a quick snifter?'

'Don't mind if I do,' he said, surprised.

What he didn't know was that she had noticed a small lapse in security on his part. He had forgotten to log himself off his computer for the night. And if she could make sure he was in his room before she got back to it, she could shore up her defences in the unlikely event of a few waves on the phone-voting front. She had covered her tracks fairly comprehensively but it was always worth having one more back-up plan. Marvellous, she thought gaily, as they walked through the moonless night together. I am marvellous.

Sunday had not been a marvellous day for the Fallons. There had been a major fight with Eleanor after Issy's mother had rung up to complain that her daughter had been led astray. She had left nothing out. So, when Eleanor had arrived home, Rod had torn her off a strip and grounded her for a month. She had stood there sullenly, and then shouted, 'I *hate* you. It wasn't my fault. They weren't my drinks. Issy and I just wanted to have some fun.' And when it had been pointed out that it didn't matter whose fault it was, she was old enough to make her own decisions, Eleanor had said, with vehemence, 'You don't listen to anything I say. It wasn't my fault. I don't care what you do to me. I hate you,' then gone to her room. A slight waft of cheese escaped as the door slammed.

The Fallons had exchanged a look, and Rod had asked, 'Do all teenagers smell like that?'

CHAPTER THIRTEEN

'I'm definitely going to get Katie to introduce me to Flynn O'Mara,' said Dee, as she flopped into the makeup chair on Monday morning, clonking her plaster cast as she did so. 'Did you see it over the weekend?' she asked Vanda, who was washing her hands ready for the day's ministrations.

'Sure did. Cancelled a racy evening out entirely so I could sit down and watch it on my ownsome.'

'What racy evening out had you been planning?'

'Supermarket. I hate it. I put it off until there was no time. Can't be doing with weekend shopping. Too many children.'

'Aaah,' said Dee, with a smile. 'I love them. Mad little midgets. They make me laugh.'

'Your brain must be wired up wrong.'

'Anyway. So. What do you think of Paul Martin now, eh?'

Vanda sighed in a swoony way. 'I think he is the most handsome man. But I can't understand why he's making such a big thing of flirting with Katie when he knows she's going out with Adam.'

'Mm. Yup. I agree,' said Dee, nodding, as Vanda put the makeup wrap around her. 'It's very confusing. I don't know whether it's because I quite fancy him myself, but I do wonder whether Katie's going to succumb. Which would send the newspapers insane.'

'What would send the newspapers insane?' asked Keera, gliding in. She had been on her way to the wardrobe department but, at the magical word, she had done a body swerve.

Without looking round, since Vanda was rubbing cream blusher on her cheeks, Dee said, 'If Katie went off with Paul Martin on *Celebrity X-Treme*.'

'Why should she do that? She's got Adam Williams.'

'Yes, of course,' said Dee. She didn't want to discuss Katie's love life with two-faced Keera Keethley who, she suspected, sold stories about them to the nationals.

'Anyway, I was saying *if*. She wouldn't go off with him because, as you say, she's going out with Adam.' She closed her eyes to prevent further talk, and Vanda silently applied makeup, until Keera's footsteps could be heard going down the corridor.

'Toe-rag spawn of Satan,' said Dee, quietly. Then added brightly, 'So where were we?'

'About the newspapers going wild. At the risk of sounding like Keera, why would she mess up a relationship with Adam?'

'Why did she mess up her relationship with Bob?'

'There is that. Is it because of her background? Did she grow up in a stable environment?'

'Neigh!' whinnied Dee.

'Stop giggling. You're messing up my perfect eye-shadow application,' said Vanda, her hand hovering with a fresh load of Christian Dior.

'Yes. Her parents are still together. They're lovely. I've met them a few times. Barking. But really nice. No. I think Katie just likes flirting. I know she's not after a husband or anything.'

'Unlike the rest of us.'

'Oi. Speak for yourself. I had one, and they're dreadful. All they do is mess up your life.'

'If Oliver asked you, you'd say no, would you?'

Dee had her eyes closed. After a minute she said, 'I don't know.'

'Aha.'

'I didn't say I would.'

'But you didn't say you wouldn't.'

Dee was imagining the scenario: Oliver on bended knee, looking up at her and asking her to marry him. Oh, yes. She'd say yes. Deffo. She smiled.

'You see?' said Vanda, understanding.

'No – I'd gone off on one and suddenly found myself thinking about underwear,' she lied.

'Specifically what?' asked Vanda, not believing her.

Dee cast around her brain cells and came up with 'Teddies.'

'Teddies,' said Vanda, with scorn. 'One of the most awful inventions of the eighties. Do you remember how the poppers underneath would burst open if you sat down too quickly?'

'Or trap everything so you ended up walking with a wince,' Dee said.

'Or they'd start riding up, and you'd have the two bits inching their way up your waist.'

'And the shoulder pads they were holding in would start slipping.'

'And they flattened your boobs. They were a nightmare. Almost as bad as thongs.'

'I *love* thongs,' pronounced Dee.

'How can you? They're so uncomfortable.'

'Get bigger ones. You need them in extra large. Or large, at least.'

'And they look cheap when you bend over and you can see them.'

'I won't argue with you there. Mascara?' Vanda handed it to her. Dee opened her mouth as she put it on, then put the wand back into the tube. 'Strange how you can't put mascara on without having your mouth open.'

'Like how you can't look in a mirror without doing a mirror face,' added Vanda.

Dee smiled. 'But is that a mirror face, or just the face you're pulling to reflect how you feel?'

'Is this one of those psychological conversations?'

'At this time in the morning?' asked Dee. 'Talking of which, I need to go and choose something to wear or I'll be doing it in

222

these day pyjamas.' She gestured to her tracksuit bottoms and the sweatshirt with a stain on it. 'Oops. Wonder what that is.' She raised it to her nose and sniffed. 'Coffee. I'll see if Derek can sort it out. Maybe he'll wash it for me if I do a really major creep. Wish me luck. I'm going over the top, Captain,' she said dramatically, as she disappeared round the corner to Wardrobe.

Derek was steaming one of Rod's suits and a luminous yellow shirt.

Dee goggled at it. 'Haven't seen that one before. Does it come in any other flavours?'

'Strawberry. You naughty girl,' said Derek, who quite liked Dee. 'What will you be wearing this fine ... erm, what day is it?'

'Monday. All day.'

'Oh, God,' he groaned, 'you mean I have four more of these to go before the weekend?'

'I know,' she said. 'It does feel like it goes on for ever and ever. You get up, and it's another day. It's like Groundhog Day. It's like Groundhog Day. Isn't this like Groundhog Day?'

'It's coming round awfully quickly. Could have sworn you said Groundhog Day a moment ago. Now, tell me what you want to wear,' he said, as they walked into her dressing room together. She picked out a plum dress.

'Good. Nice and subdued. Rod's banana can shine through.'

'I don't really want to think about Rod's banana, thank you,' said Dee, grimacing.

'Know what you mean,' said Derek. His ears pricked up. He put up his hand to stop any more conversation, and popped his head out of the door. 'Morning, Rod,' he said, as Rod pushed open his dressing-room door. 'I've done a nice navy suit and a lemon shirt for you, with a choice of two ties. OK?' He brought his head back in.

'Lemon!' whispered Dee. 'If that came with my gin and tonic, I'd send it back.'

But actually, on air, it worked surprisingly well.

Keera was wearing a pale yellow dress, which somehow took the edge off it.

She was in an imperious mood. 'Phil,' she said, to a cameraman who was bent over his camera, 'why are you fiddling with that crane? Can you please do it somewhere else? That's right in my eye line.'

'I'm splitting the tension wire back on the roller,' he said, and thought, Like you know what that means.

In their earpieces, they heard the countdown to the end of the VT.

'Coming up, we're going to be talking to a family whose house was almost destroyed by the recent floods,' said Rod.

'Although it does look like it only needs a lick of paint,' said Keera, as the pictures rolled.

Rod paused to let her idiocy sink in with the nation, then continued smoothly, 'And we'll be talking moths – specifically, endangered moths and how we can help.'

The *Hello Britain!* music came up. But the soundman had forgotten to fade Keera down, and she could be heard quite clearly saying, 'Who wants to help moths, for God's sake? They eat my clothes.'

As the adverts went on in the background, the floor manager asked them if there was anything they wanted. 'I'd love a herbal drink,' said Keera, 'maybe a lemon-flavoured one. How strange. I wonder why I want a lemon-flavoured one.' She tried out her new laugh again as she fingered her yellow dress – in case anyone had missed the point. If she wasn't careful, she thought, the laugh had a tendency to go quite Sid James.

'Anything involving plums for you, Dee?' asked the floor manager, with a wink.

Dee shook her head.

'Rod?'

'No, thanks. Is this moth on its way in here?'

'Twenty grand's worth of moth is currently being primped and preened ready for its television appearance by its handlers. I think it may be in Makeup having a wing dusting. But you've got the parking-meter thing first.'

'That's a down-the-line, isn't it? No guest in the studio?'

The floor manager checked his notes. 'Yes. And then it's Keera doing the moth.'

'I thought I was doing the moth,' said Rod.

'No. You're parking, she's mothing.'

'I am mothing without you,' Dee muttered, as she checked through her graphics in front of the chroma key.

Keera moved her ankles together and admired her sheer tights. She liked these ones: they gave a good sheen. Her ankles really were superb. And she liked the way her shoes gave her toe cleavage.

Rod picked up the phone with the direct link to the senior producer. 'I thought I was doing the moth.'

'Oh, sorry. Forgot. We had to drop the bus story. So Keera's doing the moth.'

'Well, thanks for letting me know,' said Rod, curtly, and semi-slammed the phone back on its cradle. He sat back on the sofa. He was in a bad mood, and had been all morning. Eleanor had been unbearable, and he had slept badly.

'Coming back to the studio. Five … four … three … two … one … on air.'

The ident came up, and Rod read the autocue. 'We're celebrating – if that's the correct word – the half-century of the parking meter. Fifty years ago today, the first meter was unveiled in London. This report from Rick Merkney.'

It began with pictures from Manchester and Glasgow of parking wardens, then switched to black-and-white footage.

'Shall I caption them as library pictures?' asked the PA.

'Kind of obvious, really,' said the director. 'What else would we put up? Pictures just in? Latest news?'

'Um. Get your point.'

Rod's interview afterwards was lacklustre to say the least. But nobody expected much of him any more.

And while it was going on, a man and a moth snuck in to sit on the sofa. 'Good morning,' the man whispered to Keera, so that the microphones wouldn't pick it up. 'I'll take the moth out after we've talked about her. She might be a bit difficult with the lights.'

'All right,' she whispered back. Boy, she loved television. Being in control. If she'd said, 'Take it out now,' he would have done. She stifled a smile. Take it out now. That was a bit rude. She smiled. Her guest smiled back. Idiot, she thought, and turned to face Rod as he finished his interview.

'It's twenty past seven and you're watching *Hello Britain!*,' she said. 'Now. Moths. Some of them are in danger of becoming extinct. And we can help …'

In her earpiece, she heard a shouted: '*But* we can help. *But* …'

She didn't know what he was trying to say, so carried on, 'They're in danger of becoming extinct, and we can help. Here's Rachel Barrington.' As the report was going out, she explained to her interviewee what she wanted from him while Rod gritted his teeth in annoyance.

Keera put on her fake smile as the VT ended. 'And here is one of the endangered moths, along with its handler.'

He opened the cage to bring out the most enormous specimen. And it flew straight up into the lights. 'Oh dear.' He grimaced. 'I'm not sure we'll be able to coax her down. She's eaten already.'

Keera did her tinkly laugh. 'We'll let her sit up there for a moment while we talk about her and others like her.'

The moth sat on the light, refusing to budge, as the interview continued. Rod watched her as she wiggled her feelers. She was beautiful. All sandy brown feathery wings. He liked moths. It was strange how everyone liked butterflies, dragonflies and bees and generally nothing else on the insect front. You didn't find people propounding the merits of beetles or ants. Yet some beetles were stunning. He had seen a lime green one in Jamaica. Or had it been America?

The floor manager passed him a handwritten note: 'Apparently it's worth twenty grand.'

As Keera wrapped up the chat, Rod leaned over. 'Sorry about your moth,' he said. 'She's having a nice time sitting up on the lights. And I hear she's worth twenty thousand pounds.'

'Yes, she is. And that is exactly why we won't be going anywhere until she comes down.'

'We'll keep you supplied with hot drinks until that happens,' said Rod, and he turned into a two-shot to continue with the programme.

The cameras turned away from them, to pick up a young indy band who were to perform their first hit.

'Rod,' said Keera, sweetly, 'that was my interview that you just signed off. And I saw you being handed a note. You should have passed it to me, since it was my item. Can you do that in future?'

He smiled a smile that didn't reach his eyes, and said as sweetly as she had, 'Of course I can, Keera.' He pulled one of the tabloids off the desk to check a fact for his next interview.

Keera examined her fingernails. She loved her hands. Hands were worth looking after. They showed your age. She had noticed that some of the guests who were young had old-looking hands. Maybe she'd give hers a good exfoliation this afternoon, cover them with heavy moisturizer and encase them in white cotton gloves. There might be a fifties musical she could watch while it was all soaking in.

Dee, trying to sort out a microphone problem with the sound department, couldn't help enjoying this morning's bickering. If Katie hadn't been in Norway, she would have phoned her up to bitch about it.

Adam would also have quite liked to speak to Katie. He had enjoyed Paris, and particularly his dinner with Cécile d'Ombard, but he had come back to tabloid pictures and stories from *Celebrity X-Treme* that seemed to suggest his girlfriend had exceeded her brief. As humans are wont to be, he was jealous and angry because he had done a very similar thing. The difference was that he had done his misbehaving – if misbehaving it was – in Paris, without witnesses. Actually, he didn't even acknowledge that he was feeling jealous and angry. He put his peevishness down to the fact that he hated his advice being ignored.

So, when he went into Wolf Days Productions that Monday morning, he was not in the best of moods. The producers, Gemma and Rose, were chatting inconsequentially, as usual. This morning, they were discussing breakfast.

'Bacon sandwich. Ketchup,' said Rose.

'Cereal. No milk,' said Gemma.

'What? In a bowl?' asked Rose.

'Do you two really have nothing better to do or do I pay you to talk about your bloody breakfast habits?' growled Adam, as he strode through the office, leaving a waft of something expensive and peppery in his wake.

Rose sniffed appreciatively. 'He smells *so* yummy,' she said, gazing after him hungrily.

'And his clothes are always *so* cool.'

'I think it's the way he wears them. He's fit.'

'Would you prefer to be fit and thick, or fat and clever?'

Rose crunched a Hobnob from a packet she had found on her desk, and pondered for a minute. She noticed a crumb on the computer, picked it up and ate it, then made a face. 'Yurk,' she exclaimed. 'That was disgusting. I thought it was a bit of biscuit and it tasted like scab. Do you think I've eaten a piece of scab that someone's picked off? That is so gross.'

'Or maybe it was a piece of crunchy dandruff. Like when it's psoriasis.'

'How revolting,' Rose grimaced.

'Yup. Anyway. Fit and thick or fat and clever?'

'Are you still on that? I may be dying from scabitis. Or bogeyitis. Urgh. I feel sick.'

'Sick or thick?'

'Sick. As in I'm going to vomit if I've actually eaten someone else's scab.'

'Well, take your mind off it and discuss. Cool but dim? Nerdy but brainy?'

Rose went to the water-cooler for a drink to wash down whatever it was she had swallowed. She came back and said, 'Actually? As I am. Very cool. Very clever.'

'Right. So you aren't going to answer?'

'I don't want to be one or the other. It's impossible. I don't want to have to be fat and anything. I refuse to have an option where I can't change. If I'm fat and clever, I want to be able to stop eating so that I can be slim and clever. And if I'm fit but not that bright, I want to be able to study and improve myself.'

'Ooo-er! 'Ark at you.'

'Well, it's daft. If you're going to do those either-or things, there has to be no way of changing. Like the shag, marry or over-the-cliff one.'

'All right. We'll do that, then. Let me have a look in today's newspaper,' said Gemma, reaching over for the *Daily Telegraph*. 'Taken at random, who would you shag, marry or throw off the cliff? John Prescott. Robert Mugabe – no, too easy. Ho hum. Robert Kilroy-Silk and—'

'Gemma,' called Nick, from his office.

'I'll marry *him*,' whispered Rose, as Gemma stood up.

'He wasn't on the list,' she threw over her shoulder.

Nick looked slightly bemused as she went in. 'We're going to see if we can find anything suitable for Keera Keethley.'

'Keera Keethley? But Katie would *kill* Adam,' burst out Gemma.

'Yes. I must say, I'm surprised. But to put you in the picture, her agent phoned me up to ask about possible programmes.

I've just spoken to Adam, and he's said we should. Look at possible programmes, that is. I don't think it's up to us to decode what's going on there, do you?'

'No, sir.'

'Don't be cheeky.'

'Yes, sir.'

'Gemma ...' he said, with a warning look.

'Oh, all right. But why ask me? You know exactly what we've got and what we're working on.'

'That's correct. But you also have friends – as do I – who work at other companies. You have your ear to the ground, and you're also being paid to come up with ideas and proposals. Obviously I know that there's nothing that would suit Keera at the moment. Could you think something up, do you reckon?'

'As you know,' said Gemma, 'she turned us down for *Dare to Bare*. And, as you know, I was greatly relieved, because apparently she's a bit of a mare.'

'Is she?' he asked. Like most men, he thought she was gorgeous, if dim. He didn't think it mattered that much for some programmes – particularly if you looked like Keera.

'Yes, she is,' said Gemma, firmly. 'She's gone over to the dark side.'

He laughed. 'What *are* you talking about? Gone over to the dark side? You've been watching too much *Most Haunted*.'

'I mean she's done that thing some presenters do, where they believe their own publicity and are falser than false, and it's all about how they look and not about the programme. And they're demanding.'

'Hmm. I'm not sure that constitutes nightmare.'

'And she can't do the job,' finished Gemma, dramatically.

'Well, *Hello Britain!* seems to rate her. To use a dreadful Americanism, this is a heads-up that we may have to look for something.'

'I can't believe he'd do that to Katie.'

'As I said, ours is not to reason why.'

'As you said,' said Gemma, going back to her computer.

'What's going on?' asked Rose.

Within fifteen minutes, everyone knew that Adam was pissed off with Katie.

Every day that she woke up in Norway Katie promised herself she would get on with the job in hand, make friends with the muddle-headed Crystal and the asinine Peter, stop sneering at the oafish Dave Beal and absolutely stop flirting with Paul Martin. She was all right with Flynn O'Mara, who was a nice woman with a strange job.

But no sooner had she stretched and gone through to the kitchen to make a cup of tea than she had snapped at Dave, had a go at Peter, tutted at Crystal and smirked conspiratorially at Paul. She gave herself a mental shake. Most of the time, she now forgot that the cameras were there. But when she remembered – and recently it was only when the eviction was announced – she felt guilty. She wondered – seriously wondered – whether she still had a boyfriend. Could she explain it all away? At least she hadn't kissed Paul Martin. That was the one thing she was holding on to.

Paul wandered over as Crystal and Peter gazed admiringly at each other.

'I know,' he said. 'Those love birds, eh?'

'Um,' she said, trying to adhere to her rule of being nice to and about them. 'I once had a very sweet friend who was a perfect widgeon. You couldn't go out with her if you needed to have a deep and meaningful conversation. But she didn't have a malicious bone in her body. It was like going out with Winnie-the-Pooh – not intellectually stimulating, but she made me happy. They have their own unique take on life, people like that.'

'She still a friend?'

'No.' She laughed. 'You know, she once told me that some people steal your sleep – and I could see her point. She also thinks that when you get *déjà vu*, it's because there's been a time crease. And that the word "tentacles" is rude.'

'Oh, OK,' he said and, with a gesture to Crystal and Peter, 'So they're a pair of tits and we should beat them to death with spades in case they're infectious.'

She laughed. 'I didn't even remotely say that. We can't all like current affairs and reading books. And even to my ears that sounds snotty and stuck-up. But on the other hand, I really can't be expected to carry on a conversation with someone who thinks that an abdication is when you've got a flat stomach.'

'Your friend? Or Crystal?' he asked.

'Well, OK. I made that up. Neither of them said it. Good line, though.'

He ran his hand through his thick hair and gave her a searching look. 'You bored with all this?'

'No,' she said, with feeling. 'I am, surprisingly, enjoying myself. You?'

'How could I not be when I'm in here with you?'

She shook her head. 'There you go again. You're determined to get me into trouble. If you carry on, I'll have to dedicate myself to talking to Crystal and Peter about *High School Musical* films.'

'Instead of talking to me about what matters. Love. Marriage. Children.' He gave her a meaningful look.

And maybe because she was tired, maybe because of the promise she had made to herself that morning, or maybe because he had a spot on his chin, she was irritated. 'Enough already.' She put up one hand. 'I'm not in the mood. Now is not the time or place.' She walked away.

'My place some other time,' said Paul, looking towards a camera.

'Good one,' whispered Siobhan, as she wrote down the time details on her pad.

CHAPTER FOURTEEN

Bob had woken up grumpy, and was made grumpier by being forced to listen to Radio 4: his temporary housemate had it on very loudly in the kitchen. There was never anything happy on the *Today* programme. Unremittingly bad news. Which was why he preferred XFM. Or even Radio 2.

He threw on his clothes and shuffled downstairs, his sandy blond hair sticking up in all directions. He rubbed his stubbly chin and yawned as he went into the kitchen.

'Good morning,' Jack said chirpily. 'I have a horrible feeling I've woken you before you normally get up. I was trying to find a whisk. I had to open all the drawers before I found it. And you've got a sticky one,' he indicated the drawer he had pulled out completely, 'so I'll sort that out today.'

Bob couldn't help smiling. Nobody who had stayed at the house had ever done anything but eat, drink or make merry before.

'I was thinking coffee and omelette?' Jack suggested.

'Excellent. Need any help?'

'No, thanks. Think I've got all I need now. Cheese, tomato and onion all right?'

'Perfect.' Bob went to sit at the table, his feet in odd socks, his grey cashmere sweater tucked into his jeans at the back.

'Did you sleep well?' asked Jack, twisting round from his position at the kitchen counter. 'Apart from being woken up far too early by that old man in the kitchen, that is.'

'Yes, thanks,' said Bob, ruffling his hair vigorously to try to energize himself. 'Got out of bed on the wrong side, I think. Sorry. Not exactly mine host today.'

'Oh, don't you worry,' said Jack. 'Here. Do you need ketchup?'

'Does the Pope pray? It's in the pantry.'

They sat eating the fluffy omelette, and sipping coffee as the *Today* programme gave way to *Start the Week*. Sunlight was slanting through the window, showing up streaks and smears. 'I'll wash the windows for you, today,' Jack said, taking the plates to the sink.

'You don't need to,' said Bob, 'honestly. You're welcome to just hang out.'

'No. I can't tell you how grateful I was when you said yes to my request out of the blue for a place to lay my head. The least I can do is the sort of odd jobs I'd be doing at home.'

'Well, thank you, then,' said Bob, picking up yesterday's newspaper and turning a page.

'Do you never use the dishwasher?' asked Jack, who had noticed that it looked rusty round the edges.

'Nope. I used to. But you take a week to fill it up, by which time there are no mugs left and you keep on having to get them out again. And then the stuff's all caked on. You can only do it so long before you think it's a health and safety hazard.'

'Health, I can understand. Safety?'

Bob thought for a moment. 'Spontaneous combustion?' he suggested.

'Listening to the news, that's the least of our worries,' Jack said, washing out the omelette pan. 'War, pestilence, famine, global recession or depression – even champagne is an issue. Did you hear that this morning? More people are killed by flying champagne corks than bites from poisonous spiders. And a lot of them are at weddings. Not that I suppose you get many poisonous spiders at weddings.'

'My mother-in-law came to mine.'

Jack wiped his hands on the tea-towel and nodded sympathetically. 'Yes, they do tend to.' He hung the tea-towel on the radiator and leaned against it. 'I obviously don't want to get in your way. So what are you up to? I was thinking fish for dinner. Not that you have to have dinner here, if you have something else planned. I could have a quiet one on my own.'

Bob smiled up at his guest. 'Fish would be lovely. I should be getting on with a project that has to be sorted by the end of the week. Instead I've spent the last week procrastinating, and I'm probably going to carry on putting it off until the last possible minute. Time stealing.'

'Are you enjoying it, though, the procrastination?'

'No. I think that's why I'm in a bad mood. I know I'd feel better if I got on with it. But I can't be bothered to start. I watch television or do other things – and feel guilty doing them so don't enjoy the experience. It's ridiculous. I should just get on with it.'

'Can I help, then, by making life so uncomfortable everywhere except your office that you have to do your work?'

'I'd get on the computer and write emails. Or look out of the window and plan new planting.'

Jack went over to the window. 'It looks beautiful,' he said.

Bob joined him, his hands on his hips. 'It does, doesn't it? I love this time of year. Actually, I like all times of the year, even the dead of winter. It's nice when there's snow everywhere and you suddenly see the shape of the garden. It can give you ideas.'

They silently surveyed the scene.

From the radio, a voice said: '… so we discover it's a Burne-Jones. Which doesn't actually make it any better.'

Without moving his head, Jack murmured, 'It would make it better for me.'

'And me,' agreed Bob. 'Unless, of course, I'd thought it was a Picasso.'

'Easy mistake to make,' said Jack. 'Now, in all seriousness, is there anything else that you need me to do? Otherwise I'm going to do the windows, finish that drawer, potter about finding other little jobs for myself, then cook dinner. And I'm afraid you'll have to do a little bit of shopping for me. I'd do it myself but I can't because of the danger of running into someone who would tell Lynda. And I'll insist on paying for the ingredients, no matter what you say – if you were going to say anything in the first place, which I suppose you might not, but in case you were – because I'd like to.'

'Write me a list, and I'll go immediately.'

'Oh, it's not that urgent,' Jack assured him.

'If I don't go now, it'll be dinner time before I do. When I get my procrastinating head on, there's no knowing when it'll come off. And Caligula will keep you company until then. He loves curling up at home if there's someone to stroke him.'

Caligula could tell he was being spoken about. He stood up, stretched, spread his paws, put his tail out and marched over to the cat-flap. He checked to make sure they were watching, put his ears back and climbed out.

'As I said. He loves being inside curled up on a day like today.'

Eleanor Fallon was at war with her father because he had grounded her for a month. She had decided that her desperate desire to be a journalist could be achieved with the added bonus of getting back at him. She would shop him. She sat in her geography class, imagining his face when he found out. Or was it better if he didn't?

Oxbow lakes, drumlins – when was this going to be relevant? Seepage point, she wrote in green ink, without thinking.

Would it be better to get her father to help with her career? No. That would involve having to be nice to him. And, second, he was in television. She was going to be the editor of a tabloid.

Also, he didn't seem to know anyone useful. She wrote 'alluvial deposits' and underlined it.

During the lunch break, she phoned the *Daily Mail*. She explained what she was offering.

'And are you expecting payment for this article?' asked the feature writer to whom she was eventually put through.

'That would be good, obviously.'

'There is a slight problem because of your age, which might mean we need parental permission.'

Eleanor was silent for a minute. Her father was hardly going to agree to an unflattering article. 'If I didn't get money, would there be something else available?'

'Like what?'

'Like maybe doing interviews with bands, that sort of thing?'

'For money?'

'Not necessarily.' For being the girl at school who interviews sexy boys, you moron, she was thinking.

'Well, it's certainly something we could look at.'

'Good. And maybe work experience?'

'Hang on a second while I just ask about the article …'

There was a mumbled conversation.

'Eleanor? What we could do, to protect both you and us, is chat to you, get the information, and then we'd have to confirm what you've said through other sources.'

'So would my parents know it was me?'

'No. Not from the quotes. We couldn't attribute them to you.'

'But if I wanted to I could tell them it was me who did it? Or not?'

'Obviously we can't stop you saying whatever you want to your parents.'

Later, doing her homework, the only thing she was worried about, was what 'see page ...' meant.

Richard and Louise were late sitting down to watch *Celebrity X-Treme* that Monday night, and were having a swift bet with each other as to who would be voted off.

'Daisy. Bed,' said Louise, without turning round.

Daisy, standing in the door jamb, stayed perfectly still.

'I know you're there. I can smell your unwashed teeth. Go to bed. And clean your teeth.'

'Oh, Mum, why can't I watch it?'

'Because it's school tomorrow, and I don't like you whining about being tired. Go to bed.'

They turned the television down until they heard her going up the stairs.

Louise put the sound back up. 'I can't believe they got rid of Flynn O'Mara last night. I'd have voted that hideous apology for a comedian out. He's a rancid little nonentity.'

'Katie's still giving good television,' said Richard, as she appeared on screen.

'Dee looks great these days,' said Louise.

'She's lost weight,' said Richard. 'And she's got Oliver, of course.'

'Are they going to get married?'

'Who can tell? She looks happy.'

The shock was that Dave Beal survived another vote. Crystal Blake was out.

'Well, there's a turn-up for the books,' said Louise, going to make herself a mint tea.

'It goes to show that the public can be discerning,' said Richard. 'Can I have one of those? There's a limit to how much superficial, brainless idiocy anyone can put up with. Although Keera's managed to indulge in it for years. Vacuous woman. She probably thinks "negligent" is a man in a petticoat.'

'You've nicked that from somewhere, haven't you?' asked Louise suspiciously.

'Course I have. I haven't got time to go round making those things up. Good one, though, isn't it?'

In Norway Siobhan's plan of a double relationship had been stymied by the eviction of Crystal – although the irritation factor of Dave Beal was high, and keeping the viewers hooked. And she had nailed her stooge in every way in case anything did come to light.

As a lover, Mark had been sadly lacking. She was unaware that this had been entirely due to his shock when she had appeared without her heavy layer of makeup. She had looked like a different person, and he had had to concentrate hard to make any headway at all. He didn't want to renew the acquaintance. And since Siobhan had no urge to repeat the performance, they were both as satisfied as they could be under the circumstances.

'Let's go through tomorrow's programme, then, now that Crystal has been evicted,' she said. 'Mark, what are your feelings?'

'Well, it's three guys and one girl.'

'Yes, patently.'

'So perhaps tomorrow we should use those messages from loved ones back home instead of saving them for when there are just three of them. It always reminds people that they do have outside lives. And we get the crying stuff, which would be good.'

'Not a bad idea,' said Siobhan, thoughtfully.

'And then, maybe, we should have a task outside that involves them all helping each other. Apart from the one we already have, I mean. I know they've got to do that slide thing but maybe we should get the guys to rustle up something that not only has funny potential but also shows who is the most genuine …' He tailed off.

'Anyone else got any ideas?'

Another producer piped up: 'I wonder if we should write the scripts a bit earlier. It's always such a rush.'

'Wonder again, then,' retorted Siobhan. 'You can't shape the script until all the tasks have been performed. Anyone else? No? Well, in that case, Mark, you get on to the designated family and friends and get some VTs in the bag. If they can't get to a proper studio to record them, do a phono and we'll put a picture up.

You don't need me to tell you to keep on at them until they do it in a short soundbite. And the more sentimental the better. We want damp eyes at the very least, if not a full-on boo-hoo. Right. Get on to it.'

Mr Ben Fisher, consultant anaesthetist, younger brother of Katie Fisher, had been enjoying dinner with friends when he got the call. He didn't recognize the number, but he was sufficiently worried about one of his patients to take it.

'Hello. Mark Jarvis here, from *Celebrity X-Treme*. Sorry to bother you, but would it be possible for you to get into our central London studio tomorrow for a very quick interview about Katie?'

Ben had not been enjoying watching his sister on television. He'd known she was a flirt, but this was something else. He assumed his father was watching (and therefore Bob), and supposed he ought to phone his mum at some stage and ask her how she was getting on without him. Jack had done as much as he could to make sure she knew he was all right without revealing where he was.

'Erm, can you get to the studio?' asked Mark again, as there seemed to be no answer forthcoming from Katie's brother.

Ben sighed. 'Yes, I probably can. Is there a particular time?'

'Any time at all, to suit you.'

'I'll do it on my way in to work, then.'

'Thank you so much,' said Mark, aware that Ben Fisher was not happy about doing it. Shouldn't have a sister who was prepared to reveal all on a national television show, then, he thought.

A thought echoed by Ben as he rejoined the table.

'Bad news?' asked Oliver, who knew he was concerned about a patient who'd had an operation that afternoon.

'No. Well ... no.'

'Nothing you want to tell me about?'

'Nothing to do with work, if that's what you mean. Katie ...' He let her name trail.

'Sisters,' said Oliver, with feeling.

'You haven't got any,' said Ben, accusingly.

'I know. But I can imagine. I only ever wanted a sister so that she could bring home her friends. I had to find all my own girl-friends from scratch.'

'Whereas you've used my sister to get your girlfriend.'

'Ha. *Touché*,' acknowledged Oliver.

'And from your lack of conversation on the matter, I assume that side of your life is still going well.'

'Yes. I may even take it on a stage,' he said.

Ben raised his eyebrows. Oliver nodded.

'Hey,' said Ben, to the rest of the table, 'Oliver's getting married.'

There was a raucous response.

Oliver put up his hands. 'I did *not* say I was getting married.'

'Yes, you did,' said Ben.

'I did not.'

'I raised my eyebrows. You nodded. Confirmed.'

'Have you asked the little lady yet?' drawled a haematologist, in a *faux*-Texan accent.

'No, I bloody haven't. And, frankly, none of your bloody business.'

'Oooooh! Tetchy. Calm down, girl,' minced a fellow proctologist.

'Well, shut up, the lot of you.'

There was a tiny silence, and then somebody said, 'Or shall we buy a bottle of champagne to celebrate Oliver getting shackled? And because we can't believe that anybody's agreed to marry such a complete nadger-brain?'

Ben waved a waiter over, as Oliver shook his head.

'You know what this is all about?' He raised his voice to be heard. 'This is all because Ben has got a sister who puts it about a bit.' He realized immediately that he'd gone too far. He had forgotten the golden rule: never diss the relatives. He grimaced. 'Sorry, Ben. Sorry. You know I didn't mean it.'

Ben got up and left the table.

'Bloody hell, Oliver. You really are a twat,' said the haematologist. 'Although, to be fair, Katie isn't doing herself any favours in that programme. I'd be seriously pissed off if I was Adam Whatsisname. But you can't go round casting aspersions. Really not your place. Always quite fancied her myself, actually. That lovely hair.'

'I suppose I'd better go and have a word,' said Oliver, getting up to follow Ben. He found him having a conversation with a waiter. When he had finished, Oliver apologized again. And again.

'Oh, it's all right. Forget it,' said Ben, eventually. 'Just don't repeat it.'

'What is it you heard about Katie, anyway?' asked Oliver.

'They want me to go and record something tomorrow morning to be shown to her. It'll go out in the evening. And I don't want to do it, but I agreed when she went in.'

'What are you going to say, then?'

'What I *want* to say is that she should stop it now. Quit while she's ahead. Or quit before she does any irreparable damage. And you know they won't let me say that. Or if I do they'll just cut it out.'

'You could say that you're looking forward to her getting out so that you can hit her squarely in the snout.'

Ben laughed.

'Or that you can't wait for her to be evicted so that you can rip her guzinters out,' said Oliver.

'Guzinters?' Ben queried.

'Animal innards. I think. Heard it in Australia. Filed it away for future use.'

'A little excessive, perhaps. Honestly, she is a dingbat, though. If we're going 'Strine. She carries on with one of my best mates, cocks that up, finds a decent bloke who has a good job, then cocks it up on air. In front of millions. I swear she never used to be this much of a mess.'

Oliver didn't say anything. Ben, who had been admiring a waitress with a short skirt and an excellent pair of legs, dragged his attention back and noticed Oliver's face. He snorted. 'Oh, all right. She's always got herself into pickles. It's just that this one is public. So it feels worse.'

'Look, mate, do the thing tomorrow morning and make it as bland as you can. Say something like you're looking forward to her coming home so you can sink a couple of martinis together. And if they try to make you say that you're missing her, say that you've been far too busy making sure people don't die under surgery to miss anyone.'

'And if they try to make me say that I think she's doing really well, and I'm proud of her – which is what they always do on these reality shows?'

'Then you say that it's nice she hasn't broken anything yet. Unlike my girlfriend, who breaks her ankle in a ruddy loo.'

'Girlfriend … future wife?' said Ben, with a twinkle.

'Stop it. That's how we ended up standing here by the cloakroom, instead of sitting with our friends at the dinner table.'

'All right. To *le table, mon ami.*'

'*Bien sûr, mon frère.*'

'*Mon* best man at the wedding …'

'Shut it,' said Oliver, in a threatening manner, as they walked back to join their friends.

CHAPTER FIFTEEN

As it was, the message from Ben was never played out …

The *Celebrity X-Treme* contestants had an early start the next morning and were on the snow at six o'clock. The challenge involved an obstacle course through mini igloo tunnels and over snow bricks. It didn't sound that hard, but with thick Arctic suits on, it was exhausting.

'I feel ever so slightly glowy,' announced Katie, as she clomped across the finishing line.

'That will be the close proximity to me,' leered Dave Beal, who had gone first and was standing cheering the others on. 'It's the pheromones – they're phenomenal.'

She looked at him gurning and said dampeningly, 'Oh. And there I was wondering if it was the mumps.' She brushed snow off her shoulders. He was a revolting smeggy turd and she hoped he'd be voted off that night. Give them all a break.

She watched Peter limbo his way down the course. He was like a racehorse, she thought. All sleek and shiny. And about as intelligent. She wondered if he shied at plastic bags and was scared of pigs.

And, finally, Paul Martin, who gave her a wink as he went past. She was looking forward to getting back to England. Wearing something different. Getting out of her wretched thermal suit.

They were done with the challenge by mid-morning and were driven back to the hut on skidoos. The sun was glittering through the trees, and Katie was suddenly glad that she had come. Nature. It made you feel happy, she thought, breathing in the fresh air – and the fumes of the skidoo in front.

They were back in the hut by eleven for desperately needed hot drinks. Katie put the kettle on. 'Brrrr. Why is it that even though we wear snowsuits it takes such a long time for your bones to warm up?' she asked nobody in particular. 'We should be able to take the bones out and leave them near the stove or in the oven on a low heat so they're nice and warm for later. Although that could be an issue with the boneless body. It would be difficult to get them back in again with your fingers all flappy. Maybe we'd have to have special seams, like a tent ...'

Two of the three men looked bewildered.

Katie stopped speaking as she noticed. And smiled in collusion at Paul Martin.

'Are we all having tea?' she asked, and crouched to get some biscuits from a low shelf. Paul reached over her to get the mugs from the cupboard. He had just put them on the counter when Katie stood up quickly and smacked her head smartly on the open cupboard door. She was only aware of the most incredible pain behind the eyes. The next thing she knew, she was being held in the arms of the handsome doctor. 'Well, good morning,' he said, relieved.

'A very good morning. Am I ill?'

'That depends. You had a nasty knock, and you've got an enormous bump on your head.' He smiled.

'Nice smile,' she said woozily.

'I just need to check that you haven't done any major damage, Katie,' he said. 'How are you feeling?'

'Annoyed.'

'Anything else?'

'A bit sick.'

'Right. Always horrible when you bang your head that hard. So what day is it today?'

'I don't know. But I don't think I knew before you asked me.'

'Who's the President of America?'

'Ah. General knowledge. Is it Batman?'

One of the producers, watching on the monitor, put his head in his hands. 'Oh, God. She's really concussed. Nightmare.'

'Don't be a moron,' said Mark. 'She's always doing that sort of rubbish joking.'

'Katie, I need you to be serious,' said the doctor. 'Otherwise you'll have to have a lot of unnecessary tests to discover the extent of the brain damage.'

'Barack Obama.'

'And how many fingers am I holding up?'

'Two spring onions and a tree.'

'She's fine,' he announced, 'even if her jokes are still as bad as ever. But I'm afraid she's going to have to go to hospital for twenty-four hours' observation.'

'Oh, no,' groaned Katie, while secretly quite pleased that she wouldn't have to continue. She didn't think she had a chance of winning – and this way she retired hurt but with her pennant still held high. If that was the right expression.

She tried to get up, and her head swam. 'Oops. That doesn't feel so good,' she said, as a severe attack of nausea and light-headedness attacked her.

The doctor held on to her. 'Can someone call an ambulance, please?' he asked in a general way, knowing that the cameras were still rolling, and that someone would react to the request.

'Call an ambulance,' bellowed Peter Philbin, in his best soap-opera voice.

In the control room, Siobhan's face was like thunder. An all-male final was not what she had planned, and her revenge on Adam Williams was not quite complete. Damn. Damn. Damn Miss Katie Sodding Fisher. Throwing a spanner in the works. Typical. Outwardly she was ringing for an ambulance. 'Can someone get the insurance company on the phone for me?' she shouted, then spoke into the phone slowly and exaggeratedly as she explained what the ambulance was needed for. The Norwegian telephonist – who spoke perfect English – told her in a very slow and exaggerated way that it would be sent as quickly as possible.

'It will be about two hours,' Siobhan said into a walkie-talkie.

It crackled into life: 'Two hours?' came back, with disbelief.

'Well, we're not exactly on the main road, are we? And I'm assuming it's not urgent. Or does the doctor want me to tell them we need an air ambulance? And he can pay the insurance company when the quibbling starts.'

There was silence. Then the answer came back. 'No. He says it's all right. Unless Katie faints or something.'

She could hear the echo coming through the cameras, as they continued to roll and record.

'The insurance company's on the line,' said Mark.

'Transfer it through to me, can you?' she said.

The conversation wasn't a long one.

'Can someone call the phone company to get Katie's voting line blocked?' she shouted. 'I need to go out and check on something. Can you cover for me, Mark?' she asked, with a quick smile.

'Sure,' he said.

Siobhan walked out of the building and, in case anyone was watching, made as if to go to the celebrity house, veering off at the last moment to duck behind a small outhouse, where she made an international call.

'Hello, it's Siobhan Stamp here … No, I can't speak any louder. Pin your ears back. I'm paying you enough for this. Stop the programme, if you can.' She listened intently, her eyes peeled for interlopers. 'Will it come up on their phone bill that calls were attempted? … Good. And then it automatically disconnects? … Fine … Your money will be in your bank account at the end of the job. Goodbye.'

The voice at the other end of the line continued to speak.

'No. We agreed the fucking money beforehand. The fact that you have belatedly realized how important it is is neither here nor there.' She listened again.

'I think you'll find that if you try to blackmail me, you'll come off very much worse, you little worm. You should be grateful for the opportunity I've given you to pay off some of your student loan. Don't you dare threaten me.' She pressed the end-call button.

Her heart was beating rapidly. That was not what she'd wanted to hear. Thank goodness she had her fall guy. She hoped it would work. Otherwise … Of course it would. You had to have faith.

She returned to the control room. Mark remarked on her pink nose, and the blast of cold air she brought in.

'Possibly something to do with the precipitation from clouds in the form of ice crystals formed in the upper atmosphere,' she said sarcastically.

'Really?' he asked, pretending not to know what she was talking about.

'Also known as snow, you idiot.'

'Oh. Is that what it is?' he asked sweetly. Boy, was she in a mood. That was what happened if you determined the outcome of the programme from the beginning, he thought.

You want two couples and you end up with three blokes. Maybe he should suggest a farting competition. Or who could piss the furthest. Or highest. Or longest. He looked at Siobhan's set face. Maybe he wouldn't suggest anything.

She was staring at the computer screen while dialling a number on the phone.

'Hello, Mr Fisher. Siobhan Stamp here from *Celebrity X-Treme*. Your son gave me your telephone number ... No, nothing to worry about. But, yes, it is actually something that has happened to Katie. She stood up too quickly and banged her head on an open cupboard door, and may have concussed herself. We're having her taken to hospital for observation. She'll be in for twenty-four hours. Which means that she won't be continuing in the show ...' dammit '... although we hope she'll be making an appearance when we have the winner ...'

Jack Fisher had been skinning a rabbit with a clingy cat round his ankles. Caligula was winding in and out of his feet, rubbing his fur desperately against the chef's corduroys in an attempt to get a whole undressed animal for lunch. It had never happened so far in his entire feline life – but hope sprang eternal.

Then Jack had been distracted for a moment by the phone ringing. It was all it took. Caligula gathered himself together and, concentrating all his power in his haunches, launched himself at the counter. He had the rabbit by its tail and had dragged it onto the floor just as Bob came into the kitchen and spotted him.

Caligula let out a low growl, his teeth clenched on the meat, his eyes fixed on Bob. He began to back slowly towards the cat-flap, knowing that, once there, he was home and free.

Bob was having none of it. He advanced cautiously, murmuring in a low, reasonable voice, 'Caligula, if you don't put that down, I will rip your legs off and beat you to death with the furry ends.'

All Caligula heard was the threat. And he didn't care. He had a rabbit that was as big as him and smelled like Paradise. He carried on towards the cat-flap.

Bob rushed him, and his escape route was cut off. He dived round with a grumble in his throat, but the rabbit was bulky and slowed him down, and he was caught, and lifted off the floor still attached to it. He did what he could to hold on, but eventually his teeth gave out. With a yowl, he fled through the cat-flap, his tail like a stiff, stripy catkin.

Inside the kitchen, Jack was apologizing profusely. 'Sorry, Bob. It was the phone call. Took me by surprise. Katie's been hurt.'

Bob's heart did a somersault. 'How is she? What happened?' he asked, suddenly breathless.

'She's on her way to hospital. Or will be. I think they said an hour or something. I don't think I was really concentrating. But she's going to be all right. Apparently she banged her head on a cupboard.' He stopped, then did a short laugh. 'Ha. Bloody typical. She goes on an extreme-sports type event, and ends up knocking herself out on a cupboard.'

'Concussed, then?'

'Yes. Out like a light. She's got to have twenty-four hours of observation.'

'Standard stuff for that,' said Bob, his heart getting back to its regular beat.

'And then, I assume she'll fly home. Or maybe not. Oh, no. I think the woman said she'd stay for the final. Well, I'm sure they'll phone to let me know. But I am sorry about the rabbit. Can it be salvaged, do you think?'

Bob looked at the two major incisor marks on its back leg. 'I would say so. I don't know about you, but if we give it a wash and cook it thoroughly, I'm willing to take a risk on getting scabies or whatever you can get from cats.'

'Catamarans?'

'Catapults?' countered Bob.

'Catarrh?'

'Leave it on a good one, I say. Anyway, what do you reckon?'

'A jolly good scrub and a stew.'

'That sounds like a sketch from *The Two Ronnies*.' Bob grinned. It was so like being with Katie that he wanted to hug the older man. I think I love your daughter, he wanted to say, but didn't. What was the point? She had ended their affair, and was ensconced with a man who was in her world – and very rich, by all accounts. And not bad-looking, he had grudgingly to admit. A bit primped, perhaps. Looked like he spent a lot of time in front of the mirror. And waxed his eyebrows, he thought bitchily. Probably goes for manicures every week. I bet he doesn't know how to skin a rabbit. Or bleed a radiator, for that matter, he thought randomly.

Adam was also on the list for a phone call if anything happened to Katie. Siobhan made Mark ring him. 'What did he say?' she asked.

'Why didn't you call him, if you wanted to know what he said?'

'Don't be impertinent,' she said, as though she was talking to a ten-year-old. 'What did he say?'

'What you would expect him to say,' said Mark, getting as stroppy as she was.

'Which was?'

'Phone him yourself,' he said, and walked away from her. She was such a bitch. He couldn't believe he'd shagged her. Yes, he could. She'd looked all right with makeup on.

Siobhan was incensed, but could hardly threaten him with the sack. Or should she? Would that work better if he was going to be her stooge? *Could* she have him sacked? After a moment's reflection, she realized she couldn't. They would ask why she hadn't made the call herself. She could hardly have said that Adam had not succumbed to her advances and had gone out with her rival – who was now in the programme she was executive-producing. No. Revenge was a dish best eaten cold.

* * *

Dee got ready to watch *Celebrity X-Treme*. She prepared a tray full of food.

Carrots and celery (because she was oh-so-healthy) with hummus (because she was oh-so-healthy, even if it was a little bit fattening), tsatziki (because she was oh-oh-oh-so-healthy and it was yoghurt, which was good for the digestion), deep-fried prawn balls (because a girl's got to have fun) and a tumbler of red wine (because it's good for the heart). It looked lovely, and she had all the major food groups and vitamins covered.

She went into the bedroom on a tilt, trying to stop the wine slopping over the side of the tray. Then, since every surface in her flat was cluttered, she gingerly set it down on the carpet, teeth clenched on her bottom lip. At the last moment, the wine tipped. 'Fishcakes!' she exclaimed, and went to get some kitchen roll to put on it. Was there something else you were supposed to do? She could never remember. Salt. That was it. She went and got a tub and poured it in a satisfying heap on the stain. The wine started to soak into it. She turned the television on while it performed its cleansing act, and sat on the bed in her tracksuit bottoms and long-sleeved T-shirt, absent-mindedly picking at a yellow, crusty flake on one sleeve. It came off, and she smelled it. Egg, perhaps? When had she last had an egg? She sniffed it again. No. Maybe it was a piece of Crunchy Nut Corn Flake. She ate it. Yes, Crunchy Nut Corn Flake. Yesterday's breakfast. Nice.

She got off the bed to look at the stain, and stood there for fully five minutes, debating. It might be best to leave it until it's dry and then hoover it up, she thought. What's the worst that can happen?

She began her dinner as the titles for *Celebrity X-Treme* came up.

At *Hello Britain!*, an overnight producer was watching the programme to see what clip could be used for the item on Katie's exit. They had rung her brother to see if he would do a quick piece with them, and also her mother. They hadn't bothered to phone Adam. He had made it clear that he would not be talking on the subject. In the absence of family or lover, they decided to leave it to Dee to comment.

Richard, who was outputting, asked a researcher to ring her, and tell her to watch the programme if she wasn't already so that she could talk about it.

'And tell her we'll have live pictures from Bournemouth for the chroma key tomorrow. If she cares.'

The researcher was riffling through a pile of yesterday's papers before chucking them away. 'Hey, that's interesting,' he said, looking at one. 'Fifty years ago, Pope Pius the Twelfth declared St Clare the patron saint of television. St Clare. How weird is that? And Prince Charles was officially made Prince of Wales.'

'Can you phone Dee, please?' Richard reminded him, and looked back at his screen, trying to see where time could be saved. 'What the hell can we cut at this late stage?' he moaned. 'They organize all these people dayside and we have to ditch them. Unless we can interview four people about diabetes in under three minutes. And tell the band to sing their song in twenty seconds. And only do the temperature and cloud cover in the weather. And get someone to tell Keera to shut up and stop wasting our time.'

'That's what people tune in for,' Kent piped up, defending his favourite presenter.

'Yes, of course it is,' Richard said sweetly. 'They love the quick-fire wit and repartee emanating from the dynamite combination of Sagacity Keethley and Wisecracking Fallon. Personally, I always find the adverts very stimulating.'

Kent threw him a darkling look and walked away.

The intake editor sitting on a nearby desk said, without raising his eyes from his computer screen, 'You do enjoy winding him up, don't you?'

Richard smiled. 'Sure do. You know, I admire him for sticking to his guns. And I also know that he probably passes on my comments to Miss Keethley. Or a version of them. Keera and I both know where we stand in each other's estimation.'

'I know where she stands in yours ... what about vice versa?' asked the input editor, now looking up from the computer.

'Lower than the runner, I'd have thought.'

'That high, eh?'

Celebrity X-Treme finished, and Dee phoned in.

'Wotcher,' said Richard.

'Well,' said Dee, 'thoroughly enjoyed that. Were you watching?'

'Of course. Can't let the Fisher down. You know how she'll be on to us the minute she's *compos mentis*, demanding to know whether she did the right thing, and did her bum look big in that snowsuit.'

'And we'll tell her ...'

'That she looked super-thin, hardly bigger than a tooth-pick.'

'And then someone who isn't you or me will tell her that they edited it to make it look like she was permanently on heat.'

Richard ate another of his stash of chocolate biscuits, feeling the need of a sugar rush. 'I've discovered that a friend of a friend has been working on the show. And he's appalled at what they've done. Apparently, they've been slashing and editing so that the whole meaning has been completely skewed. Sadly, I bet the bloke concerned won't back her up publicly because he'll be wanting another job.'

'So she hasn't been a super-slut, then?' asked Dee, aghast.

'*Weeell*, slut, but not super-slut.'

'Same old Katie Fisher. I bet Adam's not too keen on how it's come out, eh? Anyways ... I was phoning in to see what you wanted from me tomorrow morning.'

'About two minutes on how she did, and how she'll be feeling,' said Richard, leaning into his seat to ease his back.

'Oh, Gawd, I don't know. Can't mention the unmentionable, can I? The flirting between her and Paul Martin?' queried Dee.

'She did do other things, you lemon.'

'Did she?'

'Fell down on the skiing. Underpants on her head – that still makes me laugh. Hot-tub nonsense. Tidying up everywhere. Not winning Monopoly. Ever played Monopoly with her?' asked Richard.

'No. But I remember her telling me about how she and her brother used to play it with their parents, and how she used to insert a hotel up her brother's nose if she was losing. Apparently she'd hold him down and, next thing, they'd be on their way to hospital to get it out. Fitted perfectly up his nostril. She reckoned it was why he became a doctor. He enjoyed the visits so much.'

'Maybe better not tell that story or we'll have mothers complaining that it's promoting sticking small items up children's noses. Let's confine ourselves to the stories that have come out of the programme, eh? Have you spoken to her?'

'I sent a text. Maybe you're not allowed to have your mobiles on in hospital.'

'I spoke to her briefly. She sounded surprisingly jaunty. But it would be better if you could speak to her yourself. Give her a ring now.'

'Will do. See you tomorrow, then,' said Dee. 'By the way, do you know how you get red wine stains out of carpet?'

'Put soda water on it, I think.'

'Oh. I put a whole load of salt on it. It looks like a snow turtle. Pink round the edges. Quite lovely. But I don't know what to do now.'

'Neither do I. I always thought it was soda water. Or white wine. Let me ask.'

There was a muttered conversation before he returned to the phone. 'Apparently you need loads of kitchen towel. Get rid of the salt. Then you press on the stain with kitchen towels until it's all gone.'

'I *knew* there was something I'd forgotten to get the last time I went to the shops. Do you think loo paper would work?'

'How would I know? Good luck. Go and get some sleep. See you tomorrow morning.'

CHAPTER SIXTEEN

The moon was a silver disc in the sky as Keera left her flat to go to work. The black Mercedes, which was there to pick her up, smelled of Magic Tree. There were those who hated the synthetic tones of air-freshener, but it reminded Keera of dolly mixtures and she sniffed appreciatively. 'Good morning,' she said pleasantly.

'Good morning, Miss Keethley,' said her driver, as he opened the door for her.

She slid in, knees together, since she was wearing a micro-mini under her long black coat for a meeting at Wolf Days Productions after *Hello Britain!*. And since she was in a good mood, she responded to the driver's conversation.

'There's going to be a demonstration on Park Lane today. A big one,' he said, as Smooth Radio played in the background.

She couldn't hear him terribly well over Neil Diamond. 'Demonstration? What for?'

'Trucks, I think.'

'Pro or anti drugs?' She wondered whether the news desk knew about it. Always nice to be able to go in with some breaking story.

'Trucks,' he reiterated.

'What are they going to do?'

'Deliver a coffin to Ten Downing Street, I think.'

She hesitated, then asked, 'Why would they deliver a coffee to Downing Street? What's that got to do with drugs?'

The driver didn't answer. He was tired, it was the end of his shift, he couldn't be bothered to explain.

Keera liked Thursdays. It was almost the weekend. And she felt more cheerful, knowing that Matthew Praed was still working on her career. She blushed to think of their last meeting. But it couldn't be helped. Too late now. She wouldn't think about it. And she hoped he would sit there in today's meeting, seeing what he was missing. What would she do if he did ask her out for dinner again? She toyed with the idea of snubbing him. No, that would be too foolish. He was a powerful man. She did wish she hadn't succumbed, though.

She needed more publicity. The front page of a glossy magazine. Her face gazing down from a hundred and one magazine racks. And maybe today on air she would accidentally on purpose make a gaffe. It was the easiest way of making money in the world. It would go off to a bloopers show, and could be shown again and again, earning money for each airing. Ker-*ching*. She smiled in the darkness, and breathed in the smell of Magic Tree.

The darkness was beginning to lift as she arrived at *Hello Britain!*. 'Good morning,' she said gaily, as she went through Security. They knew better than to stop her.

The newsroom was quiet. The final pieces of the jigsaw were being slotted into place.

'Hi, Keera,' said Richard, as she threw off her coat theatrically to reveal her outfit.

Kent gasped. That was the shortest skirt he had ever seen in his life. Was it legal?

Even Richard was shocked. 'My God. I hope you're wearing sturdy underwear.'

She tried out one of her new laughs. It sounded more like a drain being cleaned than the sexy, throaty growl she'd been practising. More work required. Nobody could possibly know, she thought, how difficult it was to get things right.

She logged on to the computer and started to look through the scripts.

'Incidentally, do we know that there's a demonstration on Park Lane today about drugs?'

'Is there?' asked Richard. 'No. I don't think we do. Anti-drugs, I assume – unless it's a load of lost hippies, ravers and junkies campaigning for more?'

'I don't know.' She cast her eye down the running order. 'Why are we doing this thing about Katie Fisher?' she asked, trying not to sound peevish.

'It's a story. And I think our viewers still want to know about those who used to be our top presenters here,' said Richard, passively.

'You've put it down for two minutes, though. That's a long time to talk about somebody who's banged her head and is out of a reality show.'

'Is that actually your item, Keera? I thought I'd put Rod down to do it.'

'Yes, you have. Doesn't stop me having an opinion, does it?' she asked.

'No. I suppose not.' Richard carried on typing away on his keyboard.

'So?' she eventually asked.

'So, er, what?' he asked, now involved in trying to work out how to move one guest out and another in during the link between the items.

'So are we going to spend two minutes on this item?'

'Yes, we are. How do you feel about doing one of your items in front of the chroma key to help me out with swapping guests?'

She looked mutinous, but realized the futility of carrying on the argument.

'Of course. Anything to oblige,' she said shortly, and turned to face her computer screen again.

A researcher came over to Richard. 'I've checked it out. There is a demonstration on Park Lane but it's the one we've already got as a short news item. It's a whole load of lorries demonstrating about petrol prices and taxes and so on.'

'Thanks,' said Richard. He hadn't really expected Keera to come in with a news story they were unaware of. Although he did wonder how she had got drugs and petrol mixed up. Great party guest – ask her for a quarter of black and she'd turn up with a gallon of diesel.

When Keera had finished looking through her interviewees, she went down to Makeup and was surprised to see Rod already in the chair, the cape thrown around him. 'Pre-record,' he said briefly, before closing his eyes again.

'Why are you doing a pre-record?'

'Because it's with someone in LA who doesn't want to stay up until two o'clock in the morning for the dubious pleasure of talking to us live.'

'Sleep well?' she asked. Not because she wanted an answer but because it was the sort of thing you were supposed to ask your co-presenters. She really had no interest in whether he'd slept well or slept *in* a well. Hey. That was a good line. She'd try to find somewhere to use it.

'No,' he stressed. 'I didn't. Children. Who'd have them? Teenagers are a pain in the arse. I can't wait for her to leave home.'

'Hmm. Know what you mean,' said Keera, who had stopped listening and was gazing in rapt admiration at her reflection in one of the mirrors. It was at an angle where she could see the stunning curve in her back, the trim waist and the pert bottom encased in its tiny skirt.

Rod flicked his eyes open. 'Do you have experience of looking after teenagers, then?'

Caught out, Keera answered, 'I was a teenager once,' and left before he could ask anything else.

'Did you watch *Celebrity X-Treme* last night?' asked Vanda.

'Course,' said Rod. 'Bet the producers aren't happy they've got three men in the final. Always nice to have a bit of fluff to look at.'

'Paul Martin's got to win it, hasn't he?'

'Nope. Peter Philbin will walk it. Think about the voters. Women or girls who watch soaps. It'll be Peter,' he said, with conviction.

'I can't quite believe Dave Beal made it through to the end. No accounting for tastes,' she said, moving her lipsticks to make room for the two new eye-shadow sets she had bought the day before.

'Oh, I think the viewers are canny enough when it comes to these programmes now. They like to leave someone in who shakes the tree. You want to throw things at the screen when he's on. Doubt if he'll get much work out of it, though – he's just enhanced his reputation as a poor comedian with a penchant for sexism, racism and any other ism. Whereas Peter has won – no matter what. As has Paul. Nobody had heard of either of them. Depends how wisely they make their next move.'

'And Katie?'

He pursed his lips. 'Hmm. Difficult to tell. Maybe she'll be offered a show on UK Living based on that old Paul Simon song, "Fifty Ways To Leave Your Lover".'

'I know. That's going to be very interesting. A sort of accidental dumping of the boyfriend,' said Vanda. 'And she didn't
even win.'

Paul Martin actually knew that he was going to win because he
had been told he would by Siobhan. But he missed sparring
with Katie and was sorry to see her go. He had no doubt he
would see her again, and was fairly confident that he could
tempt her into a night out. Would she leave her man for him?
What a fantastic tale that would be for the newspapers. And it
would be a win-win situation for him. Win *Celebrity X-Treme*
and win the girl. He was going to enjoy the after-show party.
Maybe that was where he would make his move on Katie. He
knew she liked a drink, and a tipsy female was a fairly safe bet,
in his humble opinion. Beal would go this evening, he'd bet a
pound to a pinch of salt. And then there would be the run-off
between him and Philbin. He had no doubt that his triumph
would be greeted with surprise, and he hoped he could do a
convincing goodness-little-old-me-winning. And he also
hoped that Siobhan was happy with his performance. But not
so happy that she would want another close encounter of the
horizontal-jogging kind. He didn't think he could countenance
another round of tapeworm grappling.

Katie was excited that she had been given her mobile. She
hadn't realized how isolated she had begun to feel without it.
She phoned home. 'Hi, Mum. I can use my mobile again until I

go back for the final. Sorry I couldn't speak for longer yesterday afternoon. Draughty place for the phone. Just to tell you that I should be out of hospital soon.'

'How are you feeling?'

'Fine. A comedy bump on the top of my head. Apart from that, it's all OK.'

'Good. Good.' Her mother sounded distracted.

'Is Dad there?' asked Katie. The line went so quiet she thought she had been cut off. 'Hello?' she asked loudly.

'Hello. Your father is not here at the moment.'

'Where is he?'

'He's, erm … out.'

'You're being very peculiar, Mum. Where is he? Has he gone dogging or something else embarrassing?'

'I have no idea what that is. I also have no idea *where* he is.'

'What do you mean? What's going on?' asked Katie, puzzled by the way her mother was responding to her questions.

'Well,' her mother sighed, 'you'll no doubt hear it from your brother anyway. Your father appears to have left me.'

'Left you?' asked Katie, disbelievingly. 'Left you? When?'

'About the same time as you went into *Celebrity Dream*.'

'*Celebrity X-Treme*, Mum,' corrected Katie. 'What's happening? What did you do?'

'Thank you for being so sympathetic,' said her mother, waspishly.

Katie bit her tongue, thinking that it was always her mother who was unsympathetic. 'Poor Mum,' she said, glad that her mother couldn't see the face she was pulling. 'But, really, what happened?'

'Nothing. Or nothing out of the ordinary. I came in to find a note in the kitchen.'

'And you have no idea where he's gone? At all.'

'As I said, no. I phoned your brother. He said he was sure he was safe. There's no point in me worrying. He'll come back if he wants to.'

Katie couldn't believe the way her mother was dealing with this bombshell. Her concussion felt like it was coming back. 'Have you told the police?'

'He's not missing, Katie,' said her mother, sounding exasperated. 'What would I tell the police? My husband's left me. And they would do what? I have to go. Hercules is whining. I'm glad you're all right. I'll see you when you come out of that house or whatever. I'm sorry I've been the bearer of bad tidings.'

Katie phoned her brother and left a message. He was never there when you wanted him. Why had her father left home? Should she have seen it coming? Where would he have gone?

In Hawes, Jack had been watching *Hello Britain!*. He turned it off as it ended.

'Yes, I thought they might do something with Katie. She sounded well. Very perky.'

'Hm. She did, didn't she?' agreed Bob.

'And she's going to be back on Saturday. Which is good. Another coffee?'

'Yes, please.' Bob was aware that something else was being debated.

Jack had planned to stay away from his wife until the weekend. But then the phone call had come about Katie bashing herself up, and he suddenly wanted to go home. Six days was enough to miss someone, Jack reasoned. He certainly missed Lynda. 'Faint heart never won fair maid,' he said to himself, as he went up to pack his few belongings in the suitcase. He took it downstairs.

Bob looked up from his newspaper enquiringly.

'Yes. I know. Earlier than planned. I'll make us both a fatboy's breakfast, and then I'm going to take a taxi home,' explained Jack.

'I'd offer to take you, but the battery on the Land Rover's buggered again. And I'd take you on the back of the bike, but I think either you or the bag would fall off.'

'And I feel inappropriately dressed for that,' said Jack. 'There's a severe lack of leather about my raiment. Not even an elbow patch.'

'Good heavens above, my liege,' said Bob, in mock-horror. 'No leather elbow patches? What were you thinking, going about dressed thus?'

'There are those would say that I'm fit for purpose,' said Jack, with dignity. He continued, 'And talking of purpose, I'm very hungry and must needs eat. For my farewell breakfast, I will be offering either the full English or eggs Hollandaise with trimmings. Or an omelette. Or anything you damn well fancy.

As a massive thank-you for putting up with a daft old man who wanted to shake up his life a bit.'

'It's been an absolute pleasure,' said Bob, standing up. 'I've enjoyed being cooked gourmet meals for, and having someone to share my sofa and television with. And I hope it's been worth putting up with my poorly equipped larder. I had no idea I was missing so many important staples. How could I have lived without organic saffron?'

Jack left after a breakfast of smoked salmon and scrambled eggs, and Bob kicked disconsolately round the house for an hour, moving things that didn't need to be moved, and giving the cat a thorough brushing – which so surprised Caligula that he let it happen.

Jack arrived home a short while later and let himself in quietly. He was half hoping that Lynda would be out so that he could have a minute to gather his thoughts.

It was not to be. She was standing in the kitchen, her eyes wide, her hands grasping a hard wooden conch crusher he had brought back from a Caribbean island decades ago. A pot of tea steamed on the table, with a fresh cup beside it. 'You beast,' she said, and burst into tears.

He bustled forwards and took her in his arms. 'It's all right, Lynda. It's all right. I'm sorry.'

'Sorry about what?' she muffled into his shoulder.

'About frightening you.'

'I wasn't frightened,' she muttered, pulling away from him slightly.

'Of course you weren't,' he said, pulling her back into his embrace.

'What the hell have you been about, going off without a word?'

'I left you a note,' he protested.

'Saying you were going away. You didn't say for how long or anything. You could have been anywhere. I've been worried sick.'

'Good.'

'How can you say that? What would you have said if I'd been murdered in my bed while you were off gallivanting?'

'That sounds more like my Lynda,' he said approvingly.

'But really,' she said, trying to push him away.

He held her closer. 'I wanted to make you remember that I was around,' he said, 'to remind you. You know why I went. I've been feeling like a drudge, and when I've tried to have a conversation, you shout at me. Or dismiss it. I needed to make you see that I really meant it. You have to stop the sniping or I'll have to leave for good. You know, I cook for you, look after you, make you tea in bed. And you just accept it, and then have a go at me. All the time.'

She looked at him mistily as he explained. 'Do I?' she asked, in a small voice, trying to find a tissue in her skirt pocket. 'Never got the skirt with pockets in when I need it.' She used her jumper sleeve to wipe her eyes.

'Yes, you do. We used to laugh together. Have fun. Be silly. But over the years it feels like we've drifted apart. Or, rather, I feel like I've stayed on the shore and you've drifted off to other pastures.'

'You should never mix your metaphors. You're on dry land or you're not.'

He laughed. 'Am I forgiven?'

'You can't be forgiven just like that.' She snapped her fingers.

'Can't I? You could do it if you wanted to. And you do understand why I went? That I couldn't think of any other way?'

She moved over to the kitchen table. 'Oh, all right. Yes, I suppose I do,' she said, looking down, then up again with a martial light in her eye. 'I don't know why we're standing up when there's tea in the pot and my cup's getting cold.'

'You are a terrible old woman.'

'Yes, all right. All right. What do you want me to say?'

'I don't want you to say anything. Except. How about saying you love me?'

'You know I do.'

'Well, say it, then.'

'Love you,' she mumbled.

'I can see I'm going to have to leave again.'

'Well, if you don't want to come home, don't. Don't do anything you don't want to do.'

'Stop being so bolshy.'

'I wasn't being bolshy. But you march in here as though nothing's happened ...'

'I did not.'

'You did. And then you expect me to forgive you,' said Lynda, getting annoyed where, just moments before, she'd been willing to take him back under almost any circumstances.

Jack began to get annoyed too. 'It is actually your fault that I left,' he snapped.

'Oh. Now it's all about whose fault it is.'

And all of a sudden, the reconciliation was turned on its head. The cup of tea continued to cool.

'I can see this was a bad idea. I wish I hadn't bothered. It was all a terrible mistake. This time …' he said dramatically, picked up his bag and left again, slamming the door.

Yes, he did know that he was partly to blame – because he had let it happen, instead of dealing with it when things had first started to go wrong. But that was the problem with life. It crept up on you. The speck of dust became a plank of wood. You had to deal with that grit when it was still manageable.

Bugger, he thought, as he trudged back to the road. He sat on his suitcase and phoned for a minicab. It had all seemed so easy.

Dee and Katie were having a textual relationship.

'Hey, Batface,' wrote Dee, 'has your head come off yet?'

'Thanks for the sympathy, you miserable old crow,' wrote Katie. 'Head still here. How have I been looking?'

'Like the ugly cow you are. When you back?'

'Saturday. Party tomorrow night. Adam being weird. What's been going down?'

There was a pause before Dee wrote back. 'Celebrity X may have stitched you up. May be why Adam being weird.'

Katie read the text twice. First the bombshell about her parents, now this.

She knew it. Admittedly she had flirted with Paul Martin but that had been the deal, hadn't it? It hadn't meant anything.

Mark, the producer, was waiting for her in the hospital reception area. He led her outside to a plush four-by-four. 'How are you?'

She felt as if she'd burst with worry, but forced herself to think of the show.

'Fine,' she said, fastening her seatbelt, and flicking down the sun visor. She gave herself a quick glance in the vanity mirror. 'Although I felt fine anyway, apart from the ridiculous lump on the top of my head. But I can't deny it was nice to be lying down in clean sheets and having handsome doctors – well, some handsome doctors – checking me out.'

'I hope you don't mind, but we've got cameras waiting for you back at the camp.'

'That's OK. I signed up for cameras. And, obviously, it saves my phone bill if everyone knows I'm all right.'

'Lots of texts and messages?' he asked, in sympathy.

'Tons of them. Didn't get through them all …' She trailed off.

Adam got her text message as he was having a conversation with Keera Keethley in his office. He had seen it and sent a terse one back, feeling a mixture of guilt and smugness. Two can play at this flirting-and-messing-with-the-emotions game, he thought. He hadn't been able to concentrate fully on the meeting. Keera's skirt was so short that he found his eye constantly drawn to the shadowy triangle where her thighs met.

If he hadn't seen evidence of the skirt when she came in, he would have sworn it wasn't there.

When she went through the office, there had been a hush – an envious silence from the women, a lascivious one from the men. As soon as the office door had closed, Gemma and Rose let her have it.

'She looks utterly ridiculous,' said Gemma. 'I mean, there's party gear and there's office gear. And that is Pink Rhino gear, no question.'

'Don't know why she turned us down for *Dare to Bare* when she's showing her knickers to all and sundry,' said Rose.

Gemma took a noisy slurp of her black coffee. 'The bitch does have a cracking pair of legs, though.'

'I bet she doesn't eat. Ever,' said Rose.

'Unlike you,' added Gemma, thoughtfully, 'who eats other people's psoriasis crumbs.'

'Will you never let me forget that?' huffed Rose, wrinkling her nose.

'Absolutely not. Highlight of my year. Licked any good ear wax recently?'

'Why are you always so gross? Did your parents drop you in something when you were a baby? A bag of poo or something?'

Gemma giggled. 'I love the word "poo". And "pong".'

'Sounds like a dim-sum place.'

'What's Adam going to offer Ms Knickers, then?'

'Nick says it's something to do with the fashion world. I don't know that it's actually been commissioned, mind you.

But if it is, she'd just have to drift around looking beautiful. Which, let's face it, is about all she can do. Her interviews are *so* crap.'

'She *is* stunning, isn't she?' said Gemma, wistfully.

'You wouldn't want to look like that, though, would you?' asked Rose, dismissively.

They both looked at the office where Keera was. And then declared in unison, 'Yes.'

Gemma added, 'I would. But I wouldn't want to be her. It must be very boring in her head.'

'Beautiful but thick, or clever but ugly?' asked Rose.

'I'm having a funny sense of *déjà vu*.'

'Are you having a funny sense of *déjà vu*?' asked Rose.

'Yes. Only it's not very funny.' Gemma drank the dregs of her coffee. 'I suppose I'd better get on with my programme treatment. I've got to get this in to Nick by the end of the day, and I've only half written it. Every time I look at the computer screen, my eyeballs feel tired. Or maybe it's my brain that's tired. Sometimes I hate my job. I want to be at a supermarket passing products over the beepy thing. Beep. Beep. Beep. Your own bag, madam? Unidentified item in the baggage area. Beep. Beep.'

'You wouldn't last a day. You'd have a row and throw your pinny on the floor.'

'"Pinny". That's a good word. I wonder if I can get "poo", "pong" and "pinny" into this treatment.'

'Bet you can't.'

'You're on.'

Gemma began typing. 'Hey, you know Daniel's been given a warning about his expenses?'

'No!' gasped Rose.

Gemma stopped typing. 'I really do have to get on with this. But, yup. Apparently went out for lunch with some mates. Put it through as dinner with contributors. Nick recognized the date – Mothering Sunday.'

'What bad luck,' said Rose, sympathizing with Daniel. 'The amount I put through that probably wouldn't stand up to scrutiny.'

'Not lunch with four people, though. Would you?'

'No. I'm a scaredy-cat. Always think I'll be spotted. But I got a jumper through.'

'No!' exclaimed Gemma.

'Yeah. Having said that, I did have to buy it. I was freezing my tits off on a shoot. I'd have got frostbite if I hadn't bought something warm. On the other hand, I should have taken a jumper in the first place.'

'Do you remember that presenter at Sky who put through a whole load of clothes from Harrods? He hadn't noticed that they'd all been itemized. He could have got away with the sweater, but the blouse and skirt …'

Gemma went back to the computer. 'This wretched treatment. I've only written three words.'

'"Poo", "pong" and "pinny"?'

'Exactly.'

CHAPTER SEVENTEEN

There are few things more gratifying to those who work behind the scenes in television than having those out front ripped apart by a national newspaper.

When the papers were delivered to *Hello Britain!* late on Thursday night, the double-page feature in the *Daily Mail* detailing Rod Fallon's critique on the other presenters and his bosses was the most fingered. No one was surprised by his view of Keera – few people would defend her intellect, apart from Kent. But they hadn't known that he felt himself so superior to absolutely everyone. Dee was an airhead. Simon, the editor was feeble. The Boss was an idiot.

'Who do you think this "source close to Rod" is, then?' asked one of the researchers.

'Whoever it is has got his turn of phrase down a T,' mused Richard, rereading a particularly pungent description of the editor.

'Could it be someone here, do you think?'

'If it is, then it's someone who's prepared to take a great big risk. One whisper and they'd be down on you like a ton of bricks. You'd be out on your ear. Not that Rod's wrong on some of the points. It's going to be a fun morning.' He made a face. 'Better not give him any of the happy stories. And the morning meeting's going to be interesting. No doubt he'll deny all the statements. Only thing he can do. I thought he sounded a bit subdued when he phoned in earlier to check on what guests he was doing. Well I never.'

Normally Rod would have been asleep by eleven o'clock at night. But he was lying in the darkened bedroom going over and over his recent conversations.

It had been at four o'clock that afternoon that the nightmare had started.

A woman called Sarah from the *Daily Mail* had phoned to ask if he had a moment to respond to an article that was going into the next day's paper.

How the devil had she got his mobile number? was his first thought. Followed by horror at what she had revealed.

She wanted a response to the litany of vitriol that had spewed from his own lips on everyone from The Boss down. And the worst of it was they had him bang to rights. Every quote was accurate. Every turn of phrase was his. It was as though his *alter ego* had written the entire article as a resignation letter. To each comment, though, he had said, 'That's utter bollocks,' his heart beating so wildly he thought it might come out of his chest.

'Come on, Rod,' said Sarah, reasonably, as he continued to say that it was rubbish. 'We know from two separate sources that these are your views. Do the people concerned know what you think of them?'

'Since it's all rubbish, there's no reason for me to have a conversation with anyone about it, is there?'

As soon as the call ended, he rang the head of the press office at *Hello Britain!*. He had to dial three times, his hands were so sweaty.

'Hello, Rod,' said the chief press officer, warily. He hated phone calls from the presenters – it usually meant trouble. His instincts weren't wrong. He listened quietly as Rod talked, jotting down a few words on the pad he had beside his computer for just such occasions. 'So. First things first. Where have all these quotes come from?'

'I honestly have no idea. I mean, obviously not me. I wasn't planning on leaving the company any time soon.'

'Well, take a minute and try to think of anyone who wants to stitch you up. Anyone you've been out with for a beer, whom you might have spoken to, or someone who might have over-heard.'

He thought. 'No. No one.'

'If you think of it later, let me know. I don't know how much difference it's going to make in the damage-limitation stakes, mind you. Right. Is there a photographer outside your house?'

Rod went to the door and opened it. 'Can't see anyone.'

'Well, there will be one. More than one, I would imagine, if they're going big on this, as you suggest. So make sure you walk out with your head up. And make your expression as neutral as possible. Don't try to avoid being photographed – it looks like you're guilty. Be friendly to the photographers. Ask if they want a picture, and pose for them, before getting into your car. I'll have a word with the car company and make sure they're directly outside your house and waiting with the door open so that you can get in and be driven off. I suppose you read your scripts in the back of the car?'

Rod assented.

'Keep a semi-smile plastered on your face as you're doing it, in case they follow you.'

'OK,' said Rod, humbly. His hands had started to shake now. Who could have done this to him? If he ever found out … He could feel bile in his throat. He'd kill them. How could they do this to him? 'Sorry. Missed that,' he said, as the chief press officer had continued to talk.

'I asked if you'd spoken to any of the parties concerned?'

'In what way?'

'As in, have you spoken to Keera, Simon and The Boss about what you've said?'

'Allegedly said.'

'I think we can be honest between ourselves, Rod,' he said nastily. 'I assume you haven't. In which case, I suggest you do it as soon as possible. And call your agent so that they're on-side. I'll ring the *Mail* now and try to put a spin on it, but I doubt if I can do much if they've double sourced. And, finally, don't mention the article on air. No point in having everyone rushing off and buying the paper. Giving it the oxygen of publicity. I'm going to phone Keera, Simon and The Boss too. I'll give you a ten-minute start.'

'Which order do you suggest?' he asked humbly.

'Whichever order you want. Make it snappy, though. I need to get on. Try not to make the situation worse.' The chief press officer put the phone down, then rang Sarah Nicholls. 'Hello. It's Christopher Dingle from *Hello Britain!*. I understand you have an article running tomorrow about one of our presenters.'

'Actually, it's about all of your presenters. And your bosses, too,' she said sweetly, making sure her pen was working, and writing 'chief press officer' at the top of a new page on her notepad.

'Could you tell me what the gist of it is?' he asked, knowing full well what it was.

Sarah told him.

'Well, regarding Rod and Keera, off the record – and this is strictly off the record – they actually do get on well together. They socialize outside work. They went to the Christmas party together, for example. And you'll have seen that photograph – I think it may even have been printed in your august organ – of the two of them shopping together.' No one needed to know that it was a set-up by Keera with her publicity agent when she'd felt she needed more press. 'On the record, I'd like to say that they're highly professional people and of course they get on. It's ridiculous to suggest they don't.'

'Thank you for that,' said Sarah. 'But what do you say to the incident in which Rod walked off the set saying he couldn't believe Keera had been given the job of interviewing the Prime Minister when, and I quote, "one of the runners could do a better job"? Yes, I have that right. Just wanted to check my notes.'

He remembered that incident. Keera had lodged a complaint. 'People are up very early. It's a live show, and things go wrong. Tempers flare. But that was an isolated incident,' he said.

'What about the views he expresses about his bosses? That essentially they're incompetent and overlook Keera's obvious shortcomings because of the shortness of her skirt?'

'I'm not going to dignify that with a response.'

'No comment, then?'

'I did *not* say "no comment". I said I would not dignify the statement you just made with a response. Please do not write "no comment".'

At the end of the fractious conversation, he called the Boss on his mobile.

'Problem?' he asked brusquely, answering on the first ring.

'Yes. An article in the *Mail*. Unfavourable. Quoting Rod Fallon – but he has no idea where from.' He explained the situation.

'Does Keera know?'

'I'm about to tell her. Rod may well be on the phone to her now.'

'Well, remind her to keep a dignified silence.'

Christopher gritted his teeth. Like he didn't know his sodding job. 'Of course. I'll also tell her to tone down her clothing. We don't want a photograph of her looking like she's forgotten to put her skirt on.'

'Oh, I don't know,' said The Boss, 'but you're probably right. Remind me of the exact quote he used to describe me.'

'Ignorant numpty with your head up Keera's arse,' said Christopher, regretfully.

'Thank you. I'll let you get on.'

The penultimate call was to Simon.

'Well, well. Dull, boring Rod, eh? I'll make sure he remembers who allows him to live a comfortable life in a big house in an expensive part of London Town. He'll get a nice hand on his entrance from me tomorrow morning. I'll warm up that hand right now,' declared the editor.

Keera was having a pedicure when he called. 'Yes, I know all about it,' she said. 'I'm just off the phone to Mr Rod Unpleasant Fallon.'

'Is someone listening to this phone conversation?' asked Christopher. 'Because if they are, I suggest you don't use those sort of words. Not when there's something like this happening.'

She made no answer.

'Anyway,' he pressed on, 'I wanted to mention a few things. There may be photographers. Have a quick picture taken and move away. Be friendly. Do not make any comment other than that you two are friends.'

She made a noise.

'I know that's not necessarily true but you say it, all right? And you must not mention the article on air. Ignore it. And, I'm sorry, I have a feeling this might rumble on for a week or so.'

Oh, goody good, thought Keera, already planning what she would be wearing. She was glad she had on her bottom-skimming skirt and that her makeup from the morning was still looking alright. She reached over and got out the vanity mirror from her handbag. 'Sorry, didn't get that,' she said, her phone having slipped slightly from her ear.

'I said it would be helpful if you were wearing a reasonable-length skirt tomorrow. Make you look more like a professional presenter.'

The cheek of the man. She hoped there were photographers outside right now.

'Of course,' she said sweetly. 'Anything to oblige. Do you think he'll be sacked?'

'I think I said that it was perhaps better if you didn't use those sort of words while there was the possibility of someone overhearing.'

'Oh, it's all right. They don't speak English,' she said.

* * *

Iwona, carefully painting Keera's big toe, assumed she was being described. She made a mental note to go and buy the papers the next day.

Keera lived by the motto that all publicity was good publicity. She phoned her publicist. 'There's going to be a big story about me in tomorrow's *Daily Mail*. Not very complimentary. So I could do with a big picture to go with it, and today would be a good day to have my photo taken. Can you phone round and tell them I'll be drinking tea outside Starbucks on the King's Road for the next hour, and after that I'll be walking in Holland Park near the Orangery?'

She reapplied her lipgloss and swayed down the road from the nail bar, looking at herself in the shop windows. She lingered in front of a hairdresser's, her image reflected through hair products, then moved a few doors down and feigned interest in boots and shoes. If she moved her head slightly to the left, her reflection showed her wearing odd shoes as earrings. Interesting. Would that be a good photograph?

At the coffee shop, she had a quiet word with the manager, who went out to apologize to a couple who were sitting at the best table. They moved, and Keera took their place with her skinny latte. She got out the book she had just bought, and sat there in the weak sunshine, supposedly engrossed in Dostoevsky's *The Brothers Karamazov*.

* * *

In Norway, it was early evening, and Katie found herself with the first spare time she'd had in weeks. It was crisp and quiet, and she had seen the northern lights the night before. It had been so special that she wanted to share the vision. She phoned Adam, and left a message on the answerphone. She looked at her watch, wondering where he was. Then she phoned Dee, who was contemplating a mountain of stuff that had emerged from a rather small cupboard in her sitting room, debating whether she really had the energy to tidy or whether it would be better to push it all back in again. She felt much as a woman with a hideous teenager must feel, she mused.

'Hey, Katie,' she said, when the phone rang, 'you would *so* approve of what I'm doing now. I'm organizing a cupboard.'

'As in throwing things away?'

'Not as such. Or not yet, anyway.'

'As in what, then?'

'As in taking it all out and deciding what to do with it. Although I'm not sure that I could actually throw things away. How can you bear to do that when so many of them have memories attached?'

'I'll tell you in a minute. But, first, can I tell you that I was standing outside in the frosty air of northern Norway last night, watching the northern lights? And that they're beautiful. So gorgeous they take your breath away. Green lights dancing and flickering. Lovely.'

'Aaah,' said Dee.

'Exactly. Meanwhile, back in your cupboard. Take me through three of the items in front of you. I'll tell you what needs to be done with them.'

'You're hundreds of miles away.'

'All the better to advise you. Shoot.'

'A really nice vase, which I bought in a little shop in Holloway when I was married.'

'Your ex-husband was a shitemeister. He had an affair. The vase reminds you of him. Give it to the Oxfam shop.'

'But it's pretty.'

'Is it chipped?'

'No … not much.'

'When did you last use it?'

'Yes, all right. Not since I left him. But that's because it's in the cupboard.'

'Throw it. Next.'

'I can't bear this. You're too harsh. You'll tell me to throw it *all* away.'

'You're right. Get rid of it all. You live in a giant manifestation of a waste-disposal pipe. It needs to be recycled. You don't need it, and there are others who would be very grateful of a small pot into which they could put a nice bunch of dandelions.'

'Dandelions don't last in a vase.'

'Nettles, then.'

Dee sank down, sticking her legs out in front of her, leaning against the cupboard door and wriggling her toes to get rid of the cramp that had just come on.

'What exactly is cramp?' she asked.

'Eh? What's cramp got to do with it?'

'Got cramp from squatting uncomfortably in front of the cupboards and sorting them out.'

'I don't know. Ask a doctor. Don't you know any nice doctors you can ask?'

'Oliver is a bottom doctor.'

'And bottoms never get cramp? No, actually, I suppose they don't.'

'I was just wondering what the point was in human terms? You know, you get the surge of adrenalin in a tricky situation because the body needs to get ready for fight or flight. And goose-bumps make you warmer because they tighten the pores to stop the cold getting in. Or something like that. But what's the point of a cramp?'

'To remind you that you're stopping the blood getting round and you're in danger of getting gangrene. Talking of which, how is your ankle?'

'Every day in every way, it's getting better and better. But, oh, so dull. It's like all these things. Exciting at the beginning. Then progressively more irritating because of the things you can't do. And itchy. Talking of dandelions, do you know where the word comes from?'

'Isn't it *dents de lion*, meaning lion's teeth, because of the shape of the leaves?'

'Oh, Miss Know It All,' said Dee, in disgust, 'I knew I didn't like you.'

Katie laughed. 'You know I can only remember strange facts like that. Nothing useful, like people's names or dates or who came next in the kings and queens of England. Or who I've interviewed in my life. Ask me what I did yesterday, and I can't remember.'

'What did you do yesterday?'

'Actually, I can remember that. I knocked myself out.'

'Oh, yes. So you did. How is your poor head now?'

'I have to have extra time to brush my hair, to get over the bump.'

'Ouch. But no lasting damage?'

'Not perceptible. Yet.'

'Hey, should I wear a dress or trousers on Saturday night?' asked Dee, brightening.

'What are you doing on Saturday night?'

'No, I asked you the question. What's the answer?'

'Hotpants. What are you doing on Saturday night?'

'Going out for dinner with Oliver. He said it was important.'

'Did he indeed? Important, eh? Do you think he's going to ask you to marry him? Eh?' shrieked Katie.

'I dunno. Maybe. Do you think he will?' asked Dee, excitedly.

'Abso-bloody-lutely, to use a tiny tmesis.'

'Tmesis?'

'One word inserted into another. Like fan-bloody-tastic. Another of my essentially useless bits of knowledge. Of no great interest. Unlike your news, which *is*.'

'So do you really think he is?'

'Abso-bloody-lutely,' said Katie, dramatically. 'To use a tiny tmesis. As I said before. What else would Oliver consider "important"?'

'Oh, I hope he does.'

'You'd say yes?'

'Of course I would,' said Dee, without hesitation.

'Dee Greene. That sounds like you're going to make the lawn a nasty brown colour. I'm degreening the lawn.'

'No, it doesn't.'

'Oh yes it does.'

'It's not the panto season.'

'Dee Greene. As in where dee golfers play.'

'Can you point me out to dee green?' giggled Dee, in an Irish accent.

'Anyway, why else would he say it's important? Unless he's pregnant. Or leaving you.'

'Don't be horrible. Leaving me? Of course he isn't. Oh, God. Maybe he's shagged someone else and needs to tell me. Oh, no …' she wailed.

'Don't be such an idiot. Of course he hasn't. He's not the type. You've found a good one. And you're lovely. If messy. Wear that purple dress which shows off your waist.'

'It's got a rip in the sleeve.'

'Sew it up, then.'

'How about that black dress with the polo neck?'

'You look like Maria von Trapp in it. Wear the purple.'

'Or that short tartan kilt?'

'He *will* leave you.'

Dee sighed. 'All right, I'll sew up the purple.' She went to the sofa, moved a pair of knickers and an old milk carton, then sat down.

'But enough of this,' said Katie, 'and do keep me informed of Mr Greene's movements on Saturday. Regarding wedding, that is.'

There was a pregnant pause.

'By the way, I understand I may not have been getting the best newspaper coverage in the world,' Katie said.

Dee might not have known what to wear on an important Saturday night, but she did know that you never tell a friend the unvarnished truth. 'Er. Yes. Perhaps. They've been making something of your flirtation with Paul Martin. Who, I have to say …'

'No, you don't have to say. No court order has been taken out against you.'

'Who, I have to say, is rather gorgeous.'

'Yes, he is, isn't he?'

'And I'm sure it's just the way they've been editing it, but you know how they do those voiceovers and make it sound worse than it is …'

'You're saying it's bad,' said Katie, baldly.

'Well, it's perhaps not good,' said Dee.

'Anything else?'

'And you fall over a lot.'

'That's true enough.'

'Perhaps through drink.'

'Not true.'

'I know. That's what I mean. I know it's not true. I can't believe Adam doesn't think it's not true either,' she said, suddenly confused over how many negatives there had been in the sentence.

'Hmm.'

'What did he say when you spoke to him?'

'I haven't, really. Spoken to him, that is. Briefly, after it happened. And I've left a message.'

'And, erm, also,' said Dee hesitantly, 'just to warn you … that, er, Keera has been spouting it around that she's going to be working for Wolf Days Productions.'

There was silence on the line.

Katie felt like she'd been thumped in the solar plexus. That would be the outside of enough. To be shafted once by the wicked witch was bad enough. To be shafted twice … 'Doing what?' she managed to ask.

'I'm sure it's nothing. You know how she bigs things up. But she's been saying some fashion series. You do know what she's like? She was having a meeting this morning, apparently. And doing all that they're-so-desperate-to-get-me-they're-throw-ing-money-at-me rubbish.'

Katie sniffed. 'Well, she's not going to get away with her scheming this time.'

'Good. What are you going to do?' asked Dee.

'I don't know. But I'm going to bring out the big guns. Flynn O'Mara. She'll know what to do.'

'Yes, I can see Flynn O'Mara as a massive great grenade-launcher,' Dee said, a smile in her voice. 'Just to get off pig-scarer Keethley for a minute, I love Flynn. Will you introduce her to me?'

'Course I will. Oh, and the other thing. My parents seem to have split up.'

'What? You wait until now to tell me your parents have split up? When? Why? They haven't really, have they? That's awful,' Dee gabbled.

'It didn't seem right to rain on your parade,' Katie answered. 'An awful lot of things appear to have happened. Ben says that Dad was staying with Bob. Which is very odd. But he's not now. He hasn't got a mobile. Dad, that is. And obviously I can't phone Bob. I don't know what the hell's happening.'

'Oh poor you,' said Dee, getting up to rescue a comb she had spotted under the armchair. 'What does your mum say?'

'She's being her usual taciturn self. Not saying much. Won't say why. Says she isn't worried.'

'What does Ben say?'

'That Dad is old enough and ugly enough to look after himself. Oh, I don't know. Of course he is. But I want to know he's all right and not moping. Or whatever dads do.'

'As long as you don't think he's a danger to himself or anyone else, you're just going to have to let them sort it out. Bloody nightmare, though. Awful for you and Ben. But what can you do? Nothing. Parents. Who'd have 'em?'

Katie laughed. 'Can't live with them. Can't kill them. Right. Anyway, I suppose I've got to get on. On a lighter and more inconsequential note, who do you think is going to win this wretched show?'

'Peter Philbin.'

'Same here.'

'Although Paul Martin has got a very attractive smile.'

'Are you after Mr Martin now, you floozy?'

'No, I am not. I have a very nice man already. I'm not like you, trying to gather them like onions on a kebab stick.' There was a pause.

'Thanks,' said Katie, tight-lipped. 'Maybe you could tell Adam that.'

'Oops. You know I didn't mean it,' said Dee, feeling guilty.

'The awful thing is, I know that deep down you do,' said Katie.

When she had phoned Adam, he had dropped her call. He was feeling uncharacteristically grinchy and didn't want to say anything that might be used against him in future. He had done too much of that with his previous girlfriend, Naomi, to want to repeat the experience. She never forgot a single slight, and he still had a scar above one eyebrow from a hurled egg-cup. He had been surprised by how much an egg-cup could hurt – then pleasantly so by the rakish scar that had been left behind.

But did he want to continue with a relationship if the general feeling was that he had been cuckolded? How much did he care what everyone thought, if what they thought was not accurate? He had to wrestle with that before he talked to Katie. He thought about Cécile in Paris. An elegant woman who would never talk about 'snogging' and 'shagging' but of 'affairs' and 'passion'. Yes, OK, it was the same thing, but it sounded less tawdry. Less childish.

He sighed. What he needed was a large glass of chilled Sancerre. He left the office and went round the corner to a gloomy bar he sometimes used for evenings when he didn't want to bump into anyone from the trendy world of television. He spent three hours there, getting unusually maudlin as he drank his way through two bottles of wine and ate a small portion of olives before going home. He stopped at a late-night shop to pick up some milk and an early edition of Friday's *Daily Mail*, which had a strap line promising revelations about the stars of *Hello Britain!*. He flicked to the double-page spread as soon as he got home. And laughed out loud at the photo of Keera halfway through *The Brothers Karamazov*. You couldn't help admiring the girl.

CHAPTER EIGHTEEN

Katie Fisher being out of *Celebrity X-Treme* meant less money for the production company from the voters. Her designated phone number had immediately been frozen after a code red warning was put out to everyone on the programme – and the phone company – that Katie was on her way to hospital and might not be back to continue the show.

'How about we put Katie back in?' suggested Siobhan, silkily, at the production meeting that night.

'Hmm. Not a bad idea,' said one of the senior executives, 'although, of course, we'd have three in the final, which wouldn't be what we'd planned. Bloody viewer voting. If we didn't make so much money out of it … Why don't you ask her if she'd be prepared to go back into the house?'

Siobhan didn't care either way, but it always paid to show willing. She drove over to the hotel where those who had been in the contest were now enjoying five-star luxury.

Katie had finished breakfast and was reading a fax of the *Daily Mail* article, which Richard had sent to her, starring Mr Rod Fallon as Blofeld. She looked up as Siobhan walked towards her, thinking that she really was a striking woman, with her strawberry hair and slim figure – today in a white shirt with her jeans tucked into high boots.

'Hello, Katie. Just the woman I was looking for. Can you talk?'

'Only if I open my mouth and make noises.'

Siobhan pretended to smile. It really was sad how Katie thought she was funny. 'We were wondering whether you could be persuaded to go back into the hut for the final?'

'Why?' asked Katie, enjoying her freedom and the fact that she had managed to escape with an honourable discharge. Then she pretended to brighten. 'Would I get more money?'

Venal woman, thought Siobhan. 'No,' she said, 'but you'd obviously get more air time.'

'I think we both know that, the way I've been edited, I've probably had more than enough,' said Katie, with a tight little smile.

'Well, the executive producers wanted me to let you know that they would be more than happy for you to go back in for the final.'

'If you could tell the executive producers that I would rather not?'

'Fine. Enjoy your article,' said Siobhan, having noticed the headline. She hoped that *Hello Britain!*'s viewing figures were sinking through the floor and that they were being roundly beaten by the BBC. She walked away, pleased with the outcome. It would have been quite nice to see Katie trounced by Paul Martin. But it really didn't matter.

It seemed to Rod, as he sat in The Boss's office at *Hello Britain!*, that he was having an out-of-body experience. His mind had gone into a constant refrain that filled it with such a buzz there was no room left for anything else. It had been there since that blasted phone call: 'Who told them? Who told them? Who told them?' And the trouble was, it was the first question The Boss had asked him.

'Who told them, Rod, do you think?' He had waited for an answer, but none was forthcoming.

Rod was thinking that some of the quotes had been so scarily accurate it was as though Sarah Nicholls had been in his sitting room, listening to his conversation. If he didn't trust his wife so much, he would have accused her of being the mole. He looked up. 'I have no idea,' he said miserably. 'No idea at all. Obviously I'm very sorry for any upset I've caused. I've already apologized – I don't know what else I can be expected to do. You know that sometimes we say things in the heat of the moment that are perhaps not, erm, exactly, er, political. Or correct, even,' he ended.

The Boss knew what he was trying to say. However, he did get a degree of pleasure from seeing his presenters squirm. He picked up the newspaper in front of him. 'So I am not, as it says here ... Let me look at this again ... "an idiotic numpty" with my head up Keera's … What is that word? It's always difficult when there are so many asterisks, don't you find?'

'No, of course I don't think that.'

There was a silence as The Boss stared at him.

Rod had not taken his agent into the meeting – a decision he was now regretting.

'I do think, Rod, that it might be as well in future if you remember how your mortgage is paid. You're on a cushy number here. I could sue you, of course, for lowering me in the eyes of right-thinking members of society …'

Rod examined his shoes. He wriggled his toes. This was excruciating.

'… but I won't. To parrot our chief press officer, I will not dignify the slur with a response. You can go now.' And he turned his seat slightly, and picked up the phone.

Rod stood up, adjusted his trousers, which were sticking to his sweaty legs, and left. Phew, he thought, as he made his way to the reception area, and was brought up short by the view of about twenty photographers outside. He ducked back into the loo and checked his reflection in the mirror. He looked as white as a sheet. He splashed water on his face and gave it a scrub with the roller towel to bring the colour back. He tidied his hair, and left, his face carefully arranged into what he hoped was a bright but contrite expression.

The Boss called the chief press officer in. 'What do you think?' he asked, standing up and going to the window.

'Could go either way. You know how it is. Sometimes we get more viewers when something like this happens. They tune in to see how the, er, miscreant is coping.'

The Boss could just see the reflected flashlights going off at the exit to the building. He turned and smiled. 'He really isn't one of our finest appointees, is he?' he mused.

The chief press officer was not that easily drawn. He made a noise that was a cross between a cough and an 'ahem'.

'Even his insults in the paper were grey and uninventive, didn't you think?' continued The Boss.

No answer came.

'How's everyone else?'

'Well, as you saw on air this morning, Keera appears to be handling it in her own way.'

The Boss now laughed out loud. 'Oh, yes. I think we can safely say she actually enjoyed herself. It's hardly new, co-presenters slagging each other off behind their backs. Won't be the first or last time, eh?'

The chief press officer left to continue fielding calls from other publications.

Keera, meanwhile, was speaking to her publicist, giving him a complete rundown of her day to make for optimum press coverage. 'Can you put it out there that I've been offered another high-profile job?' she asked. 'You don't have to mention Wolf Days Productions, obviously. Is there anything else I should be doing?' She suddenly had a blinding flash of inspiration. Why on earth hadn't she thought of it before? Nick Midhurst. He was perfect. Rich, handsome, and not as much of a player as Matthew Praed. He'd be grateful for the attention. And – this was the genius of it – they would be more famous than Adam Williams, who was hardly maximizing his publicity potential with that overweight old biddy Katie Fisher.

She hurriedly ended the conversation and rang Matthew. 'I know you're busy. I don't mean to hassle. But have you heard back about the show for Wolf Days?'

He assured her he would get on to it, but it was early days. The meeting was only yesterday. He was pleased to hear she sounded less peeved than previously. Peevish people were particularly pointless.

'Would it be terribly unprofessional if I gave them a call myself?' she asked sweetly. She couldn't see him raise his eyebrows in surprise. But she could tell from his silence that she had stumped him.

'It would be perhaps a little singular,' he commented eventually.

What did 'singular' mean when it was used like that? 'Is that good or bad?' she essayed.

'To what end?'

'Well …' she started. 'Well, maybe I could persuade them to let me do something else for them, if this fashion programme doesn't work out.'

'I'm not sure,' he countered. How long had she worked in television, for God's sake?

'No matter,' she said gaily. 'What's the worst that can happen?' She checked the time on her new Chanel watch, then did it again because she liked the look of it on her wrist. She spread her fingers and held her hand towards the sun. A look of horror came over her face. Was that an age spot? She brought the back of her hand slowly towards her face and, with her index finger, touched the blemish. It moved. She brought it up to her nose. Oh. Coffee. Relief coursed through her. It would be just too, too hideous to have an age spot. Heather, one of the producers, had a cluster of age spots on her forearms. Sometimes it was hard to concentrate on what she was saying because of them.

She looked at her watch again, having forgotten to take note of the time. Eleven o'clock. By half past, she had secured an early-evening drink with Nick Midhurst.

Nick had been as confused by Keera's phone call as her agent but, like most men, he wasn't about to turn down the offer of a drink with a very attractive woman. It was one of the perks of the job. He wasn't unaware of his appeal. He didn't think he was bad-looking, and he knew he was rendered more attractive by his job, his sufficiently deep wallet and his friendship with a number of famous people. He just wished he hadn't been away from the office when Katie Fisher had become available. He would have told her not to do *Celebrity X-Treme*. He would have developed a programme specially for her.

He didn't understand Adam and his don't-want-to-be-seen-promoting-nepotism rubbish. Secretly, he was quite enjoying

Adam's obvious discomfiture over the stories in the newspapers. '*Schadenfreude*' – a wonderful word for such a mean emotion.

He leaned back in his chair and stretched, his thin black Prada jumper coming slightly adrift from his trousers.

Rose, on her way past to the water-cooler, faltered and almost stumbled as her eyes were drawn to his taut stomach. God, he was gorgeous. She loved him. She loved her job. She *loved* her job. Last night, she had dreamed they were having dinner and he was proposing to her. Of course she had hesitated before saying yes. She had got as far as the bridesmaids' dresses before the alarm went.

She decided she would make him hers. She and Gemma had been reading a book that essentially said you could have whatever you wanted. You just had to put the thought out there, visualize it, and it would come to you. They were addicted to it.

One of the other producers had pooh-poohed it over drinks after work, saying they'd be better off just getting on with their lives. 'Get out there. This sort of crap panders to the viewers of reality shows. You don't have to work hard, just wish for it to happen. It's all shit. Sixteen-year-olds are "visualizing" themselves as TV presenters, leaving school with no qualifications and filling in application forms for every reality show going. Because that's how you do it. Yeah. Right,' he had sneered. 'And it works. For one in a million.'

They had tried to explain that it wasn't like that. But he was having none of it. Nobody was going to change their mind, so they'd had another round and moved on to a discussion about pointy elbows and, more specifically, that it's physically impossible to lick your own.

Nick came out of his office and almost bumped into her. 'Looking very serious,' he said. 'What's up?'

Rose blushed.

'What?' he asked again, looking bemused.

She could hardly tell him she'd been daydreaming about his upcoming marriage proposal to her. 'Oh, nothing,' she said, feeling quite hot round the back of her ears.

He walked through to Adam's office. 'Women.' He laughed.

Adam looked up from a DVD he'd been viewing. 'What about them? Found a new place where you can buy them by the metre?'

'Ha. No. Got a phone call from Keera Keethley. I think she wants to jump on my bones,' he said, with a slow swagger over to the bookcase. There were few books on the shelves, just rows and rows of DVDs, tapes and industry tomes.

'Oh, really?' asked Adam, pressing the pause button and addressing himself entirely to his friend.

'Yes.'

Nick straddled the chair on the other side of the desk. 'She phoned me up and did that slightly, erm,' he made a face, 'slightly strange laugh – and then virtually invited me to dinner.'

'You dirty dog,' responded Adam, with a smirk.

'I know. Obviously she thinks we're not working hard enough on a proposal for her. I'm supposed to be meeting up with my mates Sam and Thomas tonight, but since it looks like I'm on a promise, I'll ditch them. I said I'd have an early drink with her. I'll see how the land lies, and take it from there.'

'That skirt was something else,' said Adam, nodding at the memory.

'I know,' said Nick, smiling. 'And I bet she'll be wearing something special tonight, too.'

'I think that's a fairly safe bet. Well, good luck to you.'

'When's your bird back, then?'

'Tomorrow, theoretically.'

'Do you think it was worth it? Going into *Celebrity X-Treme*?'

Adam stood up and went to the window. It was a breezy day, and each gust of wind rattled the window casing. 'Must get this ruddy window sorted. Drives me insane. I don't know. I suppose it depends what Katie gets offered afterwards.'

'And at least tomorrow you'll find out her version of events.'

'Yes. Exactly,' said Adam, going back to his desk and shuffling a pile of paperwork. 'Now I must get on with this. I promised the lawyer I'd have it all done by the end of the week and, as usual, I've been procrastinating. So sod off and let me at it.'

Since Nick had never seen Adam procrastinate over anything, he merely inclined his head and left the room.

In Hawes, Bob was missing having Jack around. He had a desultory breakfast of cheese on toast and a cup of coffee, fed Caligula a handful of dried cat food, then mooched about. The trouble with being self-employed was that there was ample opportunity for doing nothing. He stood by the window, and gave his head a good scratch. Nothing quite like a good scratch. Except maybe a good stretch. He tried one. It didn't work when it wasn't done as an urgent response to a need to stretch. He bent down and touched his toes. Good flexibility, he thought. He lay on the floor in the kitchen and did a few sit-ups, flipped over and did some press-ups. Maybe he should go for a run. No. He couldn't be bothered. He reached over and closed a cupboard door. It was a bit wonky. He went to fetch his tools and was midway through adjusting the hinges when his phone rang.

He answered it.

'Blimey. That was quick. Sitting on it, were you?' asked Harry.

'I'm bored out of my box. I was altering a hinge.'

Harry whistled. 'Well, I hate to interrupt you in the middle of such a major job, but are you doing anything this evening?'

'Friday night? You kidding?'

'Oh,' said Harry, sounding disappointed.

'Which means that, no, I haven't got anything on this evening. Originally, I was going to be having a house guest so I didn't organize anything. What are you up to?'

'Can you babysit?'

'And there I was thinking you were going to invite me out for drinking, cheap women and carousing until dawn.'

'Yeah. Right. Now … you know how Elizabeth loves you …'

'Uh-huh. And your babysitter's dropped out at the last minute …'

'... And the babysitter's dropped out at the last minute, yes. Could you help me out of a pickle of the large, brown variety? I promised Sophie I'd take her to some Opera North thing in Leeds and we'd stay at this hotel she's always going on about.'

'Ooo-er. Well posh. Will you be wearing a sparkly number?'

'Of course. But only if you babysit. Can you? Go on. You know you want to.'

'All right, you old scrote. In the absence of anything else to do. But tell Elizabeth that I'm reading a fairy story of *my* choice. And I demand a selection of salty snacks. And I want the hot-water bottle with the Barbie cover.'

'Those are pretty stiff terms. But since beggars can't be choosers, I'll have to give in to your ridiculous demands. Thanks. I owe you. Can you come at four?'

'I can come now, if you like.'

'No. It's all right. Thanks for the offer, but I have things to do. And if you came round, we'd sit drinking beer and playing computer games.'

'Got some new ones?'

'I'll show you when you get over.'

'You temptress, you.'

'You should see what I'm wearing right now, big boy.'

'Is it pink and lacy?'

'It's like you have X-ray vision. Spooky. See you at four.'

Bob went back to the cupboard door. And since he'd got the screwdriver out, he did a few other jobs. And then, because he'd worked up a sweat, and had something to do later, he went for a long, bracing run.

The clouds were scudding across the sky and some of the smaller trees were bent almost horizontal. He loved Yorkshire. The light had a purple edge to it, and the weather somehow felt more personal.

He got back to the house and took a leisurely shower, before getting down to the work he had been putting off all morning. Suddenly he was in a rush. Where does the time go? he wondered.

Dragging on his motorbike helmet, he gave Caligula a stroke and a large bowl of tinned meat. 'See you tomorrow. Help yourself to the mice,' he said, as he locked the door, while Caligula tucked his tail round his paws.

The Triumph fired into life, and ten minutes later, Bob was being bounced over by his goddaughter. 'Daddy's been farting a lot,' she pronounced.

'No, I have not,' declared her father, smiling over her head at Bob.

'You have. Don't lie. You always tell me not to lie. And then, Bob, he says that it's better out than in. He *does*.'

'Well, they do say better an absent landlord than a friendly tenant. Is that the right expression?' asked Bob.

'I thought it was better an empty flat than a bad tenant. But I quite like your version,' said Harry. 'I'm just going to nip upstairs and throw a few things into a bag. I'm picking Sophie up on the way. You OK?'

'Cool. You get on with it. Elizabeth and I are fine, aren't we?'

'Yes. Can we watch television?'

'I don't know. Harry, can we watch television?'

'Elizabeth knows the rules. If she eats all her vegetables, then she can watch television.'

'Vegetables smell,' she said mutinously.

'Of course they do,' said Harry, mildly. 'They smell delicious. Peas are yummy. You love peas.'

'What we're going to do is cook our dinner together, aren't we?' Bob grabbed Elizabeth and blew a raspberry on her stomach. She squealed. 'Aren't we?' he asked, and immediately tickled her.

'Stop it!' She giggled.

'Aren't we?'

'Yes. Yes. Yes,' she gasped, between tickles.

Harry left them rolling around on the sitting-room floor and went to pack his bag. A few minutes later he was back. 'Be good, Cuddlechops,' he said to Elizabeth, giving her a hug.

'Don't go, Daddy.' Suddenly she was crying.

'What are you on about, Elizabeth? You know that Mummy and Daddy are away for the night. You're going to have a laugh with Bob. See you tomorrow. I might bring you a nice present back from Leeds if he tells me you've been super-good.'

The tears stopped. 'What might you bring me?'

'I don't know. And I didn't promise you anything. I said I might. It's up to Bob. If he says you've been good …' He let the words hang.

'She'll be fine,' he said quietly to Bob, as he straightened up. 'She's going through a clingy stage.'

'What time does she have to be in bed?'

'Half eight at the latest. But sooner if she looks like she's drooping. I must get off.'

'Have a good time. Send Sophie my love.'

'And I was thinking we should have a weekend in London with some of the lads. Maybe go to the theatre or a comedy gig, if you fancy that.'

'Sounds great.'

'See you tomorrow about lunchtime.'

Bob closed the door and Elizabeth immediately wailed and clutched her doll to her chest as if it was her only friend in the entire world. 'Do you want some chocolate cake?' he called through from the kitchen, having found a piece in the fridge with a note on it from Harry: 'FOR EMERGEN-CIES'.

There was a sniffle and a subdued 'Yes, please,' as she shuffled in with damp eyes.

Two hours later, they had played at shops, where Bob had bought an assortment of vegetables for eighty pounds, and they had pretended to eat plastic food, which Elizabeth had cooked for him on her child-sized cooker. They had played hide and seek, run all over the house, worn each other out, and eaten a small amount of vegetables with a pie.

Now Elizabeth's eyelids were drooping.

'Bed,' he said determinedly.

'No. Don't make me go to bed. I want to stay up with you,' she moaned, bottom lip protruding.

'You know I don't like whining. Big girls don't whine, do they?'

She looked at him sideways through her eyelashes. Girls, he thought, certainly learn how to flirt early.

'*Pleeease* can I stay up with you?'

'Tell you what. You can have a bath, clean your teeth and get ready for bed. Then we'll tuck you up in your duvet and you can watch a bit of television with me. Deal or no deal?'

'Deal,' she pronounced solemnly.

They missed the opening credits of the final of *Celebrity X-Treme* because she couldn't find her beanbag rabbit, but they were on the sofa in time to watch the highlights of the series.

'You know her, don't you?' asked Elizabeth, snuggling down into her pink duvet.

'Yes, I do,' he said.

'Her name is Katie.'

'Yes, that's right.'

'Why don't we see her any more?'

'Because she's in Norway, my little cauliflower. Now shut up and listen to the television.'

In Norway, Siobhan was quietly confident. She had settled a couple of scores rather cleverly, and produced a bloody good series in the process.

The director moved the shots around to get the best close-ups of the two remaining contestants in *Celebrity X-Treme*.

Peter Philbin really was extraordinarily handsome. And she knew what she knew about Paul Martin. He was a man after her own heart. Ambitious. Single-minded. Ruthless in pursuit of his own goals.

The other contestants were ready to join the winner after the announcement. She could see them all jostling for position – apart from Katie Fisher. Pretending she wanted to go at the back. Pah! She hated dissemblers. No point in being on television unless you were *on* television. Self-effacement was wasted. Tanya Wilton was easing herself right to the front. Well done. And Alex Neil. Yes, let's get the gay thing going. Had Denise Trench been at the celebratory champagne? She made a quick note on her pad to check who had been slack enough to leave the bottles unattended – or if anyone had let the drunken old soak have first dibs.

She looked at the red figures on the clock as it counted down to the moment. And then there it was. There was the usual massive pause, which went on for ever …

'And the winner of *Celebrity X-Treme* is …'

She knew there would be people up and down the country mouthing their favourite at the screen, unaware that from the start there had only been one possible outcome.

'…'

Really, it was quite ridiculous how drawn out these things had become. She could have cut all her toenails and filed them in the time it was taking to announce the winner.

'…'

She felt a stiff hair poking through on her chin and fingered it lightly.

'… Paul Martin!'

Peter Philbin's face fell. She could tell he had been expecting to win. But he immediately put on a smile and turned to hug Paul, who was doing an expert job of looking shocked and amazed.

In Yorkshire, Bob watched Katie with hungry eyes. She looked beautiful, if tired. She had lost weight, he thought. Was she giving more attention to Paul Martin than anyone else? He couldn't tell, but he was jealous of everyone who was there and hugging her.

He heard a little snore. Elizabeth was asleep. She had done her best to stay awake but had fallen in the final furlong, her head back. Bob wrapped her securely in the duvet and took her upstairs, giving her a feather-light kiss on her forehead as he turned on the fairy lantern by the side of her bed.

CHAPTER NINETEEN

The after-show party was wild. The hotel's reception room had been swathed in red and white satin. There were huge bowls of punch on some of the tables, bottles of beer marching together along one bar and an enormous vodka luge.

Paul Martin was the last to make an appearance, wearing an intricate gold crown. He got a standing ovation – although it would have been difficult to do it sitting since there were very few chairs. This was, after all, a party, and the production company was hoping for dancing and inappropriate behaviour, which could be cobbled together for an 'and finally' programme, to be slotted in wherever the schedules allowed.

Katie had been looking forward to it to take her mind off an unsettling conversation she had had with her brother Ben that afternoon. Their father had apparently been overcome by an unusual bout of intransigence and was even talking about divorce. He was living with a friend of his they had never heard him mention. 'He's turning into a bit of a dark horse, is Dad,' he had said.

'You're making it sound like a joke,' said Katie, tersely.

'They're grown-ups. They can do whatever they want to do. If he's had enough of Mum or she's had enough of him …'

'Hardly likely.'

'Whatever … well, it's up to them to work it out. Nothing we can do.'

'Yes, there is.'

'What?'

'Give them a good talking-to. Explain why it's imperative they stay together.'

'But it's not imperative,' he asserted.

'It is,' she stressed. 'I'd come from a broken home.' She sensed him smiling even though he was hundreds of miles away. 'Yes, OK,' she admitted, 'I concede that it perhaps wouldn't make any difference to the outcome if we did speak to them. But you must find it as upsetting as I do.'

'You've had less time to get used to the idea, that's all,' he said.

In the intervening time, she had been mulling it over in her head. She kept imagining scenarios that would bring them together. Whatever the ruse, though, it foundered on the stubbornness of both parties. Jack was usually the emollient one and if he couldn't be budged …

Eventually, she had taken the bull by the horns, and phoned her dad on the number he had given at his friend's house, with little idea of what she was going to say. The conversation had lasted more than an hour, and towards the end she had become acutely conscious of the bill that must be racking up on her mobile.

'I'm sorry, Katie,' he had said, 'but you haranguing me isn't going to make me change my mind. Your mother and I have always had our differences, and in the past we've worked through them. But there comes a time when you've had enough of pulling in opposite directions. When you yearn, positively yearn, for a quiet life. I feel unhappy. What else can I say? You talk to your mother. I'm sure she'll tell you her side of the story. I can't live with the non-stop grumbling, griping and sniping. You've been at the sharp end long enough to know how it eventually wears you down. I can't cope with what she's become, and that's the truth. She's turned into a harridan. I can barely put down a cup without it being moved. Whatever I say, she contradicts me. She's sucked out my energy. I don't want to end my days feeling like I'm in the way and always in the wrong. Do you understand?'

Katie was silent.

'Katie?'

She sniffed, and blew her nose sideways into a tissue, with the phone still clutched to her ear. 'Yes. I'm still here. I didn't realize it had got that bad. Would it do any good if I called Mum?'

'Of course you should call her. I can't at the moment because I'm so angry.'

And hurt, she would bet.

She splashed cold water on her face and composed herself.

Her mother had sounded robust. 'I know what you're going to say, Katie.'

'No, you don't. You can't,' she responded. 'I don't even know myself.'

'Fine. Go on, then. I assume you've been speaking to your father. When you next talk to him, can you tell him the dog's pining for him? If he gets somewhere settled, he can come and pick Hercules up.'

This was awful. It was like watching a depressing French film in black-and-white. 'Mum, don't be silly. How about going to Relate?'

'At our age? Don't be silly, to quote you back to yourself. I know that it's a shock, Katie, but I've come to terms with it. Lots of women manage very happily on their own.'

'But you're not one of them, Mum.'

'Oh, don't be ridiculous, Katie. Anyway, shouldn't you be getting on with filming?'

'You know it's all over. The only thing now is the party.'

Her mother could be heard drumming on the hall table. 'Do you think you did the right thing by going into it?'

Katie frowned. 'Has *Celebrity X-Treme* had something to do with why you and Dad have split up?'

Her mother was a little too quick to deny it. 'You always think you're the focal point of everyone's lives. You aren't,' she said briskly.

'Thanks, Mum. Of course I think I'm the centre of everyone's lives,' she said sarcastically. 'But did you and Dad argue over it?'

'We had a small disagreement.'

'And I know exactly whose side you'd have been on,' said Katie, pointedly.

'You're being very snippy. We had a disagreement over whether it was a good idea for your future career, that's all. It was a spurious argument because it was entirely your decision, obviously. Now I need to get on. Tell your dad about the dog, won't you?'

Katie was incensed. Parents. You couldn't leave them alone for a minute without them doing something stupid. She could have banged their heads together. She humphed quietly as she recognized her mother's expression. But it was beyond the pale. She couldn't bear the thought of not going home to 'Mum and Dad'. They were an entity. She never thought of one without the other.

She went and had a shower and got ready for the party.

So by the time Paul Martin entered the room, she had downed a couple of glasses of punch and some vodka shots and had the bit between her teeth.

Paul saw her immediately, as he accepted the felicitations of the cast, crew and fellow celebrities. He thought she looked stunning. She was wearing a green dress, which was moulded to her newly honed body, and her auburn hair shone in waves down her back.

He made a leisurely tour and, near a sneaky camera hidden by one of the columns, slipped his arms round her and gave her a hard, meaningful hug.

She flushed slightly. 'Well done,' she said, smiling and looking up into his eyes.

'Thanks. Do I get a congratulatory kiss?' he asked.

'Don't see why not,' she said. She lifted her face as he bent his head towards her and pressed his lips to hers.

She knew she should have stopped him. Of course she should have. But she was an addict. Kissing was like drinking the finest wine. More often than not it had no more meaning than that. A moment of supreme deliciousness. An indulgence.

And he was the most marvellous kisser. Strong and swift and dominating. Oh, it was so wonderful to be held and given such a thorough mauling.

She was brought up guiltily by Siobhan's voice.

'Adam will find that an edifying sight, no doubt,' she said caustically, as Paul withdrew his mouth, but left his arm draped casually across Katie's shoulders.

'Only if someone takes the trouble to tell him,' sparked Katie.

'There are cameras here, in case you'd forgotten,' she said.

Katie bit her lip. 'It doesn't have to go in, though, does it?' she mouthed to Siobhan, so that any lurking microphones couldn't pick it up. Siobhan simply smiled at her and walked away.

This was dreadful, thought Katie. She blamed the punch – it was obviously stronger than it looked.

Paul turned her towards him again, and it seemed as though he was going to make another attack on her lips. 'No. No. Stop it,' said Katie, angrily, and slightly slurring. 'Not here.' She left the room. He followed.

'You knew about the cameras!' she accused him.

'No, I didn't. Well, I suppose I sort of assumed there might be some somewhere,' he said.

She narrowed her eyes. 'Am I part of your game plan?'

'I don't get you. I think you're bloody gorgeous. I've never made any bones about that.'

Funny expression, she thought, woozily. Making no bones about something. Would it involve an awful lot of grinding?

'And you obviously don't care enough about the bloke you're with,' he continued, 'or you wouldn't be here. And you wouldn't be responding like this …' He pulled her towards him again. Although she put up a token resistance, there were no cameras in sight and she gave herself up fully to the luscious feeling. Bliss. He was a god. She loved him. Or she loved kissing him. This was what life was all about. Her parents' troubles receded. Adam receded. There was nothing but the fizzing in her blood.

On Saturday morning, Katie had such a big hangover that she could barely blink without a throbbing pain thumping through her skull. What the hell had been in that punch? She tried to lift her head off the pillow. It wouldn't go. It lay there, like a medicine ball. As parts of her brain began to activate, the memories started to seep in, then avalanched, building up into an unbearable catalogue of beautiful but ultimately terrible sequences. She pressed her hands to her eyes and tears leaked out.

She was a mess. There was no other word for it. She had, willingly or not, buggered up a perfectly good relationship for the instant gratification of a kiss. And she was seeing Adam today. She would have to make a clean breast of it, and leave it up to him to decide whether or not they would carry on. When had she heard herself say that before? She dragged her mind back to a similar incident involving a man at a nightclub.

If this was America, she thought, I'd be phoning a helpline this instant. Be seeing a therapist.

My name is Katie Fisher. I am a kissing addict.

Was it so bad?

Why was it so bad?

She wouldn't mind if she found out that Adam had been kissing someone else.

Or would she?

Yes, but the thing is, men never stopped at just kissing. Kissing for them was a prelude to sex. Women could enjoy it for the sheer delightfulness of it. But men didn't understand that. How could one explain it to them? It was like trying to describe the taste of an Irish whiskey to a teetotaller.

In the bus to the airport, she was unusually quiet. She had her huge sunglasses on and sat next to Dave Beal, knowing it gave neither of them any pleasure. She turned her face to the window and pretended to look out, but her eyes were closed as her discombobulated brain tried to find a way through.

Paul tried to talk to her, but she put up her hand and moved quickly away.

Eventually she came to a conclusion. She would think about it tomorrow. I'm turning into Scarlett O'Hara, she thought. She'd be pining for the red earth of Tara if she wasn't careful.

Paul Martin was hoping she would be pining for him. He was hoping that the footage of their kiss would precipitate the end of her relationship with that stuffed-shirt boyfriend. Not only did he find Katie seriously sexy, but it couldn't do his career any harm if he started dating a television presenter. Looking at her this morning, he thought it was a job done, and he was wise enough to let it go.

The flight was uneventful, the arrival back in Britain curiously flat after the hot-house atmosphere of *Celebrity X-Treme*. There was a clutch of photographers at the airport, but it was all over swiftly, and as afternoon verged towards evening, Katie let herself into her flat.

'Hello, flat,' she said, pleased to see that the cleaner had been in while she was away. There was a nice smell of wood polish, and a huge bunch of flowers in a vase on the table.

She put her bags in the bedroom before going to read the card. 'Welcome home. There's a little something in the fridge. See you tonight. Eight p.m. at Sheekey's. xxxxx'

Aaah. A wave of guilt threatened to engulf her. He was lovely. Truly lovely. She didn't deserve him. The flowers were beautiful. Pink and orange gerberas. She caressed one of the soft petals. If only they had a smell, gerberas would be the perfect flower.

They were so bright and so tidy. None of those pesky leaves to deal with, or polleny bits to cut off so they didn't stain where they fell.

She padded through to the kitchen. In the fridge she found a tiny bottle of champagne with a red ribbon round it, and a card saying: 'Drink me.' Next to it was a chocolate brownie from Maison au Chocolat with a card next to it, saying: 'Eat me.' She smiled. *Alice in Wonderland* – a book she occasionally quoted from.

She pulled out her mobile phone and sent him a text. 'No need to look for the Cheshire Cat – she's here. Love you. Thanks. See you at eight. xxxx'

First things first, though. The suitcases needed to be unpacked before she could do anything. As the washing machine set up its pleasant drone, she fixed herself a cup of coffee and sat down to make a call. 'Well, good evening, Mistress Dee,' she said, as the phone was answered, 'and I hope you're getting yourself ready for this evening's momentous event.'

Dee sounded breathless. 'I sort of am.'

'As in?'

'I can't find my dress. My shoes have gone walkabout. And I put a conditioning treatment on my hair and it's gone as limp as a lettuce. And I think I'm developing a spot.'

'Hmm. So, situation normal.'

'And if he *is* going to propose, I'm going to look like shit.'

'No, you won't. You're working yourself up into a state. Tell me what you can see in the bedroom.'

'Your idea of hell. Clothes everywhere.'

'Can you see one dress – any dress?'

'Yes. It's that boring black one. And it's got a funny stain on it.'

'Right. Well, that's what you're wearing. You've got time to wash it in cold water, after getting rid of the stain …' And Katie talked Dee down from panic. 'Don't forget to say yes,' she admonished her.

Having done her good deed, she slurped the dregs of her coffee and went to get the bottle of champagne and the chocolate brownie. The knowledge of her perfidy hung over her head like a halo of thorns. It was almost impossible to see a way through that would allow her to converse in a normal way. It would be hovering there, waiting to make itself known. She knew that some things were best left unsaid. Was this one of them? What did it mean, after all? A drunken kiss … like every other drunken kiss she had indulged in. And lost the love of her life. She caught herself up guiltily. Did I just say that? Did I just use the expression 'love of my life'? About Bob?

Anyone looking in on the scene would have recognized a woman wrestling with a dilemma. She sat on the sofa, a glass in one hand, a brownie in the other, knees together and feet splayed, gazing out of the window at the river. As the washing-machine went onto spin cycle, she sighed and got up. Things to do, places to be. No time like the present. Idle hands make light work. What was she on about? She ought to get on. She strode determinedly through to the bedroom.

* * *

A few hours later, she was having her coat taken from her at the restaurant and was enveloped in an enormous hug by Adam. He was so handsome, she thought, her body thrilling to his touch.

'Thank you for my gifts,' she said, green eyes sparkling up at him. She had supplemented the champagne with a few vodka shots for Dutch courage.

Adam recognized the signs, but didn't say anything. He beckoned the waiter over. 'Shall we continue with the theme?' he asked her, and, with her assent, ordered a bottle of Krug.

'How lovely. My favourite.'

'I know … So tell me …' he said, as it arrived, both of them aware of the metaphorical elephant in the room '… how did you leave Mr Martin? Was he well?'

'I know what you're thinking. I saw what the newspapers were saying. I was given some of them after I got the bump on my head. I left a message for you about it.'

'Yes, I know.' He smiled, his eyes crinkling attractively. 'Your lovely long message that went on right through two meetings and into an early-evening drink.'

'It did not.' She laughed, her heart beating uncomfortably hard. Now that the moment had come, she was wondering whether she ought to 'fess up, as their father used to say when she or Ben were caught doing something naughty.

'And?'

'And it's out of all proportion to what actually happened. They were making out that I was having an affair with him. And I was categorically not. Absolutely not.'

She felt like Clinton and his 'I did not have sexual relations with that woman' comment. It wasn't a lie. It just wasn't quite the truth.

Katie pressed on: 'Compared to you, he's a munter. Why would I risk losing you for the dubious pleasure of an affair with a two-bit columnist?' she asked, appealing to his vanity.

And Adam, having come to a similar conclusion, was willing to leave it there. He had decided to broach the subject now and find out the details later. He had clean sheets on the bed, breakfast organized, and he wasn't about to ruin the evening. 'I believe you. Thousands wouldn't,' he said.

It was the one expression he used frequently that annoyed her. But she was in no position to bring it up now. Suddenly her dress felt less constricting. And she was glad she was wearing stockings. It was all looking a lot more positive.

Apart from that niggling doubt at the back of her mind. Was Bob really the love of her life? And if he was, what was she doing playing out this other relationship? Unconsciously, she began to compare the two men. The one so very fitting for her city life. The other an altogether kinder prospect. A man for all seasons. She wondered how it was possible to be thinking these thoughts while listening to Adam telling her *his* thoughts about the show and the fallout from it. Then he stopped, and she realized that, actually, it wasn't possible, because he seemed to be requiring an answer, and she hadn't heard the question.

She fell back on the traditional response she used in these situations. 'I'm sorry,' she said, 'I wasn't listening. Just kind of gazing at you and thinking that you are, without doubt, the most attractive man alive.'

'You are incorrigible,' he said, shaking his head. 'If you weren't looking so utterly sumptuous yourself, I'd be walking out right this minute.'

Inside, he was more than a little peeved. But he had sat through enough business meetings in his life to be able to hide his emotions fairly easily. He was not sure that this relationship was going to last the course, and had unconsciously begun to compare her unfavourably with the elegant Madame d'Ombard.

Across town, Dee and Oliver were sitting in their favourite little family-run Italian restaurant, where Dee was generally able to tell the next day what she had enjoyed by the sploshes on her clothes. She could never resist spaghetti.

Tonight, however, she had not managed to eat much of it because of the butterflies in her stomach. She wanted Oliver to ask her to marry him more than she had wanted a guinea pig when she was eight. The spaghetti *vongole* was removed, and she dabbed ineffectually at a few of the oily marks she could see on her neckline.

In the middle of her ministrations she looked up to see a small velvet box on the table in front of her. With shaky hands, she opened it. It took her just moments to accept and to upset most of the crockery on the table in the rush to hug her new fiancé. Oliver's happy nod to the waiter brought the bottle of champagne.

The antique square-cut diamond ring was beautiful. She stuck her hand closer to the candle to admire it and the smell of singed skin rose to her nostrils. 'Whoops. Think I've burned my hand,' she said gaily, anaesthetized by ecstasy.

Oliver reached out to take it and examined it as closely as he could in the flickering light. 'You should go and run it under the cold tap,' he said solicitously.

'All right, Doctor,' she said, only too thrilled to go and have a better look in a brighter environment. She kissed him fully on the lips, caressed his neck, and went to the loo, grasping the opportunity to send Katie a quick text: 'He did. I said yes.'

CHAPTER TWENTY

April stood aside for May, and clothed Britain in a cloud of blossom and blue skies.

Katie had almost begun to believe she had got away with her random act of kissing Paul Martin. Amazingly, the footage had not appeared anywhere. She wasn't to know that Siobhan had combed the pictures and failed to find a single frame. She had refused to return Paul's texts and phone calls, and he had gradually been overtaken by a whirl of meetings to capitalize on his new-found fame. He had also discovered that his appearance on *Celebrity X-Treme* had gained him an army of female admirers, and was busy availing himself of their ample charms. He believed it was only a matter of time before he found one who was as sexy, witty and, frankly, newsworthy as Katie Fisher.

She kept in touch with Tanya and Flynn – and Flynn had done Oliver and Dee's astrological chart. They looked very compatible. Katie thought she might buy them the biggest blanket box in the world as a present so that Oliver could throw all her junk straight into it, bypassing the clutter-on-the-tables stage. Katie was saving the chart to hand over at the wedding in September.

The others from *Celebrity*, she saw frequently in the newspapers during the immediate aftermath of the show, and then more infrequently, apart from Crystal and Peter Philbin, who were now something of a fixture on the nightclub circuit.

For herself, she was pleased to reveal to those who asked that she had a new series she was working on, involving women's issues. It would mean travel to a number of places and she was passionate about it. Actually, she was looking forward to doing anything that didn't include a whole load of people being manipulative, or flirty, or stupid, or a combination of all three.

The weeks following the end of *Celebrity X-Treme* had been busy. Adam had whisked her off for a weekend in Paris and shown her his new flat. It was airy and pretty, all beige and white. Very elegant. But although their relationship appeared to be back on an even keel, a certain matter was unresolved. He had appeared to accept her explanation about Paul Martin at face value, but occasional barbed comments had been made. She had tried to ignore them, but they had a habit of resurfacing at romantic moments. Adam had dead-batted her attempts to 'have it out', and she had decided that eventually he would stop picking at the scab, as it were.

There was also the problem with her parents. They were still living apart, and the longer it went on, the more entrenched both sides seemed to be. And despite her brother saying that they had to be left to it, Katie felt that enough was enough. She had called a powwow for Friday night.

'I don't want to be sitting here in two years' time with hideous step-parents. The idea of Dad and some revolting young floozy is too disgusting to contemplate. Or Mum and some young stud muffin. Yergh.'

She had had to tempt him to the dinner by promising to bring Tanya.

Bob rang Ben to see if he wanted to be involved in a boys' weekend in London. Harry had bought tickets to see Bill Bailey, and one of their friends had pulled out at the last minute.

'It's supposed to be brilliant,' said Bob.

'Actually, I *am* free on Saturday night,' said Ben, 'so you can definitely count me in. And ... erm, tell you what, Bob, thinking aloud on this one, what are you doing on the Friday night?'

'We're driving down to London. ETA about pub opening time, then we'll be going to a selection of strip bars, Stringfellows, a clip joint and finally a massage parlour, where four women inadequately dressed for a chilly night will waft us away to Paradise.'

'Right.' Ben laughed. 'I assume that the only factually correct part of that sentence is the pub.'

'Yup.'

'So how do you fancy coming for dinner with Katie and Tanya, her new bessie mate from *Celebrity X-Treme*? Now, don't say anything straight away. Have a think about it. I realize you have two friends with you, but maybe you could meet up with them later. It's just that Katie's insisting we have a push to try to sort out Mum and Dad. And you obviously have something to bring to the table since Dad stayed with you for a week. If Katie's up for it, would you be?'

Bob hesitated, unable to decipher quite how he felt about the prospect of seeing Katie for the first time since they had split up for the second time.

Ben pushed on: 'Don't make the decision yet. Have a think and phone me back. But it would be useful. Even if you came for a starter. Or a glass of tomato juice.'

'Bugger me, what an incentive. Almost impossible to resist,' said Bob, with mock-appreciation. 'You're right. I do need to have a think about it. When do you need to know by?'

'As soon as.'

And an hour later Bob had texted his acceptance.

Ben then sent a text to Katie.

When she finally opened it – being involved in a tricky spot of fridge cleaning – she stood looking at it for a while. Her initial feeling was to say, no, it was out of the question, but the more she thought about it, the more sense it made – he had housed her father for a week, after all. And she refused to acknowledge the rapid beating of her heart that accompanied the text she sent to Ben. She also convinced herself that it was mere forgetfulness that led to her not mentioning Bob's dinner attendance to her boyfriend.

* * *

When *Celebrity X-Treme* finished, Siobhan Stamp was – to her immense satisfaction – immediately approached by another production company, impressed by what she had achieved. She accepted with alacrity, and took a well-earned holiday in Dubai, where she succumbed to the advances of a rich American businessman who paid for all of her dinners and gave her an expensive watch as a parting gift. She loved a man's company – as long as he owned it – but she was pleased that he went before the end of the holiday so that she could enjoy herself and not have his fat, sweaty body all over her, even if she had enjoyed the charms of his wallet.

And she could luxuriate in the knowledge that she had done a fine job of getting back at Adam and Katie. She had pulled the strings to make Katie look like the fat, silly slapper she was, and had therefore put a thorn in her and Adam's relationship … while having, rather cleverly, made Adam pay – literally.

She applied a little more suntan lotion to those areas of pale skin that were exposed to the elements, and went back to her book.

At Wolf Days Productions it was full speed ahead with *Behind the Seams*, the new programme that had been written with Keera Keethley in mind.

Adam had explained to Katie that it was nothing personal. 'Surely you're big enough to see beyond this,' he had said, when she had challenged him about working with her usurper at *Hello Britain!*. And because she had felt guilty about Paul

Martin – would probably feel guilty for the rest of her life – she had said nothing further.

Nick, meanwhile, had confined himself to a working relationship with Keera. Their dinner meeting had remained that, a dinner meeting, much to her chagrin.

What she couldn't have known was that he shared one major trait with Adam: a fear of boredom. And that she had been so amazingly tedious on the subject of Keera Keethley that he couldn't even summon up the energy for bedroom frolics. He had no objection to sex with bimbos, but it was not worth the aggro if he was going to end up working with her. And, weeks down the line, he was glad he hadn't. It made his job easier, since he was the one who was dealing with the programme. They had agreed that Adam would be fairly hands-off the project in deference to his girlfriend.

But, in the midst of negotiations with fashion correspondents, designers and manufacturers, Adam opened a phone bill that threw the cat among the pigeons. It was for at least a hundred thousand pounds more than usual. He took it through to Nick's office. 'Look at this,' he said, throwing it onto the table.

Nick looked stunned. What a bloody big bill. Is it definitely ours?'

'I'll call the phone company. Just wanted to check with you before I did. Any ideas?'

'No. We haven't started working on Katie's programme yet, so no massive international calls. Is it worth getting it itemized?'

'It'd probably take so much paper, we'd have to get the foundations strengthened.'

'How's it going with *Behind the Seams*?' asked Adam, rolling up the sleeves of his favourite navy Armani shirt.

'Fine. We've had a query over presenters from the BBC, though. The top bod there wants us to go in for a meeting with Keera.'

'Strange,' said Adam. 'Never known that happen before. Why?'

'I don't know. But it's no problem. I'll go and see some other people while I'm there.'

Keera had been unbearable at *Hello Britain!*. There was no one who didn't know that she had a new series lined up for prime time. 'I think it. It happens,' she said to herself, as she gazed into her eyes in the dressing-room mirror. She thought back to how she had seen herself reflected in a shoe-shop window, surrounded by shoes. 'And now, here I am, doing a programme about shoes. And about clothes.' She hoped she'd get loads of designer freebies. They were hardly going to let her do a show about high fashion without putting her in designer outfits, were they?

Derek came in to ask her what she was wearing on air.

'These shoes.' She indicated the tan Patrick Cox platforms she had on. 'So choose anything, really.' She wafted a hand in the direction of the suits and dresses, and swayed off to the makeup department.

'Will do, madam,' mouthed Derek, to her departing back. 'Anything else madam will be requiring? A wipe of the royal arse, maybe?'

Vanda was applying a light layer of foundation to Dee's face.

'I'm trying so hard to lose weight,' Dee said.

Vanda reached for the concealer. 'It's beyond boring going on diets, though, particularly when you get up at this time of the morning, and your body clock's all over the place,' she said.

Keera went over to the big mirror on the other side of the room, and began to use the straighteners to iron out any kinks in her thick black hair. If either of them had any self-control … she thought, as she sprayed hair-protector on a section and applied the tongs. They were probably a pair of pigs. Would she have the body of a goddess if she didn't go to the gym every day except Sunday, and limit herself to a thousand calories a day?

'Pigs,' she said accidentally, surprising all three of them.

'Talking about us?' asked Dee, startled.

'Sorry,' said Keera, a tinge of flush to her cheeks. 'I was just, erm …'

'Joining in,' said Vanda, none too kindly, 'and claiming we were pigs.'

'No, I wasn't,' said Keera, blushing hotly now.

Dee turned back to the mirror, smiling at the rather sniffy Vanda. 'I'm wearing lilac today. Can I have that nice Mac purple eyeliner you've got in your special bag for special people?'

'Ah. The liquid eyeliner with glitter? Yes, *you* can,' Vanda said pointedly.

'You know, going back to the food thing, I reckon my body just can't be bothered to sort it out,' said Dee, thoughtfully. 'With most people, it starts dealing with, say, a meat pasty by sending the protein to the muscles, the vitamins to the skin and eyes or whatever, and then what's left over gets stored as fat. I think my body says, "Let's stuff everything on the bottom and thighs, and we'll divvy it up later." Then it just messes about and never gets round to it.'

Or maybe you eat too many doughnuts, thought Keera, putting a small amount of gloss serum through her hair.

'So, have you thought about the wedding dress?'

'Cream. Heavy satin. Tight bodice, with a dropped waist and a skirt that flows out the back just a bit. A long, thick wrap affair for over my shoulders. Hair up. Discreet makeup with light pinky lipgloss. A posy of cream roses. And cream shoes from Emma Hope. I bought them yesterday, along with a beautiful pair of Fogal stockings with lacy tops. And pure silk knickers from Myla. Oliver's promised to buy those for me. Although he'd better get large because I can't be doing with tight pants,' she finished.

'Nothing definite yet, then – still all up in the air?' Vanda snorted.

'Ha-ha. I know. But I couldn't be more excited.'

'More exciting than the first time?'

'Yes. I love Oliver.'

'You must have loved the first husband?'

'I honestly can't remember. I suppose I must have *thought* I loved him. But he was a – a—'

'Man. And that's the problem,' said Vanda, emphatically.

'Aw. Poor men. They do get a raw deal, don't they?' asked Dee.

'Just because you're all loved up,' said Vanda, sourly. 'I'll give you a couple of years and you'll be coming in saying, "Why can they never find anything, even though they're looking right at it?" And "Why does their helping round the house consist of them sitting in front of the television?" You know, I could write a Top Ten of rubbish things about men.'

She did a Fluff Freeman impression, using a brush as a microphone: 'At number ten we have leaving the loo seat up. Coming in at number nine, "Where are my socks?" At number eight it's the dropping the clothes *by* the laundry basket, not *in* it. Number seven – a real climber here – "I'm hungry. Why is there nothing in the fridge?"'

Dee laughed, as the sound girl came in. 'Number six,' she joined in, putting the belt round her waist for the microphone and talkback equipment, '"I'll do that in a minute." Followed by number five, "I've *said* I'll do that in a minute. Stop hassling me."'

'I know,' said Vanda, 'and in the end, you do it yourself and they get all annoyed, and accuse you of trying to undermine them. They're a nightmare. My mum was right when she said there was only one way to a man's heart.'

'Through their stomach, mine used to say,' said Dee.

'Nope. Through their chest cavity. Are you going to have loads of children, do you think?'

'Oi. Hang on. Haven't got married yet.'

'What? And you'd be the first person down the aisle with a bump?'

'I'm not dieting to get into a dress and ruining it by being pregnant. No way,' said Dee, disappearing out of the door to get ready for her first weather bulletin.

Rod and Keera were already sitting on the famous sofa as she went to stand in front of the green screen. In her earpiece, she heard the director saying, 'Dee's chroma needs to be tweaked.'

She held her microphone up to her mouth: 'Oh, I do like a thorough tweaking of a morning.'

She heard the director laugh, but he was having a bad moment. 'What's going on with this mixer desk? Graphics don't come up. And I've just tried firing one of the VTs and it won't come on.'

One of the producers working on the news bulletins could be heard shouting: 'Rewrite on 253, the dustbins item.'

'A new mixer isn't going to help with that,' said the director's assistant.

Keera had not been able to resist sniping at Rod ever since the article in the *Daily Mail*.

'We'll do a quick ad lib about Spain after this VT,' said Rod.

'Mmm,' said Keera, 'I was thinking it reminded me of California.'

'I don't think we've got long enough to go round comparing Spain to America. We've only got thirty seconds, not three minutes,' said Rod, tetchily.

The VT ended.

'I *love* Spain,' said Keera. 'How do you think it compares to America, though?' she asked sweetly.

One–nil, thought Dee.

In the morning meeting afterwards, Rod was overheard telling a producer a joke very loudly as Keera entered the room. 'What do you call a beautiful woman who is also intelligent?' he asked. And before the producer had time to respond, he said, 'A rumour,' and laughed at his joke.

One–all, thought Dee.

Keera smiled a smug smile. 'Be careful, Rod. You know how your little sayings sometimes make it into the papers.'

Game, set and match to Miss Keethley, thought Dee.

Rod had been horrified to discover that it was his daughter who had stitched him up, in retaliation for being grounded. He had come home shaken after being carpeted by The Boss and told his family he was now worried his job wasn't safe. Eleanor had told her mother first, then cried all over Rod until he had forgiven her.

'Nobody died,' he had said finally, when her sobbing threatened to wash away some of the furniture. And, as he told his wife later, 'At least she's got her work-experience week sorted out!'

* * *

Friday was shaping up to be one of the worst days on record for rainfall and high winds. Katie phoned her brother to check what time they were meeting that night.

'I assume the dress code is wellies and sou'westers.' She laughed, looking out of the rain-lashed windows. 'What awful weather – a proper Thomas Hardy day.'

'I have no idea what you're talking about,' said Ben, who only read books featuring psychopathic killers or CIA operatives.

'Pathetic fallacy. Or is it prophetic fallacy? No. Must be "pathetic". Oh, I don't know. Whatever it is, it means when nature reflects what the character is feeling.'

'So you're feeling wet and windy? As a doctor, I'd suggest an incontinence pad and some charcoal tablets.'

'Thank you. But no. It doesn't mean that. It means you'd be feeling sad. Rain equals tears and wind equals … well, just a turbulent emotional period. Or something. It's been a long time since I did A-level English. Anyway,' she lengthened the word, 'it's eight o'clock this evening, right?'

'Yup. Can I say I'm very much looking forward to meeting your new friend, Tanya?'

'Yes, you can say that. I hope she's up to a conversation about Mum and Dad, since that's what we're there for. You will remember that, won't you?'

'How could I forget? Although I still think it's not up to us …'

'Grrr. We've been through this before, Benjamin Fisher. I'll see you at eight.'

Katie had still not told Adam that Bob would be at the dinner. There had been moments when she'd felt it on the tip of her tongue, but she had bitten it back. Better to let him know he had a pink ticket and was free to do what he wanted because she was having a Parent Summit. No point in rocking the shaky boat.

She was annoyed that her heart would not obey her command to stop racing and lurching when her brain thought about Bob. Bodies. Couldn't live with them. Couldn't live without them. Or you'd look bloody odd without one. She giggled.

Almost a whole day to get ready. What luxury.

Hundreds of miles north, Bob was on his Triumph, concentrating hard in the hideous weather as he sped along the country roads to Harry's house. He arrived soaked to the skin.

'Oh, for goodness' sake. It's the man from Atlantis,' said Sophie, as she opened the door.

Bob smiled as he unzipped his motorcycle jacket and waterproof trousers and left them in the porch, along with his boots. 'Sorry. I appear to be a bit damp. The Landie's stuffed again. I'm hoping my overnight bag hasn't suffered too much. I put everything in a plastic bag inside it,' he said, dumping his small rucksack on the floor and opening it to check.

'Why didn't you tell Harry to come and pick you up *en route*?' She tutted.

'Because he's doing me a favour by driving to London in the first place. Otherwise I'd have had to go down on the bike in this shitty weather, or taken the train. Look, I'm dry underneath – apart from a damp spot at the back of my neck. Motorbike clothing is superb, these days. Where is Harry?' he asked, looking around.

'Primping,' she said, nodding upstairs. 'Go up if you want. He'll be applying the first layer of moisturizer and under-eye lotion.'

Bob laughed and went up.

'I'm in here,' called Harry, having heard his arrival.

He was in the bedroom throwing things willy-nilly into a tan leather holdall.

'I was in the middle of a tricky timepiece and got absorbed. I'll be ready in a minute.'

'Your wife said you'd be moisturizing.'

'What does she know?'

'I am a big fan of moisturizer. You can never be too soft.'

'You're not wearing that for your special dinner, are you?' asked Harry, standing up and eyeing Bob critically.

'Fuck off,' said Bob, calmly.

Harry smiled.

'You look very pretty. Is that a Paul Smith blouse?'

'It's actually Kenzo for Hommes,' responded Bob.

'Ooo. Posh. You look good in blue, I must say. It matches your eyes,' said Harry, with a gay flourish.

'Why thank you, kind sir. Can we get a move on, or we'll be late?'

'You looking forward to it?'

'With trepidation.'

'Ah. Are you going to tell her how you feel?'

'What do you think?' asked Bob. 'She's got a boyfriend. He's everything I'm not, plus he lives in London.'

'Well, all right. But I don't see why you can't put the thought out there,' said Harry.

'Sort of "Hello, Katie, if ever you give up that rich bloke, the sad loser from the north is still available"?'

Harry zipped up his bag. 'Right. Done. We can talk more in the car.'

'Is Ed with us?'

'Nope. Meeting us there. He's in Nottingham today, so he'll go on the train. He's coming back with us on Sunday. Assuming you're not happily ensconced in Miss Fisher's bed.'

Bob shook his head. 'You're an incorrigible optimist. For all I know, she's spitting tacks that I'm going to be there, and has only agreed because I was the last person to see Jack before he walked out.'

'It's unbelievable, his walking out like that after all these years. And well done to you for taking him in, I say. Thousands wouldn't.'

'I really like him. And, strictly between you, me and the gatepost, I loved having him around. Not only did he cook for me, but it was like having Katie there in the background. You can see where she gets all the bad puns and silly word stuff from.'

'Well, let's hope this is third time lucky for you.'

CHAPTER TWENTY-ONE

Although Ben Fisher had booked a table at a restaurant with no celebrity clientele, someone must have let the newspapers know. He arrived to find a gang of paparazzi already gathered, and his sister inside, seething. 'How did they find out we were here?' she hissed, as he kissed her cheek.

'No idea,' he said, his face set. 'It wasn't me. Do you think Tanya phoned them?'

'I did tell her it was going to be a quiet one, so I hope not.'

And when Tanya arrived, she confirmed that she had told no one what she was up to that evening. 'Sometimes they find out through friends of friends,' she said.

'Or through the restaurant ringing up for more publicity,' said Katie, with a darkling look.

'Well, whatever, it's happened. Let's make the best of it. Should I phone Bob and warn him?'

'What can he do? Put his head under a handy blanket?' asked Katie. 'Anyway, it's all about Tanya and her love life, these days, isn't it?' She winked at her friend, who wriggled in the seat and smirked at Ben. He was every bit as good-looking as he was in the photos Katie had shown her in Norway.

Bob arrived unmolested by the paps. Katie's heart constricted as he smiled his hellos. He was so handsome. His hair stuck up rakishly, his eyes were as blue as she remembered, and the shirt he was wearing clung to his taut stomach. Her own stomach lurched as he kissed her cheek chastely. It was all she could do to stop herself moving her mouth closer and fastening it on his. God, what kissable lips he had. That thought was swiftly followed by the stern reminder that she had a boyfriend. In any case, she and Bob had already tried twice. What on earth was she thinking? This was madness.

Bob, too, had a racing pulse. Katie was wearing a soft green plunging top, revealing a hint of lacy bra beneath, and a small diamond necklace. He didn't want to stare, but he wondered if it was the one he had bought her after the reconciliation in Dorset. That night had almost made up for the wrench of their split. There was nothing quite like making love with heightened emotions.

While Bob and Katie quietly assessed their responses to each other, Tanya and Ben were busy flirting. Ben had not had a long-term girlfriend for years, claiming the pressure of work. Katie reckoned it had more to do with his list of non-negotiable attributes – he was too damned fussy – and Ben capitulated: there was no point, he thought, in giving up a comfortable bachelor existence for anything but perfection.

He wouldn't have considered Tanya as a girlfriend if he hadn't been forced to watch *Celebrity X-Treme*. She had crossed his radar as a mistress to an MP, and that was it. But he had decided he liked her forthright way of calling a spade a spade, and her readiness to laugh at herself and at the vagaries of the press that had vilified her.

As Tanya entertained Ben, she studied the body language of the other two from the corner of her eye. Something was going on between them, she thought. There was unfinished business there.

The conversation got very silly, very quickly.

'And not only did I end up with those wretched pants on my head virtually on day one,' said Katie, giggling as Tanya egged her on, 'but I had some Canesten cream in my sponge-bag – due to *you*,' she wagged a finger at Ben, 'telling me I should always carry some in case I got any fungal infections. It's good for everything from athlete's foot to ringworm, Tanya, apparently, and I mistook it for my toothpaste one night. And there I was, wondering why it didn't foam up. How to look like a total moron.'

Ben put his hands up. 'Yes. I confess I did tell her many years ago about the Canesten. And when she was eleven I told her to go into medicine. So she doesn't always take my advice.'

'Can you imagine me as a doctor? Really?' said Katie. 'You saw me on *Celebrity*. If I don't like people, I don't like them. I'd want to cull them. Dave Unfunny Beal, for example. Take him out and shoot him. Keera Keethley. I'd force her to play in the snow in a tank top and shorts.'

'Very horny image,' said Ben, nodding. 'I'd suggest that too.'

'You have no discrimination. She is a brainless bitch from hell.'

'Tell us what you *really* think, why don't you?' said Ben, eating ten skinny chips in one go and washing them down with a big gulp of wine.

'Ah, but when Katie likes people,' said Tanya, without thinking, 'she *really* likes them.' She had meant to say it in reference to Bob but, coming hot on the heels of talk about *Celebrity X-Treme*, they were all suddenly uncomfortably aware of what had gone on between Katie and Paul Martin. She made a face. 'Whoops,' she said. 'That was a right clanger, wasn't it? But, look, she didn't do what they said she'd done with that bloke. Did you, Katie? Hey, defend me, won't you?'

Katie smiled. 'You really are a ruddy hazard. Ben already knows that it didn't happen as they suggested. And Bob probably doesn't care.' She looked at him.

He had cared. Very much. He had watched her flirting with the columnist and had hoped she was doing it because her relationship with Adam was on the rocks. He was still confused, but couldn't see any way to bring it up that wouldn't lay himself open. 'I know that clever editing can imply all sorts of things,' he said. And then, because Katie was gazing at him in a way that made him feel hot and bothered, he called a waiter over for the wine menu. 'Shall we have the same again?' he asked generally.

'By the way,' said Katie, in the lull in the conversation, 'can we have a moment to talk about why we're here tonight?'

'Oh, no,' groaned Ben. 'Can't it wait? It's not as though anything disastrous is going to happen if we don't do this now. Can't we have a nice evening with friends?'

'But you know that's why I organized this,' said Katie, narrowing her eyes.

'Oh, all right,' said Ben, wearily. 'You OK for this, Bob? And you, Tanya? You don't even know the protagonists.'

Tanya put her hand over his. 'It's fine. I was warned. And I come from what is colloquially termed a broken home, so I can maybe offer my own insights.'

Bob raised his glass of wine. 'And, of course, it's why I'm here,' he said simply.

'How was Dad when he stayed with you?' asked Katie.

Bob considered. 'Erm, I'm assuming you know why he left your mother?'

'Well, he said it was because he was fed up with being taken for granted.'

'Yep. That's what he told me too. And then he went home after you had that argument with a cupboard, imagining that it would all be back on track. But he said she immediately started having a go at him.'

'She told *me* he'd gone boring on her and spent all his time doing cooking and gardening – oh, and fishing with you, Bob,' said Ben.

'And that's all possibly true,' said Katie, 'except that she goes off on her own and does all her stuff. What was he supposed to do?'

'I know I'm the interloper here,' said Tanya, 'but do you think they've really fallen out of love with each other, or that they've got set in their ways and haven't worked out what are probably quite small differences? I say small in that if it's him feeling taken for granted and your mum saying he's boring, then it isn't that difficult to see that they need to do some talking.'

There was a moment's silence as they digested her comments.

'But how do we get them talking again?'

'I could take them both fishing,' suggested Bob.

Katie laughed. 'Oh, I can so see Mum dressed in waders, spending three hours up to her thighs in cold water.'

'You don't need to go that far, surely,' said Tanya. 'I mean, you could think up an excuse as to why you need them to be at a family gathering.'

'Hmm,' said Katie. 'But what would we need to talk about that requires them to be there at the same time?'

The waiter arrived with the new bottle of wine and Bob sampled it. 'That's fine,' he said, gesturing to the man to fill the glasses.

Ben was gazing into the middle distance. 'Yes, usually only births, weddings and deaths bring families together. And that ain't happening any time soon. Or is it?' He raised an eyebrow at Katie.

She shook her head emphatically, hoping that Bob was taking note. He was.

They sat sipping their wine.

'Hey, I've had an idea,' said Tanya, suddenly, her eyes sparkling. 'You live nearby, right?' she asked Bob, who nodded. 'So, why doesn't one of you,' she gestured at Katie and Ben, 'speak to your parents and invite them to a special dinner at Bob's?'

They looked confused.

'You know,' she rushed on, 'Katie phones her dad and says there's a dinner at Bob's and she needs him to be there as her date, or whatever. And Ben phones your mum and says the same. And then – God, I'm so brilliant – when they turn up, there's just the two of them. The dinner's in the oven. The candles are lit. But you've all scarpered. And they have to speak to each other.' She looked at their faces, seeing doubt that it would work. She pressed on. 'And maybe you've got bunches of flowers everywhere and there's a card on them, saying, "Sorry. I love you", with kisses and things. Not addressed to anyone. But they think they're for them. Obviously, because no one else is there.' She raised her eyebrows questioningly.

Katie was the first to break the silence as they digested the suggestion. 'But as soon as they found out we'd done it, we'd be back to square one,' she reasoned.

'Only if they really don't want to be together,' said Tanya. 'That's why I asked whether they wanted to be together but were going through a sort of late mid-life crisis.'

'You know, it might work,' said Bob, thoughtfully.

'You reckon?' asked Ben.

'Well, it's not the worst idea in the world.'

'Hey, thanks,' said Tanya, in a mock huff.

Bob smiled at her.

God, thought Tanya, what a devastating smile. If Katie didn't mind, she might have a pop at him if Ben didn't cut the mustard.

Bob liked her. He thought she was an open and generous woman. But his entire being was hard-wired to Katie, who at this minute was chewing her bottom lip in concentration. He wondered how she would respond if he asked to take over from her teeth. He couldn't stop a small laugh escaping.

Katie looked at him with enquiry in her green eyes.

He recovered quickly. 'I was imagining the scene,' he said.

'Yes,' she said. 'Funnily enough, it works for me. Big bunches of flowers. Food in the oven. And presumably in the fridge. If we *were* to do this, then who would cook?'

'Well, we could all lump in, couldn't we?' asked Bob.

'I think you're forgetting that Ben could cock up slicing a tomato,' she said caustically. 'He's famous for his burnt offerings. Mum and Dad would turn up along with the Fire Brigade and have to rescue the singed cat.'

'OK. So you and I do the food,' said Bob, trying to make it sound casual. 'Ben sets the table, buys the flowers, writes suitably contrite messages and does the wine.'

Katie felt a warm glow invading the lower quarters of her body. The idea of her and Bob in his cosy kitchen, knocking up a meal for her parents, was very appealing. 'I'm up for it,' she said.

'In the absence of anything better, so am I,' said Ben. 'As long as you're OK with my parents getting it on in your house, Bob.'

'Should I put plastic sheeting down?' Bob laughed.

'That is *not* a good thought,' said Katie, making a face.

'Anyway, it's fine by me,' said Bob. 'Anything to help my closest neighbours. It may mean that I never have to eat Sunday lunch on my own again.'

The evening wore on and many bottles of wine were consumed, so that when the bill came, it was a lot bigger than any of them could have imagined.

And Katie had been wrong when she assumed that the photographers would not recognize her ex-boyfriend. The flashguns virtually blinded them as they emerged from the restaurant together. Bugger, she thought drunkenly, as she smiled guiltily. But at least I haven't done anything really bad.

When she surfaced from slumber on Saturday morning, there was a moment of semi-consciousness when she felt surprisingly cheerful. Now, what was it? Why was she feeling so happy? She came fully awake. Oh, yes. Bob. She smiled and stretched in the bed, feeling the cold sheets in the area where she hadn't been lying. And then the headache kicked in. Ouch, she thought. And as the evening's events came back to her, she stood up gingerly and padded to the bathroom for some paracetamol.

She probably ought to ring Adam and put him in the picture. Not the full picture, just the section she wanted him to look at. She couldn't articulate to herself exactly what the full picture was because it involved being truthful about her feelings, and she wasn't ready to do that just yet. She would think about it tomorrow. For the moment, she would dwell on the lingering kiss she had shared with Bob last night. The farewell kiss before he had gone off to his friend's flat. The one that was supposed to be a kiss on the cheek but had turned into a full-blown, romantic, woozy-making, beyond-anything kiss.

She would phone Adam after she'd had a stiff coffee.

Adam was drinking a cup of green tea, puzzling over the news he'd received as he'd left the office the night before. The phone company had come back with a break-down of the numbers rung to make up the massive bill – and there were literally thousands and thousands of them for a premium-rate number. Further investigation revealed they were for one of the numbers on a programme called *Celebrity X-Treme*, the voting line for a certain Katie Fisher.

His head of IT was tracing, with some urgency, which extension had been used, and would report back to him personally. He didn't want the story getting out before he had the full details.

He couldn't come up with any reason why one of his staff would be so determined to keep his girlfriend in a reality television show. The only other alternative – which he was loath to contemplate – was that one of his staff wanted to stitch him up. But what would have been the point of that? He would find out, surely, and then that person would be sacked. The more he pondered, the more confused he became. For a minute, he even considered Nick. After all, he'd made it clear that he thought Adam had stolen a march on him when he'd made a move on Katie in the immediate aftermath of her split from Bob. But he dismissed the idea. He knew his friend better than that. Or did he? It was very perplexing.

He spread a rice cake with pickle and added a small slice of low-fat cheese, and as he ate it, he allowed himself to mull over his relationship with Katie.

Was it ever going to get back to its pre-*Celebrity X-Treme* status? Why did the beautiful Cécile d'Ombard keep coming into his head, along with a vision of her in lingerie? Or less. He was suddenly overcome with lust.

He stood up swiftly, threw his gym clothes into his bag and stalked determinedly out of his front door.

In a flat in Croydon, a young man with an unfortunate haircut was drinking a cup of builder's tea, with two sugars, and reading the *Sun*. He had been keeping a weather eye on what had happened to those on *Celebrity X-Treme*, and was pleased to see that, since their experience, his favourites were doing well. He had a huge soft spot for Crystal Blake, and was happy that her relationship with the soap actor Peter Philbin appeared to be going from strength to strength.

And then he noticed the small box at the bottom of the story about their love for each other.

He wondered how much money the newspaper would be prepared to pay for his story, and whether it was worth sacrificing his friendship with a fellow computer enthusiast. Was it the sort of figure that might wipe out his gambling debts and get him back the girlfriend who had ditched him after she had come face to face with the bailiffs at his flat one morning? It was certainly worth a phone call, he reasoned.

In separate locations, Jack and Lynda were performing similar acts. They were sitting drinking cups of tea and staring moodily out of their respective windows.

An uncharacteristic lassitude had descended upon Lynda. Since Jack had walked out for the second time, she had found it hard to work up any enthusiasm for the variety of activities that had kept her so busy since he'd retired. It was an effort sometimes to have a shower, get dressed and do anything at all. There were days when the only thing that got her out of her nightie was that she could hardly take Hercules out for his walk in it – tempting though it sometimes was just to put a coat over the top.

When she had told Jack that he should take the dog, he had huffed and told her Hercules was too old to be uprooted from his home – even if he himself had been.

She could have kicked herself. She could have been eating some of Jack's homemade bread and marmalade right now. Instead, she was spreading a sugary, tasteless commercially produced version on sliced white. She couldn't even be bothered to get decent bread. And she couldn't remember the last time she'd had a proper meal. She would snack on stuff straight from the fridge. Occasionally she would put a pie in the microwave and throw some frozen peas into boiling water. But, really, it was all such an effort.

She finished her cup of tea and went to stand in front of the hall mirror. A disconsolate figure looked back, its shoulders drooping. She put her hands through her hair. She was a mess. Did she care? No. Did Hercules care? He looked up at her expectantly from his supine position on the doormat.

'Walkies,' she said, trying to summon a *soupçon* of enthusiasm. He recognized the half-hearted statement and simply thumped his tail on the floor, as if to say, 'If you're willing, I'm up for it.'

The phone rang, making her virtually jump out of her skin, so self-absorbed had she been.

'Hi, Mum,' said Ben. 'Are you OK?'

'Fine, fine,' she said. And then, when he asked, no, she wasn't doing anything. Saturday would be fine. What was it for again? Yes, of course. And why was it at Bob's house? Right.

Ben kept the story simple. He said that Bob was pitching for business and needed to have a dinner round at his house to show off the garden. He and Lynda would be there to stop it becoming a weirdly intimate occasion.

'And why doesn't he just have a lunch?' she asked reasonably.

Ben thought quickly. 'Presumably the other person can't do it. I don't know, Mum. Bob asked me if I could come and bring someone. I thought of you because you live down the road, and it'll be nice. Don't come if you don't want to,' he ended, with fake nonchalance. She had to bite, or it was back to the drawing board – and he couldn't face any more Katie hassle.

'All right. Yes, I will. Next Saturday? What time?' she asked.

'Seven for seven thirty so he can show the garden while it's still light.'

Ben hung up and phoned his sister. 'All sorted on the mother front,' he told her. 'I'm going to phone Dad now.'

Jack had drunk his tea and was disconsolately washing up the plates from his frugal breakfast. The friend he was staying with had gone for an early game of golf, and would not be back until late.

He hated being beholden to someone for his bed and board, even though he was paying him – had insisted on it. He wanted to be back at home with his wife. He missed her. He missed the dog. He was even beginning to miss being shouted at. He smiled. Heaven forfend! Missed being shouted at? What was he like? Maybe he should get a job. Go and stack shelves. Anything to get out of the appalling lethargy that had come over him. He'd never thought there would come a day when he wasn't excited about a new recipe he wanted to try out or a new plant. Not that he could do anything with a new plant at the moment, he thought sadly. He supposed he ought to consult a divorce lawyer.

With that depressing thought, he wandered through to the hall to pick up his coat for the morning stroll down to the local newsagent for a paper.

His new mobile phone rang. He looked at caller ID, and answered it, brightening. 'Good morning, Ben,' he said.

'You sound very chipper, Dad.' His son explained what he wanted.

'Of course,' Jack agreed, with alacrity. Anything to get out of the paralysing state he was slumping into. 'Maybe I'll give Bob a ring and offer to cook for him.'

'No need,' said Ben. 'He's got some friend of his to do the catering. By all means ask him, but I think it's all in hand.'

'Oh,' said Jack, his nose slightly out of joint.

'Dad,' said Ben, clearly having guessed his thought process, 'he didn't know you were going to say yes. He asked me to organize it. So it'll be you, me, Bob, Sophie – you know, his friend Harry's wife – this woman and her friend. Six of us. So dress smart. It's important. He really wants this job.'

Ben phoned his sister. 'Right. All done. It had better bloody work.'

'Well, if it doesn't, we can comfort ourselves in the future with the thought that we did as much as we could,' she said emphatically.

CHAPTER TWENTY-TWO

Katie spent the rest of Saturday trying to work out what the hell she was going to do. This is beyond the pale, she thought. I have a wonderful man who is also helping me out with a job I don't want to lose. And he's gorgeous, if self-obsessed. Bob lives bloody miles away. And we've tried twice. And. And. And. There were so many ands and buts that it was almost impossible to wade through them. They were standing up like an impenetrable forest. She needed help to cut them down. Talk about not being able to see the wood for the trees. All she could see was the would but for the reprise. Hey, she thought, not bad for a hangovered person. Bob would appreciate that one.

And that was the point. The one big point. Bob would. Adam wouldn't.

On the other hand, she thought … and how many other hands were there? Many hands make light work.

In the middle of her heavy thinking, Adam rang to discuss the evening.

'I've got tickets for that old French film you said you wanted to see on the South Bank.'

'Oh, fantastic,' she said, shamefaced. What was wrong with her? Adam was perfect. She had told him ages ago about *Romuald et Juliette*, and he had remembered. And here she was, harping on in her head about someone else.

'How was dinner last night?'

'A long one. I'll tell you all about it later.'

'Who did you drag along in the end?' he asked.

'I told you that Tanya was coming along, didn't I? For Ben. And then, erm, Dee came along to offer her insight,' she lied.

'Ben overwhelmed by oestrogen, eh?' laughed Adam.

'Yes,' she said. I'll be struck by a bolt of lightning, she thought.

She spent the day doing a mountain of paperwork, trying to avoid thinking in the hope that Fate would intervene somehow and make everything all right. Whatever all right was.

Adam's issue with the phone numbers made him so preoccupied that he barely noticed her reticence on the previous night's dinner when they met at a little bistro before the cinema. The film hardly registered with him, but he liked the fact that Katie obviously enjoyed it, sniffing copiously at the end and groping for her tissues.

'I love a good romantic weepie,' she declared, as they came out into the balmy evening.

They decided to have a drink at a small bar nearby before going home.

And there was Bob.

They saw each other at the same time.

She turned to Adam, almost tripping him up because of her sudden stop.

'How about we just go home?' she asked. 'I feel like I might have a headache coming on. Probably all that crying. And there's such a queue at the bar. We could open a bottle at home, after all.'

'OK,' he said. 'You're right about the crowd at the bar.' He turned to go back out of the door, Katie hurrying along in front of him.

'It's also very stuffy in here,' she said, smiling with relief that they were getting out.

At the bar Harry, who had witnessed the incident, demanded an explanation.

Bob shook his head. 'No idea,' he said, hoping that the delicious kiss he and Katie had shared the night before was wreaking the same kind of havoc with Katie's emotions as it had with his.

Katie, feeling maudlin, had asked Adam to drop her back at her flat, claiming that her headache was really bad now. 'I'm sure I'll be right as a trivet in the morning,' she said, giving him a small, hard kiss as she got out of the taxi.

His mouth set as he watched her walk to the door. Something was going on. He had never known her to have a headache – at least, not one that had come on that swiftly. And now he came to think of it she had been uncharacteristically quiet all evening. Curious.

The next morning, after he'd seen one of the Sunday papers, he realized why. He rang her immediately. 'I now know why you feigned a headache last night,' he said, the newspaper in front of him showing his girlfriend with her arm round her ex-boyfriend, coming out of a restaurant.

Katie's heart thumped loudly as she heard the words. Could this be the point at which she took a hand in her fate? Said the words that she could feel in her throat? Or should she – as she was sure she could – put a spin on the picture he was talking about that would render it harmless?

'Katie?' said Adam, sounding tight-lipped and angry.

'Yes. I accept it doesn't look good.'

'Why didn't you at least have the decency to say that Bob was at this dinner?'

'Because …' she said weakly.

'Right,' he said.

'Ben asked him,' she said. 'And then I thought it would sound more than it was if I told you he'd be there.'

'And this was?'

'The night before. Honestly,' she said.

'I'm not sure I can believe in your honesty,' he said cuttingly.

'But that's how it happened,' she said.

'And the picture in the paper?'

'Well, we used to go out together,' she said.

'You know, Katie, this is a habit with you, isn't it? And I'm not sure I can cope with it. It's rude. It implies that I'm not worthy of the great Katie Fisher's honesty.'

She was silent.

'You flirt with Paul Martin in front of millions of people. And now there's this photograph. It makes me look stupid. Do you agree?'

'Yes,' she said, in a small voice.

'Do you want to continue with this relationship, Katie?'

She said nothing.

'I'll take it that the answer is negative, then. It would have been nice if you'd had the guts to say so, rather than letting me find out this way. I'd thought more of you. Thank you for everything. I hope I've been useful. Goodbye. And good luck.'

Adam pressed the end-call button with vehemence. And then, in high dudgeon, phoned Cécile d'Ombard.

Katie tried to cry. She wanted to feel sorry. But she couldn't. All she could think was that next Saturday she was going to see Bob. And not only was she going to see him, but she was going to see him at his home.

She might not have a new series any more. She might not have a high-powered boyfriend any more. But her life was looking up, and she felt optimistic. Positive. Positively happy.

She got out of bed and checked in the mirror.

'I'm heppy.' She spoke in an upper-crust accent and smiled at her reflection, feeling the urge to skip.

* * *

On Monday, Keera Keethley dressed with her usual care and attention. After the programme, she was going straight to the BBC for a meeting about *Behind the Seams*. She hesitated between a skirt or trousers. Trousers, she thought, having put them on. They fitted so snugly over her perfect, taut bottom. It was a shame that the jacket covered it. But if she wore a silky long-sleeved shirt, she could take off the jacket and reach up somewhere to hang it. Or bend over to pick up her bag. She mimed it in the mirror. Bending over was good. Her hair flowed forward in a raven's wing. Standing up again gave it a mildly dishevelled look, which was very pleasing. She struck a pose, one hand on her hip, the slinky shirt clinging to her body. Perfect.

At *Hello Britain!*, Dee was holding court in the newsroom about her lunch with Oliver on Friday. 'So I come out of the restaurant. And, obviously, I don't know that upstairs there's been this big Hollywood A-list event. Really major stars. I mean big, Brad Pitt-type names. And I come out with Oliver into this barrage of flashlights. And then, quite clearly, I hear one of the photographers say, "Yes, the camera is definitely working." How hilarious is that?' She laughed.

Keera went to the executive producer to see if there was anything special about the programme she needed to know. 'You've got the entertainment slot today. A man who used to be a car mechanic and is now an opera singer.'

'Oh, I've heard of him,' she said enthusiastically. 'He was on the radio last week. Apparently, he literally rocketed into the number-one slot after an appearance on local television.'

'Did he?' asked Richard. 'How interesting. Wonder how much fuel that involved. Anyway … you're doing a swift interview with him while he's at the mike stand, then he'll take it away and sing his song. The rest of it is pretty much as you see it on the computer.'

Keera enjoyed the show that morning – all the more so because she felt superior to everyone. Who else was having a meeting later about a prime-time series?

She smiled and nodded graciously as the guests came and went.

'What's up with her this morning?' asked Dee, of the floor manager.

'No idea,' he responded, 'but it's like being in the presence of the Queen of Sheba, isn't it? Any minute, I'm expecting her to ask me to kneel while she knights me.'

Dee giggled. 'I know. Hysterical, isn't it? I'm enjoying her new laugh, though.'

'Oh, yes,' said the floor manager, appreciatively. 'It's much better now that she's added the trill at the end. Like 'avin' parakeets in the studio.'

Unaware of the speculation, Keera left the building with a jaunty step.

She got to the BBC with time to spare, and pulled open the *Daily Telegraph* as she waited for Nick Midhurst and the producer of *Behind the Seams* to appear. It was such a dreary paper. So much foreign news. Who cared? She examined a photograph in the television pages. What an enormous head that man had. Or was it the way the photo had been cropped? No. His ears seemed a normal size. And a man who looked like Gollum was hosting a new quiz show. She wondered how anyone who wasn't as beautiful as she was ever got on screen. There should be a … what was that word? … a crematorium? something like that … on ugly people on television. Shouldn't be allowed.

She looked up as Nick arrived.

'Hello,' he said, smiling at her as she folded her newspaper carefully.

'Good morning.' She returned the smile, standing up gracefully.

'Now, I think I told you,' said Nick, as they waited to be taken through, 'that this meeting is to confirm you as the host of this show. Or, at least, I think that's what it's about. To be honest, it's all rather odd. It's not the usual way we do business. But you know how it is. New commissioners. New series producers. Et cetera. Et cetera. You look great,' he finished.

'Thanks,' she said, acknowledging that she did. And slightly miffed that he should mention it. She *always* looked great.

A girl came to pick them up from Reception, taking them past Security and showing them to an empty meeting room. 'They'll be here in a minute,' she said, and offered them a drink. She came back with a cup of herbal tea for Keera and a black coffee for Nick.

There was a knock on the door, and two women and a man came in. Keera put her cup down and stood up to shake hands. She frowned slightly at the face of one of the women. 'Hello,' she said. 'Haven't we met before?'

'Yes,' replied the executive producer, smiling. 'The last time I met you, you were on a train, sitting in my seat and refusing to give it up. And then, if I remember rightly, you tried to wipe out some poor woman who was sitting in the next seat. Oh. And you had forgotten your name.'

The meeting went by in a blur, and Keera was not surprised to find out the next day that she was not to be the presenter of a new series showing behind-the-scenes footage from the world of fashion.

For Katie, the week went by in a whirl. She bought a new outfit for Saturday night – even though she was only supposed to be going to an old family friend's to help cook dinner for her parents. She needed new jeans anyway, and the shirt was expensive, but good quality really never went out of fashion, she reasoned.

She hadn't trusted herself to talk to Bob. Their discussions had all been on email. She had sent a cheque to cover the cost of the food, and had bought a train ticket for early Saturday morning. Ben would already be with her mother, having travelled up on Friday night after work.

She had had no further communication with Adam, and was content to leave it at that until she had a clearer view of what was going on in her life. But on the Thursday before the big day, she had a call from a newspaper. She immediately referred it to her agent, and quickly rang him before the journalist could get to him.

'Jim,' she said, 'there's a reporter going to call you about some sort of dodgy phone line or something on *Celebrity X-Treme*.'

'And good afternoon to you,' he said.

She laughed, 'Sorry. I'm rushing around. I don't know what this is about, but it all sounds weird. Apparently, some computer spod has put some link onto a computer at Wolf Days, which meant that I was illegally – or not illegally but wrongly, maybe – voted for in *Celebrity* so that I stayed beyond when I should have done … or something like that,' she ended, having not made the case clear at all.

'Slow down. What?' he asked, finding somewhere to put his cup of coffee and picking up a pen.

'I know. I just listened to this reporter and phoned you. So I'm not sure I have it correct in my own head. You know the viewers' voting lines?'

'Yes. Of course.'

'So, apparently, someone put a program onto a computer at Wolf Days that voted for me constantly from the moment the lines were open.'

'As in Adam had a computer man put your number in on a computer to skew the votes?'

'You'd think so. Although out of character. And he didn't care. Anyway, no. It didn't sound like that. And, anyway, I'm not sure it's illegal or anything. But I think the paper's suggesting that someone on *Celebrity X-Treme* did it.'

'Why on earth would someone on *Celebrity* do that? Instant dismissal. What would be the point?'

'I don't know. I have no idea. I'm just phoning you to tell you what the reporter's going to say. He asked me for a comment. I don't want to say anything. In case.'

'I'll deal with it. I can hear the other phone line going. I'll speak to you when I know more.'

But by the time he got off the phone he was really no clearer. What a very odd story. He phoned Katie to say as much, and advised her to 'scrub up' in case the newspaper decided to take a photograph of her.

Meanwhile, Siobhan Stamp had picked up an email on her BlackBerry about voting for Katie Fisher and Paul Martin, and while her heart had thumped uncomfortably as she read it, she believed she had enough safeguards in place.

Katie was half expecting a phone call from Adam, but when it didn't arrive, she believed the story had disappeared. Obviously it had not stood up to scrutiny. She was not to know that Adam was in Paris having scratched the itch that was Cécile d'Ombard.

She packed a small overnight bag and took the train to Yorkshire.

She was reminded of when she had travelled this route to see Bob – it felt like light years ago – and virtually fallen off the train into his arms. She had then been violently sick into a clump of stinging nettles and given herself a rash on her forehead. Today she confined herself to two cups of tea and a seemingly plastic croissant, which she had bought at a shop on the way to the station. If she closed her eyes to get a fix on what it tasted like … it was … mmm … pork pie. Nice. Not.

By the time she arrived at the station, she was sparking with excitement and trying to contain it. It was as though there was a champagne bottle in her head waiting to pop. She was single, and so was Bob. The words felt more like: BOB IS SINGLE. I AM SINGLE. Even knowing that she was there to try to bring her parents together was not enough to squash the thoughts to the side of her brain. It was like an entire army of Bobs and Katies were taking up all the space in her cranium, packed in like plums at a jam factory.

As she went into the car park and Bob flashed his lights, she felt like she was having an out-of-body experience. She saw herself walking towards him – and not doing a particularly good job of it. How come she suddenly had so many legs? Why weren't they under her control?

Bob, waiting for her, thought she looked beyond gorgeous. Her hair, newly washed, was blowing softly in the breeze. Her orange shirt brought a splash of colour to the station forecourt. He had a feeling that life was going to be all right. The universe was unfolding as it should.

'Well, good morning, Miss Fisher,' he said, as she threw her small bag into the back of the Land Rover and jumped into the front seat.

'Good afternoon,' she corrected him, smiling into the blue eyes.

'Good trip?'

'Very uneventful,' she said. 'I read two newspapers and all I can remember is that coffee has more effect on men than women. And that fear is contagious. Research shows, apparently, that we secrete a sweat that has a different smell. It means that … say, the plane is bouncing all over the sky, even people who aren't scared of flying will start to feel fear. Herd instinct.'

'And the point of that is?' he asked, pulling out into the road and slipping into second gear.

'Hm. Can't quite recall. Maybe it's like being scared of woolly mammoths in the Stone Age.'

'But then we'd have starved,' he said reasonably.

'There must be some sort of atavistic reason, though,' she said, thinking.

'Nice.' He nodded approvingly. 'Atavistic, eh?'

'Oh, you know,' she laughed, 'as in what our ancestors did but we don't do any more. Or is that what it means? I don't know. I misuse and mispronounce …'

'I would never misunderestimate you, though,' he said, using a mispronunciation of which he had become inordinately fond.

'Words. Lovely, lovely words. So many words and so little time to use them.'

'I found one the other day that I thought you might like. "Matutinal".'

'Excellent. Something to do with a mutinous mat?'

'It means active or wide awake in the morning hours,' he declared, as he swung the Land Rover down a small leafy road.

Katie sniffed happily. 'Fresh air. Can't get enough of it. It smells of plants and growing and good things. Hey, I saw one in a book written by a man who read the whole of the *Oxford English Dictionary*. "Finifugal".'

'That is superb,' he said, changing gear as they pulled out of a junction. She looked at his forearms. She loved them. Strong. Manly. A sprinkling of golden hairs. The big watch on his wrist.

'What does it mean?' he added, casting a sidelong glance, aware of her attention.

'Shunning the end of anything,' she announced, resolutely facing forwards, 'I suppose like someone who can't bear to watch the end of a film.'

'Or finish a relationship,' he said, without thinking. And blushed. What an idiot, he thought.

She gave a short laugh. 'I think we're quite good at that, aren't we?'

He took his eyes off the road for a second to glance at her. They exchanged rueful smiles.

As they arrived at the house, Caligula meandered out to meet them, weaving in and out of their legs, depositing cat hairs – ever hopeful that, with enough of a welcome laid on, he could improve his lunch menu.

'Well, hello, you handsome young thing,' said Katie, bending down to stroke him firmly down his back.

'Lucky cat,' said Bob, meaning it.

Katie looked up, faint colour coming to her cheeks. She felt breathless. It was all going to happen again.

Which was just what Bob was thinking as he reached out to stroke her mane of hair.

And without the bags being taken in, without conscious thought, they were together again. Lost in lust. Lost in remembrance of things past. Lost in the passion of the moment.

In the grand tradition of romance, Bob literally took her in his arms and swiftly strode into the house, heading for the bedroom.

Later, so closely entwined that it was hard to see where one limb ended and another began, Katie finally spoke. 'So ...' she said, without quite knowing where she was going with the sentence.

'La ...' he sang, after a moment.

'Ha,' she declared, 'or should that be tee?'

'Doh,' he pronounced in the manner of Homer Simpson.

'Very much so,' she said, moving her head back slightly so she could look at him.

He smoothed a strand of hair back from her face. 'A lot of water under the bridge, eh?'

'Shall we pretend it didn't happen?' she asked.

'Not exactly pretend it didn't happen,' he said slowly, caressing her arm where it lay on his thigh, 'but maybe not discuss what's been happening to us in the interim until we feel a little more secure in this. In us. In whatever this is.'

She nuzzled her nose in his chest hair. 'I've missed that.' She sighed.

'And I've missed you,' he said, pushing her away so that he could look at her, an answering smile in her green eyes.

Katie traced his eyebrows, gazed into his blue, blue eyes. Fell into their depths and fastened her lips on his.

And, for a while, nothing more was said, as the sun continued its arc through the sky.

Caligula had quite given up his perambulations on the landing by the time the reunited lovers emerged from the bedroom, having suddenly noticed the time and remembered that there was cooking to be done.

CHAPTER TWENTY-THREE

Ben had got away from work early the day before and driven up to Yorkshire, taking the pretty route. Even the most clueless of pop psychologists could see that his mother was missing his father, and that, but for a curmudgeonly disinclination to admit she was wrong in any way, she would be back with Jack in a heartbeat. Katie's plan may just work, he thought, that night, as he and Lynda ate steak and fried potatoes with slightly under-cooked broccoli and boiled carrots, before sitting down in front of the television.

'What a treat,' he said, slumping on the sofa and flicking through the channels with the remote control, stopping for a few minutes on each station, then rolling backwards and forwards through those he found vaguely interesting.

Lynda gave him half an hour before bursting out, 'Could we just watch one programme for longer than five minutes, for God's sake? Honestly, you're making me feel seasick.'

'What do you fancy?' he asked, not taking his eyes from the screen on which *Top Gear* had appeared. 'Do you think this show's on a permanent loop? Whatever night, wherever one or more stations cluster together for warmth, *Top Gear* is on.'

'I have no idea,' she said dismissively. 'I only use the first five stations. As you know, it's your father's toy.'

'I don't believe you've never checked out the other channels,' he said. 'I bet you're constantly surfing. And probably ending up like the rest of us watching *Sexcetera* in the absence of anything else.'

'If that's the late-night dodgy channel, I tend not to linger in case I get charged.'

He smiled. 'It's a programme. And they don't charge. You can watch it all for free.'

'I used to like that afternoon painting show with Hannah Gordon,' she said wistfully, 'and you can't go wrong with a black-and-white film. How's Oliver, these days?' she asked, knowing that Dee was engaged to him. Even though Katie had left *Hello Britain!*, she still watched it, and was up to date on everything that was going on there.

'Unbearably happy,' he said, 'and already talking about stag nights or stag weekends, even though it's months before they get married.'

'I think she's lost weight,' said his mother, getting up to make a camomile tea. 'Do you want a herbal?'

'No, thanks. According to Oliver, Dee's down at the gym most mornings after work. He called me an ugly middle-class tosser yesterday after I told him he ought to shape up as well.'

'How very, very hurtful,' said his mother, smiling. 'You're not middle class.'

'Drrrrrr-dum.' Ben pretended a comedy drum roll.

'So what's the drill tomorrow night?' She raised her voice from the kitchen.

Ben tried to sound nonchalant. 'I think Bob said any time after seven. I'll ring him tomorrow and check.'

'And smart?' she asked, coming back in from putting the kettle on.

'Ballgown,' he said promptly.

'Gloves?' she asked.

'Obviously.'

'Should I wear a hat?'

'Naturally.'

'Or should I do a Katie and wear a pair of underpants on my head?'

'Only if they match your earrings.'

'You know, between you and me, I rather enjoyed that *Celebrity* programme.'

'Now there's an admission, Mum,' Ben said, surprised. 'I thought you and Dad had a falling-out about it.'

'Oh, I didn't enjoy Katie making a spectacle of herself. But considering I wouldn't normally have watched something like that, I actually had a good time. I found myself caring about what happened. I didn't go so far as to vote for anyone ...'

'Not even Katie?'

'As if my vote would've made any difference.' She snorted. 'And I didn't feel I could vote for her because I wanted her out of it. Did you vote for her?'

'No. I wanted her out, too.' He laughed. 'She got paid the same no matter what.'

'Oh, please stop this aimless trawl,' she said wearily, and grabbed the remote control out of his hands. She pressed button three and Hugh Grant appeared as the Prime Minister. 'Not the best film in the world, but amiable enough,' she pronounced. 'Anyway, as I was saying, I started to care about who was evicted on *Celebrity X-Treme*, while secretly hoping every night that it would be Katie.'

'Did you like Tanya?' he asked, in what he assumed was a casual voice.

She gave him a funny look. 'Yes, I did. I was prepared to dislike her because of poor Howard Elph. But then you heard her story, and suddenly you understood a bit more. Not that I could ever condone that sort of thing.'

He said no more about it.

She stood up again as the news came on. 'I'm off to bed. Do you want anything?'

'Aston Martin. A holiday in the Seychelles. House in the Hamptons. Bigger feet. A canteen of cutlery. Cuddly toy. Usual stuff,' he said, flicking through the channels again.

The next morning as Katie was on a train to a rendezvous with destiny, he phoned Bob to check that everything was in order.

386

'I've done an early shop, organized a florist to come and do some flowers – it's all right, she's a mate – and I've got meat being delivered about now. Everything appears to be on target. A-OK. All systems go. Do you think it's going to work?'

Ben lowered his voice in case his mother was loitering. 'I think if he gave even the smallest sign, she'd welcome him back with open arms,' he said.

'From my knowledge of your dad – and not presuming anything here – I reckon he feels the same,' said Bob.

'Well, let's hope it works because otherwise that wretched sister of mine will be thinking up more twattish schemes to get them back together again.'

'I thought she said that she wouldn't do that, if this didn't work.'

'Yeah … right. Now, I've told Mum and Dad the same time. Dad can be relied on to turn up on the dot of. I'll make sure Mum does.'

At five o'clock Lynda began to get ready for the evening. She was unaccountably excited about it. She had her beloved son with her, and although it was only a small dinner party, she anticipated good-quality conversation. It was always nice to be with those from a different generation. It kept you young. Otherwise you were in danger of sliding into top-trumping each other's death stories.

She came down from the bedroom wearing a long dress in muted pink tones and a cream cardigan.

Ben looked her over critically. 'Very nice, Mum. But are you going out in those?'

She glanced down. 'Of course I'm not, you ugly middle-class tosser,' she said, haughtily, and went to take off her slippers.

While she was out of the room, Ben phoned Katie. 'All sorted?' he asked quickly.

'Fine. Dad's on his way here,' she said gaily. 'We're on the finishing touches, then we'll be leaving. How are you going to get her in there without you?'

'Leave me to do my job, and you get on with yours,' he said, and clicked the phone off as Lynda arrived back in the sitting room.

'Better?' she asked, raising her eyebrows.

'Perfect,' he said. 'Shall we go?'

Jack, at that moment, was driving down the country roads, keeping a weather eye out for rabbits and badgers. He was wearing his favourite green corduroy trousers and a checked shirt, smart casual, as he had been instructed.

'Oh, and could you park further down the lane?' Bob had asked. 'Just that I've got to rearrange things in the drive, and could do without having to move cars. Is that OK? Got to go,' he had added quickly, before Jack offered to help out.

As Jack turned down the lane towards the house, he noticed a slightly steamed up Land Rover near a gate. Strange, he thought, as he continued towards the Old Coach House. It had looked a bit like Bob's.

He parked, and got out the bottle of wine he had bought in town that morning. He had decided to go for quality and not quantity. A 1989 Pauillac, and some chocolates from a delicatessen.

He approached the house. It felt oddly deserted. He was about to ring the bell when he noticed that the door was ajar. 'Helloooo,' he called, as he pushed it open. A Mozart piano concerto he vaguely recognized was playing as he went through to the kitchen. And in front of him a table had been beautifully laid for two, with a card addressed to him propped up against one of the wine glasses.

He opened it. There were just four words.

He turned as Lynda came silently through from the front door.

She saw the table and him standing there, as though he was waiting for her. Saw him as though for the first time, and fell into his arms.

'I'm sorry, too,' he said, slightly confusingly.

Although she suddenly understood as she opened her own card and found SORRY. I LOVE YOU written inside.

'Should we phone them, do you think?' she asked later, as they sipped their wine and debated whether they were too full to do justice to the strawberries and cream that were sitting, already prepared, in the fridge.

'Do it the young person's way,' he said, leaning back expansively. 'Text them.'

'What shall I write?'

'"Mission accomplished"?' he asked, smiling lovingly at his wife as she came round to the back of his chair and dropped a kiss on his head.

Siobhan Stamp was having the worst Saturday of her entire life. Her carefully laid plan had completely unravelled. Her computer nerd, despite the – to him – vast sum of money she had paid him to keep quiet, had sung like a canary the moment that the police had got involved. He had meekly handed over his meticulously detailed diary of events, and her protestations of innocence had not been believed.

She had tried flirting with the attractive police officer, to no avail, and had finally confessed all. Suddenly, in the cold light of a police station, it started to sound remarkably petty, even to her ears. Although it really had been an almost perfect stitch-up. Adam Snobby Williams having to pay a huge wodge of cash for the pleasure of watching his girlfriend shafted in more ways than one … and unable to reveal it because his company had rung the voting line thousands and thousands of times.

As Jack was 'tarting up' the strawberries ('A little bit of black pepper and balsamic vinegar would improve the flavour no end …'), Siobhan was trying to paint herself as a wronged woman. 'It was a victimless crime of passion,' she was explaining, crossing her legs and giving the detective an eyeful of frothy lingerie.

And, suddenly, she noticed the gleam in his eye. Excellent, she thought, giving him the benefit of a full-wattage smile.

Never mind what her mother used to say about the gleam in a man's eye being just the sun shining through a hole in his head – she had recognized that look. It was what she thrived on.

She wondered if, after all, she would get away with it.

On Sunday morning, while Jack and Lynda were waking up in their marital bed, Bob and Katie were tangled in a duvet in Hawes.

'What a night.' She sighed, stretching one arm up and rumpling his hair.

'Mmm. Almost as good as the day I discovered an old copy of *Penthouse* in the hedge when I was eleven,' he said, grasping her hand and kissing the palm.

'I knew it was going to be a momentous one,' she said, laying her head on his chest with a sigh. 'And Mum and Dad are back together – despite you doubting Thomases saying it wouldn't work.'

'Doubting Thomasum.'

'Doubting Thomasii.'

'Doubting Thomasamus.'

'Are they the ones with the really big flowers?'

'Enormous,' Bob pronounced, his eyes crinkling attractively as he smiled down at her.

'I've missed this rubbish-speak,' she said.

'So have I,' he said, pulling up the duvet to cover her shoulders. 'It's like slipping into a warm bath.'

'Like pulling on a pair of suede underpants.' She laughed. 'Like being stroked with a fan made entirely of boneless cats.'

'Talking of which,' he said, 'I notice Caligula's looking smug. I have a horrible feeling that your dad fed him leftovers last night.'

'Oh, he'll be fine. Maybe you should lubricate him to make sure that he doesn't get stretch marks.'

'Does your dad often suffer with stretch marks?'

She giggled. 'You know, I think Ben's going to get it together with Tanya. She seems very keen. And so does he.'

'Is that all right with you?'

'More than all right. Fan-bloody-tastic.'

'To use a tiny tmesis,' he said.

'You remembered,' she said, snuggling onto his chest hair and blowing it gently so that it went up her nose.

'You must have said it a million times.'

'I know. Miss Didactic,' she said. 'Hey,' she sat up suddenly, 'do you think if you had a dinosaur who liked teaching, he'd be called a Pterodidactyl?'

'Like the one-eyed dinosaur, D'yerthinkhesaurus?'

'The one-eyed deer?'

'No idea.'

'We could be here all day,' she said.

'What a lovely thought,' he said, 'staying here all day with occasional forays down to the kitchen for toast.'

The smile he gave her chased all thoughts of toast away, and at the next break in proceedings, it was time for lunch.

'You happy?' he asked her, watching her pad about the bedroom in his favourite old blue shirt, trying to find something to tie up her hair.

She came to sit beside him as he lay propped up on the pillows. 'I couldn't be happier,' she said.

'Couldn't you?' he asked seriously.

'Meaning?'

'Is there anything in the world that I could do to make you the happiest girl in the world?'

'Truly?' she asked huskily, her heart beating quite hard.

'Really,' he said, taking her hand.

A small gust of wind rattled the window pane as they sat in stillness.

'In that case,' she said, her voice deep with passion, 'would you mind lending me a pair of socks? My feet are freezing.'